MW00681672

IF I SHOULD DIE BEFORE I DIE

Also by Peter Israel

I'll Cry When I Kill You
The Stiff Upper Lip
The French Kiss
Hush Money
The Hen's House

PETER ISRAEL

IF I SHOULD DIE BEFORE I DIE

THE MYSTERIOUS PRESS

New York • London • Tokyo

The Mysterious Press, 129 West 56th Street, New York, N.Y. 10019

Printed in the United States of America

First Printing: February 1989

10 9 8 7 6 5 4 3 2 1

Library of Congress Cataloging-in-Publication Data

Israel, Peter, fl. 1967–
If I should die before I die / Peter Israel.
p. 304.
I. Title.
PS3559.S74I35 1989
813'.54—dc19 88-14731
ISBN 0-89296-364-6 CIP

For Elie Israel and Alexandra Emily Israel
The King of Snails and the Princess of Eagle Rock Way

IF I SHOULD DIE BEFORE I DIE

PART ONE

CHAPTER 1

By 9:30 A.M. I already knew it'd be one of those days. I'd slept through the radio for starters, and it wasn't till I realized that I'd heard the sports report at least once already that I jumped awake. It was 8:17. I'd set the alarm for 7:00. The alarm, though, was in the bedroom. I'd just awoke on the living-room couch. My neck and shoulders ached, and the lights were on, and there was a half-full bottle of Moosehead on the floor.

I kicked the Moosehead over when I swung to. It spilled onto some papers.

I remembered being at Laura Hugger's the night before till after midnight. We'd had a fight, not the first in our on-again off-again relationship. Maybe our last. I'd been unable to sleep when I got home. I'd sat up with a Moosehead six-pack and a folder on the Magister case, and at some point I'd stretched out, and the papers must have slipped onto the floor.

I started to clear up the mess, but it hurt my head too much to bend over. I showered instead, and shaved, dressed, and listened to the news and weather along the way.

There was only one news story that morning: the Killer had struck again, the first time since July. The city, I figured, would be like a zoo again, only the women who'd been wearing blonde wigs all summer long were going to have to do something else. Like shave their heads. Ditto on avoiding Brooklyn. This time the victim was blonde—a first—and married—another first—and she'd also been discovered in her own Riverside Drive apartment.

Also a first: Manhattan.

She'd been smothered, as usual. This time she'd also been violated.

The case was weird in a lot of ways. Because of differences in detail and the seemingly random rhythm, it had taken the police four murders to discover the links. And quiet too, almost without violence or struggle, as though the victims knew their killer. Once the media had got hold of it, though, and the so-called Pillow Killer had been christened, the city's brunette population had gone into a frenzy such as we hadn't seen since the days of Son of Sam.

Now a blonde, now Manhattan. In September.

Even Revere's Full-Moon Theory had been shot full of holes this time, for the moon, I found out later, had been in a quarter phase that night.

I realized with a start, hearing the radio report again, that the Riverside Drive address was only a couple of blocks from Laura Hugger's apartment. I started to call her. Then I remembered our scene the night before and thought better of it. Then I felt lousy about thinking better of it, so I hit the streets.

The radio had predicted partly cloudy followed by clearing, but the sky hung low and dribbling when I headed east. It had been that way for days, a sky the color of ashes, the kind of weather where you can't tell what the temperature is because the wet air chills you one minute and stifles you the next. I couldn't find a cab, the corner of Columbus and 86th was overflowing with people huddling for the crosstown bus, so I headed toward the park on foot. I slanted toward the Seventies along the sodden paths. You couldn't see the towers south of the park for the fog, and the co-ops and condos of Fifth Avenue loomed dimly out of a gray nothingness. I passed a few late joggers, trudging in hooded sweatshirts through the murk. All male, I noticed. Most mornings I'd have been one of them, though an hour or two earlier, and there'd have been as many woman as men. But the Pillow Killer had struck again.

Nine-thirty, then.

I'd just rounded the corner at Madison, heading for the brick townhouse where I work and hurrying because I was late and the Counselor would be pacing the floor, when a beige blur hit me thigh-high, wet paws on my London Fog: Muffin, the Counselor's Wife's cocker bitch, yanking her owner behind her.

This too was out of sync. By the time I reported in most mornings, the spaniel had already been walked and the Counselor's Wife had already left for her own office, a few blocks north on Park. But if I was an hour late this morning, she was even later.

What's more, she was crying.

It took me a moment to realize it. She's almost my height, with angular features and ash-blonde hair that billows around her when she unpins it, and a graceful, athletic body even when the cocker bitch is pulling her this way and that. She's made the Ten-Best-Dressed lists, the only shrink, I imagine, ever to be so honored, and the adjectives the media usually use to describe her are *striking* and *stunning*. *Beautiful* too. To me, her eyes are her best feature. Shrink's eyes, I've always thought, because they can be wide, limpid blue pools one minute, the kind even the most bottled-up neurotic could open up to, and sharp blue glitters the next, with crinkles at the corners, when she knows she's got the upper hand.

She was wearing a red rainslicker and matching red fisherman's hat. Not a Ten-Best outfit, you'd say, except it would have been hard for her to look bad in a burlap sack.

Maybe I'd seen her blubber before but never the eyes red-rimmed and puffed, and the wet glistens on her cheeks were tears all right, not rain.

"Nora," I said. "Hey, Nora, what's the matter? What's wrong?"

Or some such.

She couldn't answer though. She started to, but the words seemed to stick. Then she shook her head and lowered it, ducked, like she didn't want to see me or me her, and pulled west, tugging Muffin behind her.

I watched them go, her red hat bent into the mist, the spaniel still surging back toward me. Then I headed down the street and in, under the white lintel above our doorway, with the white half-columns and the polished brass plaque that says:

Charles Camelot
Attorney-at-Law

* * * * * * *

CHAPTER 2

Roger—pronounced Ro-jay—LeClerc was sitting at the reception desk in our entrance foyer, paging through the *Daily News*. That at least was normal. Roger's black, probably gay. As far as his color's concerned, he'd be quick to inform you that he was born in the Ivory Coast, in Africa, and reached New York via Paris, in France, with accent to corroborate it, whereas if you ever called him gay to his face, you'd be offending him unalterably, eternally. He comes on like he's at least as important to our operation as the rest of us working stiffs, whereas in fact he's as close as we get to superfluous.

Roger, I should add, was the Counselor's Wife's touch.

"Philippe . . . ," he began, glancing up as I strode past his desk toward my ground-floor office.

"I know, I know," I said back, halfway out of my raincoat, "he's been calling for me all morning, etcetera, etcetera . . ."

"Not at all," Roger answered, imperturbable. "He's not even down yet."

"Not down yet?" I echoed, surprised. The Counselor's

office is on the second floor of the building, his living quarters on the third, fourth, and fifth. Ms. Shapiro, his secretary, and Charlotte McCullough, our resident accountant and computer genius, also work on the second floor, LeClerc and I on the first. I couldn't remember a morning when the Counselor hadn't been in his office, open for business, by 8:30, 9:00 at the latest. Much as I hated giving Roger the chance to upstage me, I said: "What's going on? And what's with Mrs. Camelot?"

"With Nora?" he said, gargling the *r* in her name. "All I know," his accent Frenchifying, "she ask me to call her off-eece, tell them to cancel all her appointments. Ze whole day. Zis I did.

"And Philippe," he called after me as I went into my office, "Shapiro said he wants you to go downtown without him. And Monsieur McClintock? He called you. *Deux fois*. Twice."

I'd made his day, I thought, closing my door. I buzzed Ms. Shapiro. She confirmed what Roger had said: the Counselor wasn't down yet, I was to go to the Firm alone. Then I called Laura Hugger's office. She was in a meeting. I left my name. Then I punched through to McClintock and got his secretary.

"Is he there?" I said.

"Who's calling, please?"

"Phil Revere."

"Oh yes, Mr. Revere. I know he wants to talk to you, but he's in a meeting now. I've got you and Mr. Camelot down for 10:30 this morning, is that right?"

"That's right as far as I'm concerned. But Mr. Camelot's not coming."

"Oh?" McClintock's secretary said.

"But tell your boss I'll be there."

I hung up, supposing that the meeting at the Firm might suffice to explain the Counselor's absence. Their relationship—his and the Firm's—was an unusual one. More than a decade before, he'd been a partner there. In fact that's where I'd first met him, when I was a summer intern trying to squeeze out enough of a living to get myself through law school. When he'd left to, as he liked to put it, "go private," he didn't, however, cut all his ties. We still use the Firm for various services. Our computer, for one thing, is cabled into their mainframe, they keep our database, and we have access to their electronic law library. The Firm, in exchange, gets to print a discreet "Charles Camelot, of Counsel" on its letterhead, an asset many New York law firms would pay handsomely for, and certain matters, usually of a sensitive nature, pass back and forth between the two offices, including the one McClintock was supposed to brief us on that morning.

I could imagine the Counselor saying it: *If Doug McClintock wants to brief us, let him come uptown.* The truth was that the briefing was for my benefit, not the Counselor's, but such is the protocol between attorneys that we had both been invited, and accepted, while the Counselor had orchestrated things in such a way that he could always back out at the last minute.

Which is what had happened.

The drizzle had stopped when I went outside again, and the sky had lightened considerably. The avenue was full of empty cabs by then, and two of them raced to a dead heat to get me. The Counselor still hadn't ventured downstairs, and, more surprising, the Counselor's Wife and Muffin hadn't returned either.

A matter of a sensitive nature, I said. The Magister Will. Wills and estates are usually among the most boring of legal work, if the most lucrative, but the Magister Will was, to say the least, an exception, and Margarethe von Heidrich Magister—known to the media as Margie, Margie with a hard *g*—had become a celebrity that year of a dimension New York hadn't seen since Jackie O came home from the Parthenon.

To summarize:

Robert Worth Magister III, chairman of the board, chief executive officer and principal stockholder of the Magister Companies, Inc., had died earlier in the year of a massive coronary, just a week before his eighty-second birthday. He'd held his job for around half a century. Starting in the Depression with a near-bankrupt group of magazines which he'd taken over from his father, he'd built a "communications empire" which, at its height, had included twenty-three television and radio stations, a baseball team, part ownership in a film company, part ownership of a cable television network, forty-four magazines, eleven newspapers, three book publishers, a lumber company and chain of paper mills, and enough real estate from New Jersey to California to build, if it could all have been put together, a good-sized city. Though the company, or companies, had slipped some from his heyday and pieces had been sold off and Wall Street, during the last years of his life, had called the enterprise "ripe for takeover," Bob Magister still owned or controlled enough shares, at his death, to block the raiders. His personal estate, which had so far received more attention than the fate of Magister Companies, had been valued in the nine figures, which works out to the hundreds of millions.

Bob III had five surviving children, four sons, one daughter, ranging in age from forty-nine to twenty-nine, and a train of grandchildren behind them. Two of the sons and the daughter ran Magister companies and sat on the board. One of them, it had always been assumed, would succeed their father as chairman, but which one?

The answer, at least for the moment, might be: none of them.

Some three years earlier, while traveling in Europe, Bob Magister had suffered a stroke, a mini-version, say a four on the Richter scale, compared to the one which later took him for the count. He had convalesced in a house he owned on the Riviera, attended by an Alsatian nurse. When he came back to New York that fall, the nurse had graduated to "companion," and about a year and a half later, over the vocal objections of his children, she became Margie Magister.

That was Margie with a hard *g*, Margarethe von Heidrich Magister. Bob III had left her fifty percent of his estate, including the bulk of his shares in Magister Companies. The balance had been divided into fifths and left not to the children but to a series of trusts for their benefit. In other words, the will treated them as though they were still children. Worse, at least for the three who held executive positions in Magister Companies, it made their stepmother their boss.

The challenges, predictably enough, hadn't been long in coming. Several of the children, each represented by a different attorney, had already filed suit to contest the will. Then the siblings—maybe this was also predictable—had begun to squabble among themselves, in full view of the media, and most recently Margie, after spending the summer "in seclusion" and represented by yet another attorney, had countersued two of them for slander.

At first the media, by one of those weird choices which maybe aren't even choices but are dictated by what sells the most papers or gets the most people switching the knobs on their TV sets, had tended to make Margie their heroine. They depicted the children as silver-spoon types, independently wealthy no matter what happened in the courtrooms, whereas the French widow had been born in the aftermath of World War II, in one of the most war-ravaged parts of Europe, of simple origins, had plied her honorable profession in some of the most respected hospitals of Europe, then had devoted herself and her energies, while still young, to a sick and elderly man. That the sick and elderly man happened to be rich couldn't belie the fact that he had loved her, or that she had loved him. Etc., etc.

It was a Cinderella story of sorts. To put it another way, it was as though Margie Magister had won the lottery, the biggest lottery of all. And clearly she deserved it. And now "they" were trying to take it away from her.

Recently, though, the pendulum had begun to swing the other way. Maybe it was the end of her "period of seclusion" that did it. Once Margie was back in the Magister penthouse duplex on Fifth Avenue, the media all but camped out across the street. They criticized her when she wouldn't talk to them, made fun of her accent when she did. She was pictured getting into a limo on Fifth Avenue, "a diminutive figure, her dark and sulky expression half-hidden by bangs," and her clothes were reported, identified, priced, also that the limo was owned by Magister Companies, and where she went for lunch, who with, what she ate, drank, what it cost. Once the media found out that the "von" in her name was a fake, even though she'd added it over a decade before, they wouldn't let her, or anyone, forget it. And when, after the Magister kids had announced their suits, she hired Roy Barger to represent her, it was—you could feel it—time to take the gloves off. Roy Barger may have been a streetfighter by reputation, but he was also, or had become, a street-fighter for the rich, and his relationship with the media was strictly love-hate.

By the morning I'm talking about, you'd begun to hear people say that Margie's shadowy past had to be hiding something, didn't the fake *von* prove it? Wasn't Alsatian half-German anyway? Maybe she was a Nazi; maybe she was Jewish. In any case, she was foreign, and who knew what she'd been giving Bob III all that time along with the prescribed medication? Whereas the Magister kids, all right, so they'd been born with the proverbial silver spoons, but they were at least Americans, weren't they? Their father's children, weren't they entitled to something?

Evenly divided, maybe even tilting toward the kids.

And either way, the Firm was caught squarely in the middle. And trying hard to duck.

Which is what brought the Counselor into it.

Douglas McClintock, senior partner, was clearly steaming.

"What in hell can we accomplish if Charles isn't here?" he asked, still standing behind his desk.

"Do you want me to leave?" I said, starting to rise from my chair.

"No, I didn't say that," McClintock answered, waving with one hand as though to brush away the suggestion. He is a small, humorless Scotsman, more or less contemporary to the Counselor and absolutely impeccable. Steel-rimmed glasses, thinning gray hair that looks lacquered to his skull, economical gestures, blue serge, conservative tie over a white and cuff-linked shirt. Every bit the high-level corporate attorney, in sum, with the polished no-nonsense manner to go with it.

"No offense, Revere," he went on. "This isn't directed at you. But how can we have a strategy session without Charles?"

"I thought the strategy had already been decided," I said.

"Oh?" he said. "Then you tell me what that is."

He sat down, steepling his hands on the desk top.

"Do you want it straight?" I said. "Or beating around the bush?"

"Straight, please," glancing at his watch.

"All right," I said. "The Magister situation has you—the Firm—caught in the middle. You're counsel to Magister Companies, but you also represent Robert Magister's estate and are one of its executors. The companies are without a head right now, the estate is being sued, you . . . the Firm in any case . . . are going to have to testify in court as to the circumstances in which the will was drawn up, and you can't afford to take sides because if you pick wrong, you risk losing one of your biggest clients, which is Magister Companies."

"In point of fact," McClintock put in, "the companies aren't without leadership."

"Sure," I said. "The board's appointed Young Bob acting chairman." Robert Worth Magister IV, the oldest son, seemed to be stuck with "Young Bob" even though he was closing in on fifty. "But the board only serves at the whim of the stockholders, and if there's ever a stockholders' vote, you, as executor, are going to have to choose."

"Unless we resign as executor."

"Unless you resign as executor," I repeated. "But I gather that's one option you don't want. It's too bad Magister named you."

"I always advised him against it," McClintock said, "but he insisted on us taking care of his personal affairs. He told me that if we wanted to keep the companies as our client, we could damn well draft his wills out of our retainer."

Maybe, as they say, that's how the rich get richer: by stiffing their attorneys. I'd have bet the Firm had never once dared bill him for personal services.

"I see you understand the situation," McClintock said. "But what we do about it is another question."

"The strategy, in other words," I said.

"Yes."

"Mr. Camelot tells me you want a settlement. Any settlement will do, you don't care what it is as long as there is one."

"I never told him that!" McClintock retorted angrily. "We want a fair and equitable solution. Our position is one of strict neutrality."

"Whatever," I said, getting a small pleasure from his reaction. "But some kind of settlement. Only you can't go directly to either side, because whichever one you go to will think the others put you up to it. Actually, Mr. Camelot says you already know of a proposition the family's ready to accept."

"*Some* of the family," McClintock corrected. "And it's a range, not a proposition. Did he tell you what it is?"

"In substance, yes. Mrs. Magister gets to keep all her personal property. She gives up her shares in the companies. She's guaranteed no less than a million dollars a year. For life."

"After tax," McClintock added.

And not bad pay, I thought, for three years' work.

"Only nobody believes she'll accept it," I said.

"We don't know that," McClintock said. "It's a start, a point of departure for further negotiation."

The problem was that nobody was volunteering to take it to Mrs. Magister, not the Firm, not Young Bob's attorney or any of the others representing the family members.

And that, the Counselor guessed, was because of Roy Barger.

McClintock denied this that morning. The Firm wasn't afraid of Roy Barger. What made everybody cautious was that *any* offer taken to Mrs. Magister, no matter what restrictions were put on it, was going to be leaked to the media as long as Roy Barger was involved, and once it was known publicly that the children were ready to settle, the psychological tide would start working against them. Roy Barger, at least by reputation, was a master of manipulation.

Enter Charles Camelot. A like master.

There was a further problem, though. I knew it; McClintock did too. Before the Counselor could talk settlement with Barger, he needed bargaining chips. Leverage in other words, something that would make Barger think twice before he went the route with the case. As if right then, Barger had nothing to gain by getting his client to settle and nothing to lose by going to trial, which would mean a ton of publicity and a fat fee at the end whether he won or lost. We needed something either on Margie Magister or, less likely, on Barger himself. As of right then we had nothing.

Which is where I came in.

A little later, McClintock passed me on to Henry Rand, a tall associate with a prominent Adam's apple who was in his early thirties and well up the ladder toward success in the Firm. Chances seemed good he'd make it the rest of the way: he'd graduated from the right schools, had the right social connections, and had hitched his career to the right star, meaning Doug McClintock. Meanwhile, while he sweated out his progress toward partner, which would give him a cut in the Firm's annual profits, he did most of McClintock's dirty work.

Hank Rand and I spent much of the day going over the Firm's files on Margie Magister. We worked in one of the smaller conference rooms, allegedly so that we wouldn't be interrupted but really, I guessed, because Hank's office was several notches below McClintock's in size and appointments. Hank's secretary, an eager damsel with a big polka-dot bow tie, brought us the papers we needed, plus sandwiches and coffee, plus a Perrier for Hank and a beer for me.

As executors, the Firm had at least formal approval over Margie Magister's expenditures, and from what Hank Rand showed me, the bereaved widow had been spending as though tomorrow would never come, or just in case it didn't. Bendel, Gucci, Cartier, Mark Cross, all of them were there, and art dealers, antiques dealers, and many of the watering holes and eateries around town which survive, or don't, on the largesse of the rich and famous. None of them was going out of business that season, thanks to Margie, and you could say Bob III's death was the first good thing that had happened to New York's pleasure merchants since Imelda Marcos lost her credit cards.

In addition, the Firm controlled Margie's payroll, or "household staff," the maids and housekeepers and gardeners and cooks and chauffeurs and "personal secretaries" without whom, you had to assume, the bereaved widow couldn't so much as get out of bed. There'd been a heavy dosage of young male employees, I noted, plus a lot of turnover; apparently Margie was hard to satisfy. In addition to names and dollars, to which they were entitled, the Firm had a lot more, and I was glad to see my sometimes accomplice, Bud Fincher, had been making an honest living. Bud runs a medium-sized private investigations agency, one of the better ones around town, and as far as I could tell, he'd done a pretty thorough work-up on the Magister staff, past and present.

"So much for strict neutrality," I commented to Rand as I went through the paperwork.

He looked at me with a quizzical expression.

"That's what McClintock told me," I said, quoting: "'The Firm's position is one of strict neutrality.'"

"Well," he said huffily, "that's substantially correct. What other position could we take?"

"In that case," I said, "why aren't we going through the same material on the rest of the family? You've got it, haven't you?"

He hesitated, like he wanted advice on how to answer. But then he thought better of it.

"Off the record?" he said.

I nodded.

"The answer is no," he said. "But that doesn't mean we couldn't develop it if we wanted to."

"Of course you could," I agreed.

The point, though, was that they hadn't. Margie Magister,

the Firm had clearly decided, was their target and Roy Barger their enemy.

I took some notes on items I thought could use further investigation, and Rand's bow-tied secretary photocopied some of the documents for me, but the message I took back uptown that afternoon, clear as it was, was one I knew the Counselor wouldn't want to hear.

"Essentially they've got nothing," I told the Counselor. "They know she's been on a spending spree, that she's got some good-looking young studs on her payroll, also that she's been chasing around with a pretty fast-and-loose crowd recently, but that's about it. Some smoke, but nothing you could light your pipe with."

The Counselor was in one of his fouler moods. He sat behind his desk, a massive figure in the usual late-afternoon working costume of shirtsleeves, bow tie, and suspenders. He chewed on an unlit pipe while I gave my report, his jawline gleaming in the light. The air-conditioning unit and his pipe smoke had been fighting for control of the atmosphere when I got there. The unit had won, but only temporarily, because when I finished, he kept me sitting there while he fussed with matches, then, failing to relight the old pipe, discarded it and found another, which he stoked with tobacco, then lit. The usual ritual, I thought, but I noticed one detail that wasn't: the bow tie and the suspenders didn't match. In fact, they clashed. The Counselor's Wife, I thought, would have a fit.

"What does Fincher say?" he asked, glowering at me.

"I haven't had a chance to talk to him yet."

"You haven't?"

I caught the accusatory tone all right.

"No."

"Well, and what have they got on the rest of the family?"

"I asked the same question," I answered.

"And . . . ?"

"Nothing. They haven't even looked."

"Assholes," he said, pulling the pipe from between his teeth. I didn't know for sure if he was referring to the

Magister children or the Firm or both, but I knew enough not to ask.

We sat there, eyeing each other. I could feel it mounting in him, call it tension, anger, whatever, but it was par for the course and I was used to it to the extent that I would ever get used to it.

"We'd better get off our butts, Phil," he said finally. "What else are you working on?"

I mentioned one or two matters of no great consequence. Nothing, in fact, that couldn't wait.

"Drop them," the Counselor said. "I want you full time on Magister. And not just the widow. I want them all. Now."

"But the Firm . . . ," I started to say.

"I don't give a damn what McClintock wants or says he wants. *We* want to know who's going to win."

I sat there a moment, waiting, but his head had already turned away, and then he rang for Ms. Shapiro.

I stood up and crossed her in the doorway.

A foul mood all right, but I put it to his gearing up. At the beginning of any case the Counselor feels at a disadvantage, and the feeling communicates itself to the rest of us. Usually, when the Firm calls us in, the feeling is double because nothing irritates the Counselor more than, as he puts it, the Firm's incompetence at handling its own matters. Even though, needless to say, their incompetence helps pay our bills.

Anyway, I was used to it like I said, and the foul mood, I expected, would dissipate once we began to get a handle on the case.

Only this time it didn't, and I was only partly right in the cause I gave it.

There was an envelope waiting for me when I got back downstairs. It was marked "By Hand," and I thought I recognized the writing, but all Roger LeClerc said was that a messenger service had delivered it.

Strange. The more so since the handwriting was the one I'd thought it was.

"Phil," the note inside said, "I need to talk to you in

private, to ask your advice, maybe your help. I'd prefer not to do it at home. Could you come over to my office any time between five and seven today? I've got to do my show after that, but I'll be here until seven-thirty. Please try to make it. It's important."

And the signature read: "Nora."

I looked at my watch. It was 5:20. I put in a call to Bud Fincher's office, not to talk to him but to find out where I could reach him later. Then I left the office and walked up Park to the apartment house where the Counselor's Wife, a.k.a. Nora Saroff, does her shrinking in one of the ground-floor suites.

As it turned out, I didn't get Bud Fincher till the next day. And if I thought I found out why the Counselor's Wife had been crying that morning and why she'd canceled her appointments, well, I turned out only to be partly right there too.

In other words: you win some, you lose some.

CHAPTER 3

"I find myself in a strange position," she began. "Strange to me at least. I've never had anything like it happen before."

I sat across her desk from her in a padded armchair where, I supposed, her patients confessed their secrets when they weren't lying on the couch behind me. I'd been in the outer area once or twice before, where the receptionist and waiting patients sat, and I knew that the Counselor's Wife shared the setup with another shrink, but I'd never been in her private office.

The effect of the room and its furnishings was quiet, neutral, maybe a touch feminine. The Counselor's Wife used a long white parson's table for a desk, and there was a large white vase at one end filled with fresh flowers in water, also a tape recorder, a white jar for pencils and pens, a telephone (also white), and very little else. Behind her, framed by floor-to-ceiling bookcases, hung a large oil painting, lit from above, which depicted ballet dancers at rest. A couple of them were holding on to those practice bars, another group was talking in a cluster, and a single girl leaned forward on a bench, head down, like she was trying to relax her neck. The painting was signed, but I couldn't read the artist's name. I assumed it was a good one, probably valuable.

The lighting was indirect and on the dim side. Beige drapes completely masked the two windows which, I figured, gave out onto the Park Avenue sidewalk. The carpeting was of a reddish brown tone and the upholstered furniture, including my chair, was covered in a nubby beige fabric. I had the weird feeling that I'd been there even though I knew I hadn't, and it wasn't till later, when I went along with her to the television studio, that I realized why.

"The professional ethics are muddy," the Counselor's Wife was saying. "Of course there's the confidentiality of the therapeutic situation . . . that's what you're taught in school. Whatever a patient says inside this room is held to be secret and sacrosanct, the same as in a priest's confessional. Or, if you like, a lawyer's office. But only up to a point. After that, you're on your own. Only there's no one to tell you where that point is, or when you've reached it, or what you should do once you have."

As though amused by something she'd just said, she smiled, showing her white teeth.

"God knows it's not like me to beat around the bush this way," she said. "It's also not like me to be the one doing the talking. Here, I mean. In this room. Maybe we ought to switch sides." She eyed me, crinkles in the corners of her eyes. "I bet that's what you're thinking too, isn't it?"

I shook my head. Actually I'd been wondering what it was that had choked her up that morning. Whatever it had been, though, I saw no sign of it now. Maybe she felt self-conscious inside, or was beating around the bush, but outwardly she seemed perfectly composed, cool.

"Here's the point, Phil," she said. "I think one of my patients may have committed a crime. Or crimes. A terrible crime, or crimes. And I don't know what to do about it."

She stopped there, eyes on me, head slightly tilted.

"Do you *think* it?" I asked. "Or do you know it?"

"Both," she answered. "Both think it and know it. And

neither. Sometimes I think I'm crazy even to think it; other times I'm dead certain."

"Certain enough to tell the police?"

She shook her head.

"Hardly," she said. "You'd have to understand the dynamic of the . . . damn, excuse the jargon. You'd have to have sat here where I sit to believe it, heard what I've heard, felt what was behind the words. Even then. Just hearing myself say it out loud makes me think I'm all wrong, that I might be doing him . . . someone . . . a terrible injustice."

She paused again, leaving a gap.

"What does Mr. Camelot think?" I asked.

"I haven't told him," she answered coolly.

I felt something in her then. Call it a stiffening.

"Then why me?"

"I felt the need to talk to someone outside the profession."

Another silence. It unnerved me a little, along with the cool, blue-eyed stare that invariably makes me feel like I'm being measured.

"Look, Nora," I said, "if you don't think you should tell me about it, don't. Not to worry, I'll forget you ever mentioned it. As far as I'm concerned, I never . . ."

"Not to *worry*?" she repeated harshly, turning it into a question, her eyes now large and fixed on me. "For God's sake, Phil, I think I may know the one who's killing those women!"

"You mean the Killer?"

"The Pillow Killer," she said. Then, tossing her head angrily, she repeated it: "The Pillow Killer. That's typical, isn't it? Men on the loose, anonymous, so sick and twisted and frightened that they'll commit horrible crimes, and we don't know who they are so we give them funny names. We invent their names for them. The Zodiac Killer, the Boston Strangler, the Mad Bomber. Son of Sam. The Pillow Killer. We don't know who they are, so we make them into celebrities with funny names. Did you ever stop to think why we do it?"

"I guess we all need our heroes," I said.

She laughed quickly.

"Funny," she said. "That is, unless you're a woman. Then it's not so funny. But that's the point, isn't it? After all, isn't it men who give the funny names to men who prey on women? You ought to try it sometime. I mean: try being us. Try walking in the street, or waiting in the subway, an elevator, at a supermarket checkout, and not knowing whether the man standing behind you is thinking about suffocating you with a pillow. We're supposed to be hysterical, paranoid, and everybody jokes about the blonde wigs and the scarves. You ought to try it sometime."

It would have been hard to be male in the last decade or two and not have heard similar suggestions. Hard too not to have learned that it's pointless to answer.

"I'm sorry, Phil," she said. "I didn't mean to subject you to Feminism 101. It's just that I've had a tough day as far as the sexes are concerned."

She didn't elaborate. She put her hands on the parson's table, palms flat, and gazed at me.

"I want to play you some tapes," she said. "It won't take long. I won't do all of it for you unless you want to hear more, and I didn't tape every session, far from it. I wish I had now. Or hadn't taped any of them. You'll see what I mean."

While she fiddled with the machine, she filled me in on the case history, or at least the parts she wanted me to know. She never called the patient by name, only he or him. He was young, twenty-five when he first came to her, which had been about a year before. He came from money, a lot of money, she said. New York money, what she called "your basic poor-little-rich-boy background." His father and mother had separated when he was a baby; then his father died when he was three. He had no recollection of him. Then his mother—he and his mother—had lived with another man for several years. The man had moved in with them. Then, when the boy was nine, his mother remarried, not to the lover but to another man. The boy had gotten into a lot of trouble. He'd been shipped off to boarding school at twelve and had been kicked out of a number of places through the years—for cheating, stealing, at least once for possession of drugs. He'd never finished college. When he'd first come to the Counselor's Wife, he'd been between jobs, though after she'd started seeing him, he'd gone to work for a bank. His stepfather had got him the job. It hadn't lasted. He no longer lived with his parents. He had a trust fund, enough apparently to pay for an Upper East Side apartment where he had a succession of roommates, male and female—"a kind of free-floating living arrangement" she called it—and enough, for that matter, to pay for the Counselor's Wife.

She wasn't the first shrink he'd been to. He'd been in and out of treatment a number of times. But she was the first one he'd picked out himself. Actually he'd watched her on television, and he'd come of his own volition.

"He has a sex problem," the Counselor's Wife said. "He announced that right off the bat, the first session. Almost before he sat down. He said he could do sex in the sense of getting an erection, doing intercourse, but it didn't go anywhere for him. That was what he called it: doing sex, doing intercourse. He said he didn't get aroused, didn't feel anything particularly. Nothing happened. He didn't come. Finally the erection would just go away, either because he got tired or else bored.

"You should know that it's not uncommon at all, although I've never met a male patient who didn't think it was unique to him. There's a whole body of case literature on the subject. But that's not the point. He wanted to deal with it, for me to deal with it, like . . . like it was an abstraction. I mean, I was a sex therapist, wasn't I? Well, if all he wanted was to have pleasure in sex like anybody else, he didn't see why I was interested in what he'd dreamt as a child. The usual stuff.

"Anyway, it turned out not to be so simple. It never is, otherwise . . ."

She got the recorder going then.

To listen to all she'd taped would have taken a lot longer than the time we had, but even the playbacks she'd selected had a kind of mind-numbing effect. Maybe shrinks are used to it, maybe they can listen to a disembodied voice and fill in the blanks, but I didn't know what he looked like, couldn't see the body language that went with his flat, nasal, preppy-sounding accent, and I couldn't help focusing on his verbal tics, like the way he had of tacking "you know?" on to the back of his sentences, turning every other sentence into a question. There were the pauses too, long ones sometimes, when you imagined him sitting in the chair I was sitting in or just lying on the couch and the Counselor's Wife waiting, just waiting, and even though I knew that part of being a shrink is getting the patient to bounce words off the blank wall of the shrink, I didn't see how she could stand it.

To hear him tell it, he and his peers spent most of their nights hanging out in a bunch of East Side bars, waiting for the "bridge-and-tunnel bunnies" to show up. They called it "trolling." The saloons were the kind that cater to the under-age crowd. The bunnies were girls from Brooklyn, Queens, the Island, out for high times and kicks and sometimes getting more than they'd bargained for. The Counselor's Wife may have called it group sex; to me it sounded like gang bangs, sometimes uglier than that, and the wonder of it was that this Carter McCloy—for that turned out to be his name—hadn't long since had the shit kicked out of him by vengeful bridge-and-tunnel fathers and brothers.

He hadn't. He claimed that he didn't take part in the rough stuff. Maybe so. But he also told about one of the schools he'd been expelled from years before. A faculty daughter had claimed that Carter McCloy had beaten her up. According to Carter McCloy, the faculty daughter had made him do it. The scandal had been hushed up; McCloy had been sent home.

If he hadn't taken part, then he'd certainly watched. He described it in detail, and it took me a while to realize that the detail was for the Counselor's Wife's benefit. Because, to hear him tell it, he didn't feel a thing.

"Why don't *you* ever say anything?" he said at one point, and you could hear the irritation in his otherwise flat voice. "I mean, you're always asking me stuff like: 'How did you feel about that? Did that give you pleasure?'" Pause. "The great Dr. Saroff. Why don't you tell me what *she* feels?"

Pause.

"I wasn't there," came the Counselor's Wife's answer.

"But I'm telling you about it, you know?"

Pause.

"How do you think I should feel about it?" the Counselor's Wife asked.

"There you go. Very clever. Answering questions with questions, turning it back on me, you know? But seriously—I mean it!—how do I know what you think? Maybe you'd like to get spread-eagled yourself, how do I know? Would you like your wrists tied down? I want to hear that. Maybe you'd like to be a sandwich, you know?" Laughter, then another pause. "All right, I know what you're thinking, go ahead and say it. 'Is that what I think most women want?' . . ."

"Well?" the Counselor's Wife said on the tape.

"Sure they do, lots of them. They want to be scared. Most women are excited by being scared. It turns them on, you know? But I want to hear that from you. What turns you on, you know?"

Pause.

"Why is it so important for you to know what turns me on?" asked the Counselor's Wife's cool voice.

No answer.

Silence.

End of tape.

Increasingly, in the chronology of the tapes, he got more pointed, personal, more graphic too. And angrier, when seemingly nothing he said got to her. I could hear that clearly, and I kept thinking meanwhile that if the bridge-and-tunnel fathers and brothers hadn't done it yet, somebody sure ought to.

Still, that didn't make him a killer.

I said something of the sort to the Counselor's Wife.

"Wait a minute," she said, head bowed and fiddling with the machine. "There are a couple of more things I want you to hear."

McCloy was very quiet in the next selection, at least at the beginning. He'd start to say something, then he'd fall silent. You could hear him cough. Even though I knew it was part of the technique to wait for him to talk, I didn't see how she could just sit there, listening to him cough.

Suddenly, on the tape, she was the one who spoke:

"You once said you thought women like to be scared, that being scared made them sexy. I wonder why you think that's so?"

"What makes you ask that now?" Tone of irritation.

"Curiosity, that's all. I also happen to think it's not true, so I wonder why you think so."

"It's been . . . well, it's been my experience, you know?"

A conversation-stopper, but only for a minute.

"What frightens men?" the Counselor's Wife asked. "I've only heard you talk about scaring women, about what scares women. But what scares men?"

Pause.

"I don't know. I'm never scared."

"Never? Not even when you were little?"

Pause.

"I don't remember ever . . ." Pause. "Not really, you know?" Silence again. Then he started, slowly at first, then his voice picking up speed. "I've got this friend . . . Hal, you know? I've told you about him before . . . You want to hear something really weird? He says that when he was little . . . real little . . . do you know what he was scared of? I mean like *really* scared? Of falling asleep, you know? He says he was scared to death of falling asleep! And do you know why? Guess. Go on, guess."

No answer from the Counselor's Wife but it didn't matter, the voice rushed on:

"It was the kid's prayer. His mother made him say it every night. You know the one I mean: 'Now I Lay Me Down to Sleep,' you know? 'Now I lay me down to sleep/I pray the Lord my soul to keep/If I should die before I die/I pray the Lord my soul to take.'

"It made him an insomniac, you know? He was convinced that if he let himself fall asleep, he was going to die, you know? Can you imagine that? He did everything he could think of to keep from falling asleep! To this day, he won't sleep with anything on him, not a blanket, not even a sheet.

He won't even use a pillow, you know? In the middle of winter he'll turn the heat up but he won't put anything over his body. Oh yeah, and he sleeps with the lights on!"

Toward the end he started to laugh, and then you could hear his snorting sounds on the tape.

Then silence.

"Why did you say it wrong?" the Counselor's Wife said.

"What do you mean, 'say it wrong'?"

"Don't you realize you said 'If I should die before I die' instead of 'If I should die before I wake'?"

"That's not what I said."

She recited it then, the lines from the kid's prayer, the way he'd said it.

It agitated him all right.

"What're you trying to do, twist my head?" he accused.

By way of answer, she told me, referring to some notes on her desk, she'd rewound the tape and played the passage back for him.

". . . deal, you know?" he was saying when the tape picked up again. "Big Freudian slip, you know? So what?"

"Why *did* you say it?" the Counselor's Wife asked.

"How should I know? It was a mistake, that's all. You're supposed to be the expert on Freudian slips, why don't you tell me what it means?"

"If I knew," her voice said mildly, "I'd tell you."

Her tone, though, had no effect on his rage. You could hear it gargling up in him, how she was no different from all the others, how all they wanted to do was play mind trips on him and twist his head and then, when the going got rough, they dropped him like a hot potato. He had the language to go with it too. He threatened her. His voice trembled with it. She was so smug, he said. That was what stuck in his craw, he said: that she was so *smug*.

Finally, a lull. Then you could hear a rustling sound on the tape, and she said:

"I think that's all we'll have time for today."

"That's what *you* think!" he retorted. But if anything more had happened, the tape didn't have it, because that's where it ended.

She played me parts of one more, from the next session and, she said, the last one. She dated it at the beginning of July.

I didn't understand, listening, why she wanted me to hear it. McCloy was all whiny and apologetic. He'd had no right to blow his cork the last time. He'd figured it out, he thought. The real reason he'd blown his cork was because he couldn't stand not seeing her again till September. The Counselor's Wife interrupted the tape to explain to me. The patient, she said, had gone a little bananas when she'd announced that her office would be closed the month of August. Most therapists closed in August, she said, and it was common enough for patients to have trouble with it. There'd even been a novel written about it. In any case, McCloy's "revenge" had been to announce back that he himself wouldn't be coming any more in July. He was going to Alaska. She'd spent a lot of time, she said, trying to convince him that by not coming in July, he was really punishing himself, not her, and suggesting that he postpone his trip till August. But to no avail. His friends were going, the whole gang.

The tape went on. A drone of self-pity was what it sounded like to me, but quiet, flat even. At one point, he'd asked her what would happen if he canceled Alaska. Would she reconsider about August in return? Would she find a way to see him then? No, she'd answered, that would be impossible. Well, he'd said, in that case there wasn't much more to be said.

She let it play through to the end.

"I think that's all we'll have time for today," her voice said. Apparently she ended every session that way.

Sounds of movement.

"Okay," his voice answered. "But you know? I think I'd like to shake your hand anyway."

"Good," she'd said.

End of tape.

Yes, I thought, and there'd been no more murders during the summer.

The Counselor's Wife looked up at me, shaking her hair back behind her shoulders.

"What did it feel like?" I asked for no particular reason.

"What did what feel like?"

"His handshake."

She laughed, and her hair tossed.

"Funny you should ask that," she said. "Sweaty, to tell the truth."

I watched the smile drift from her face. She was gazing intently at me, waiting for my reaction.

"I don't get it," I said. "I mean, I guess he sounds sick enough. And all that 'Now I Lay Me Down to Sleep' stuff and sleeping with the lights on, I guess he was talking about himself there and not a friend. Is that right?"

"I'm not so sure, but I assumed so too."

"So maybe he's afraid of pillows. But that doesn't make him a killer, does it?"

"What makes a killer, Phil? Do you know?"

"No," I said.

"Neither do I."

I think I've called her face angular before, but not thin, and when she's looking right at you and talking animatedly, which is about the only way she talks, it seems full, broad even. Only now it did look thin, small. Chiseled. She looked distracted, or maybe just tired.

"I spent a lot of time going over it today," she said. "I'd canceled all my appointments, not because of him but because something else came up. A good thing, though, as it turned out. Or maybe a bad thing, who knows? By the way, I don't tape all my sessions, only with certain patients and they have to agree to it. Anyway, I went over the material today, the tapes and my notes, and I called up a friend at the *Times* for the dates, and there's a correlation. I'm sure of it, Phil."

"What dates?" I said.

"Look," she said. "There's no way you could have spotted it, just listening. I hadn't either. But what I call the crazy sessions? The really angry ones? There was a rhythm to them. What you just heard was nothing like having been here. You could feel the electricity in him, Phil. Palpable almost. And building up. It was like . . . like . . . well, like when you feel a lightning storm building. I've seen them in the Hamptons. I've seen the ground actually smoke when the lightning bolts hit. It was like that. Once he almost put his fist through the wall. Sheer rage, and always directed at women. At me mostly, the surrogate Mommy according to theory. But then, by the next session, it would be as though exhaustion had set in. Utter exhaustion. I always thought it was because he'd worked it out himself the time before, or worked it out of himself, and that if we did that enough times, working it through . . ."

I'd heard the rage all right, particularly on the next-to-last tape. And then that kind of relapse on the last one.

"They coincide, Phil," the Counselor's Wife said quietly. "I've verified the dates. Each one of those murders took place in between."

But there she lost me, at least for the minute. It was like my Full-Moon Theory. Besides, the last session she'd played for me had taken place in July. We were now in September.

"Did he go to Alaska?" I asked.

"I don't know."

"But when's the last time you saw him?"

"I haven't," she said. "Not since then. He was supposed to call the first week of September to make an appointment. He did call. I scheduled him for last Friday."

"And . . . ?"

"He never showed up. Didn't call, anything."

"And the Killer killed again last night."

"That's right."

"Well," I said, "if he's the killer, then at least you can't blame this last one on yourself."

I'd meant it as a joke, but it didn't make her smile. Instead, she reached out and handed me something across her desk.

"When I got here today," she said, "I found this waiting for me."

It was a white envelope with the top slit open. I took it, glanced at the front, which simply said "DR. SAROFF" in typed capitals, and pulled out a single sheet of paper folded in three. There was a one sentence message inside:

WHAT MAKES YOU SO SURE YOU COULDN'T BE THE NEXT ONE

and it was signed:

A FRIEND

The Counselor's Wife had put her hand over her mouth while I read it, an involuntary gesture I hadn't seen before. I studied the page again. It looked like it had been typed on one of those cheap memory-writer machines because you could see the little dots that made up the letters. The letters were all in capitals. There was no punctuation.

"How did you get this?" I asked her.

"Alice gave it to me. Our receptionist. It had been slipped under the front door sometime during the morning, before I got here. Actually, one of Bill's patients spotted it on the way out and handed it to her."

"Who's Bill?"

"Bill Biegler."

Biegler was the name of the other shrink who shared the suite.

"Could anybody have seen whoever delivered it? One of the doormen?"

"I asked, but you know how they are. Sometimes they're in the lobby, sometimes not. Besides, the whole ground floor is doctors' offices, people come and go all the time."

"Who else have you told about it?"

"Just Bill. Some of it."

"Could one of your other patients have written it?"

"I thought of that. I don't see who."

"Or anybody else?"

She shrugged, a jerky movement.

"So you think McCloy."

"I don't know. One minute I can't believe it. The next minute I believe it."

"Then why don't you take it to the police?"

"But how could I do that?"

"Easy," I said. "They've got hundreds of people on the case, a whole task force. They could trace the paper this was written on, the typewriter. They're tracking down leads a lot flimsier than this one."

"But I'd have to tell them about Carter, wouldn't I?"

"Yes."

"And what would they do to him?"

"I don't know. Probably they'd haul him in for questioning. They'd . . ."

She was shaking her head, slowly, side to side.

"I couldn't do that," she said. "Even if he did send the note, suppose that was just his idea of a joke? It would fit his sense of humor. And suppose the rest of it . . . the correlations . . . were just coincidence?"

"Suppose you're wrong, in other words?"

"Yes, suppose I'm wrong. I couldn't do that to him. It would be just one more betrayal, a woman betraying him, which I think is his deepest fear. I don't want to go into it, but believe me, subconsciously he sees all women as betrayers of men, starting with his mother. Suppose the note is just a test? He's always tested me, that's obvious on the tapes."

Maybe *testing* was what a shrink would call it.

"Anyway," she said, and then she shook her head slowly again and smiled at me, one of her dazzlers, "and here comes the confession. Oh, I tell you, it's been a great day for self-criticism. Yes, I couldn't do that to Carter, and that's true enough as far as it goes. But I also couldn't do it to myself. If I went to the police and it turned out I was wrong, it would ruin me professionally. I mean," with a wave at the room, "I couldn't do this anymore, not for a day. I'd have to go eat bonbons, whatever. It'd be just one more case of a woman too hysterical to do a man's work, do you know what I mean?"

I did, but I didn't say anything.

"At the same time, I'm frightened. I'm not supposed to be, but I can't help it. I've never felt in danger from a patient before. And I tell myself: all the killings have been random, so the police say, and even if Carter McCloy was a murderer, he's incapable of matricide, which is what his neurosis is really about. Or even surrogate matricide, meaning me. Yes, I know that's right clinically, but if it's supposed to reassure me, it doesn't. Because what if I'm wrong? What if he's charged? The victim this time—last night—was older than the others. And blonde. The first blonde. And I'm blonde. And I know that's irrational, hysterical, but what if it isn't? So I'm a little freaked out, Phil. Not a lot, but a little. But here's the point: in order for me to do anything, like going to the police or anything, I need to be surer than I am now. I've also decided I can't just wait—for him to show up or make contact again. Or for the killer to kill someone else."

I waited for her to continue, but that was all she had to say. We stared at each other across the desk.

"So that's what brings you to me?" I said.

"That's what brings me to you," she said, smiling.

"And you haven't told Mr. Camelot?"

I watched the crinkles vanish, and her eyes went that deep blue, and her voice, when she spoke, dripped icicle water from some underground pool.

"He doesn't know anything about it. I don't want . . ."

She glanced at her watch and suddenly started.

"My God, Phil, it's almost eight! Why didn't you tell me? The limo's late, I'm going to be late for the show! God, I've got to run!" She stood, rushing and reaching at once, then, as quickly, jerked back at me, her eyes on mine. "But please, Phil, please come with me. I need someone with me tonight, I can't help it. I mean it. Besides, I've got more to tell you about him. I . . ."

I hesitated. In fact I had nothing on for that night. Laura Hugger maybe, but she hadn't called back. Actually, I think I'd been tilting toward Chinese take-out, a rental video, and my feet up. But she already decided everything: that I was coming with her, that I was going to investigate Carter McCloy for her and determine if he was the Pillow Killer, and God knows what else.

Simplify it: it was hard to say no.

By way of explanation, I ought to say something about our relationship, undefined though it is.

We're close to the same age, and probably because of that

there's a kind of running banter that goes on between us. Usually it takes this form: (a) I'm a hopeless and sexist philanderer; (b) I'm a confirmed and generally prudish bachelor; (c) since (a) is unacceptable and (b) is wasteful, somebody (she, namely) has to take me in hand and fix me up permanently from a seemingly endless roster of available candidates.

I've never taken her up on the available candidates.

On occasion—rare occasion—the teasing has threatened to get out of hand. It never has, though. By presumably mutual consent.

After all, she's the Counselor's Wife and I work for her husband.

In some weird way, I guess that makes us friends. At least I imagine that's what she'd say, and it's why it wasn't so strange that she'd turned to me in the Carter McCloy situation. Or that, in the end, I went along with her in the limo provided by the television station, she leaning back in the seat and talking animatedly as we drove to the studio way west in the Fifties. Or that I sat in the studio way west of the Fifties. Or that I sat in the studio audience, the only male in the joint, it seemed, except for the cameramen, while she did the show.

If you go in for that kind of thing, and a lot of people seem to, I needn't describe "Nora Saroff's Hour" because you'll already have watched it. The set turned out to be an almost replica of the office we'd just left, except that there were three chairs adjacent to the white parson's table for her three guests: a women's magazine editor, a well-known sculptress I'd never heard of, and an allegedly $1000-a-night call girl who called herself Carrie. The subject (what else is new?) was Female Orgasm. To tote it up: the sculptress said she never had one, Carrie claimed she always did, the magazine editor never pronounced herself (nor, really, did Nora) and the studio audience, in that part of the show where Nora goes out and interviews with a portable mike, seemed about evenly divided. But the topic seemed to turn them on enough that, even after the broadcast part ended in a shouting match with Nora standing behind her desk, hands raised and smiling broadly at the cameras, they kept at it for another good half hour.

She didn't want to go home afterward. We ended up in one of those overpriced checkered-tablecloth Italian joints in the West Forties and ate spaghetti and meatballs and drank red wine into the second bottle while the limo waited outside. She also emptied the bread basket, the salad bowl, and had *zabaglione* for dessert, and critiqued the show, signed three autographs for people who recognized her, and gave me data on Carter McCloy, which I noted down. I told her that, with a full-time job myself, I'd have to hire in from the outside. This was all right with her, provided I didn't use Bud Fincher or anyone else who worked regularly for the Counselor. She said she counted on me for total discretion.

If she was still freaked, in short, she'd stopped showing it at the restaurant. The awkwardness came outside, where the limo driver held the passenger's door open and an umbrella over our heads.

I told her I felt like walking, that I thought I'd walk home.

"You can't do that, silly," she said. "It's raining again."

Was it raining? Yes, it was. I hadn't noticed.

In that case, I said, I'd take a cab. No good. Then I suggested that I see her home in the limo and either ride it the rest of the way or walk across the park. No good either. We were already on the West Side, wasn't it stupid to go over to the East and then back again?

We got in. So help me, as we drove up Tenth, which turns into Amsterdam, and the windshield wipers *wickwacked* against the night lights, I thought about whether I'd made the bed that morning. I knew I hadn't.

The Counselor's Wife must have got the picture. As we crossed the 72nd Street intersection where Broadway and Amsterdam meet, she started to giggle softly. Then, a little later, taking my hand:

"You're so sweet, Phil. I couldn't have gotten through tonight without you. I thank you, dear Phil. But I'm not getting out with you, not to worry. Don't misunderstand: another time, with pleasure. Right now, I can't explain . . ."

We were at my corner, stopped. I had the door open. She

pulled me back, then, with her hand reaching around my neck, kissed me.

"Please call when you find out something," she said, letting me go. "Please call anyway. I'll be in my office all day tomorrow."

I watched the limo pull away, thought I saw her wave through the rear window. I still didn't get why she'd insisted on taking me home first, and when the truth finally hit me—I remember I was eating a sandwich at my desk with the door open—it was because I realized the cocker bitch was no longer in the house.

CHAPTER 4

"He had five children," Bud Fincher said. "The oldest, Bob, is forty-nine, the youngest twenty-nine. Then you start over again with grandchildren, starting at twenty-six and working down to eleven months. Then . . ."

"I can count," the Counselor growled. "I also know their names and that they breed like rabbits. What's that you've got there?"

What Bud had, and handed over, was his first report on the Magisters. It ran some twenty pages. Some of it was warmed-over data, the kind any city paper would have in its morgue: names, dates of birth, education, marriages, divorces, principal assets; and Bud, after an intervening call from the Counselor, had had full access to the Firm's files. But there was stuff in it that was fresh, including items I was pretty sure the Counselor didn't know about, and even though Bud's organization had had only a few days to develop it, it already pointed to one conclusion: that when push came to shove, the Magister children's worst enemy wasn't going to be Margie so much as each other.

Bud's report, in sum, was precisely what the Counselor had ordered. I knew this because I'd helped him edit it.

The Counselor glanced at it momentarily, then flung it into the debris on his desk.

"What's in it that Roy Barger doesn't already know?" he said, glowering at me and reaching for a pipe.

Why don't you give it to Barger and ask him yourself? I thought but didn't say. There is no point, at such moments. The trouble was that his mood had been like that for almost a week, unappeasable, stormy. I'd been spared the brunt of it mostly, but when Doug McClintock, senior partner at the Firm, took to calling me to find out if the Counselor had called Barger yet, and when Ms. Shapiro was reduced to tears as she had been that morning—a first, in my experience . . .

"And what's Fincher Associates' fee for this?" he went on, through clouds of smoke and gesturing at Bud's report. "What would you guess, Phil, all in? Ten thousand dollars? Fifteen? What's in there that Roy Barger doesn't already know that's worth fifteen thousand dollars?"

It would have been pointless, like I say, to tell him his number was exaggerated, or to remind him, for that matter, that Bud's fee would be passed through to the Firm, along with an hourly charge, overhead included, for my own participation.

"Well," Bud Fincher said beside me, "that Sally Magister may be a practicing lesbian, for one thing."

The Counselor's reaction lay hidden behind a bank of smoke.

"May be? Or is?" he said gruffly. "There's a difference."

"May be," Bud answered. "We think we can prove it, though. At a price. But I wanted instructions from you before we took it further."

"Even supposing it's true," the Counselor said, "or supposing it turns out she prefers animals? What difference would that make in today's day and age?"

"A lot," I said.

"How so?"

I knew he knew the answer, but I laid it out for him

anyway. Sally Magister, the second child and only daughter of her generation, had been the Magister black sheep for years. Three times married, three times divorced, mother of four, she also ran the Magister magazine division. Ran it into the ground, some said. Ironically, the one bright spot in her otherwise faltering empire was *Fem*, once known as Sally's Folly because she'd allegedly sunk millions into it but which had somehow turned out to be what women in the Eighties wanted to read. Without *Fem*, so Wall Street said, the Magisters would long since have either folded or sold off their magazine interests.

In any case, Sally was the obvious weak link in the family's solidarity against Margie. Her contempt for men in general, and her brothers in particular, had been widely publicized. As long as their father lived and, as the dominant shareholder, wielded effective control of the company, Sally could shout all she wanted. But with him dead, and his shares split, and control of the company up for grabs?

Actually, Sally had been quiet since Bob III's death. She'd sided with the family in contesting the will, had accepted Young Bob's appointment as acting chairman without complaint. Without public complaint anyway. But I could think of several ways a clever lawyer like Barger could use the information Bud had dug up, even if Sally didn't give a damn who knew what about her private life, and I guessed the Counselor could think of more.

"Push it," he told Bud Fincher. "And you," he said, turning to me, "you go after the widow."

It wasn't just that he called me "you." His tone was accusatory and anonymous at the same time, like a sergeant giving orders to a new recruit.

"What do you mean," I said, "'go after the widow'?"

"Find out what she really wants."

"How? Do you want me to ring her doorbell and ask her? Or should I ask Roy Barger for help?"

An attempt at sarcasm, I guess. I'd already reported that McClintock had been after me to get him to call Barger, also that I'd told McClintock I thought there was no way he'd call Barger till we had some bargaining chips. But the Counselor's pipe had gone out. He rummaged on the desk, looking for something to attack it with, then found a paper clip and worked at unbending it.

"That's up to you," he said. "But if you want to ask Barger, he'll be here this afternoon. I want you to sit in anyway."

I looked at Bud Fincher; Bud Fincher looked at me. The Counselor jabbed the straightened paper clip into his pipe bowl.

"Who called who?" I asked.

"Whom," the Counselor corrected, banging the pipe bowl into an ashtray. "Barger did. He wants a meeting. Says there's no point our clients running up legal bills if there's a common ground."

"But how did he know we're invol—?"

"I don't know," the Counselor interrupted. "But if he's really pushing for a settlement now, it's because he knows something he doesn't want us to find out."

He stared into the pipe bowl, then, apparently dissatisfied, picked up a substitute, and started to stoke it with tobacco. Then he looked at me, his eyes deep and expressionless in the craggy head.

"Find it out," he said.

You work for anybody long enough, you learn to pick up even small shifts in mood, and the Counselor and I go a long way back, back in fact to the Firm, in the days when he was a senior partner among other senior partners and I was a paralegal trying to scrounge together a living while I struggled through Torts and Wills. Like I've said, I know he's at his worst in the early stages of a case, when he feels himself at a disadvantage because he has to wing it. *The Law is 95 percent preparation* is one of his dicta. At various times I've heard him put the other 5 percent to luck, brains, or connections. But his mood that week had been blacker than the Magister situation called for, like there was something underneath that drove him to beat up on all of us that had nothing to do with the Magisters or any other legal matters he had pending.

As, in fact, there was.

In addition, I brought something of my own to the party. This wasn't the first time I'd carried out an investigation on my own. Though I'm not licensed to do anything more in New York State than drive a car, I've functioned as a sort of para-PI on more than one occasion, and on my own account. But this was the first time I'd done it, at least in part, on "company time," and the first time without the Counselor knowing about it.

With the Counselor's Wife's approval, I'd turned over the Carter McCloy legwork to an independent I knew, an ex-cop called Bobby Derr. Bobby was a handsome smoothie still in his twenties. The way he told it, he'd resigned from the NYPD because you couldn't be a New York cop in the 1980s unless you were on the take. Other people, who knew something about what had happened, told other versions. He'd worked for a time for Fincher Associates, which was where I'd met him, but then he'd gone out on his own. He looked equally at home in Banana Republic and Brooks Brothers—one reason I'd picked him for the job. For his part, he assumed he was working for the Counselor even when I asked him to bill me direct, and he'd guessed our clients were McCloy's parents. I hadn't led him to believe that, but I hadn't exactly told him he was wrong either.

"You're going to get billed double-time on this one, Philly," he'd said when we met for breakfast that morning.

We'd gone up to the Roosevelt, the last of the great West Side cafeterias, where you can sit all morning on one mug of coffee and they serve the best honeybuns in town. My kind of place, in sum.

"I've been up . . . let's see . . . ," he said, checking a notebook, "three A.M. one night, one-thirty another—that was the early bird, last night—and the grand finale, that was on Staten Island: seven-thirty in the morning. He and his buddies picked up three broads at Melchiorre's on Third Avenue, danced the night away, and took them home. Six studs, three broads. They live in a condo over there, the three broads. They're secretaries down on Wall Street. Not bad either. What they did in there is your guess, but two of the studs came out at 6:45, including your boy Carter, and his buddy drove him home. Drives an Alfa. How the rest of them got home I don't know, or if the broads ever made it to the office. D'you know Melchiorre's, Philly?"

"By name," I said.

"Yeah," Bobby Derr said, chuckling, "you'd stick out like a sore thumb there. Too old. Even me, I just manage to get by. It's kind of a singles joint for the preppy set, y'know what I mean? Most of the customers are under age, 'specially the broads. That's how I got Alfie to tell me a thing or two."

"Who's Alfie?"

"Alfie Leonard. Owns the joint, bought it from the Melchiorres a couple of years ago. I know some people he pays, and he knows I know. So even though he made me, he lets me sit around, tells me a thing or two. I've slipped him a few bucks, it's on the bill."

"What did he tell you about McCloy?"

"Alfie says he's okay. Drinks too much but quiet, non-violent. No problem. Not like some of his crowd. Alfie thinks he might be gay, closet-fag variety. They use the joint like a kind of club, anywhere from six to a dozen of them."

"You mean they're there every night?"

"Most nights anyway, according to Alfie. He lets them run tabs. Sometimes they eat there, though Alfie himself says the food's terrible, but anyway, they show up and drink till they pick up some action. Then they hit the discos, Rosebud's mostly. Some nights they close up Melchiorre's, some nights not. D'you know Rosebud's, Philly?"

"No," I said.

This made Bobby laugh, a white-toothed laugh that could have passed in a toothpaste commercial.

"Shows your age, ole buddy. It's down off the Bowery, used to be a stage theater of some kind. They gutted the insides, put in lights, mirrors, bars, a coat room as long as Grand Central Station, and all the latest electronics shit. Big screens all around. It's a kind of *Rocky Horror Show* environment. The kids lap it up. They're not too particular who they let in, 'cept for the over-thirties. You gotta have an ID proves you're under thirty. I doubt you'd make the cut, Philly."

He thought that was pretty funny too.

"Any drugs?" I asked him.

"Drugs? You gotta be kidding. The grass is so thick at Rosebud's they gotta be growing it in the johns."

"I didn't mean Rosebud's. I meant McCloy, his group."

"Not that I saw. Alfie says the preppy set's back into booze mostly nowadays. Booze and sex. Says they're like rabbits, least that's all they talk about. Even with AIDS. I could've been picked up half a dozen times myself if I hadn't been on the job."

Bobby Derr looked the part. He might have been up late every night, but sitting at the Roosevelt that morning, clean shaven, in a yellow button-down Oxford shirt open at the neck to show some chest hair, and jeans, and a brown tweed jacket, with his raincoat slung over the back of his chair, you'd never have guessed it. He had the Ivy League look, and though the way he talked didn't say Yale or Harvard exactly, it didn't say not-Yale or not-Harvard either, not in the 1980s.

He had some other stuff for me too, and not bad. He'd greased the super at McCloy's building and had learned that though Carter McCloy lived there, he didn't own the apartment. Some corporation did, the super said. The super had nothing on McCloy in particular, but the apartment, 9B, had been in trouble off and on. Late-night parties, neighbors' complaints, people coming and going at all hours. The police had been called in a couple of times, and the super knew the apartment had been brought up at the co-op board, but nothing had happened. Bobby thought the super knew more than he'd let on, but he wasn't sure.

"You're in twelve hundred bucks so far, Philly," he said at the Roosevelt Cafeteria. "Round numbers. What do you want me to do next?"

I thought about it. What I really wanted was a rundown on Carter McCloy's whereabouts on certain specific dates stretching back to the spring, but there was no way I could turn Derr loose on that without running the risk of him guessing, and I couldn't do that without the Counselor's Wife's approval. I didn't think she'd approve. I thought of narrowing it just to the night of the last murder, but that was risky too.

"Just keep it going," I told him.

"You want round the clock?"

"No," I said. "Just nights."

"Nights'll cost you double, Philly. I'm not like these guys, I don't get to sleep all day. Besides, if I keep it up, they're gonna make me. A face gets familiar after a while. What do I do then?"

"Let it happen," I said. "Get in the middle of it. Get to know them."

I watched him think about it. The money was okay, I figured, and the possibility of getting laid on the job wouldn't bother him either. But something did bother him. Call it pride if you want to, but I think he was looking for an angle.

"What's Camelot after?" Bobby Derr said. "Wouldn't it be easier if you just told me? What's he really after?"

"It's not Mr. Camelot," I said. "I've told you that before."

"I know, I know," he said, grinning, "it's not Camelot's money, it's the client's. But who's the client? McCloy's folks? And what are they after? Drugs? Do they think little Carter knocked somebody up?"

I told him I couldn't answer him on either ground. I was pledged to confidentiality.

"There's something else I don't get," Bobby Derr said. "You guys always use Bud's outfit on this kind of deal. Why me this time?"

"Two reasons, Bobby," I answered. "One is that Bud doesn't have anybody for this kind of job, nobody who could get as close as you. The other . . . ?" I hesitated long enough to let him do some speculating on his own. Then: "Well, you know Bud, Bobby. Let's see how it plays. Maybe we'll have some other things to talk about, once this one's over."

This did the trick. I guess Bobby's no different from most people, in terms of his ego and his dreams, and maybe I'm not much different from people who'd make use of them.

Anyway, I worked through one other idea with him. I

wanted somebody I could talk to myself, who knew Carter McCloy. He didn't think that would be easy; from what he'd seen, the broads were mostly one-night stands; besides, hadn't he told me they wouldn't let me in at the Rosebud? But he said he'd keep his eyes open.

Money, I told him, might help.

He seemed to like that suggestion.

Breakfast with Bobby Derr wasn't the only work I did for the Counselor's Wife on "company time." I could use Bobby up to a point without telling him why, but there was no way I could call any of our regular contacts at the NYPD or the media and not arouse suspicion. Not when a whole task force was, as it was put, "combing the city" for the anonymous killer and every tip, or shred of a tip, was being tracked down and women on the streets and in the stores, blondes as well as brunettes now, were wearing scarves around their heads. The media, of course, had been full of it all that week since the Riverside Drive murder, complete with criticism of the police, scientific explanation of death by suffocation and capsule rundowns of the four previous crimes, and an enterprising reporter on the *Post* had even got hold of, and run, the police file on "open" homicides involving women victims over the last two years. The reporter suggested that the Pillow Killer might have been operating for much longer, only that his modus operandi had changed.

But knowing that the media have a way of changing things over time, dropping this or that detail in order to fit a developing story, I wanted to look at the original reportage, so I put in some time in the Periodical Room at the New York Public Library on 42nd Street, and from it I abstracted some interesting facts and discrepancies.

Of the first four murders, the first had taken place the previous winter, then three in the spring and early summer. They had all happened in Brooklyn, the first in Cobble Hill, the second way out in Bensonhurst, the third in Park Slope, the fourth in Brooklyn Heights. The victims had all been white, brunette, single. The oldest had been twenty-seven. All had worked. All but one of them—the last—had lived alone. All but one—the last—had been murdered during the night. All have been called "party girls" by the media, connoting something south of prostitution but north of the straight arrow. None appeared to have known or been linkable to any of the others. All dated frequently. The kind, in sum, who might have been found in places like Melchiorre's on the Upper East Side, or discos like the Rosebud, though neither of these two was mentioned in the accounts.

The third murder, the Park Slope one, was the only one where there'd been signs of violence. The police had found blood traces on the victim's bed. It was their only forensic evidence in all four cases, but they'd never been able to match it with a suspect.

The fourth murder, the one in Brooklyn Heights, differed in several respects. The victim, Annette Costello, had a roommate, and the killing had taken place on a Sunday in broad daylight. The roommate, away for the weekend, had discovered the body when she returned that evening. There was evidence that Annette Costello had been out shopping in the neighborhood before she was killed, possibly in the company of the killer. Witnesses claimed to have seen a young man with her in a local supermarket, but none could agree on what he looked like and that lead too, like all the others the police had uncovered, had apparently evaporated in the course of investigation.

Annette Costello had died on a Sunday, in Brooklyn, during the daylight hours. She was twenty-one.

Then the Killer had taken the summer off.

Then Rosemary Stevenson Sutter had died in September at night, in her bedroom above Riverside Drive, in Manhattan. Rosemary Sutter was blonde, thirty-seven, married. Her body had been discovered by her husband in the early morning hours, when he returned from a business trip. She too had died by suffocation, but unlike all the others except one she'd had sex that night, with either her killer or another man.

The Sutters, as portrayed by the media, had had a pretty open marriage. Alan Sutter had "business interests" outside the New York area, it was pointed out, and the papers invariably used the quotation marks. Friends of Rosemary Sutter had said that she was "estranged" from her husband (quotation marks again) and had taken solace from time to time with other men. Younger men, it seemed. Alan Sutter himself was in the clear: he'd been in transit at the time his wife was murdered. The media, picking up on the differences in this case, wondered out loud if it had been a copycat killing. The police, emphasizing the similarities, thought not.

In other words, sure, Carter McCloy *could have* killed the five women. But at that point you could have said the same thing about thousands of other people, and that was substantially what I told my "client" when she called in that day on my direct dial, at about 1:30 P.M., while I was brown bagging it at my desk.

For the record, I was eating a Revere Special: Muenster cheese and sliced tomato, with mustard, on bagel, and a bottle of Moosehead. You can have the bagel toasted or plain. I normally go for plain. The office was in its usual midday lull, which is probably why she called then. The Counselor was off at La Gonzesse, the French bistro over on Lexington where he usually goes for lunch. He'd be back around 2:30 because we had Barger at three. Charlotte McCullough had taken a sick day. Ms. Shapiro was also eating at her desk because we ordered in from the same deli. Roger LeClerc was either out or upstairs, conning lunch in the kitchen from Althea, the Camelot's cook and housekeeper, because the front door was locked and all incoming calls were routing upstairs to Ms. Shapiro.

Normally at such times, Muffin, the Counselor's Wife's cocker bitch, makes her rounds. She knows not to cross my threshold, but she'll walk past anyway, wagging her tail if I look at her, and sometimes hunker down outside the door for a few minutes. Dogs never give up hope entirely, I guess. But Muffin didn't show up, and I realized then that I hadn't seen her since that morning on the street, when her owner was crying in the red slicker and the red fisherman's hat.

"These are your choices," I told the Counselor's Wife on

the phone, after summarizing for her what Bobby Derr had dug up. "We can let Derr go on, which will cost money, time, and probably end up nowhere. Or we can go to the police with what we have. Or we can drop it, at least for now."

"I'm not worried about the money," she said calmly. "We can't go to the police. You know why that is. But we can't drop it either, silly as that may sound to you. At least I can't."

She was giving me an out, I guess, but I didn't take her up on it. I thought of asking her if she'd told the Counselor yet, but I now knew the answer to that one without asking.

"How's Muffin?" I said.

"Muff—? Oh, she's fine."

"Well, and how are you?"

"Me?" A short laugh. "Oh, I'm okay. I'm fine too."

"Where are the two of you living these days?"

Pause.

"Look, Phil, maybe someday I'll tell you all about it. Or maybe I won't. I'm in a state of flux right now about a lot of things."

"Does that mean you've moved out of here permanently?"

"I don't know."

"Well. Is there anything else I can do for you?"

"No, but it's sweet of you to ask."

"But suppose I have to find you over the weekend? About McCloy, I mean? Where can I reach you?"

"Just leave a message on my answering machine at the office. I'll be calling in regularly."

For a woman who'd just walked out on her husband—after how many years of marriage?—she sounded remarkably cool. Also for a shrink who suspected one of her patients of homicide. But it sure explained the prevailing atmosphere in our office. I don't know if I was the last of the Counselor's staff to catch on or the first. Nobody had said anything, at least not to me. But it explained the tension, explained Ms. Shapiro's tears, even maybe Charlotte's absence. And of course it explained the Counselor himself.

Like I've said, he'd never exactly been a piece of cake to

work for. But that week? Well, come to think of it, he'd acted exactly like a man whose wife had just walked out on him.
Against his will, I figured.

"No, I've never had the pleasure," said Roy Barger, extending a plump hand toward me in the Counselor's office, "but I've surely heard of Phil Revere. Do you know what they call you around town, Phil? Charles Camelot's Secret Weapon. Not so secret at that. But listen, my friend, any time you're tired of playing slave to the Counselor here, you give me a call, will ya?"

I'd never met Barger either, though I'd have recognized him from his pictures in the papers. He was a bulky man, a little shorter than I'd have guessed, with a florid complexion, lively blue eyes set in a large head and wavy gray hair, a lock of which frequently wandered across his forehead. His clothes fit him well: gray worsted suit, blue-striped shirt with white collar, black tie with a blue polka-dot design, black tasseled loafers. He came originally from somewhere in the South, still had a trace of the accent and the speech cadence and the ingratiating manner. As an attorney, though, he had the streetfighter's reputation, also the headline-seeker's, based in part on several notorious criminal cases, and though his firm now had several names after his own, it was, make no mistake, Roy Barger's firm. An expensive one too, by reputation. He was also the first person I'd ever heard call my boss "Counselor" to his face.

"I'm here to try to cut through the tall grass," Roy Barger began, once the niceties were over and he was seated across from the Counselor, I at my usual end of the desk. "Why for once, Counselor, can't we save our clients some money and ourselves some precious time?"

I watched the Counselor reach for a pipe.

"I think first we should define who our clients are," he said. "I . . ."

"Right there," Barger interrupted with a wave, "do you see what I mean? Why can't we dispense with all that, Charles? I know, I know, McClintock represents the estate, the Magister children have their own attorneys, and you're just a consultant to McClintock. Is that why you've got your own investigators climbing all over my client, trying to find out what she had for breakfast this morning?" He paused—good timing, I thought—but when the Counselor didn't answer, he turned to me with a broad smile: "If you really want to know what she's having for breakfast, Phil, why don't you just call me? Or call Margie? We'll be delighted to give you the menu." Then, back to the Counselor: "The point is, Charles, for every forkful of dung you can fling at Margie Magister, we've got truckloads we can dump on the family. Even the numbers are on our side. You've only got one Magister. We've got five Magisters to start with, and not only do their closets have skeletons in them, but their skeletons have baby skeletons. You know that as well as I do. What's more, the will is going to stand up. Whatever you say, no court will overturn it. The man was competent when it was written; he was competent till the day he died. But that's self-evident. For once, I say let's not litigate. That's what I've recommended to my client, and she agrees. And that's why I'm here. I'm here to talk a deal. I'm here because I'm empowered to talk a deal, and I'm talking to you, Counselor, and nobody else because you alone have the intelligence to understand the elements."

Ingratiating, like I said. *Flattering* would be better, but flattery in such broad strokes as to put even the most naive on guard.

"One question first, Mr. Barger," the Counselor said, holding a lighted match over his pipe bowl.

"Roy, please," Barger said, brushing the stray lock of hair back off his forehead.

"Roy," the Counselor repeated. He sucked flame from the match, puffed smoke clouds, then with a snap of the wrist extinguished the match. "What's your rush?"

"What's my rush?"

"That's right. You come barging in here—no pun intended—all full of the urgency to make a deal, or talk a deal. At the same time you're convinced your client is lily-white and simon-pure, and a sure winner in any legal contest with the Magisters, if there is such a legal contest. In that case, I can't but ask myself: Why is Roy Barger in such a hurry?"

Clearly the Counselor meant to throw him off guard, but it didn't work. Outwardly, anyway. Barger didn't bat an eyelash.

"I'm always in a hurry," he answered smoothly. "And this time there's good reason. The stock market for one. Have you followed what's happened to Magister Companies lately? Down, down and down, even in a generally bullish climate. The stock's on everyone's sell list. You know what the analysts are saying as well as I do: that the company's in chaos. What's more, you know that it'll stay that way till the leadership question is resolved."

"Which could be to somebody's advantage in a buy-out situation," the Counselor said.

"From the buyer's point of view, yes. But is that what you're suggesting?"

"I'm not suggesting anything," the Counselor said, blowing smoke. "I'm waiting to hear what deal you have to offer."

"It's very simple," Barger said, crossing his legs. "My client wants control of the company. She wants to run Magister. She believes it's what her husband would have wanted. She also believes it's to the company's best interest."

He paused, glancing at me, then back at the Counselor, as though leaving room for comment. I watched the Counselor, trying to gauge what he was thinking. He drew on his pipe, one of those curved jobs with the silver ring at the joint, and puffed smoke, which eddied upward, wreathing his head. Then he took the pipe out of his mouth, stared at it briefly, then sucked on it again. I saw his jaws work, a sign usually that he was either thinking or angry, or both, but otherwise he simply stared at Barger, dark eyes set deep under shaggy graying brows.

"That's what your client desires," he said at length. "But what's the deal?"

"It's very simple," Barger repeated. "Essentially it's whatever the children want. If they want to stay in their current jobs, including their seats on the board, she would welcome them with open arms. She's totally ready to extend the olive branch."

"And if that's not what they want?"

"Then she's prepared to buy them out, at a price to be negotiated but well above market. In fact we're ready to go beyond that. We're ready to make a tender offer, at the same price, for *all* the outstanding shares of Magister Companies."

If I'd caught his shift from *she* to *we*, I knew the Counselor had too. I also guessed he'd be wondering: where would she—or "they"—get the money? The estate held approximately 25 percent of the outstanding shares. This would be enough, practically speaking, to block any "unfriendly" takeover attempt, because it was written into the company bylaws that any sale of the company had to be approved by 75 percent of the outstanding shares. Old Bob had set it up that way. But if his will stood up, and Margie and the children, each with half of Old Bob's 25 percent, ended up in a shoving match, then either side would be able to bring in outsiders.

"What makes you think she's competent to run Magister?" the Counselor asked. "I didn't know she had experience in business."

"She doesn't," Barger answered. "In fact she says it would be the greatest challenge of her life."

"That's not what I asked," the Counselor said. "I wanted to know why *you* thought she was competent."

"Me?" Barger said. He thought about it a minute, uncrossing his legs, then recrossing them in the other direction. "I'm just a lawyer," he said then, the Southern coming up in his voice. "A country lawyer at heart. But I think two things. If you look at the histories of family businesses, you'll find that the second generations mostly aren't up to it. Young Bob, they tell me, is one of the nicest fellows in the world, but that doesn't make him chairman of the board material. His sister, I understand, is something of a flake, and her . . . er . . . sexual predilections would make for difficulties. Mind you, Margie . . . Mrs. Magister . . . is very fond of all Bob's children. That's an important point. She wants nothing but good for them.

"But the other thing is this: Margie Magister is one of the most remarkable women I've ever met. I truly believe that anything she set her mind to she could accomplish. Yes, I'm truly convinced of that. She could have been a film star; she could run for political office; and, yes, she could manage a company."

He paused, as though to let the strength of his convictions sink in on us. For my part, it occurred that "all Bob's children"—at least Young Bob and Sally—were in fact older than their stepmother, also that, as far as we knew, her only professional qualification was that she'd been trained as a nurse.

"I've a suggestion for the two of you," Barger went on, his eyes now glistening with sincerity. "Suspend all judgment until you've met her yourselves. I'd be happy to arrange that, at your convenience. Or if you're too busy, Counselor, why don't you just sent Phil? And meanwhile," looking from one to the other of us, "why don't you call off your dogs? Frankly it's a waste of your time and an annoyance to my client. There's nothing you'll find out that she wouldn't tell you herself. Yes, she's been leading the high life, yes, she's been spending rather freely, but hasn't she paid her dues? Of course she has."

I looked to the Counselor, waiting for some rejoinder that would cut through Barger's smooth talk. But it didn't come. The more Barger went on, the more he simply sat there, impenetrable, pipe in hand.

It was as though he was thinking about something else.

Maybe he was.

Somewhat to my surprise, he accepted Barger's invitation. Barger made the call then and there, and we were set up for lunch at Margie Magister's.

Still more to my surprise, he went.

As soon as Barger was gone, the Counselor himself took off. No postmortem, no instructions. I heard Ms. Shapiro calling the garage for the car to be brought down. This in itself was not unusual: it was still September, their house in the Hamptons was still open. But normally they'd wait till late Friday night or Saturday morning to avoid the traffic.

When I got home myself, I found a message from the Counselor's Wife on the answering machine. She wanted to talk to me urgently. Carter McCloy had called. He'd asked for an appointment the next week. She'd given him one. But when I phoned back, all I got was her own machine, and by the time I left to go out, she still hadn't called back.

CHAPTER 5

"Come on, all you kids out there, all you boys and girls, all you mothahs of both sexes. . . . Let's shake a leg! Let's vacillate a limb! Let's GO-O-O-O-O-O-O . . ."

The speaker was a king-size black man with a Rastafarian hairdo and gold chains inside an unbuttoned yellow silk shirt. He hovered over his consoles in the smoky air on a platform raised above the dance floor, and when he straightened up to harangue the throng below him, his teeth flashed gold.

The beat of "Gimme Shelter" boomed over the giant sound system, drowning his voice, and multicolored globes in the rafters rotated slowly, sprinkling blobs of light over the five hundred couples, give or take a few, who began to gyrate underneath, as well as a huge billowing floor-to-ceiling Orson Welles, blown up from the movie poster of *Citizen Kane*. The place was Rosebud's, an abandoned movie palace on the Lower East Side that had been converted into a vast bar and disco. For the well-heeled presumably, because it cost you twenty bucks a couple to get into the joint, two bucks a head at the coat check, four bucks for a beer at the mirrored orchestra bars and seven-fifty for a watery Scotch and two small ice cubes. The dancing, upstairs in the converted balcony, was free. Bobby Derr had called it a *Rocky Horror Show* environment. To Laura Hugger and me, the decor was a combination of high-tech and Forties movies, with bright lights downstairs and a lot of smoked-glass mirrors and dark corners where they couldn't figure out what else to put in. Add some neighborhood winos and contemporary flower children, who were let in free, I figured, for local color, plus a troop of shirtless high-stepping gays, black and white, wearing bib overalls cut down to their hipbones, and you had the recipe for nightlife success. Or so it seemed, because people were lined up out in the street in a drizzling rain, waiting to get in, and by midnight you had the feeling that one more body on the dance floor and the whole joint would explode.

Earlier that day Laura Hugger and I had declared a truce, and we'd gotten together after work at one of our favorite Chinese eateries on the Upper West Side. Meanwhile, without telling her, I'd left a trail for Bobby Derr in case he needed me. But Bobby didn't call. Then we went home to Laura's place, and it was there—*in flagrante*, as they say—that Bobby found me. The whole gang, McCloy and Bobby included, were about to leave Melchiorre's for the Rosebud.

"How did he know to find you here?" Laura said when I hung up.

She listened in bed, the sheet now pulled up over her body, while I explained some of the situation to her. I censored out the Counselor's Wife. Laura was known to be sensitive on the subject. Even so, the more I explained, the more I got ready to duck. Instead, and to my surprise, she got up and went into the bathroom to get dressed, saying over her shoulder that Gee, wasn't it a good thing we'd gotten the sex out of the way early because she'd always wanted to party with a bunch of rich young hoods?

Ms. Hugger, in case I haven't mentioned it, has a pretty sharp tongue when it comes to priorities. Especially mine.

She's also a pretty flamboyant dresser. She came out in a

black mini-skirt and hot pink top, with a gold choker tight around her neck and heels high enough to bring her almost up to my height.

I must have raised an eyebrow.

"If you're going to try to pass, Phil," she said, "you'd better do it right."

Anyway, that's how we found ourselves on the dance floor at the Rosebud, shaking and baking to "Gimme Shelter" while the oversized Rasta boogied behind his consoles up above and Carter McCloy, a few couples away, revolved in the general direction of his partner, like a statue turning slowly on a pedestal.

He was a tall kid with a shock of straight brown hair that fell over his eyes a lot and which he got rid of either by a toss of the head or a flick of the hand. He had on loafers without socks, jeans, a blue blazer over a tieless white shirt, and a white silk scarf draped around his neck. Laura Hugger said he looked like a college boy, a handsome one at that. A very handsome one. Ralph Lauren, Laura said. He also looked stoned to me. He'd downed four double Scotches while I watched him across one of the downstairs bars, plus whatever he'd had before, but there was something else besides booze, I thought. His pupils were like pinpricks with the light gone out of them, his complexion pale, his expression vague, almost vacant. He moved like an automaton, like his mind was a million miles off, or nowhere, and on the dance floor it was his partner who did the work.

The girl was a freckle-faced youngster, pretty in a chubby sort of way, with brown hair piled on top of her head and wearing one of those oversized rhinestone-studded sweatshirts with the fake labels on them over a pair of black stretchpants. She was also chewing gum. According to Bobby Derr, in a hurried conversation at the bar, she was a pickup at the Rosebud, not one of the original crowd.

Bobby had given me a quick who's who, names included. There were six of them. They looked to me, well, like the Yale football team a little gone to seed: beefy, square-faced types in their twenties, preppily dressed, and one little guy they called Shrimp. They had, it seemed, great senses of humor. At least they made a lot of noise. Their girls, the bridge-and-tunnel types Bobby had described, matched them drink for drink and laughed at their jokes and snuggled up for more.

Plus Bobby. I had to hand it to Bobby Derr, he fit right in, Yale or no Yale. And one of the girls, it looked like, was his.

The Rasta disc jockey spun us out of "Gimme Shelter" and into some Heavy Metal number, then, announcing another "oldie goldie goodie," into "A Hard Day's Night." The Beatles, for some reason, drove the young crowd wild. Midway through it, I saw McCloy's partner pull him by the arm and shout to him, then lead him off the floor. He followed, unsteady. So did we. Strangely, because he'd hardly danced, his face was glistening with sweat, and he mopped at it with the silk scarf. Then I lost sight of him in the crowd going up and down the staircase, to pick him up again, across the main orchestra bar, heading for the men's room.

I parked Laura Hugger at the bar and followed.

The Rosebud men's room was one of the few places I've ever been where you get high and sick both, just while taking a leak. The acrid smell of grass was fighting a war with the disinfectant, and the contact high was winning. All the urinals were occupied, and a group of young white studs was passing a roach from hand to hand, and I couldn't locate McCloy for a minute.

Then I did.

He was standing in one of the cubicles at the rear, the door half-open behind him. Head down, scarf dangling, hands holding onto the tops of the metal panels on either side. He was puking his guts out.

While I watched, he heaved and threw up some more. He didn't look like much of a murderer, right then.

I think I pushed the door open for a better look—maybe I heard somebody call out "Where's Cloy?"—but simultaneously something hit hard into me from behind and my head clunked the door jamb.

"What d'you think you're doing?" somebody shouted behind me.

Maybe I said the same. I spun around to somebody who grabbed my shirt front and pulled.

His face was red and boozy, hair blond. Powell by name, one of McCloy's buddies, surrounded by the rest of the Ivy League offensive line.

I shook loose, and they crowded me.

"What's this, some kind of fag?" one of them asked, the one called Halloran.

"Are you okay, Cloy?" called another.

"Hey, where's McCloy? Is he all right?"

"Let's teach this fag a lesson."

Adrenaline time. I couldn't take them all, but the blond one was sure going down with me. Right, and there was already blood or something on the side of my head from the door post so what the hell, bring on your armies! I let one fly at the blond, or started to because somebody was grabbing me from behind then—who else but my old pal, Bobby Derr?—and then the blond unloaded a shot, a good one, that caught me somewhere south of the diaphragm and north of the navel and set lights to spinning in my head that had nothing to do with Rosebud lights. I skidded, my feet went out from under, and down I went on Rosebud tiles.

I covered up, because the blond had his leg back and his foot aimed.

"Hey, leave him alone, Booger," I heard Bobby Derr call out. "It's party time, let's get the show on the road!"

"Where the hell's Cloy?" somebody else shouted.

"Here he is, Hal!" came the answer, and a cheer went up as McCloy was led from the cubicle.

"Come on, Carter, you're up!"

"Go get her, tiger!"

From what I could see, he looked better than he had before. They helped him while he splashed water on his face, and then they took him out, Bobby Derr leading the way, singing as they went: "A-trolling we will go, a-trolling we will go . . ."

I did my own repairs, more or less. Then I made my way back to the bar.

"Jesus Christ, Phil, what happened to you?" Laura Hugger said in the din. "You look *green*!"

"Never mind," I said. "Where are they?"

"Who, McCloy, etcetera? I think I just saw them leave."

"Come on, then, let's get going."

But—small complication—she didn't want to go. The Rosebud hadn't been her idea, but now that we were there, she wanted to dance some more. I made her feel exploited, she said. Besides, why couldn't we have some fun for once in our lives without me being at the beck and call of the goddamn Counselor?

At first I thought she was kidding. She wasn't. Then I told her she could stay there alone if it was so much fun, and for a minute I thought she was going to take me up on it. But then we were outside, where it was still drizzling and the line of people waiting to get in was down to the corner, and when I spotted my group still down at the Bowery end of the block, shouting and waving in the middle of the street, I told Laura I'd have to put her in a taxi and send her home alone.

I guess it was a bad night for couples. Maybe up above the rain there was a full moon, or Neptune was in retrograde, or some damn thing. Laura Hugger told me she didn't need me to put her in a taxi. She didn't need me to do anything at all for that matter. That wasn't all she told me either, and she told it at the top of her lungs, her black hair frizzing in the damp air, and listeners in the Rosebud line sent up a cheer for her.

Then a taxi pulled up. Two young couples got out. Laura Hugger got in, slamming the door as I reached for it, and the taxi rolled off.

I headed for the Bowery corner. My group had succeeded in flagging down two taxis. Bobby Derr was organizing them, shoving bodies into the back seats in a noisy commotion, and by the time I got there, he himself had wedged into the second cab, pulling the door shut behind him, and off they went into the mist.

I watched their taillights for a second. I'd parked the Fiero a couple of blocks away. I didn't have a coat, hat, or umbrella, and my head was beginning to hurt and it was past midnight in the seediest part of town.

A bad night for couples, though, like I said.

About halfway up the next block, under a streetlight which doubled as a garbage dump, Carter McCloy was arguing with the girl he'd been dancing with at Rosebud's. The girl had a see-through plastic raincoat on over her sequined outfit, and her hair had come partly loose. McCloy had the white scarf wrapped around his neck, and he seemed to sway on his feet in the dim light.

I saw him reach for her, maybe push her. She slipped but didn't fall, and I could hear the crack when, righting herself, she slapped him in the face. He swung back, fist balled. No sound, but down she went, sitting hard on a black plastic garbage bag.

"Bastard!" I heard her shout after him. "Lousy cheap fag bastard!"

McCloy, though, seemed oblivious. He swayed up the wet deserted pavement in the other direction, diagonaling in toward the building line, then out toward the gutter. I started to trail him, but when I got as far as the girl, still sitting on the garbage bag, I stopped. People like to say the Bowery's a harmless neighborhood, but life among the local winos is still cheaper than a joint or a pint of Gallo Thunderbird, and it's no place for a Linda Smith to be alone, in the middle of the night.

At least Linda Smith was the name she gave me.

I learned too that she lived in Astoria. She said she was a theatrical makeup artist which, it turned out, meant she gave manicures in a hotel beauty parlor in the West Fifties. She said she was twenty-three.

It took me a while to get that far, though.

"Do you need any help?" I said when I got to her. "Are you okay?"

She was rocking a little on the garbage bag, rubbing her jaw, talking to herself or to nobody.

"Did he hurt you?" I asked.

". . . bastards," she was saying, head down, rocking. "How I hate the fags."

The bag she was sitting on was at the edge of a pyramid that mounted up around the lamppost. Most of the bags had split open, their contents spilling out among some soggy cardboard cartons. I picked out another closed bag and sat down near her.

"Who the hell are you?" she said, half-glancing across at me.

Her eye makeup had smudged, and the plastic raincoat packed her in, making her look plumper. But she was pretty like I said, in that freckle-faced, Cupid's mouth kind of way.

"What'd he do to you?" I said.

"Whadda you care?"

"I know him some."

"Then you're no friend of mine," she answered, looking away.

"I'm not his friend. I just know him, some. What'd he do to you?"

"Nothing."

She went on talking, though. She'd only just met McCloy, she said. At Rosebud's. All right if it made her a dumbbell, but she'd thought he was cute. Her type. Handsome even. He hadn't wanted to go off partying with the others, he'd wanted them to make their own party. That's what he'd said, and that was okay with her. He'd kept saying it when they were dancing, the whole time. But then, no sooner did the others take off then he told her to get lost.

Unbelievable. Unbelievable.

"D'you know what he wanted to give me?" she said. "He wanted to give me twenty bucks. Unbelievable. That's what he said: I'll give you twenty bucks just to get lost."

It wasn't clear whether the twenty bucks was too little or that McCloy had ruined her evening.

"Maybe you should at least have taken the twenty bucks," I said.

Her bow mouth tightened momentarily, then she burst out laughing.

"Hey, you're right!" she said. "But it felt better to slug him. Hey, who are you anyway," taking another look, "some kind of cop?"

We stood up then. She twisted and pulled at the raincoat.

"What a mess!" she said. Then, again: "You a cop?"

It was a reasonable guess, I suppose. I was clearly too old for the Rosebud and too well-heeled for the Bowery. On the other hand, I'd taken my tie off inside and my jacket collar was turned up, and, as we started to walk in the drizzle, I must have looked almost bedraggled enough to belong.

I told her I wasn't a cop. It seemed to disappoint her a little. She said she kind of liked cops, most cops. But that's when she started telling me about herself. We walked south on the Bowery a block or two, talking. We exchanged names. She even hooked her arm into mine.

But then, at a corner, she stopped abruptly.

"Hey, Phil, where're we going? I don't exactly want to walk all night in the rain."

I thought quickly, for some reason, about what Bobby Derr would have done. But I'm not Bobby Derr, and I guess I blew it.

"I'll tell you what, Linda," I said. "I'll double what he offered you, and then some."

"What for?" she said.

"You don't have to do anything," I added. "I just want to know everything you know about him."

"About who?"

"About McCloy. Carter McCloy. The guy you were just with."

"I *told* you I never met him before tonight! Jesus, what're you, another one? Isn't there a guy in this whole city who's *not* gay?"

"Wait a minute!" I called after her, because she'd torn away from me and was heading up the street. "Where're you going?"

"Home," she said angrily, when I caught up.

"How're you going to get there? I'll take you."

"Thanks but no thanks, buddy. I can take care of myself."

"Well, let me at least get you a taxi."

"A taxi to where I live costs eleven bucks."

"I'll pay for it," I said.

"Never mind," she said, pulling free again.

I spotted a cab, though, with the yellow light on in its roof, and waved it down. I called to her, then held the door open for her when she gave in.

"I'm not gay," I told her. "I just need to know about McCloy."

She stopped, just inside the door, hand out.

"Sixty bucks," she said.

"How come sixty?" I said, laughing in spite of myself.

"You said double his twenty and then some. Plus the cab. Round it off at sixty. But not tonight."

"When can we talk then?" I said, reaching for my wallet and holding on to the door.

The cabdriver swung his head around in the driver's seat and started to bitch.

"Not tonight," she repeated. "Some other time. You give me a call, my number's in the book."

I handed her three tens—on account, I said. She called me a cheap bastard but she took them. Then I let her go, shutting the door, and stood back to watch another set of red taillights disappear into the wet night.

Needless to say, her number wasn't in the book, not at least under Linda Smith. I never saw her again, only her picture in the paper. Right then, I was stranded on the Bowery, wet and insomniac, and that's how come I ended up in the wee hours, at Melchiorre's, drinking with Carter McCloy.

By reputation, Melchiorre's has been *the* preppie watering hole in New York for about as long as I can remember. It's been closed down once or twice, and one time, when the fifteen-year-old daughter of one of the city's prominent families got herself raped in Central Park early one morning and it turned out she'd been drinking in Melchiorre's, there was a move to put it out of business for good. It never happened, though. Presumably business was good enough for the protectors of Melchiorre's to up the ante. It was a darkish place, with half-curtains on brass bars in the windows and a long, heavy oak bar, oak tables, some with chairs, some long benches, dining areas in the back, and a giant old-fashioned juke box with the big half-moon glowing with neon.

I drove up there on a hunch, and for once one paid off. The action was fierce by the time I arrived, but McCloy was in the middle of it. I squeezed onto the last empty stool at the short end of the bar next to the waiter's station. I realized at some point that I was the oldest guy in the joint by plenty, and that included the bartenders and the waiters, all male, all in white shirts with the sleeves rolled up, black bow ties and white half-aprons tied around their waists. Old enough, in fact, that a couple of the damsels who got me to buy them drinks could have been my daughters, if I had any daughters.

I bought them drinks, which—sign of the times—was all they seemed to want out of me, and nursed some draft Bass Ale and kept an eye on McCloy who was holding court, the white scarf around his neck like a badge, about halfway down the long leg of the bar.

I remember thinking I should have bought stock in the Dewars Company. He was putting them away, doubles on the rocks, like tomorrow was the start of Prohibition. A couple of times he swayed off toward the back, maybe to clear his stomach like he had at the Rosebud, but he navigated pretty well and then he returned to the booze and, to use his term, the bunnies. He drew them like magnets. Well, he was a good-looking stud like I've said, of the young, tall and long-jawed kind, the straight hair slanting across his forehead like a scowl, and I guess he looked like Money, Glamor, Romance to girls who were a little short on all three. They seemed to come at him in waves, edging into the bar next to him, and I watched their different techniques. None worked. For that night anyway, he was wedded to the bottle, and he dismissed them with a sneer and a shake of the head and words I couldn't hear, and I watched them slink away to be replaced by other hopefuls.

The Bass Ale sent me off to answer the call a couple of times myself. The second time back, just as I came abreast of him, a pretty blonde in a black stretch outfit and high heels was backing off from the bar.

"You can go to hell yourself, Cloy," I heard her say.

A space had opened up next to him, an empty stool, and I took it.

"Bunnies," he was saying to nobody in particular. "Thick as flies, you know?"

I recognized the voice all right, flat and scornful, from the Counselor's Wife's tapes.

With a vague wave he summoned the bartender. He ordered another double, I a fresh Bass.

"What'd she do to you?" I said. "Or you to her?"

"Who?"

"The blonde. The one who was just here."

"Her?" he said. I saw him eye me in the mirror above the bar bottles. "Why? You want me to fix you up with her?"

He gave off some weird kind of smell. I couldn't identify it. It wasn't pleasant, musty sort of, stale. Maybe the Scotch was sweating back out through his pores. Maybe that's just the way rich kids smell. He was sweating all right, and from time to time the back of his hand did double duty, brushing away the sweat and the hair off his forehead.

"That's what I do, you know?" he said. "I fix people up with people. That's my life's work. What's your life's work?"

"A little of this," I said, "a little of that."

"Fix people up with people. You don't believe me, do you?"

"Oh, I believe you," I said. "Is it lucrative?"

"Lucrative," he said. "Lu. Cra. Tive."

"But who do you fix yourself up with?" I asked.

He didn't answer, though. Instead he waved for another Scotch.

"Double Dew," he said.

At some point we exchanged names. People called him Cloy, he said, short for McCloy, the Real McCloy. And when he heard Revere, he declaimed a little Longfellow, "'Listen my children and you shall hear,'" his glass raised in the general direction of my mirrored reflection. From then on, he called us the Midnight Riders.

I remember asking him why he called women "bunnies." He said that's what they were, wasn't it? Bunnies, born to breed? That's what they were for: breeding. I asked him if he'd ever done any breeding himself. That made him laugh. He had a snorting way of laughing, right out through the nose. He said he'd bred a couple of times, but he'd never seen the end results. He'd been too busy making money to pay the bunnies off. Now there was a lu-cra-tive business, he said: paternity suits.

I knew this to be 100 percent garbage, but I let it pass. Instead I asked him what he did to make money.

"Didn't I already tell you that?" he said. "I fix people up with people."

"Men with women?"

"All kinds," he said. "Rabbits with bunnies, bunnies with rabbits. Bunnies with bunnies, rabbits with rabbits . . ."

"You mean you're some kind of pimp?" I asked.

That made him laugh too, a full snorter.

"Pimp!" he said, breaking into some kind of song. "That's me, the King of Pimps, the Pimp of Kings!" and he called for another Double Dew and a Bass Ale for me.

"But what about Linda Smith?" I said.

"Linda who?"

"Linda Smith."

"Well, I know lots of Lindas," he said.

"This is the one you picked up at Rosebud's. She called you a cheap fag bastard. She said you offered her twenty bucks to get lost."

Whatever reaction I expected this to get out of him, though, I was disappointed. At first. His head seemed to float and wobble on his neck, like there was something loose in the swivel.

"That Linda?" he said. "You know that Linda?"

Then his head dropped down over his Scotch glass, nodding and bobbing as though from its own weight, and he was mumbling something, sounded like: ". . . l'il Linda . . . l'il Linda, doesn't know what she's . . . ," and for a second I thought he was about to pass out.

Wrong. He righted abruptly, head jerking up, and, lifting his glass, lurched it hard against my glass mug, sloshing the booze.

"Let's drink to Linda!" he said loudly. "A toast to l'il Linda!"

He downed what was left in his glass, banged it on the bar, waved for another, and then he said:

"All right, Midnight Rider or whoever you are, now answer me this: Why are you following me around?"

His eyes had mine in the bar mirror. Confrontation time.

"I didn't know that's what I was doing," I said, eyeing him back.

"You didn't *know*," he said, sneering. "What are you, some kind of private eye? You've been on my back for days asking all kinds of questions, did you think I wouldn't notice? Now here's what I want to know, Midnight Rider: Who's paying you?"

"Nobody's . . . ," I started to say, but I guess my evasion spiked his courage, and then the bully in him took over.

"D'you think I can't guess?" he said, swiveling toward me and hitting my shoulder with the heel of his hand. "The sucker. If the sucker wants to know what I'm doing, you tell him to come himself. I'm right here. Go ahead, call him now, wake him up."

He heeled me in the shoulder again. Then he said: "What's in it for you, Rider? A hundred bucks a day?"

The sneer of it got to me, the idea that somebody would do somebody else's dirty work for a measly hundred bucks a day. I turned on him. What kept me from laying him out right then, sneer and all, I can't say. Maybe I'd had too much to drink by then. Or not enough. Instead I knocked his arm away and, fixing him, said:

"I don't know who or what you're talking about, buddy. My name's Revere, you can check my driver's license. I work for a lawyer during the day; I'm on my own time now. As far as I know, this joint is open to anybody who brings money. But I'll tell you this: If you so much as lay a hand on me again, I'll take your knuckles and I'll break them off at the stems."

I saw his eyes go wide in his pale face, and then he backpedaled about as fast and far as he could, blurting apologies as he went. How he hadn't meant anything. How if I knew what he was going through, I'd understand. Etc., etc. And called for another Scotch. And told the bartender to pour me one too, a real drink, and when I passed it up in favor of another Bass, downed mine as well.

I guess his kind aren't much good at that, one on one.

On the contrary, I became like his long-lost buddy. It got me one of those drunken, rambling, more-than-you-want-to-know life stories. The sucker he'd mentioned turned out to be his current stepfather. The stepfather was always on his case, riding him, checking up on him, harassment and threats, and all because of the bucks. Other than for the bucks, the sucker didn't give a damn about him. But the bucks belonged to his whore of a mother, who didn't give a damn about him either, never had, as long as he kept out of the way.

"Chris' sake," I remembered him declaiming, "you'd think I was a criminal!"

Which brought the snorting on, violently, and tears leaking out of his eyes.

I remember him tacking off toward the john where, I expect, he puked his guts out again, and back again, amazingly, for another double Scotch. And you may well wonder: Didn't I ask him some questions of my own—like about Annette Costello and Rosemary Sutter, to name two? I wonder too. Worse, I think I even may have.

I remember the crowd at the bar thinning out, and a Last Call from the bartenders and one of them shouting out "Absolutely Final Last Call" which, for some reason, brought a ragged cheer from the remaining drinkers. I'd been paying as I went, a twenty following a twenty, but the bar kept a running tab for McCloy. Now the bartender brought it over with a pen, and without looking, McCloy scrawled his signature across the bottom.

We headed for the door, the street. At least I did. I was alone when I got to the door, and when I turned around, McCloy was arguing with one of the bartenders. I went back for him.

"Where's everybody?" I heard him shout.

"I told you, Cloy, they didn't show," the bartender answered, exasperated. Then, to me: "He's looking for some of his friends. He says they were supposed to meet him here. Well, I can't help that, we're closing."

". . . s'posed to meet . . . ," McCloy was saying.

"You mean the ones at the Rosebud?" I said.

"Rosebud's, yeah."

"They took off, remember? You came here alone."

". . . s'posed to meet!" he said angrily.

"Well, they didn't make it," I said.

"Come on, guys," from the bartender. "Closing time."

I remember getting him to the door. He still wanted to stay. Then, as suddenly, he didn't. Outside the pavements were glistening under the dim lights, but the rain had stopped and the air was cold. McCloy, though, didn't seem to feel a thing. He tacked along the sidewalk, building line to gutter, and I guess I tacked with him.

"Come on, Midnight Rider," he called out, "let's go to Rosebud's."

"That's closed," I said. "I'll get you home."

"No home. Let's go someplace else."

"No else," I think I said. "Sleep."

He stopped abruptly, turned, stared at me.

"Not sleep," he said. "Hey, where's everybody? Where's . . ."

He said some name I didn't get. But the panicky look in his eyes, in one of those weird, short snatches of lucidity you get when you're drunk, reminded me of something else. The Counselor's Wife's tapes, the story he'd told about his friend's insomnia. *If I should die before I die.*

His story, all right. Not a friend's.

He headed off across the avenue, I behind him. The traffic lights could have been green, red, or blue, but somebody protects drunks from accidents in the middle of the night.

We somehow got to his block. He careened along the wall of his apartment house. I remember one end of the white scarf now trailing behind him.

He turned toward me right near the entrance, tilting against the brick facade.

"Hey, Rider," he said. "Whatever you want. Want a

bunny? Free of charge. Want to beat up on a bunny? Want to . . . ?"

I got no chance to answer, though. In mid-sentence his body started to slide down the wall. And down he sat, on the pavement, listing to one side, head down and nodding.

Out like a light. Finally.

I stood over him for a minute. I remember thinking he looked like one poor excuse for a killer, right then. If he was a killer. If he wasn't. Either way. I peered in through the locked entrance doors of the building, spotting a black man in a cardigan sweater nodding on a straight chair just inside. I remember he had a newspaper on his lap. Maybe it was the super Bobby Derr had greased, maybe not. I rang the night bell and watched him jerk awake.

He came to his side of the door without opening it, and I pointed McCloy's body out to him. Then he unlocked, and together we loaded McCloy into the little vestibule where I held him while the black man opened the inner door.

"I'll take him up for you," I said to the black man.

"Never mind," he answered. "I'm used to it. They always come home like this, one or the other."

"I want to make sure he gets home."

"Never mind," he repeated. "He's home now. You're not." Then somehow he was standing between McCloy and me, propping McCloy up with one hand and pushing me back out the front door with the other. "You go home now too."

I guess I made it as far as the Fiero, but apparently no farther. The next thing I knew, it was 7 A.M., and I woke up behind the wheel in the East Eighties, and a blinding sun was staring right at me with its fingers in my eyes.

PART TWO

CHAPTER 6

I've probably given the wrong impression of the Counselor. Dour, cold, unfeeling, implacable—I've seen or heard all those words used to describe him, and a lot worse too, usually by people who've tangled with him professionally and lost. But he's also capable of humor, usually with a cutting edge, even of charm, even, on occasion, of warmth. His problem mostly is that he's a creature of habit. Circumstances which, for whatever reasons, break up his routine usually bring out the worst in him. For instance he'd complained about the Magister lunch ever since the meeting with Barger, and I'd have been willing to bet the house that he'd find a way to duck out.

And would have lost.

Maybe the setting contributed to his good mood. And the weather. Also, apparently, our hostess.

"Are you sure you don't want something a little stronger?" she asked, turning to him.

The Counselor, I knew, never drank anything stronger at lunch than Campari and soda, and that's what he'd asked for. To me the stuff's like drinking cough medicine, and maybe Margie Magister, her hand pausing near the bottle on the rolling bar, thought the same.

To my surprise, he answered: "What are you having, Mrs. Magister?"

"Whisky and a little water," she said. "One piece of ice. Scotch whisky. But I want you to call me Margie."

Margie with a hard *g*.

"Margie," the Counselor repeated. "Yes, I'll take the same as you."

Unprecedented.

Roy Barger ordered a white wine, I a beer, both poured from bottles stored in a silvery ice bucket, and then the four of us stood near the terrace parapet, glasses in hand, looking out over Central Park.

"How can people hate New York?" Margie Magister said with a sweep of her hand. "I think it's magical."

By one of those quirks of New York weather, we were having a rerun of summer, the temperature back in the low 70's, and the buildings lining the 59th Street end of the park and the glass business towers behind them shone in a strong midday sun. The air all but sparkled, and a soft breeze blew in from the southwest. From that point of view, that height and distance, yes, she had a point. Having nine figures at her disposal, give or take, may have helped the magic along too.

Small and chic, that's how she struck me. She had black hair cut short, with slanting bangs across her forehead, olive skin, expressive angular features, dark eyes hidden behind a pair of wraparound sunglasses. She wore a black pants-and-shirt outfit under a tailored olive-colored blazer with the collar turned up, and as dazzling an array of jewelry as you'll see in the middle of the day, even in New York. Rings on her fingers, a diamond-headed stickpin in one lapel of the blazer, and a diamond choker necklace in which the stones, you'd normally have figured, were too big to be anything but glass.

She was pretty too, in that miniature European way. The kind of woman, I thought, who probably devoted a lot of time to turning herself out to look both casual and elegant.

She served us lunch at a terrace table set for four under a

large striped umbrella, helped by a blond youth called Edward, in black pants and a white dress shirt unbuttoned to mid-chest, whom I recognized from Bud Fincher's reports. She put the Counselor on her right with, as she pointed out, the best view of the city. I sat at her left, Roy Barger across from her. She apologized for the size of the meal—a throwback, she said, to Europe, where people used to eat the big meal in the middle of the day before they learned American habits. We should eat as little, or as much, as we wanted. The Counselor maintained that the European custom was more civilized, and they discussed the finer points of the spread, things like where the smoked salmon had come from, how the roast veal had been prepared, whether strawberries were better with English-style clotted cream or crème fraiche from France. As for me, with my American brown-bagging habit, it was closer to a banquet than lunch, and when I made the mistake of switching from beer to white wine, a fruity-tasting version from the Loire Valley, I started thinking things like: well, sure, New York is magical; and why shouldn't she run Magister Companies? Because somewhere—between, say, the salad and the Chilean strawberries—the conversation had switched to business. It was Margie who'd switched it, and very directly.

"Charles," she said, "I know Roy has told you what it is I want, what is my objective, but I want you to hear it from me, okay?"

"Of course," the Counselor said, holding his wine glass up as she poured.

"I want to run the Magister business," she said, her head tilted toward him. "I want to control the business and to run it. It is as simple as that. Do you think I'm wrong?"

The Counselor seemed to consider it for a minute.

"I don't think I have an opinion as to right or wrong," he said, "but the question which comes to mind is: Why? Why do you want that?"

"Why? Well, I'll tell you why, Charles. Firstly," grasping the little finger of her left hand, "I think it would be fun. I've never done that before. Secondly," adding the fourth finger to her grip, "I think definitely I would succeed. And finally," adding the middle finger, "because of the children. The grandchildren too. But because of the children, there's no alternative."

"I don't think I understand that," the Counselor said. "Why is there no alternative?"

"Well, the children are hopeless, you see? We all know that," glancing quickly at Barger, then at me, then back at the Counselor. "It is not their fault, poor darlings. It was Bob's fault. He never trusted them in the business. I used to tell him that, but of course it was too late by then. For him they were always children. Yes, of course he took them into the business, but they were always . . ." She paused, then arched her neck and laughed aloud. "Ahhh, New York! How I love New York . . . the Yiddish language in New York! *Schleppers*, do you know the word, Charles? That's all he ever let them be in the business: *schleppers*. Not Sally so much, she's too headstrong. But the boys. They're so weak, they're not really men yet. Young Bob, do you see him running the business? He never liked me, but I don't blame him for that. His mother died; I wasn't his mother; his father loved me; his father married me; I was a threat to him. All natural things. But does that mean he should be running a big business?"

The Counselor didn't answer, but Margie didn't seem to need him to. Her voice, which had softened while she went about burying the Magister children, now took on a sharp edge.

"I know what you think. Everybody thinks the same thing. I'm an opportunist, isn't that what they say? Worse things. Well, I say to them: What's so wrong, in the land of opportunity, with being an opportunist? Isn't that how you're supposed to be, in New York? In Europe, of course, it would be impossible. Unthinkable for a woman. But in America?

"I'll tell you the truth, Charles—but off the record, please. When I married Bob, I *was* an opportunist. I made a calculation. That's *very* European. He was old, dying, when I met him. Me? I was nothing, and I was tired of being nothing. It wasn't so much of a marriage, but I made my . . . how shall I say? . . . accommodations. He needed a nurse, not a wife. He was cranky, sometimes nasty. Sometimes he wet his bed at night, so I changed his sheets. But he loved me, and I gave him . . . what? . . . two more years of life. Do you know what he used to say to me when he was in the nasty moods? 'It is better than being dead.' So. He had two more years of life because of me, is that such a crime?"

She took her sunglasses off and gazed intently at the Counselor, insistent on his reaction.

"I would have called it admirable," he said. "But is what you're trying to tell me that that gave you the right to run Magister?"

She shrugged, and her lower lip protruded upward in a sort of sulky, pouty expression.

"You're so harsh, Charles," she said. "Roy said you would be harsh. No, not the *right*. But it's what Bob would have wanted."

"Do you have documentation of that?" the Counselor asked.

"Only up here," she answered, tapping the side of her forehead with her forefinger.

By this time we'd gotten through the strawberries, with or without cream, and into the coffee and cognac. She served the coffee in those little demitasse cups I can't stand. I mean: one swallow and it's over. Anyway, I felt the Counselor start to stir.

Margie Magister must have felt it too. She reached across, put her hand on the Counselor's arm.

"Please, Charles," she said, her eyes widening. "I asked you to come here not only because I love bow ties, although I do, but because Roy told me you were the best lawyer in New York. Better even than Roy." I saw the Counselor glance at Barger, who, by way of response, simply shrugged and grinned. "I don't want you to be arrayed against me."

"I'm not arrayed against you," the Counselor began, but Margie interrupted him:

"Oh yes you are. Can't we finally be open with each other? The great big firm of lawyers wants me to give up and go away, but they don't know how to go about it because they're afraid I'll fire them, once I have control. So they call in Charles Camelot to deal with me and his master spy, Phil Revere, to dig up all my dirt, and I'll tell you, Philip," looking at me, a smile working up into her cheekbones, "what I want us to do about that part. I want you to move in with me, morning, noon and night, and take notes on all the money I spend and interview all the people I'm sleeping with—of both sexes, mind you, including goats—and make pictures of the drugs I shoot into my arms, and do you know? It won't make any difference. When you have finished, I will still be running the business."

She'd made the Counselor laugh aloud, his craggy head back, hair shining white in the sunlight. Then he leaned forward, still smiling, head now shadowed again by the umbrella.

"But where did you hear all this, Margie?" he said. "What makes you so certain that's my role?"

"Well, Sally said . . ."

But she broke off abruptly, and the hand, the one which had been holding the Counselor's arm, swung over her mouth as though to shut off the words.

Too late.

"Merde," she said, looking at Barger. The lawyer just tilted his head sideways as though to say to his client: You've dug your own hole, now climb out of it yourself. Then she looked ruefully back at the Counselor, started to say something, then thought better of that, and her mouth closed and the lower lip rose in that pouting expression.

"Okay," she said carefully, as though choosing her words. "Yes, Sally and I have talked together, what's wrong with that? We are two women. I admire her. As a woman. I mean: I, as a woman, I admire her. It is remarkable what she has accomplished in the man's world. I don't just mean her magazines, although *Fem* speaks to the women of today. But a single woman, divorced, three times divorced, and still she is working and bringing up her children. All at once. It isn't easy, you know? They're remarkable. The children, I mean . . ."

Her voice broke off, though, as though she'd lost the thread.

"You said you and Sally have talked," the Counselor said. "What exactly did you decide?"

Barger started to intervene, but Margie waved him off.

"Don't you see, Charles? Bob wanted to create an empire. I think all you men do. You don't want what you make to die. You want heirs, your own blood, to make it grow. That's what Bob wanted. But he knew the boys—Young Bob, Stafford, William—well, he knew they were no good, that they would lose what he'd built. One time he said to me: 'Sometimes these things have to skip a generation.' He was looking toward his grandchildren, don't you see?"

"Then why didn't he provide for that in his will?" the Counselor said.

"Because he thought he would live long enough to take care of it himself. I don't know why, but in spite of everything, some men think they will live forever."

"And Sally? What does she want?"

"What can I tell you? Sally hated her father more than anyone else in the world. But she loves her children to the point that she would lay down her life for them." She seemed to hesitate, as though surprised by what she'd just said. Then: "Sally wants to stay in the company. There is a place for her; she wants this place." Then, her hand reaching to touch the Counselor's arm again: "In fact, there is a place for everyone. Nobody should have to leave. We should all work together to make Bob's dream come true."

Maybe that was a little heavy, the part about Bob's dream, but taking the meal and the weather into account, I'd still have to give her performance a 9.9. Including the "mistake" she'd made, mentioning Sally Magister. The point about that was that there'd been no good reason for her to slip Sally's name into the conversation—Barger himself had surely briefed her on the Counselor's role—and I suspected she'd done it not inadvertently but, to use her own word, as a calculation. A calculation and a message.

Roy Barger summed it up for her:

"We don't want a war, Counselor. We want to negotiate the peace in good faith. But if the brothers insist on fighting, in or out of the courts, then we will fight back. And we will win."

We stood. I could guess at least some of the questions the Counselor would be turning over in his mind, but evidently he decided to keep them to himself.

He towered over Margie Magister. She had to stand on tiptoes, extending her arms. For a minute I thought she was going to kiss him. Instead, she straightened his bow tie.

"I'm so sorry you have to go already," she said to him.

"I am too."

"But you're leaving Philip with me, aren't you? To watch over me?"

She'd taken the Counselor by the arm and, turning to me, now linked her free arm in mine. We walked that way into the cool interior of the duplex while Roy Barger stayed on the terrace.

"I'm afraid Phil has other things to do," the Counselor said.

"Better things than to stay with me?" she asked, laughing and squeezing my arm.

"I didn't say better," he replied.

"Well, I would absolutely insist on it," she said, "if he wore bow ties too. Bow ties make me—how do you say it?—go weak in the knees. I think they're so cute. Do you know what we call them in French? *Papillons*. Butterflies. Big men wearing butterfly ties . . ."

I've never, I've got to say, seen the Counselor respond that way to flattery. He stood there chatting animatedly, his eyes on hers, a bemused smile on his face, and if the elevator had taken all day to get up to the penthouse, I doubt he'd have noticed.

The elevator did get there finally.

Margie Magister turned to me. We shook hands, and I got a quick kiss on the cheek, a tiptoe job, and a strong whiff of some tangy, floral scent.

Then she turned to the Counselor. Both hands on his shoulders, tiptoes, then one leg kicking out behind the other. Two kisses, European style, one for each cheek.

"I'll be talking to you soon, Mr. Camelot," she said, gazing up at him.

"I hope so, Mrs. Magister," replied the Counselor.

So help me God.

We rode down in silence, side by side, facing the door. Then the Counselor said:

"Bow ties, Phil. That's the secret."

It was almost 3:30 in the afternoon. I've never known him to get back to the office later than 3.

I was trying to wave down a cab in front of Margie Magister's building when he said we should walk. Four blocks was about his usual limit; we had a dozen to get to the office.

A day, like I said, for the unprecedented.

"So what do you think?" the Counselor asked as we headed up Fifth Avenue.

"Charming," I said. "She's a genuine charmer." Then: "Also, she seemed to take a special shine to you. And you to her, I guess." Then: "The food and the booze were first-rate."

No comment from him on any of the above. We walked on, in silence. Then he said:

"What have we got on Sally Magister?"

I pulled from memory the main points in Bud Fincher's reports. Three marriages, three divorces; four children, one by the first marriage, three from the second; took back the Magister name after the last divorce; ran the company's magazine division; practicing lesbian, according to Bud's latest intelligence; big on feminist causes.

"What about her finances?"

"Fairly well loaded, as far as we can tell," I answered. "In addition to Magister money, she got big settlements out of the first two marriages. The third was some painter, no bucks. According to what we've got, she pays him off. She gives a lot of it away too."

"Where to?"

"Feminist causes," I said, naming a few Bud Fincher had dug up. "She's a major backer."

"I want you to go see her," the Counselor said.

"How come?"

"Because they want us to," he said. "For the minute, we're going to do exactly what they want us to. But I want you to focus on her children too. There's something wrong there."

"What do you mean, wrong?" I asked.

"Margie Magister doesn't strike me as the type who'd worry overly about other people's children. And there was something Barger said about the skeletons having baby skeletons."

Another block, in silence. There were, I noticed, a lot of kids going into and coming out of the park, some on their own feet, some pushed in strollers by their nannies or mothers, these days it's hard to tell one from the other. There was a vendor selling helium balloons and pinwheels, and another selling ice cream, and a cop with nothing better to do than write a ticket for a double-parked car with out-of-state plates. A panhandler or two, but nothing else to remind you that there were homeless on the streets, and teenagers peddling crack, and somewhere a killer who liked to stalk women who had pillows on their beds.

Magical, Margie Magister had called it.

Anyway, that's more or less what I was thinking. The Counselor, apparently, was somewhere else.

"Phil," he said out of the blue, "I want to know everything that's going on between you and my wife."

Maybe I walked another block without breathing. Maybe less.

"Nothing's going on," I said. "She asked me to look into something for her, that's all."

"What?"

"I'm not sure I can tell you that, not without asking her permission."

"But you work for me, don't you?"

"Yes, I do."

"You should know that I overheard her talking to you a couple of times this weekend. Unless there's another Phil in her life, it was you, wasn't it?"

"Yes, it was."

At least this meant they'd been together after all. At the house in the Hamptons, I assumed. It also explained why she'd been in a hurry and why, once, she'd cut me off.

"It's about one of her patients, isn't it?" the Counselor said.

"It could be."

We'd stopped walking. We stood at a corner, waiting for the light to change. Then it changed, and we still stood there.

"How long have we worked together, Phil?" the Counselor said.

"Over ten years."

"And you're well compensated?"

"Relatively well, yes."

"I know I've always said to you that what you do on your own time is your own business. But I didn't know that you free-lanced."

"I don't, as a rule."

"How much is she paying you?"

"Expenses only," I said. "Out-of-pockets."

"Including Bobby Derr?"

This threw me, I admit.

"When did you talk to Bobby?" I asked.

"I didn't have to. He's been spreading the word that he's working on a job for me."

That stupid bastard, I thought. Whether or not Bobby had believed what I'd told him, he'd bragged that he was working for the Counselor, probably to somebody who worked for Fincher, and Fincher must have passed it on, either to the Firm or the Counselor himself.

We stood on the Fifth Avenue corner, head to head. He's only a little taller than I am, but he gives the impression of towering. I remember the breeze lifting his white hair.

He's never been one, needless to say, not to press home an advantage.

"Nobody likes ultimatums," he said, "but take this as one. I want to know what's going on. I want it now."

"And if I decide not to tell you?"

"Then you're out of a job, Phil. As of this minute."

Eyeball to eyeball.

Knowing what I know now, I could say that I'd been crazy to keep the McCloy business to myself. I'm not a cop, not even a PI in the normal sense. I should have made the Counselor's Wife take it to the police right away, or done it for her. You could also say I was simply relieved to have somebody else to share it with, there on Fifth Avenue, other than a woman who, at least in her own mind, had reasons beyond the Pillow Killer to be in a semihysterical state.

Yeah, and if pigs had wings, etc., etc.

In short, I blabbed the whole thing. I was sore about it all right, about the way he squeezed it out of me, but I gave him all my facts and suppositions, including some things I haven't put down yet, like my interview with the Staten Island girls that Bobby had set up over the weekend, like the surveillance I'd organized at Nora Saroff's office for McCloy's scheduled appointment, when McCloy didn't show. I also told him what Bobby Derr had dug up from his carousings with McCloy and his buddies. According to Bobby, the others had been on McCloy's case lately. It had mostly to do with sex, Bobby said, with McCloy not being able to get it up. The Staten Island girls had corroborated this. They thought "Cloy" was cute, weird but cute, and not much in bed. They thought maybe he drank too much. On the other hand, Bobby said, Cloy was the one who organized them, Cloy and Hal, and what really seemed to burn them was Cloy taking off on his own. Like that night after the Rosebud. In fact, he hadn't been around at all the last couple of nights. All of them, according to Bobby, had money to spend, but he hadn't been able to get at the source of the bucks other than their families, because only a couple of them held down regular jobs. According to Bobby, there was stuff he thought they still hadn't let him in on, drugs maybe although they themselves were booze hounds, but it had occurred to me that this could also be Bobby Derr's own way of hanging on to a good thing.

"What do *you* think about McCloy?" the Counselor asked when I'd finished.

"I think he *is* weird," I said. "In a screwed-up, rich-kid kind of way."

"But is he a killer? The Pillow Killer?"

"I don't know," I said. "I suppose there are plenty of men with sexual hangups, but that doesn't mean they go around murdering people. Other than what your wife gave me, I've got nothing. Then there's the note he put under her door, if he was the one who did it."

Outwardly at least, he didn't seem very impressed. Maybe that should have struck me as strange, but it didn't at the time.

"Do you want me to put a stop to it?" I said.

"That's up to you."

"And to Nora," I said. "I'm going to have to tell her that I've told you."

"Be my guest," he said. "What you do on your own time is what you do on your own time."

We were headed east by then, walking in cool shadows. It occurred to me in turn to ask him, ultimatum-style, what the hell was going on between him and Nora. But I didn't, and you could say that's what makes him an attorney-at-law and me his special assistant. Just before we reached the office, though, he answered it, kind of.

"There are times, Phil," he said with a grunt, "when a woman really tries a man's soul."

I didn't ask him what he meant.

"The manipulative son of a bitch," the Counselor's Wife said later, in her office. She leaned back against her white parson's table–desk, palms propped on the edge of it behind her. I sat in the patient's chair, a few feet away.

"It's okay," I said.

"It's definitely *not* okay!" she said angrily. "He's a manipulative son of a bitch. It's not fair that he drag you into what's going on between him and me. He'll manipulate anyone he has to to get what he wants."

"I didn't have to tell him either."

"Of course you did! He put your job on the line. I asked you to help me, not to put your job on the line."

This was the first time I'd seen her since the afternoon of McCloy's appointment, when he hadn't shown up. She wasn't looking good, then or now. That's a relative statement with the Counselor's Wife, because even at her worst she'd make you sit up and take notice, but her face looked drawn. You could see the lines working out from her eyes, and her ashen hair, normally swirling and full-blown, had gone scraggly. She wore corduroy pants of an olive-khaki color and an oversized overblouse of sweatshirt material, three-quarter sleeves, same color tone. No jewelry, little makeup. A Hamptons outfit, I guessed.

"Maybe it's time somebody told me what *is* going on between the two of you," I said.

She sighed, arched her chin, then lowered it into her collarbone, as though trying to relax her neck muscles.

"I've left him, Phil. Or at least I'm trying to."

"Why?"

She smiled at me, the corners crinkling next to her eyes, but there wasn't much humor in the smile.

"How long have we known each other, Phil?"

"I don't know. Around ten years, I guess."

"Ten years, yes. Doesn't it sometimes seem like it's gone by in a blur? As though you hardly know what's happened, but it's been ten years?"

"Sometimes," I agreed.

"Doesn't that frighten you?"

I didn't answer. The truth is, I deal with things like that by not thinking too much about them.

"How old are you, Phil?"

"The same as you, if I remember correctly. Give or take a couple of months."

In fact we were both still on the safe side of forty, but not very safe.

"Exactly," she said. "Except that you're a man. You don't have a time clock inside your body. A time clock that's running out."

"Oh," I said.

Actually, I had my own version of her ten-year bit. For the past decade I'd been practically living in the same household as she and the Counselor—ten years, mind you—but I knew next to nothing about their private life. The Counselor was a lot older, and once in a while the age difference showed. But they both had successful careers, they had plenty of money, they'd been written up, more than once, as having an ideal marriage, and if they were childless, well, weren't lots of ideal marriages childless? I suppose if I'd ever thought about it, I'd have said that's what they both wanted. But I don't think I'd ever thought about it.

"So you're living in the Hamptons and commuting?" I guessed.

"Where? Oh yes, more or less."

"How's Muffin?"

I don't know what made me think again of the cocker bitch, but I hadn't seen her since that morning in the rain, and I assumed that wherever the Counselor's Wife went, Muffin went with her.

"Muffin? Oh, she's fine." Then, with a shake of her head: "No, she isn't. She's not eating. I practically have to hand-feed her."

I started to say something like: Well, where do you go from here? or: What's going to happen next? but the phone interrupted us, a jangling sound.

The Counselor's Wife twisted her body, then leaned across the white desk to pick it up.

"Who?" she said. Then: "Oh. Just a minute." Then, turning her head to me with her hand over the receiver: "It's for you. How did anybody know you were here?"

Only one person did. I'd been waiting for a tip-off from Bobby Derr, and I'd given him the number.

"You gettin' any?" Bobby Derr asked me.

"That's not very funny," I said. "What's up?"

"Your coast is clear, babe."

"I want to talk to you, Bobby."

"Not tonight, babe. We're on the town tonight, me and my buddies."

"Is McCloy with you?"

"Yep. And rarin' to go. It's all yours, Philly, you got the keys?"

"I've got the keys. Remember to call—three rings—if there's a problem."

"You got it. I'll check in with you tomorrow, Philly, but not too early. Gotta go now."

And he hung up.

"What keys?" asked the Counselor's Wife.

"The keys to McCloy's apartment," I told her. "Derr got me a set. I want to take a look."

"Forget it, Phil."

"Forget it?"

"I've gotten you into enough trouble as it is. I want us both to forget it. I think I made it all up anyway. I'm a hysterical woman who wants to have a baby. Hysterical women who want to have babies can make anything up."

"You didn't make the tapes up," I said. "I heard them, remember? I also checked your correlations, they were right on. You didn't make up the note either, did you?"

"No."

"Then I'm going to take a look," I said, standing.

"But we don't know for sure that *he* wrote the note."

"We don't know anything for sure, Nora," I said, "other than that he's a rich kid with a lot of poison in him. We also know he's capable of treating women like dirt," seeing in my mind's eye Linda Smith sitting on the garbage bag, "and that he can be intimidated by men. Whether that's enough to make him kill people is anybody's guess, but you, who probably have better insight into him than anybody else around, thought it might."

"I told you: I'm a hysterical woman who wants to have a baby."

"Yeah. You're also a professional."

For once, she didn't answer. She took it in and stared back at me meanwhile: no expression. Then it must have registered because she stood up, tall, chin up, and gave me one of those dazzling smiles, with the white teeth and the crinkles darting out from her eyes.

"You'd have made a hell of a shrink, Phil," she said.

"I'll let you know if I find anything."

"No you won't," she said, taking my arm. "I'm going with you."

I argued with her. Inevitably I lost. I pointed out that what I was doing was illegal and while, if I got caught, I could probably wriggle out, if she did it would sure shoot the hell out of her professional standing. Screw her professional standing, she said. Why was everyone so worried about her professional standing? Bill Biegler, the shrink who shared the office, wanted her to forget Carter and not see him anymore, but she thought that would really screw her standing—with herself if not the profession.

Besides, she said, she was tired of hiding, tired of feeling sorry for herself.

So we ended up on Park Avenue together, walking stride for stride in the darkness. The unusually balmy weather of the day had held, and people were out, and I guess those who noticed us took us for a couple. We talked about McCloy mostly. The McCloy I'd met and described, she thought, matched the one she knew. She was worried, though, that he hadn't shown up for their appointment. On the most simplistic level, she thought he could still be paying her back for August. But she suspected something else, some revival of the unresolved conflicts that had brought him to her in the first place. Whether she wanted it or not, it was conceivable that she'd lost him. After all, she said, she wouldn't be the first shrink he'd dumped. She only hoped she wouldn't be the last.

From my point of view, having her along actually helped. I'd expected trouble getting into McCloy's apartment, even with the keys, and I think if I'd showed up alone, the night super, the suspicious black man in the same cardigan sweater whom I'd run into that drunken night with McCloy, would have tried to stop me. But with the Counselor's Wife on my arm, I'm not sure he even recognized me.

We rode up to the ninth floor, then down a nondescript corridor to McCloy's apartment. I had two keys for the door, one for a dead bolt, but the dead bolt had been left open. So much for security.

"Ucch," the Counselor's Wife said behind me, and with reason.

At first glance, you'd have said somebody had beaten us to it. I mean: ransack city. You walked into a small hall, then the living room, and the first thing you saw in the living room was a foldout couch. The couch was open, unmade, and there was a flotsam and jetsam of clothes dumped on it, around it, draped on chairs, on the cross bar of a floor lamp, hanging from the corners of the mantel over the fireplace. The second thing you saw was the TV, a king-size console job facing the couch, with a VCR on the floor next to it and a jumble of videotapes, some loose, some in those black boxes the rental shops use. To judge from the adjoining kitchen, this was one of those households where they let the dirty dishes pile up till there are no clean ones left, and then they go out and buy new ones. The contents of the refrigerator I didn't examine long enough to try to describe.

At the other end of the living room were a pair of windows nobody had washed in a long time and a door that opened onto a small terrace. The waist-high parapet, a curved affair built of brick, gave out onto the street far below. On the neighboring terrace some kind of tree was growing in a large clay tub, but this one seemed to be a dumping ground for what nobody wanted anymore: a carton containing parts of a vacuum cleaner, an old typewriter, an abandoned stereo which seemed to have been replaced by a big-speakered rig on the floor behind the couch.

I left the Counselor's Wife in the living room and explored down a back hall, off of which were two bedrooms, two baths. Whatever it was I was looking for, I didn't find it there, only more of the same: clothes everywhere you looked, on the beds, the floors, hanging in the closets, dumped on the closet floors. Men's mostly, but some women's too. And good labels if that's your taste: Brooks, Paul Stuart, Calvin Klein, Lauren. Shoes from Church. The strangest thing was that, as lived in as the place obviously was, I found very little that you'd call personal. It was more like everything was interchangeable among the people who came and went, and maybe that was the point. Like: If it fits you and it's fairly clean, wear it. Like: If you need some aftershave, help yourself. (I counted a dozen bottles, with different labels, in the two medicine cabinets. Over half of them were empties.) No drugs that I saw; no booze either except for some empty Dewars bottles; no personal mail, just some bills in their envelopes, none of which was addressed to Carter McCloy. A few posters tacked to the walls, the old Farrah Fawcett among them, and Willie Nelson too, torn, on which somebody had scrawled: "Willie sucks."

It was, in sum, the way Bobby Derr had described it, being there made it more depressing.

While I stood in one of the bedrooms, trying to figure out what it told about McCloy, or didn't, I became aware of sound from the living room, like somebody had turned the TV on. Then I heard the Counselor's Wife calling:

"Hey, Phil, come here a minute."

Then:

"Oh my God . . ."

She was kneeling on the floor in the living room, in front of the television set.

"It's my show," she said softly when I hunkered down beside her. "My God, Phil, he's taped my show."

And taped it carefully, we discovered. The commercials had been neatly zapped. Somebody had sat there, watching, working the Pause and Record buttons.

The one she was watching was the very one I'd gone to, the show about Female Orgasm, but before we quit we found half a dozen "Nora Saroff's Hours." And not only Nora Saroff. There were tapes of other television women—newscasters, talk-show hosts, anchorwomen. Diane Sawyer was there. So were Suzi Lee and Brenda Simpson. So was the one who does the news on Channel 9. But Nora Saroff, it seemed, was the local favorite.

"God, Phil," she said when I put the last one on Rewind. "You don't know how this spooks me. It really does. It spooks the living daylights out of me."

"I can't say I blame you."

"What do you think it means?"

"I don't know. Except that somebody—McCloy—is pretty fixated on you."

"Brrr," she said, and I saw her shoulders shudder. "I mean, I've seen tapes of the show before. I look at them all the time myself, trying to figure out ways to improve it. But that somebody out there should actually be taping me . . ." She shook her head from side to side, inhaled, exhaled. "God, I find that spooky."

I stood up.

"Come on," I said, "let's get out of here."

She reached up, and I pulled her to her feet. Her body swayed, and I sensed her trembling.

"How did you come across the first one?" I asked.

"It was already in the machine," she said. "I just happened to turn it on."

I found the tape in question and stuck it in the VCR. Otherwise, I didn't think we'd disturbed enough in the mess that anybody would notice we'd been there.

I'd had it set up with Bobby Derr that if he thought someone was heading back to the apartment, he'd call, allow three rings, then hang up. But the phone hadn't rung, and when we got down to the lobby, the night super was nowhere in sight.

We walked a while. I think we went south on Park Avenue, but it could have been north. Or maybe it was Lexington. If somebody was tailing us then, in the dark, I sure didn't spot him.

I told her I didn't want her to be alone for the next while, particularly alone in her office.

She said she could arrange that. There was Bill for one, Dr. Biegler. But she asked me why I said it.

I admitted that the tapes had freaked me out too.

Beyond that, neither of us said anything much.

I remember her putting her hand in mine, that it was trembling and that I held it till the trembling stopped. I remember we were both wearing raincoats and it wasn't raining. I remember thinking that she'd just dropped the proverbial shoe and where was the other one?

Then she turned to me in the street, put her arms around my neck and kissed me, hard. Then her mouth relaxed, opened, and I kissed her back.

The other shoe.

"Phil," she said directly, "I want you to make love to me tonight."

I guess I thought a mishmash of thoughts, all in simulcast. That she shouldn't be alone. That maybe the timing was good for what she wanted and I was certainly available on that score. Or that she was scared and ditto. Also that she needed a protector and there I was, Midnight Rider, one if by land and two if by sea.

Also, and you didn't have to be a genius to figure it out, that I'd had a semisecret hankering for Nora Saroff for a long time.

But also, finally, that for Christ's sake Nora Saroff *was* the Counselor's Wife.

Put it another way: maybe I wasn't ready for my own midlife crisis.

Yeah, and maybe someday, on some shrink's couch, I'll figure out why I did what I did.

"There's nothing I'd like better," I said to her, "but I think the timing's wrong. I . . ."

"How could the timing be better? I know I appeal to you. It's not some misbegotten sense of *loyalty*, is it?"

"No. Look, Nora, I'll be glad to take you wherever you want to go, to stay with you tonight, but . . ."

"Never mind. You're right, it was a stupid idea."

"I didn't say that. Let me take you home. I want . . ."

"Never mind," pulling angrily away from me, "I'm okay, I'm fine. Let me go now."

She ran out into the street, waving at taxis, and I remember shouting at her back, and, yes, it was Park Avenue because a cabbie on the far side of the island did a swerving U-turn at the intersection to beat the competition.

"Please, Nora . . ."

"Not to worry. I'm fine. I won't be alone."

"But I . . ."

Then, with one foot in the taxi and her hand on the door,

and in one of those quicksilver mood shifts of which I knew she was capable, she turned back to me. Her hair was swirling across her eyes and she was grinning at me.

"Not to worry, Phil. Besides, this only makes us even. Remember?"

And was gone.

I didn't get it at first: her limo pulling away from me on the West Side, that night after her show. About all I could think of right then, at the risk of repeating myself, was that it sure was a week for watching women ride off in taxis.

CHAPTER 7

"You got no call to be mad, Philly," said Bobby Derr. "I mean, like look at it from my point of view. You work for Camelot and you don't moonlight on the side. How was I supposed to know this *wasn't* a Camelot job?"

"Because we use Fincher when it's Mr. Camelot's business, and you know it."

"Yeah? And how was I to know you hadn't decided to dump Fincher?"

"Why would we do a thing like that?"

"I don't know," Bobby said, shrugging. "Maybe you finally woke up to the fact that Bud's a horse's ass. Besides, you said it was an undercover job, that I was to get in with McCloy and his buddies. Could you see Fincher doing that?"

He had me there. The truth was: I was madder at myself than at him. I'd let him think what he wanted to think at the beginning, and if he'd decided he was really working for the Counselor, I had nobody but myself to thank for it.

"Anyway, Philly, not to worry. I've got it all figured out."

"You've got what all figured out?"

"It's Nora Saroff, babe. She's Camelot's wife and McCloy's shrink, right? It took me a while to put that one together, why the hell didn't you tell me up front? But once I got it, things fell into place, no problem."

"Is she still his shrink?" I said.

"What do you mean?"

"Just what I said. Does he talk about her like she's still his shrink?"

"You gotta be kidding! Has he got some case for her. Did you find those tapes in the apartment? He watches them all the time. I guess it happens that way, huh? That people fall in love with their shrinks? 'specially a piece like Nora. The way I figure it, young Cloy got too hot for her to handle, maybe started working on her after hours, and she told her old man about it, and Camelot told you to fix it, and you hired me. Right?"

Doodling with my second mug of coffee, I pretended to think about it. We were sitting at the Roosevelt; it was around eleven in the morning. Bobby Derr had looked pretty green around the gills when he showed, but by now, after working his way through three eggs scrambled, with fried ham, hashed browns and a double order of toast, he'd pretty well caught up with the day.

As for me, I'd called in sick at the office. Another first. And had learned from Ms. Shapiro that the Counselor had arranged for me to call on Sally Magister. I told her I'd be there, sick or not, and at the office for another appointment that afternoon.

"Only it won't wash, huh, Philly?" Bobby asked, grinning at me.

"What do you mean?"

"Well, the way I figure it, if all Camelot wanted was to scare McCloy off his wife, you could've done that yourself, in ten minutes. Or I could've done it for you. No problem. But if that's all you wanted, why all the cloak-and-dagger stuff? I mean, I'm not complaining. I'm getting paid and I'm getting my rocks off, it doesn't always happen that way. But suppose McCloy *is* balling her and Camelot found out about it? Or even suspected it? I mean, it stands to reason, doesn't it? How old is he anyway, late fifties? Sixty? Maybe he can't get it up enough for a hot piece like Nora. I mean, what would he do about it if he didn't want anybody to know? He'd hire somebody to glue himself to McCloy and eventually it would come out, one way or the other. Well, you can tell . . ."

"That's bull!" I said, and I guess I must have said it loud. The Roosevelt is mostly deserted that time of day except for some old-timers they let hang around in the off-hours, as long as they keep a mug in front of them. But I was aware of heads turning toward me.

I lowered my voice.

"She thinks he may be the Pillow Killer, goddamn it!"

Bobby Derr gaped at me.

"What did you say?"

"I said she thinks McCloy may be the Pillow Killer."

"Well, that's paranoid," he said.

We stared at each other. I watched him reach for a cigarette, watched him light one, felt the old nicotine yearning start nagging at my nerve ends.

I watched him think about it.

"I don't buy it, Philly," he said finally, shaking his head. "I mean, maybe he likes to beat up on women—they all do—and maybe he's messed up inside. But that doesn't make him a killer, does it? I mean, he's a silver-spoon kid. Silver-spoon kids don't go around killing people."

"It's been known to happen," I said.

"Serial killers?"

I couldn't think of an actual case. At the same time, though, I didn't see that rich or poor had much to do with whether somebody committed multiple mayhem.

"Besides," Bobby said, "he's such a wimp." I watched him run his tongue around the inside of his mouth, like he was cleaning house. "Take last night. We were at Melchiorre's, just hanging out, and some of the guys really got on his case."

"What about?"

"I don't know how it got started. You know how guys are. There's been a lot of tension there. Some of them even want to get rid of him, like he kind of cramps their style. I don't get it altogether. Anyway, Stark starts riding him—that's the one they call Shrimp, the little guy? He asks Cloy about his sex life. Then they all jump in. Then somebody asks him about his shrink, about Nora, you know? Asks him has he done it yet? When was he going to do it? Or did he get enough kicks out of the tapes? Stuff like that. It got pretty personal, pretty ugly. And you could see it get to Cloy. He stiffened up. I mean, his knuckles went white, like he was about to coldcock somebody. But then you know what happened? Damned if he didn't start to cry! He hadn't even had that much to drink. And then out the door he goes!"

"What time was this?"

"I don't know. It was early. Must've been before midnight anyway."

"And then what happened?"

"I don't know. I think Hal went after him. The rest of us more or less closed the joint. Nobody much felt . . ."

"But McCloy? Where did McCloy go?"

"How do I know? I guess he went home."

"You *guess*?"

"That's right. At least that's where he was this morning. I spent the night there. He was still asleep when I . . ."

"For Christ's sake!" I interrupted. "I'm paying you to stay with McCloy, not to hang around in saloons!"

"Hey! Hey wait a minute, Philly, I . . ."

"Forget it, " I said, getting up in a hurry. "I've got to make a phone call."

I'd had one of those sudden . . . well, all right, call it a premonition. I don't believe in sixth senses, but all I saw was Nora getting into the cab and how did I know where the hell she'd gone after that?

Irrational? Paranoid? Okay, but it caught me right in the gut.

I went to the phone box which hung on the wall between the cashier's desk and the street window. I dialed her office. No, Dr. Saroff wasn't in, the receptionist said. She recognized my voice. Where was she, I asked. The receptionist didn't know. Well, had she heard from her? Yes, the receptionist said. In fact Dr. Saroff had called in, she wasn't feeling well, she'd said to cancel all her appointments. Was she sure she'd called in that morning? Of course she was sure, was anything the matter? No, I said, but where had she called in from? The receptionist said she didn't know. Well, who would know? Maybe Dr. Biegler, she said. Well, could I talk to him? No, he wasn't there either, he had no morning appointments. Did I want to leave a message? No, I said, just say I'd called. Say I'd call again later.

I hung up, took a deep breath and blew it out. Bobby Derr was staring at me from across the cafeteria, and he eyed me all the way back to the table.

"Jesus, Philly," he said, "what's got into you this morning?"

"I don't know," I said. "You got a cigarette?"

"Sure," he answered. "But I thought you'd quit smoking."

I took a cigarette from his pack, lit it, took a deep drag, exhaled and felt myself go dizzy in the head.

"I have," I said, stubbing the damn thing out in the ashtray.

"Look, Philly," he began, but I cut him off.

"I know," I said, "I told you to get in with McCloy and the others, not necessarily to glue yourself to him."

"That's right. And what the hell was I supposed to do? Like I can't divide myself into pieces. Like last night . . ."

"Never mind, Bobby."

"Shoot," he said. "You never even told me you thought he was a murderer."

"I'm not sure I do," I said.

"But how come you even suspect him?"

I gave him what I had then, including the correlations the Counselor's Wife had worked out and the note that had been slipped under her door. Even as I laid it out, though, it sounded flimsy, circumstantial. In addition, the last Pillow murder had taken place before I'd hired Bobby, and the killer, whoever he was, had crawled back into his hole since, and as far as Carter McCloy was concerned, it had been pretty much party-party.

We kicked it back and forth, working over the times

McCloy had been with the group and those he hadn't, and what the girls had said about him, including the Staten Island girls, and why the others seemed to want to get rid of him, and why McCloy let them ride him.

"Why don't they?" I asked Bobby.

"Why don't they what?"

"Get rid of him."

He thought about it.

"Part of it," he said, "is that some of them are old buddies. They go way back. Some of them went to the same school, some prep school. And maybe they need a butt, kind of. But also, in a funny way, McCloy pimps for them. I mean, the son of a gun draws women like a magnet. The bims go for him, they think he's handsome. I've watched him get them without half trying. It's amazing."

I'd seen that too. What was it? The King of Pimps, the Pimp of Kings.

"Maybe it's the white scarf bit," Bobby Derr said. "He always wears that white scarf. But your killer doesn't strangle, does he?"

"No, he doesn't. He uses pillows."

"You gotta be strong to use pillows."

By this time, I'd paid the check at the Roosevelt and we were out on Broadway in the daylight, heading south past a construction site where they were putting up another one of those block-long residential high-rises.

"Well, babe," said Bobby Derr, "where do we go from here? It's your call."

I'd been thinking about that too, thinking about the Counselor and what he'd said, and the Counselor's Wife and where the taxi had taken her the night before, and where she might be now.

She'd wanted to call it off. *I'm a hysterical woman who wants to have a baby,* she'd said. But that was before we'd seen the tapes, on McCloy's VCR.

"I want you to keep it up," I said.

"Really?"

"But narrow it. McCloy."

"Well, that'll cost you, babe. Or her. Or Camelot. I mean,

I didn't know I was working a murder suspect before. That calls for hazard pay."

I stopped him in the street.

"Cut it out, Bobby. Either that or I'll pull you off the case right this minute. You don't . . ."

"Hey!" he interrupted. Then he burst out laughing. Then stopped. "Jesus, Philly, have another cigarette, will you? I was only kidding around. Don't you know I'd work for you for expenses if you asked me to? For old times' sake? Besides, I haven't had so much free sex since high school!"

I knew this much about Bobby Derr: that there wasn't any old times' sake between us. As it was, I gave him my upcoming schedule and left him on the Broadway corner while I crossed the street to where I'd parked the Fiero. I had my hand on the driver's door when I heard him call out behind me:

"Hey, babe! I forgot to thank you for breakfast!"

Tribeca.

It stands for Triangle Below Canal Street, and that means a forgotten wedge of west Manhattan, underneath the Holland Tunnel, that up to a few years ago was a mixed bag of warehouses, sweatshops, light manufacturing lofts, and here and there a tenement thrown in. From the outside it still looks pretty much the same, and why anybody over the age of thirty, with a few bucks in his or her pocket, would actually choose to live there escapes me. But people do, a certain kind of radical-chic, I guess you'd say. Sally Magister among them. And to judge from Sally Magister's pad (if that's the word for it), I'd have to reverse myself and say there are few enough under-thirties who could afford the neighborhood now.

Sally Magister, mind you, could have bought the same space on Park Avenue, or Central Park South, or Gramercy Park. Instead she lived on the top two floors, with a roof garden, of a cadaverous, gray-stoned loft building in Tribeca, and she owned the whole building, which was why, I guess, certain features remained unchanged, like the huge gateless elevator, big enough to hold a Sherman tank and slow enough, going up, to make you feel like it was carrying one.

"How'd you like the ride?" she said, not smiling, when she let me in through a people-sized door cut into the enormous sliding panel of her landing. "I keep it that way because it slows people down. We all need that. People are too damn *agitated* in this city. Why do you think we've so many heart attacks, aside from smoking? It's because people are stressed out from noise and speed. The only rule I've got up here is no smoking. Tobacco, anyway."

To judge from Sally Magister, her theory of the slow elevator didn't always work, although I guess there's no telling what she'd have been like if it went up and down at normal speeds. As is, she was perpetual motion and yak-yak. No beauty either. The features which made the Magister men good-looking in a sort of rawboned way hadn't worked so well on a woman. She was tall, even gawky, with carrot-red hair cropped short, freckles, big teeth, an ostrich neck, and she wore a denim overalls outfit with a sweatshirt underneath and leather sandals on her feet. If I didn't like her at first blush, she, as she made aggressively clear, didn't like me any better. Not that she was singling me out either. It was men, in general.

She might have made an exception for her sons. But that's a tough call.

Her place had a similarly unnerving effect. I guess you'd call it high-tech decor, in that there were exposed pipes and ducts everywhere, most of which looked like they belonged to the original building. The downstairs was really two gigantic rooms with enormous ceilings, one of which—the "office"—had been taken over by a work crew in painter's whites. The other reminded me of an art gallery. Its floors were broad squares of black and white tiles, and it was hung with canvases too large even to get into the normal-sized living room, great splashes of color except for one that looked solid black to me, but for a thin gray line which wandered down from top to bottom. She told me that one was priceless as we passed it on our way to a tubular spiral staircase which took us to the upstairs.

We emerged into her living room, which had been converted temporarily into the office and where the regular furniture had been pushed back to the walls to make room for drafting tables, stools and other art and photography equipment and where, she told me, the people were working on layouts for *Fem*. *Fem*, the so-called Woman's Magazine of the 21st Century, was Sally Magister's great claim to fame. She stopped to look, comment, and criticize as we walked through to another room, this one walled off from the rest and a little more human in dimension and content.

Oh yes, I forgot to point out that while I was there, I didn't see a person who wasn't female. Including the work crew on the lower floor.

"I heard you were cute," Sally Magister said, gesturing me to an upholstered couch that had a scrolled wood backing that looked antique.

"Where'd you hear that?" I asked conversationally.

"I've got to tell you I don't like cute people," she said. "Particularly men. Life's too short and I'm too busy. So why don't you state your business and tell me what you want to know."

She sat across from me, first on a revolving wood stool that also looked antique, then in a stuffed chair, then back on the stool. Behind her was a massive fireplace with a broad marble mantel crowded with framed photographs, and there were more photographs hung on the walls to either side. To her left, on a pedestal table, was a life-size sculptured head of a young boy, the color of earth. The model, it turned out, had been Sally's oldest son and the artist—a little to my surprise, because it looked to me like a professional piece of work—had been the model's mother.

Which, Sally Magister would likely have said, was too cute a way of putting it.

"I made that," she said later when she caught me looking at it. "I was trained as a sculptress. That's Vincenzo, age five." She pronounced the name Italian-style, with a *ch* for the *c*, "Vincenzo the angel. My first-born, no longer the angel."

As it happened, I never did get a chance to state my

business as such. Having told me to, she did it for me. I was there to snoop, pry, dig into her closets.

"I don't like closets," she said. "I like everything outside where you can see it. I also don't like intermediaries. If . . ." and she mentioned the Firm's name, ". . . want to see me, they should come themselves instead of sending a messenger. I'm only seeing you because La Marga wanted me to." La Marga, it turned out, was what she called Margie Magister. "La Marga thinks you're cute. I'll tell you what I want. I want the magazines. The Magister Magazine Group. That's my life. For the rest of it, I don't give a damn, not as long as it doesn't affect what I'm doing."

"So you don't care . . ."

"I didn't say I didn't care. I want La Marga to take control of the company."

"Why is that?"

"Because she's a woman. I believe in women. Because she's smart, motivated, willing to roll up her sleeves and get her hands dirty. The Jerks will run it into the ground. They've already started. The Jerks will end up selling off assets, and the first asset they'll try to sell is the magazine group, and that's mine. I'm not for sale."

"I take it the Jerks are . . ."

"That's right. The Jerks are my brothers. They were born Jerks and they still are. Their father's creation. If they hadn't been born to money and power, they'd be selling stamps behind a post office counter. *If* they could pass a civil service test, which is questionable. And I'll tell you something else," jabbing a large finger at me, "yes, I prefer women to men. I make no bones about it, I affirm it. It took me a long time to recognize that I didn't have to let men ruin my life. That was a long, hard struggle, believe me. And that goes for my sexual preferences too. I prefer women to men. You could have saved your bosses a great deal of money if, instead of paying people to pry into my private life, you'd simply asked me. I've nothing to hide. But do you realize the trouble you've caused some of my friends? Who gave you the right to harass my friends?"

"I'm afraid I . . ."

"I know," she interrupted with a dismissing wave, "you were only following orders. That's all you men do: you follow orders."

There seemed, to say the least, not much point arguing. I wondered, having learned to be suspicious of people who say they've nothing to hide, what she was hiding. I also wondered how the Counselor had known to send me instead of himself, and how he would have reacted if he'd found himself in the bear pit in my place.

"Let me tell you about the Magisters, Mr. Revere," she said, changing seats again. "My father was the cruelest man who ever lived. He had no equal when it came to how he treated my mother. Her life was a living hell. People said it was because he was empire-building that he had no time for family, but that's so much nonsense. He married her for breeding purposes, pure and simple. Otherwise he cheated on her every day of her life. Not just with mistresses, he cheated on them too. And she took it, that was the worst part. She never fought back. He'd bought her, that was all. The best thing that happened to her was that she died."

She paused to stretch herself in the comfortable chair, arching her head back into the cushion as though she was doing some relaxation exercise. Then:

"I've got to hand it to La Marga. Whatever she got out of him, she deserved it. I like to think she did it on behalf of all of us, all of us women whose lives he tried to ruin. What do you think of La Marga? I admire her, don't you?"

No room for an answer, though. It was more like she was interrogating herself. The more she talked, in fact, the more she talked about herself, and the more she talked about herself, the more it seemed like she was talking to herself. She'd dropped out of college, had gone to art school. By then, nobody'd cared. Her first two husbands, she'd realized at long last, had been attempts to marry her father, pure and simple. To make him love her, notice her. It had taken her four children and two marriages to discover that this wasn't going to happen, ever, and that all she'd done was make herself into a replica of her mother. That had been the crisis of her life, and once she'd understood it, she said, she'd been able to get out from under. At great personal cost, mind you. Then she'd browbeaten the Jerks into giving her the magazines, and her father had approved. Then she'd gotten married again, the first time as a mature woman. That it had been a mistake wasn't his fault, the poor darling.

This third husband, I knew from Bud Fincher, had been both younger than she and gay. Presumably that was why he got off as "the poor darling."

"So there you have it," she said.

Maybe my mind had wandered, or at least my line of vision. That was when she caught me looking at the head of her son, Vincent, the one-time angel.

"What about your children?" I asked.

"Well, what about them?" she answered sharply.

By this time she was back on the stool, perched, her feet tucked into a rung and her arms hugging her coveralled body. The Counselor had wanted me to focus on the children.

"Mrs. Magister . . . Margie . . . said you cared a great deal about them. She said you'd lay down your life for them."

For the first time, Sally smiled.

"Did she really? What else did she say about them?"

"Nothing much. I got the impression you wanted them to inherit the company."

"Well, that would be up to them, wouldn't it? How much they wanted it. How hard they worked for it."

"Well, do they?"

"Do they what?"

"Do they want it?"

I knew, from Bud Fincher's reports, that Sally's oldest child—the one she called Vincenzo—worked in the company. Or had. In fact, he'd been in and out, most recently as circulation manager of one of the other magazines than *Fem*. The three younger ones were still in school.

"If you want to know that, I suppose you'll have to ask them," she said, looking away from me. "But why is that important?"

I shrugged.

"I guess it isn't," I said. "But Mrs. Magister . . . Margie . . . seemed to think it was."

"Oh? How so?"

"Well, she said that's what your father would have wanted."

"Is that what she said?"

"That's what she said."

For some reason, she seemed to find this funny. She laughed aloud, toothily, then uncoiled her body, got off the stool perch, and, turning toward the pictures behind her, said:

"Well, there they are. My little darlings. Not so little anymore."

I got up off the couch and looked with her while she gestured and described. The photos spanned a couple of decades and they were snapshots in style, the kind you'd find in any family album except that here they'd been mounted in frames and hung on the wall. There were pictures of babies, of Sally holding them, pictures of the boys in short pants and Sally and her one daughter in a white dress with puffy skirt and petticoats showing, pictures mostly in outdoor summer settings, on sailboats and docks, the kids on water skis or posing on the front steps of a big, Victorian-style mansion. There were a few winter scenes, one of three bundled kids standing next to a snowman wearing a black top hat, and one of a solemn-looking teenager in a school football uniform—that was Andrew, her second son—with the pigskin tucked under his arm. Sally described them with almost total recall as to where they'd been taken, at what age, and who else was there, and you'd have said, well, that's just a typical doting mother. Except for a couple of things.

One: there wasn't an adult male anywhere on the wall or the mantel, no father, no grandfather. Secondly, once you got past the short-pants age, Vincent seemed to have dropped totally out of sight.

I also noticed, almost in passing, an oddly familiar face.

The picture was of a bunch of college-age kids of both sexes on a sailboat, with froth in the water and billow in the sails. They wore bathing suits and T-shirts and sweatshirts, and some of them waved at the camera, and some had their arms around each other's shoulders, except for the one who was doing the steering and had his back to the camera. The photo had a grainy texture, like it had been blown up, and if I was right, it would have been some six to eight years old.

I was right. I'd recognized the one in the middle of the group. Maybe because he was taller than the rest, but almost certainly because of the towel draped around his neck.

"Is that one of yours?" I asked, pointing at him.

"Who?" she said, looking closer. "No, that's just Carter. Carter McCloy."

"Oh?" I said.

"Just a friend of Vincenzo's."

"And where's Vincenzo?"

"That one," she said, pointing. "The one with his back to the camera."

"Funny thing," I said, by way of covering up my surprise, "but I notice he seems to have dropped out of your family album. I mean, once you get past the kiddie pictures, there aren't any of him, except for this one with his back to . . ."

Like I say, I'm pretty sure it came out matter-of-factly, a passing comment, but she caught me up short, whirling on me angrily.

"I thought I told you I don't like cute people. I also don't like people who waste my time. If what you're after is dirt on Vincent Angus Halloran, then why don't you ask *her*? She knows more about him than I do!"

There was flash in her voice, her eyes, and her face had gone white and taut.

"Ask who . . . ?" I started to say, but she didn't give me room.

"Let me tell you something, Mister Revere," she said, with an ugly twist to the "mister." "You want to dig up dirt? Go ahead. You want to publicize that I sleep with women? Go right ahead. And if my goddamn son is sleeping with his stepgrandmother? Sure, put that in too. If that's all he's doing, who gives a damn? I've already made peace with it. You'd better be able to prove it, but even if you can prove it, do you really think that's going to stop us? And you can tell my brothers this for me, mister: if they want to start slinging mud, than La Marga and I can sling with the best of them!"

"I'm sorry, Sally, I . . . ," I began.

"And don't you call me Sally. How *dare* you? My name's Ms. Magister."

Whatever else she may have been, she laid this on me with all the cold indignation of somebody born to give orders, like the queen talking to an errand boy.

"I . . . ," I started, but that was as far as I got.

"I want you out of here now," she said, leading the way out of the room and pointing.

So out I went.

I stood outside in the diesel smoke of Tribeca, where the build-up to the Holland Tunnel rush hour was just starting to form, making and unmaking combinations. For instance, Vincent Angus Halloran, Jr., Sally's son, was already on three of my lists, but up to that point I'd missed the connections. This could have had to do with the names. I'd thought of them all as Magisters, the whole clan, but Sally's first husband had been a Halloran, her second a Cummings, and the children still went by their fathers' surnames. Vincent Angus Halloran, Jr., had appeared on Bud Fincher's family rosters and reports, and he was also down, I discovered when I checked later, as a sometimes visitor and escort to Margie. That they'd been shacking up together was news, and possibly not even true. Sally Magister, I judged, was capable of paranoia where her children were concerned.

But Vincent Angus Halloran, Jr., was, in addition, on a third list, only there he was called Hal. I'm talking about the Carter McCloy list. I'd even met him once myself, more or less, in the Rosebud men's room, and Bobby Derr had told me he was the one who usually defended McCloy against the others. And McCloy's picture was on his mother's wall.

What the implications were though, if any, I had no time for right then. For one thing, I was due at the office in fifteen minutes, when McClintock and Hank Rand were scheduled for a council of war. In addition, and closer to hand, I had company.

They were parked in a tan-colored Accord in a No Standing zone at the bottom of Sally Magister's block. I didn't pay any attention at first because I thought they belonged to a line of traffic waiting for the lights to change. But then the lights changed, the column moved forward, and the Accord stayed put. Then one of them—the driver—got out and walked toward me.

I don't know what it is about the Gentlemen of the Law, I truly don't, but you really can spot them. FBI, NYPD, DA's office, take your pick. These two didn't have that young, scrubbed, crewcut look. It wasn't the polyester either, or the London Fogs, and as for smell, all you got on that street was diesel and carbon monoxide. Maybe at that it's the eyes.

"We want to talk to you," this one said as he came up to me. NYPD as it turned out, but assigned to the DA Squad. His partner was an assistant DA.

"Who, me?" I answered in time-honored style.

"You," he said.

"Who's we?"

He showed me his wallet then, with his badge inside a plastic cover.

"Gee," I said, "I didn't know you guys got to drive around in foreign cars."

"Let's go, Revere."

So—at the risk of repeating myself—I went.

CHAPTER 8

I sat in the back while the assistant DA swung around to face me and the cop, who was driving, eyed me from time to time in the rearview. The fact that they were DA puzzled me. Usually the prosecutors only get called in late in an investigation, after the cops, as they like to say, have done all the dirty work. But the Pillow Killer investigation, they claimed, had thrown all such distinctions and divisions out the window. Both of them belonged to the Task Force.

Even so, the DA connection led me to assume that it was the Counselor himself who'd tipped them off. After I'd told him Nora's story the day before, he must have called somebody like Anne Garvey. He'd have been looking for clout and discretion, and Anne Garvey had both. She was a bitch on wheels about my age, and well on her way up in the Manhattan District Attorney's office. The day would come, according to the Counselor, when she'd either jump to a big firm or stand for office herself. Meanwhile, since the call had come from him, she'd have had one of her own follow it up: Andrew Intaglio by name.

We drove slowly through the traffic over to West Street and parked at one of the piers. After a while we got out and walked out on the pier into the river, where there was a moist breeze blowing up out of New Jersey, and they kept me in the middle so that they could take turns.

They were experienced investigators, I guess, in that they lied well. For instance, they told me they'd already picked up and questioned Bobby Derr, which turned out to be true, and that Bobby had mostly hid behind professional confidentiality, which turned out to be true too. They also said they'd been on to McCloy for some time, which turned out to be untrue, although I had no way of knowing it then.

Meanwhile, they held back the big news, but that was more omission than outright lie.

They sweated me on the confidentiality issue. The fact is that I'm not licensed either as an attorney or as a private investigator, and while I usually manage to duck behind my working for the Counselor, in this case I couldn't. What's more, they knew it.

"We want to talk to Mrs. Camelot," said Andrew Intaglio, the assistant DA.

"Well, you certainly can do that."

"The problem is, we don't know where to find her. You tell us."

"How should I know? Try her office. Try her at home."

"We have."

"What about their house in the Hamptons?"

"She's not there."

"Then leave a message. That's what I do when I'm trying to reach her."

"That's all you do?"

"That's right."

"Why do I get the feeling you're lying?" asked the cop, whose name was Walters, but Intaglio intervened.

"Why has she moved out on her husband?" the assistant DA went on.

"If she has, you'll have to ask her that."

"Has she got something else going on the side?"

"Ditto," I said.

"And where does Sally Magister fit in?"

"She doesn't."

"Then what were you doing up there just now?"

"I was there on business."

"What kind of business?"

"Mr. Camelot's business."

"Is Camelot involved in the Magister fight, the one about the will?"

"You'll have to ask him that."

"We intend to. But which side are you representing?"

"Ditto," I answered.

For some reason, this last ditto seemed to stir them up. We'd reached the end of the pier where the breeze was strongest and the river water chopped against the pilings underneath us. Intaglio stood with his back to the river, staring down at his toes. He rocked back on his heels a little, then forward on his toes, then looked at me. He said if they found out I was holding out on them, they'd hang me up by the thumbs. He said he couldn't believe I didn't know where Nora Saroff was.

I asked why it was so important for them to talk to her.

Because she'd named a suspect.

Then why didn't they talk to the suspect? I gave them Carter McCloy's name and address.

"We already got that," Walters, the cop, said.

"Why'd the two of you go up to that apartment last night?" Intaglio asked, moving in front of his partner.

"I wanted to see how somebody lives," I said, thinking fast.

"Who?"

"McCloy. Carter McCloy."

"How come he's not listed downstairs?"

"The apartment's in another name."

"And you took her with you?"

"That's right."

"Why?"

"She insisted on going."

The only person who'd known I was going to McCloy's was Bobby Derr. It made no sense that Bobby himself would have tipped off the police. That meant either they'd had McCloy's building staked out beforehand, which I tended to doubt, or they'd followed us from Nora's office. And had seen us holding hands in the street afterwards. And kissing.

"What'd you find up there?" Walters asked.

"Why don't you go look for yourselves?"

"That's our business, wise guy. Unlike you, we have to wait for a warrant."

"Where'd you go after she got into the taxi?" Intaglio asked.

"Me? I went home."

"Alone?"

"Yeah. Alone."

"Can you prove that?" Walters said.

Sometimes, in my experience, the Gents of the Law will sweat you just for the fun of it, but this had an edge of real to it. I didn't get it, not at least till Intaglio rocked forward again, saying:

"There's been another murder, Revere. Last night, we think. We just found out. It'll be on the evening news."

"An old lady this time," Walters added.

"Suffocated?" I asked.

"With a pillow, apparently. Death by asphyxiation. And he beat her up pretty bad."

"Beat her up? I thought the Pillow Killer just suffocated. No sex, no violence?"

I saw Intagilo's mouth tighten, and he glared at his partner.

"Sometimes," he said. He hesitated. Then: "Except for the Park Slope case, we've managed to keep that part quiet so far. What he does when he does it."

"Then what makes you so sure there's not a copycat involved?"

"We don't know yet, about this one. As for the others, we've got our reasons."

"Where did this one take place?"

Walters gave me the address. It was about a block and a half from McCloy's apartment. A walkup, one block south and on the other side of Third Avenue. Sometime after midnight, they thought. Apparently the victim lived alone. And so far nobody had heard a thing.

The first one, I thought, on the Upper East Side, and then my mind started racing, trying to remember what Bobby Derr had told me about the night before.

"You'd better tell us everything you know about McCloy," Intaglio said.

I did, up to a point, while we walked back in toward the city. South of us, the World Trade Towers had curls of clouds around their tops, and the darkening gray sky looked like it was closing down on the downtown skyscrapers. I told them what I knew firsthand, and what the Counselor's Wife had said, including the note she'd gotten. They seized on the note. They wanted to see it. I told them that to the best of my knowledge, the Counselor's Wife still had it. I also told them what Bobby Derr had found out, and what he was up to, and about my own one encounter with Carter McCloy.

And stopped there. Why I didn't tell them about the videotapes, I honestly don't know.

By then, we were standing next to the tan Accord. Walters opened the back door and motioned for me to get in.

"Where are we going now?" I asked.

"Uptown," Walters said.

"We want to talk to Camelot," Intaglio added.

"Do you have an appointment?"

No, they didn't.

"Then he won't see you," I said. "In fact he's got a meeting going on right now, one I'm supposed to be at. And unless I'm wrong, it's going to run late."

"We'll take our chances," Walters said.

I shook my head. The Counselor, I told them, didn't see people who just walked in off the street, not even cops. I spotted a phone booth across the street and offered to call Ms. Shapiro to make them an appointment for the next day, but they turned that down. The more I discouraged them, the harder they pushed.

Then Walters said: "We know why you're trying to stall us, Revere. Don't worry, we won't let the cat out of the bag. No problem."

His grin had a lot of leer in it. I told him I didn't know what he was talking about.

"Oh no? You mean to tell us you're *not* balling his wife on the side? You mean you're *not* scared we'll spill it to him?"

I measured him, cop or no cop. He was about my height, a little older, maybe a couple of sizes wider.

Intaglio, though, must have seen what was coming.

"Here's the point, Revere," he said, cutting in front of his partner. "This is an ugly case, and we've got no time for people playing cute with us. There's a killer out there who likes to play around with women and then suffocate them, or vice versa. We've got no idea when he'll strike again. We want him bad, and we want him now. We've got the manpower to follow every lead, and that's exactly what we're doing."

He was the second one that day who'd accused me of being cute.

"Okay," I said, "but you get two things straight. One, Mr. Camelot's not going to see you just because you're there. Besides, he doesn't know any more about the murders than what I've told you."

"Except where his wife is," Intaglio said.

"Maybe he'll tell you that, but you'd better let me call first. And the second thing," staring behind him at Walters, "there's nothing going down between Mrs. Camelot and me. If you think there is and you want to tell him about it, go right ahead. But I'd strongly recommend you be sure of your facts."

"Go ahead and call him," Intaglio decided for them.

He crossed West Street with me to the phone. I got Roger LeClerc, who said with his usual pleasure that the Counselor had been looking for me. Then I got Ms. Shapiro who said the same thing, without the pleasure. I told her to interrupt the meeting, that it was urgent. A moment later he came on:

"What's going on, Phil? You're supposed to be here."

"Unavoidably detained," I said, "on West Street, by two representatives of the law. The DA's office, in fact. They're on the Pillow Killer case. There's been another murder. They're very insistent on talking to you and Mrs. Camelot."

"Why?" he said.

"Information. I've told them everything I know."

"Tell them to be here at nine o'clock tomorrow morning."

I passed this on to Intaglio. He shook his head angrily.

"He won't accept that," I told the Counselor.

I heard him grunt at the other end. Then:

"Put him on, Phil. What's his name?"

"Intaglio," I said, handing the assistant DA the phone.

Intaglio got in the first words and the last. In between came a fair-sized pause, punctuated here and there by a "Yes, sir," and a "No, sir." Then, finally: "Yes, sir, nine o'clock sharp."

Intaglio handed the phone back to me.

"I want you back here, Phil," the Counselor ordered. "Right now."

And he hung up, without even leaving room for another "Yes, sir."

"Your boss is some piece of work," Intaglio said. "On the other hand, he did say he'd have his wife there, tomorrow morning."

We dodged across through the traffic to the tan Accord, where Walters was just hanging up the police phone inside.

"Hey, Andy," he called to his partner. "They've got him! They're bringing him in even as we speak!"

"Who's that?"

"McCloy. Revere's ole buddy, Carter McCloy."

"Let's get going," Intaglio said to Walters. Then, turning to me: "You want us to drop you off?"

My Fiero was still parked over near Sally Magister's.

"Thanks but no thanks," I said.

"Probably we'll see you tomorrow morning?"

"Probably you'll see me tomorrow morning."

"Nine o'clock?"

"Nine o'clock."

"Nice of you to join us, Phil," the Counselor said sarcastically when I showed up in his office, over an hour and a half late.

There were eleven people present, and they filled the

room to bursting. In addition to the Counselor there were McClintock and Rand from the Firm, Young Bob Magister and his brothers Stafford and William, plus their personal attorneys, plus a steno from the Firm to take notes. I sat in a straight chair which I brought in from the outer office and sandwiched between Hank Rand and the far wall. We of the local staff had long since quit lobbying for a conference room. The Counselor would have no part of it. On rare occasions we'd held larger meetings on the top floor, where the Counselor's Wife had thrown parties for up to a hundred people, but the top floor was part of the residence and the Counselor liked to keep his business separate. I also think he had the theory that if people were that uncomfortable, jammed into his office, they wouldn't stay that long.

I'd never met the Magister men before. At least they didn't look like Jerks. Young Bob looked every bit the gilt-edged executive at fifty, in blue serge, lustrous white shirt with collar pin, maroon rep tie with navy crests on it which probably signified some club or university. His brothers were similarly turned out. They all came on self-assured and articulate, and the fact that there were no less than eight people in the room whose services were being billed to them, directly or indirectly, some at high figures, didn't seem to bother them in the slightest. Probably, if it had occurred to them, they'd have liked the idea of it.

The people who were sweating, I saw quickly, were Doug McClintock and Hank Rand. I knew the Magisters had called the meeting—a "council of war," they'd said. The Firm, I also knew, had contrived to put it off for one reason or another, but now, with the apparent defection of Sally, the brothers had insisted. The Firm, in other words, was now being forced to choose sides, and I figured they'd asked for the meeting to be held at our office as a last-ditch attempt to stay on the fence.

The part I'd missed, I found out later, had been devoted largely to reviewing and assessing all the litigation-in-progress, particularly the contesting of Old Bob's will. The consensus was that the case was a loser. Nobody could produce evidence that Old Bob was mentally incompetent when the will was written. On the contrary, the Firm itself had drawn it up. Nor could anyone prove that Margie Magister had coerced him into signing it. At the same time, no one was willing to drop it, lest it be taken as a sign that the brothers were throwing in the towel.

By the time I got there, they'd shifted to mudslinging, or to mudslinging as an offensive strategy.

Young Bob put it this way:

"I don't believe," he said, leaning forward in his chair, "and by the way," motioning to the stenographer, "I want this off the record. . . . But I don't believe that any shareholder or investor in his or her right mind is going to support a Jewish nurse from Europe and an avowed dyke, even if she is my sister, to manage a corporation like ours. It's patently absurd. Does anybody disagree with me?"

"We don't know that she's Jewish," somebody said.

"Believe me," Young Bob went on. "Look, I've nothing against Jews. They run some of our biggest companies, particularly in the communications industry. But look at what you've got. You've got two women—*women*, mind you—one of who's a Jew who's never worked a day in the business, the other an artsy lesbian who lives in SoHo or wherever and who only got where she is because the old man had a temporary weak moment. We all know Wall Street. Do you think they'll leave a dollar invested in Magister?"

"In fact, Bob, Sally hasn't done so badly," his brother Stafford said.

"Let's not get into that. You and I both know that if the old man hadn't played games with the corporate overhead, the magazine group would have long since been in water up to its chin."

"Still, *Fem*'s been the best new income producer we've had in the last decade."

"I don't want to hear about *Fem*," Young Bob said icily. "What is it? Less than five percent of our annual revenues? Somebody's got to worry about the other 95 percent."

"Maybe Wall Street doesn't think anyone is, enough," Doug McClintock said calmly.

"I'm surprised to hear that from someone like you, Doug," Young Bob said, turning on McClintock.

"It's not me, Bob," the lawyer said, unflustered. "I'm simply gauging Wall Street opinion."

"And you know the reason for that. The old man kept our hands tied for years. But I'll tell you this much: If I knew for sure those bitches were going to win, I'd dump every last share of Magister I own. Right this minute."

Part of Young Bob's plan, as I've indicated, had been to get enough dirt on Margie and, more recently, his sister that they could be bought out, either in private negotiation or through investor pressure. Blackmail, in sum, by another name. He now asked McClintock for an update. McClintock turned to the Counselor, and the Counselor, not to my surprise, turned to me.

I told them I had little to report that they didn't already know. I described my interview with Sally Magister. She'd been clearly hostile toward her brothers and open about her own life, particularly her sex life. For what she'd said, everything Bud Fincher had dug up on her was true enough, and it hadn't seemed to bother her.

"All she said was that you'd better be able to prove it. She also said to tell you that if you want to start slinging mud, then she and La Marga—that's what she calls Mrs. Magister—can sling with the best of them."

"That sounds like our sister," Stafford Magister commented.

"There was one other thing I didn't quite get," I said.

"What was that?" McClintock asked.

"I haven't even had a chance to tell Mr. Camelot yet," I said, eyeing the Counselor whose long face was partly hidden behind wreathes of pipe smoke and whose eyes were half-closed. "But there's something funny about one of her children."

"Vincent. The oldest one."

"What's funny about Vince?" Young Bob said. "Other than that he's a bum."

"I don't know," I said. "But according to his mother, if I

understood her right, he's been sleeping with Margie Magister."

This revelation seemed to start everybody talking at once, except for the Counselor, and then Young Bob was shouting louder than the rest.

"I don't know what you're all getting so excited for," he called out. "We all know Vince. Did he ever finish school, Staff? I don't think he even graduated. The biggest joke of all is that she's employed him in the magazine group, can you beat that?"

"Used to, Bob," his brother William said. "I think he's out again now."

"In or out, what difference does it make? The word around the company is that if you want to get Vince Halloran on the phone before lunch, you'd better call him at home."

"Or at Margie's," someone else said. "God, that means he's shacking up with his grandfather's widow!"

"It wouldn't surprise me at all," said Young Bob. And then, to me: "Is there anything else?"

"No," I said. "Or maybe. I could be wrong, but I got the impression she—your sister—didn't like it. Not at all."

They chewed on that one for a while. Someone ventured that that's how Margie had gotten Sally to defect, by convincing her son to convince his mother. Someone else suggested that Sally had gone over to Margie in order to keep tabs on her son. As for me, I was thinking about my third list, Bobby Derr's, and Vince Halloran's old buddy, Carter McCloy, who, as far as I knew, was being interrogated by the Pillow Killer Task Force even as we sat there.

The meeting then drifted into numbers. Numbers of shares, numbers of stockholders, balance sheet items and income statements, P/E ratios, ROI's—all the stuff, in sum, that's the lifeblood of accountants, attorneys, investment bankers, and all the rest who serve and use the corporation. I half-listened because I was there, but the longer they went on, the more it seemed to me they were just marking time, either waiting for some other revelation like the one I'd brought them or, more likely, for somebody to decide what to do next. Following this train of thought, I realized that the

Counselor himself had said virtually nothing since I'd arrived. This was as usual. To watch him in a meeting, the unchanging expression, the distracted gestures, you'd never have guessed he was listening. But he was, as I knew from experience, not necessarily the way you and I would but absorbing what was said and formulating his opinions meanwhile, so that when the time came he'd be ready to hold forth.

That time took a long time coming, but it did.

I remember Doug McClintock turning to him.

"Well, Charles, what are your thoughts?"

The room, I noticed, had fallen silent.

The Counselor's chair creaked as he leaned forward. He propped his elbows on the desk and, facing the Magister brothers, pointed at them with the stem end of a pipe.

"You're not going to like what I think," he told them.

"Go ahead," Young Bob answered. "Try us."

"Very well," he said. "From what I've heard, you have only three intelligent choices, and the only recommendation I'd make is that you choose and exercise any one of them as rapidly as possible. The first would be: accept what the Magister women want. The second: sell off your own holdings in Magister. The third: look for a friendly takeover."

"But all those would mean effectively giving up control of the company!" the brothers protested, more or less in the same words.

"I think that's already happened, gentlemen," the Counselor said. "If you had effective control, we wouldn't be sitting here today. I understand that none of you may like these alternatives, but you know yourselves that you risk losing any protracted struggle, and there's a chance you'll take the company down in the process. So I suggest you take a closer look at the three choices.

"First: accept what they want. You all, I've been given to understand, have long-term employment agreements, with parachutes awarded in the event of a management change. I'm sure your attorneys here could negotiate even more favorable ones for you, which would leave you free to stay or leave under new management. If you were wrong about the Magister women and they succeeded, at the very least your own holdings would appreciate. But if you were right and they failed, which could come about not only from incompetence but from their losing interest, at least you could be there, if you chose, to pick up the pieces. By the way, I think it entirely possible that Margie Magister at least would lose interest.

"Second: sell out now. If you're absolutely convinced they're going to fail, and fail so badly that no rescue operation will save the company, then you should consider getting out now—at a negotiated and presumably advantageous price. The disadvantage is that you could always be wrong and live to regret it.

"Finally: find yourselves a white knight. I'm aware of two things you've said: one, about fifty percent of Magister stock is now held by institutions; two, the stock has, since your father's death, traded in a surprisingly narrow range. Why is this, in the face of continued subpar earnings? I suspect it's because the institutions themselves have been waiting out a takeover attempt and the chance to cash in. But this has yet to happen, and at some point they have to lose patience. After all, they have portfolios to manage, clients to answer to. At some point, if the family situation stays unresolved, they're going to start selling and the stock could go down precipitously, and then the raiders will be out in force, including some you might not want to work for.

"If this last is your choice, though, I suggest you act quietly and quickly. For one thing, I've a feeling your adversary may already have started."

"What do you mean by that?" Young Bob asked the Counselor in an accusing voice. "Do you know something that's going on?"

"Not at all," he answered. "But I know Mr. Barger by reputation. And I've met Mrs. Magister."

Bitter pill time, in sum. The Counselor had more to say, but it all added up to the same message. The Magisters heard it, and clearly they didn't like it. Even McClintock and Rand paled but in their case, I imagine, because they knew the

Counselor was right. In other words, Wall Street may not have liked the idea of "a Jewish nurse" and "an avowed lesbian" running a Fortune 500 company, but there wasn't realistically a hell of a lot Wall Street was going to do about it. Or the Magister brothers either.

The meeting started to break up, but the Counselor had one last bit of advice:

"In my judgment, the witchhunt—the 'mudslinging' as you call it, the digging up of people's private lives—serves no purpose other than to antagonize. Nothing we've learned is going to help you. I doubt anything will. I recommend that you call it off, now."

They didn't though, and after they'd left, I asked the Counselor what he thought would happen next.

"They'll tell us to keep shoveling," he predicted.

And so they did.

I briefed the Counselor on my meeting with Walters and Intaglio; on the fact of the latest murder, on the fact that the Task Force had pulled in Carter McCloy. I told him I'd been in McCloy's apartment the night before, that his wife had insisted on going along with me, but that I hadn't seen her since.

He greeted this news with a grunt.

But did he want me there the next morning, for Walters and Intaglio?

Yes, that would be a good idea, since I'd already talked to them.

But what about his wife? They were very insistent that she be there, but I hadn't been able to reach her all day.

I needn't worry about that, he'd see to it.

But did he know the police had had a tail on me, or his wife, or both, since at least the evening before?

That wasn't his business, he said. This was my case, not his.

"But it was you who tipped them off, wasn't it? After I told you what was going on? You asked them to give her protection, didn't you?"

He shook his head.

"That turned out not to be necessary."

"What do you mean, not to be necessary? You mean they already had somebody on her?"

"I wouldn't know, Phil," he said with a shrug. "It's not my business."

I didn't get it then. I didn't get his indifference either.

The Counselor, though, had something else on his mind.

"Is it true, Phil?" he said, looking up at me.

"Is what true?"

He chuckled, shaking his head.

"That stuff about Margie Magister and what's his name? Sally Magister's kid?"

"Vincent Halloran."

"Vincent Halloran. How old is he?"

"Somewhere in his twenties."

"Well?" he said, eyebrows lifted. "Are they lovers?"

I wouldn't know, I started to say, *it's not my business.* Or some such.

"If they are," I answered instead, "he's not been the only one."

I had him down for jealousy, and I guess I felt like rubbing it in some. Instead, he threw his head back and guffawed.

"I bet it's true," he said, relishing the idea. "Let's find out. But can you imagine? Isn't she some kind of woman?"

On that note, I ducked out.

Ms. Shapiro was still in the outer office—she never leaves for the day until the Counselor tells her to—but when I got back downstairs, Roger LeClerc had already closed up shop. Usually he leaves any late messages for me on a small porcelain tray on the corner of his desk, this on the theory, I guess, that it's too far to walk them into my office. I stopped to check. There was only one: Mr. Derr had called. Just then, though, Muffin, the Counselor's Wife's cocker bitch, came flying out of my office and, braking to a halt, threw her head back and let out a prolonged yowl, wagging her tail furiously meanwhile.

And behind her, standing in my office doorway, wearing the same red slicker she'd had on that morning she left, was the Counselor's Wife.

"Hi, Phil," she said.

"Well," I answered. "Hi. Are you back? Or just visiting?"

"I'm back," she said.

"Since when?"

"A little while ago."

"Does he know?" I said, nodding my head toward the ceiling.

"Yes, he does. But I wanted to talk to you. Can we talk for a minute?"

"Sure," I said, following her into my office.

My office is a pleasant room, with two windows looking out onto the street. It contains a foldout couch where I've been known to sack out when the pressure's on, some glassed-in mahogany bookcases containing remnants of our law library from before we went in for computers, Lexis and the Firm's other electronic resources, and on the walls some framed English hunting prints which had hung in the Counselor's office until his wife redecorated. I've got a computer terminal and keyboard, plus an old Adler portable electric I still feel more comfortable with, and assorted other items more associated with business than personal.

The Counselor's Wife sat down on the couch. I guessed she'd been waiting for me. There was a hardcover book opened and pages down on one arm of the couch. The cocker bitch followed us in and jumped onto the couch next to her mistress.

She didn't look good, even with one arm along the back of the couch in a relaxed position. She looked worn out, even washed out, like she hadn't slept. Maybe she hadn't. Why she was wearing the red slicker indoors I've no idea.

"Since when did you start smoking again?" she asked.

I looked down, saw that I had a lighted cigarette in my hand. I stared at the thing, not quite believing, then bent over and stubbed it out in my waste basket. Then I found the pack of cigarettes I'd bought earlier in my jacket pocket and tossed it into the waste basket too.

"I haven't," I said.

"Good," she answered.

Then silence.

Then:

"Well, I'm back," she said. "For how long remains to be seen. I did something stupid, maybe I wish I hadn't but never mind. I'd like to apologize to you. Then I'd as soon forget about everything that happened last night. Is that okay?"

"You don't have to apologize," I said. "But did you know we were followed last night?"

"No. Who by?"

"The police, I think. At least they saw us at McCloy's, and after that."

"And later? I mean . . . ," flashing a sudden smile, "after you turned me down?"

"I don't know."

"God," she said.

Then nothing.

I wanted to ask her where she'd gone, but I couldn't bring myself to do it.

"I thought it was your husband who'd brought the police in. But he said he didn't. I don't know who did."

"I think I might," she said. Then nothing again, only a stiffness in the air.

"Damn," she said. "Double damn." Then: "Well, I'll deal with that. I'm only sorry I dragged you into it."

"That's one thing you don't have to worry about," I said.

"And I want you to forget about Carter McCloy," she went on. "He's twenty-six years old, he's going to have to learn to take care of himself."

This seemed a strange thing for her to say.

"I'm not sure that's going to be possible," I said. "The police have picked him up now, did you know that? For questioning anyway. Also, there's been another murder."

"When?"

"Last night, they think."

"The Pillow Killer?"

"Seems that way." Then, when she didn't answer: "It's possible he did it. I'm not saying he did, but it's possible. And by the way, two people from the District Attorney's office are coming here tomorrow morning. They want to talk to you and Mr. Camelot. I've told them pretty much everything about your suspicions, also about the note. They'll want to see that. I also had to tell them there isn't anything going on between us."

"Good," she said. Her reaction seemed subdued, distracted even. Then, maybe because she read my expression, she said: "Look, Phil. Someday I'm going to want to tell you everything that's happened. But not today. Today, I just want to forget it. It's over. As far as Carter McCloy goes, you use your own best judgment."

"My own best judgment," I said, "is that you ought to have round-the-clock protection for the time being."

By this time we were standing. The Counselor's Wife got up first, followed by Muffin, who jumped on the floor and stretched her front legs, then her rear ones, wagging her tail meanwhile.

"That," she replied, "I think I've already got. Lucky me."

She moved forward as though to kiss me, and then she did. On the cheek this time. Without further explanation, and trailing her shoulder bag by the long strap, she crossed the reception area to the small elevator which serves the residential floors. The door slid open almost immediately, and she got in, and Muffin, after turning her head to see if I was coming along, got in too.

CHAPTER 9

I gave Bobby Derr a call before I left the office. He wasn't home. I put a message on his answering machine, telling him where to find me.

Then I went outside, making sure to turn the alarm system back on. It was dark, and the chill in the evening air reminded me that it was time to zip the lining back into my raincoat. The Counselor's Wife had said she already had round-the-clock protection, and, taking her at her word, I canvased the cars on both sides of our street. Unless he was hiding in a trunk, there was nobody on the job. I remember looking back at the building from the far sidewalk and seeing the lights on in the residential floors and figuring that what she'd meant was that her "protection" was on the inside. Mr. and Mrs. Camelot were clearly at home. But what they might have been doing or talking about I've no idea.

I rescued the Fiero from east of Park. It had gotten a ticket, which stood to reason because I'd parked in a No Standing zone and next to a hydrant for good measure. I filed the ticket in the glove compartment, noticing that the pile had become almost big enough to send down to the Firm. One of the advantages of our affiliation was their pipeline into the Parking Violations Bureau. Then I pointed the Fiero west and drove home, stopping at the deli around the corner for a six-pack and some sandwich stuff.

I tried Bobby Derr again when I got home and talked to his tape again. I remember calling Laura Hugger and listening to hers, but I hung up without leaving a message. My own phone rang only once that evening. A fruity voice said: "Hi, I'm Bill, a computer specially programmed to receive your confidential answers to the following questions," and I waited till I heard Bill's first beep, then told him, in a few carefully chosen words, exactly what I thought about computers doing market research by random dialing.

I ate some, drank some, thought some, and watched the news reports about the latest Pillow killing. The Task Force, they said, was following several leads, but I noticed they omitted any mention of the rough stuff Intaglio had told me about. I got restless, antsy. I wanted to ask Bobby Derr about what happened with the police, also—again—about the night before. I remembered him saying that McCloy had left Melchiorre's alone and that he'd still been asleep when Bobby left the apartment that morning. And, yes, I thought about the Counselor's Wife too and what it was that she hadn't wanted to tell me.

I figured she'd shacked up with somebody last night.

It could have been me. It wasn't.

Probably that was a good thing.

Around eleven, give or take, I went out again, revved up the Fiero and drove across town to Melchiorre's. It had started to rain, one of those cold fall rains that bring traffic into the saloons, and Melchiorre's was doing good business. Not, though, with anybody I recognized.

The same dark-haired bartender who'd served me the other time was working my section of the bar, and he came up to me, automatically wiping the dark wood in front of me with a white towel, saying:

"Hi there, what'll it be? Bass Ale, right?"

"Right," I said, impressed. "Is Alfie Leonard around?"

Alfie Leonard, I knew from Bobby, was Melchiorre's current owner.

"No, he doesn't come around nights much."

I watched him fill the glass mug, tilting it into the spigot, then expertly flicking off the extra head with a bar stick and refilling without spilling a drop.

"So where is everybody?" I asked him.

"Who're you looking for?"

"I mean Cloy, you know? And Bobby, Booger, Hal, all that gang?"

He eyed me, frowning a little and tilting his chin.

"Say, you're not a cop too, are you?" he asked.

"No, I'm not. How come you ask?"

"Well, you're the second guy who's been in here tonight looking for them. The first one was a cop. I didn't know him, but he flashed me his badge. Actually, he was looking for Hal. Actually, he asked for Vincent Halloran. Say, what's going down with them?"

"Beats me," I said. "I was just looking for them. They're friends of mine, sort of."

"Well, I haven't seen them tonight."

He took the twenty I'd put on the bar, rang it up and put my change in front of me. I let it lie there. He moved off down the bar to serve other customers. I worked the Bass Ale down and signaled to him for a refill, putting a fresh twenty on the bar.

He noticed it all right, even though he counted out the money from my previous pile.

"When's the last time you saw them?" I asked him.

He shrugged.

"I don't know. They're in here most nights. Some of them anyway."

"What about last night?"

He gave me that quizzical tilt of the head again.

"C'mon," he said. "If you're not a cop, what are you? A private eye?"

"It so happens I'm not, but what makes you think so?"

He grinned at me.

"Because the cop asked the same questions. He was pretty

insistent about it, who was here last night, who wasn't. Say, what's so special about last night? You're not telling me one of them's the Pillow Killer, are you?"

He said it like a joke, laughing at the idea.

"Beats me," I said. "What did the cop say?"

"I didn't ask him. It didn't occur to me till just now. But you know something? This city's such a sewer, anybody could go crazy, you know what I mean?"

"Yes, I do."

"I don't mean your friends. They play a little rough sometimes, but they're okay. The only one I can't figure out is Bobby. You know Bobby?"

I nodded.

"Well, he's not like the others."

"What do you mean?" I asked.

"He talks different, you know? I mean, not Ivy League. The others talk like Harvard, but Bobby's just regular. I mean, he's okay, but he doesn't talk the same."

"Was he here last night?" I asked.

"Hey, gimme a break, will you? Yeah, he was here last night. I'll tell you who was here and who wasn't, okay?"

He ran the list through for me then, telling me he'd told the cop the same things. Cloy, Hal, Booger, Sprague, Shrimp, Mike, Bobby. He corroborated what Bobby Derr had reported, that McCloy had left early, angry, and that most, if not all of them, had closed the joint. He thought a couple of them might have wandered off in between, but he wasn't sure which ones. And that was all I got out of him, even though I worked the first twenty all the way down in Bass Ales and added another for him.

I stayed at Melchiorre's for an hour and a half, two at the outside. Nobody tried to pick me up. Nobody I knew showed. There were reasons for that, as it turned out. The Task Force still had Carter McCloy and would hold him overnight, for which there would be hell to pay. A couple of his friends had also been picked up. And meanwhile Bobby Derr was getting beaten to a pulp on a New York street.

As for me, I got home around one, cold, wet, and

lonesome, and found Bobby slumped against the door to my apartment.

He didn't look pretty. The rims of his nostrils were caked and his right eye puffed up almost to closing. His clothes were a soggy mess, and one of his ears looked like somebody had tried to take a bite out of it.

I got him inside and helped clean him up. I offered to take him to an emergency room, but he refused. All he wanted was a drink and a cigarette. I gave him both, the cigarette from a pack, still uncracked, that I'd bought at Melchiorre's.

"I blew it, babe," he kept saying. "I didn't give them you or Nora, but I blew it. They think I work for his stepfather. Jesus, if I'd only kept my mouth . . ."

It took a while, but I finally got him calmed down enough to tell it from the beginning.

The Task Force had picked him up shortly after we'd separated on Broadway. They'd questioned him hard about McCloy. They knew he was working for me, but they didn't push the point. Because of that, and after what I'd told him at the cafeteria, he'd figured that Camelot himself had fingered him. He'd told them pretty much all he knew about McCloy, even to the point of where he thought they'd find him. Then they'd let him go.

He'd gone up to McCloy's apartment in the afternoon. Why? Well, he hadn't been able to reach me, and the last instructions he'd had were that I wanted him to stay close to McCloy. He'd found a clean-up party in progress, with a case of beer in a washtub full of ice on the living-room floor. McCloy wasn't there. Nobody seemed to know where he was. Also, they were pretty guarded with him about why, just that day, they'd decided to clean house, but he was used to them being guarded with him sometimes. He'd helped out for a while, had carried a couple of plastic bags down to the garbage room in the basement. Then he'd left, after arranging to meet them at Melchiorre's later.

He'd gone home. He still hadn't been able to get hold of me. Then Shrimp had showed up. Shrimp Stark was one of the regulars in the group. I'd seen him myself that night at the Rosebud, a short, wiry guy with a crew cut. Bobby'd said he claimed to have been a champion wrestler in his prep school days. It wasn't so unusual for him to show up like that, according to Bobby. Melchiorre's, they'd decided, was not happening; they were going to Willy's instead; somebody had remembered telling Bobby Melchiorre's so Shrimp had volunteered to collect him.

I knew Willy's. It's a pub-type joint down in the Gramercy Park area, which dates back to the nineteenth century as does, by reputation, Willy's spaghetti sauce. The cuisine there is only as good as the number of drinks you've had, but the place is always jammed, particularly with the swinging singles set, and there was no reason for Bobby to be surprised at the change.

He and Shrimp had commandeered a booth in Willy's back dining room. When nobody else showed, they'd ordered dinner. Then Hal and Booger had come in, and in a few minutes Bobby had realized he was in deep.

Cloy had been picked up by the cops. Did anybody know why? Nobody knew why. Could anybody guess why? Nobody could guess why. More, the word was out that the cops were looking for other people in the group. In fact, all of them. All of them, in fact, except Bobby. Nobody had heard Bobby's name mentioned. Wasn't that funny?

Bobby had started out playing dumb. He had no idea why the police were after them. But later on he'd told them his name might have been left out because he'd already talked to the cops.

His first mistake, he said, but he figured they already knew.

Why had he gone to the cops?

He hadn't. The cops had pulled him in.

Why would they have done a thing like that?

Because they knew he was a friend of Cloy's.

What did they have on Cloy?

Nothing, he thought. But they suspected him.

Suspected him of what?

Suspected him of being the Pillow Killer.

He remembered that this had cracked them up, the idea

that Carter McCloy, wimp of wimps, was the Pillow Killer. It only went to show how desperate the cops were.

Well, what did they have on Cloy to make them suspect him?

He (Bobby) didn't know; it hadn't seemed to him they had much of anything.

Well, what did he (Bobby) think? Was Cloy the Pillow Killer?

He didn't know. He thought he might be.

"You told them you thought he might be?" I interrupted. "What the hell did you do that for?"

He shrugged and tried to grin.

"My second mistake," he said. "But I wanted to see how they'd react."

He got a little lost then, recounting it, about what had happened at Willy's and what later. His last mistake, he said, was not making a run for it while they were still in the saloon. But it had all happened so fast. He guessed he didn't believe they'd do what they did. He also guessed, he told me, that he didn't believe they could take him, not even three on one.

Wrong.

They'd taken him all right—to the deserted yard of a small private school somewhere in the teens. He hadn't even known the place existed, but one of them had gone there. Anyway, it was night and raining, and there was nobody around to watch, and there in the school yard, taking turns, they'd systematically beaten him.

They'd thought he was a cop himself. Then, from his wallet, they'd found out otherwise. They'd worked him over on that one: Who was paying him to fink on Cloy? But he hadn't told them. Why not, I asked him. He didn't know. He only shrugged and gave me that same broken grin. Besides, some of them had guessed it was Cloy's stepfather, and he hadn't said no to that, and then they'd gotten off on why he thought Cloy was the Pillow Killer, and he'd tried to say he wasn't and not much else because of protecting Nora, and he thought he'd passed out after that.

They'd stripped him clean, right down to his shoes. He'd

found one shoe on the sidewalk outside, but not the other one.

How had he gotten up to my place?

He'd walked. In his socks.

Bobby Derr slept in my bed that night, I on the living-room couch. He was still asleep the next morning when I left for the meeting with Walters and Intaglio and probably that was just as well because he'd be hurting like a son of a gun when he woke up.

The meeting took place in the sitting room on the third floor of our building, the first, that is, of the residential stories. The living arrangements the Counselor's Wife designed are worth mentioning because they're a little strange and maybe even unique for New York City. The Camelots' living quarters are on the third floor, meaning mostly the master bedroom, a guest room, and the sitting room. The fourth floor, you could say, is for eating. It's where Althea presides, the Camelots' housekeeper and cook, along with her cat, Gorgeous, and it contains kitchen, pantry, dining room, and Althea's room. Following the theme, the fifth and top floor is for play. Or parties. It's the Counselor's Wife's pride and joy, a combination solarium and living area with plantings inside and out, and if you follow magazines like *Architectural Digest*, you'll have seen pictures of it. It has a hot-tub room, which the Counselor sometimes uses, but otherwise it's mostly for entertaining. The Counselor's Wife, when she's in form, likes nothing better than to throw parties.

That the meeting took place upstairs instead of in the Counselor's office must have been her doing. But the additional presence of Anne Garvey was clearly his, and you'd have to call it pretty even in terms of which one of them was in charge.

Not that anyone could have sensed there'd been trouble between them. In fact, they seemed very much together that morning, even to the point of sitting side by side on the wood-backed couch which, I was pretty sure, the Counselor found uncomfortable as hell. He looked positively natty, in a tweed suit and yellow bow tie—further evidence of her having come home, and she had on one of those jersey wool outfits, sweater and skirt with an oversized shoulder-padded cardigan, all in slightly different but matching shades of olive-khaki. She wore her hair swept up, the way she usually does for her professional day.

The rest of us—Garvey, Intaglio, Walters, and myself—occupied chairs grouped around the oval coffee table of thick, highly polished tiger oak. Althea had brought down coffee in a silver service and a heaping platter of those miniature Danish which Intaglio, Walters, and I largely shared.

Intaglio asked the Counselor's Wife to start from the beginning, from when she first took McCloy on as a patient, and when she began to suspect him, and why. She had a problem with that though: the confidentiality of the therapeutic session. Anne Garvey gave her the necessary assurances: one, that McCloy was already in police custody and certain statements he'd made were under investigation; two, that given the seriousness of the crimes, Dr. Saroff had every legitimate justification for breaking that confidentiality; three, that if their investigation of McCloy led nowhere, every effort would be made to keep Dr. Saroff's connection to the case anonymous.

The Counselor asked if they could be given those assurances in writing. After some debate, Anne Garvey agreed to it.

Then the Counselor's Wife led them back through it pretty much as I've already put it down: about the nature of Carter's psychological problems as she understood them, particularly his trouble with women, about the correlations she thought she'd identified between his states of mind and the earlier murders, then about his most recent bizarre behavior. She cited the no-show appointment and the threatening letter as examples of this. She couldn't be sure, not having seen the patient in several months, but if in fact Carter had written the letter, she thought it could be interpreted two ways: either something had happened in his life outside to make the therapy too threatening for him to continue; or the transference between patient and therapist had reached that key stage when the patient's emotions, particularly the strong ones like love and hate, spill over and become fixated upon the therapist. Nor did one, she said, rule out the other.

"Let me ask you this," Intaglio said when she'd finished. "Do you think he's capable of murder?"

"I can only answer that very subjectively," she said.

"And . . . ?"

"Putting it another way, the phenomenon of transference is a two-way street. What goes on in the therapist's mind is called countertransference."

"I understand that," Intaglio said. "But you still haven't answered my question."

She hesitated, unusual for her, and when she spoke it was in a surprisingly thin voice:

"All I can tell you is that I feel very vulnerable."

"Do you mean you're afraid of him?"

She clearly didn't want to answer. Then:

"If you insist," she said.

Intaglio asked to see the letter. She produced it, and opening it, he flattened it on the table between him and Walters, using the side of his palm to smooth it out. I noticed an exchange of glances between them.

"We'd like to take this with us," Intaglio said.

"What's so significant about it?" the Counselor put in.

"Well," Intaglio said. Then he looked at Anne Garvey and she gave him a brief nod. "Actually, there are aspects to the case we haven't let out so far, that not even the media know about."

"Such as this piece of paper?" the Counselor persisted. "I don't get it."

Intaglio glanced at Anne Garvey again.

"Well, Mr. Camelot," he said, "the perpetrator . . . if he's the one who writes them . . . well, we've got a regular pen pal on our hands. I mean, your wife isn't the only one who's gotten one of these."

"Who else has gotten them?"

"I'm afraid that's official business."

"But private citizens like Nora?"

"Wait a minute," the Counselor's Wife intervened. She leaned forward intently. "Let me try to guess. How about Brenda Simpson for one?"

Brenda Simpson co-hosted one of the network morning shows.

I saw the surprise on Intaglio's face.

"How did you know that?" he asked her.

"We saw the tapes," she said, looking at me for corroboration. "Brenda was one of the ones Phil and I saw on tape when we were in Carter's apartment."

"What tapes?" Intaglio asked, looking at me.

"The night before last," I said. "Dr. Saroff and I found videotapes of her television shows. Some other shows too. Brenda Simpson was one of them."

"Why in hell didn't you tell us about that yesterday?"

"I didn't know it was important yesterday," I said, which wasn't altogether true. "How come you didn't tell me about the letters?"

Intaglio glowered at me, started to say something, then thought better of it.

"They're not there now, Andy," Walters put in. "At least they weren't mentioned in the report."

"When were you up there?" I asked him.

"I wasn't myself, but we had a search warrant. It must have been late afternoon or in the evening."

"Then look in the garbage," I told him, remembering what Bobby Derr had said. "They cleaned the place up yesterday. I bet they threw them out."

"Who, McCloy?"

"McCloy or, more likely, one of his friends. Derr was there in the afternoon. He said he helped them carry stuff down to the basement."

I told them then what had happened to Bobby last night. Walters scribbled notes on a foldover spiral, and he asked me if Derr would press charges. I said that would be up to Bobby but that he was in no condition, right then, to press anything.

Then Intaglio asked for Dr. Saroff's records and audiotapes pertaining to her sessions with McCloy.

The Counselor refused. Of course, he said, that was his wife's decision, but at least until she was served with a subpoena, he would have to advise her against it. They skirmished over that one until the Counselor's Wife offered to let Intaglio listen to the tapes in her office.

And that was about the size of it, or would have been had not Anne Garvey decided to give us her prepared speech, the five-minute version, the gist of which was that private citizens have no business meddling in police work and that this situation, involving McCloy, Dr. Saroff and yours truly, was as good an illustration of it as she'd ever run into. Because if McCloy was in fact the Pillow Killer, and if Dr. Saroff had gone to the police with what she suspected when she first suspected it, then one, possibly two lives might have been saved.

I didn't think it was called for at all, and Assistant DA Anne Garvey isn't the kind, I'd have to say, who could inspire me with guilt over my civic responsibility. Or lack of. But I saw the Counselor's Wife bite into her lower lip.

"Do you really think Carter's the killer?" she asked, looking from Garvey to Intaglio and back.

"We don't know," Garvey answered.

"I know you don't know. But what do you *think*?"

Garvey deferred to Intaglio, saying she wasn't a member of the Task Force, that (glancing at the Counselor) she'd only come to the meeting as an accommodation.

"Frankly we've been up too many dead-end streets to think anything," Intaglio said. "We know we're looking for a young man, white, physically strong. That's all. As for McCloy, we're investigating some of the statements he's made to us, and you've given us some new leads we've got to follow up on."

This didn't seem to satisfy the Counselor's Wife.

"Maybe I'm missing something," she said, "but where's the connection? Haven't all the Killer's victims been anonymous, at least so far? And then you've got somebody—maybe it *is* Carter—writing threatening letters to women who are more or less celebrities. Maybe there's a crime in and of itself . . . I imagine it is . . . but it's not murder, is it?"

"No, it isn't."

"Well, where's the connection?"

"There may not be one," Intaglio said, "unless it's you." Then he caught himself and, sighing tiredly, added: "I don't mean to frighten you unnecessarily, Dr. Saroff. But the fact is that we've gotten letters from him too. After every murder, to congratulate us on our efforts to find him. The same typewriter. But we can't prove that it's the Killer who's writing them either."

The Counselor's Wife took that in, protruding her lower lip. It struck me as weird that, having just admitted she was afraid of McCloy, she now felt compelled to defend him. But maybe it wasn't weird, for a shrink. As for Intaglio, frayed and tired as he must have been, you had to admire his cool. Because what he said next proved, once you stopped to think about it, that the Task Force was grasping at straws.

He waited for Garvey to stand up. Then he stood and, turning to the Counselor, said:

"I'd like to take Revere here with us, Mr. Camelot. I think he might be able to help."

For a split-second I swear I could see the meter running inside the Counselor's head. I was, don't forget, still on his payroll. But then he smiled at me, for inscrutable reasons, and said:

"That's up to you, Phil."

A few hours later, Carter McCloy was back on the street. No charge, no arraignment, no nothing.

Here's how it happened.

They'd had McCloy in a small interrogation room downtown, one that was wired for sound, and it had one of those one-way mirror jobs, long and narrow, which must have been some kind of engraving of the Brooklyn Bridge from the inside. You could see the outline of the bridge etched in the glass when you looked through.

I watched McCloy for a while, Intaglio by my side, and I

remember I kept talking in low tones even though, Intaglio told me, there was no way McCloy could hear us. Then Intaglio went back out into the corridor and I saw him enter the room from the far side and change places with one of the other interrogators.

From the look of it, you'd have to say Carter was way ahead in chips and there was no way anybody was going to get even unless they could raise the stakes in a hurry. Which clearly wasn't happening. Even after the better part of a day and night with the Task Force, much of which had been spent answering questions, he looked laid-back. Literally. He was sprawled in a wooden armchair, arms hanging over the sides and legs stretched out, maybe a little tired around the eyes but generally none the worse for wear. He had on his usual costume, white button-down shirt open at the neck, blue blazer with the collar turned up and, sure enough, that same long white scarf draped around his neck. By contrast, his interrogators, even though they got to take turns, looked like losers in the all-night game, pale and unshaven and trying to keep the play going on coffee and cigarettes.

"He's night people," I'd said to Intaglio. "Besides, you'll never wear him down if you give him Dewars."

Strange to say, there was a bottle of Dewars on a table, next to a plastic ice bucket. McCloy, according to Intaglio, had insisted on it. To judge, he'd drunk about two-thirds of it. But for Carter McCloy, that was pretty moderate going.

The Task Force knew they wouldn't be able to hold him much longer. For one thing, the alibis he'd given them pertaining to the two most recent murders appeared to be checking out, including the one in his own neighborhood the night, according to Bobby Derr, when he'd stormed out of Melchiorre's alone. According to McCloy, he'd been drinking in another bar in the fork of time during which the crime had been committed, and he'd given the Task Force a witness to confirm it.

And then there was the little matter of *habeas corpus*.

Don't ask me to say which system is better. In most countries, the authorities have the right to hold you on reasonable suspicion for just about as long as they want to, and "reasonable suspicion" itself, in some places, is pretty loosely interpreted. But in the U.S., they've got to convince a judge. It wasn't either that McCloy had demanded a lawyer. He'd been given ample opportunity to make phone calls but had opted for Dewars instead. When the lawyer did show up—and I'll give you two guesses who it was—it wasn't because Carter wanted it but because somebody had called his stepfather.

When Intaglio took over, it was to focus on the "pen pal" and celebrity connections, and the dialogue went something like this:

Intaglio: "How well do you know Dr. Nora Saroff, Carter?"

McCloy: "Dr. Nora Saroff Carter? Only joking. In fact, I know a Dr. Nora Saroff pretty well. She's my shrink, you know? But what's she got to do with this?"

Intaglio: "Is she still your shrink?"

McCloy: "Actually I haven't been there in a while. But yeah, she's still my shrink."

Intaglio: "Why'd you go to her in the first place?"

McCloy: "I had problems. Don't we all have problems?"

Intaglio: "What kind of problems, Carter?"

McCloy (with a chuckle): "I'd say that's getting pretty heavy, you know? Like maybe it's none of your business. Something tells me I'm not going to elaborate on that particular point, you know? What's it got to do with the murders anyway?"

Intaglio walked over to a long counter and sifted through some documents, adding one from his own pocket. Then he came back toward McCloy.

Intaglio: "Why'd you stop going to her, Carter?"

McCloy: "Did I say I'd stopped? I don't know. Maybe my head has shrunk enough, you know?"

Intaglio: "Is that the only reason?"

McCloy: "I don't know. Isn't it a good enough reason?"

Intaglio selected one of the documents and put it on the table in front of McCloy. McCloy leaned forward to look at it.

Intaglio: "Have you ever seen this before?"

McCloy: "No. What is it, some kind of joke?"

Intaglio: "Dr. Saroff got this one, Carter. Somebody stuck it under the door to her office. But you didn't put it there, did you?"

McCloy: "Hell, no."

Intaglio: "And what about these?"

Intaglio put several more documents in front of McCloy, one after the other. McCloy, I noticed, didn't touch them, but he looked.

McCloy: "I've never seen these either."

Intaglio: "You didn't write them, did you?"

McCloy: "Of course not."

Intaglio: "Do you own a Canon Typestar?"

McCloy: "What's that, some kind of typewriter?"

Intaglio: "That's right, some kind of typewriter. Do you own one?"

McCloy: "No."

Intaglio: "But you're very interested in Dr. Saroff, aren't you?"

McCloy: "I don't know what you mean by that. But hey, like nothing's happened to her, has it?"

Intaglio: "Interested enough to tape her shows?"

McCloy: "Tape her shows? Well, sure, I might have taped some of her shows. I tape a lot of stuff, you know?"

Intaglio: "But you particularly like to tape Dr. Saroff, don't you?"

McCloy: "I don't know particularly, but I like her show. And she's my shrink."

Intaglio: "So you're very interested in her after all?"

McCloy: "Well, in that sense, yes, you know?"

Intaglio: "Well, what about in other senses? Would you like to shack up with her?"

McCloy (chuckling): "Hey, is that what she said?"

Intaglio: "Just answer the question. Would you like to shack up with her?"

McCloy: "Well, like if you mean did the idea ever strike me, the answer is: sure. They say everybody falls in love with his shrink sometime. At least when it's opposite sexes."

Intaglio: "Are you in love with her now? Enough to tape her shows and write her letters like this?"

McCloy: "Hey, what's . . . ?"

Intaglio: "And what about these other women, Carter? The ones on television, the ones who got these same letters? Did you tape their shows too?"

McCloy: "Hey, what're you trying to pull? Is there a law against VCR's? I told you, I tape a lot of stuff. Say, how do I know you guys didn't write these letters yourselves and are trying to frame me?"

Intaglio (breathing deeply): "We didn't, Carter, I promise you. Now just answer the question."

McCloy never did get a chance to answer. Not that it would have made much difference, as Intaglio admitted to me later. He said it reminded him of times he'd gone fishing and the fish had played with his bait all day long, poking at it but never taking the hook. From what I saw, I had the impression McCloy actually enjoyed the proceedings, like he knew all along they couldn't hook him but he got some kind of kick out of tempting them. The fish playing the fishermen.

At that point, though, somebody stuck his head in the door and signaled to Intaglio. The assistant DA went out into the hall. He was gone a while. Then he came back and called McCloy out, and a few minutes later he rejoined me.

"Son of a gun," he said. He was sweating and pale, and, head bowed, he ran a finger around the inside of his shirt collar. "If there's anything I can't stand, it's high-powered attorneys who like to throw their weight around. Do you know Roy Barger?"

"Barger? Sure I do. But what's he got to do with this?"

"He's just leaving with his client. He's threatening to sue us for harassment, can you beat that? Fat chance, but I had to stand there while he chewed us out. Actually, McCloy didn't seem to like it either."

"Is Barger McCloy's attorney?" I said.

I wondered in passing if it was just a coincidence and decided it had to be. The other way lay sheer paranoia.

"His stepfather's apparently," Intaglio said. "Somebody tipped off his stepfather."

"And you can't hold him anymore?"

"How can we hold him? We're still running down his alibis, but so far everything checks out."

"Including the last murder?"

"Including the last murder. But you know what I think, Revere? I think he's guilty of something. I can feel it. All that money and nothing to do with it, I can feel it in my bones."

"What if he just wrote the letters?" I suggested.

Intaglio shook his head.

"Maybe I'm just tired," he said. "Like played out. Tired of sitting around waiting for the next murder to happen. You don't know how many times we thought we had him. Only this time . . ." His voice trailed off. Then, as though he'd pulled himself back together: "We're going to watch this one close. Barger or no Barger. I want your help."

"How?"

"You and Derr know him better than we do, his friends, his habits, where he hangs out. Put it together with Derr, everything you got, then call us. Either me or Jack Walters. And I certainly want to know if Saroff hears from him again."

"Are you giving her protection?" I asked.

"You bet your sweet ass."

There was something bothering me when I left the building, like an itch you can't reach, and I was still reaching for it and missing when I all but ran into Roy Barger and his client on the sidewalk. Or his client's stepson. They were having some kind of argument. A limo was waiting at the curb, the back door open, and Barger, in topcoat and fedora hat, looked like he was trying to usher McCloy into it.

McCloy, though, wasn't having any part of it. I saw him knock Barger's arm away, heard a snatch of speech that sounded like ". . . screw himself."

Then Barger noticed me.

"Hey, Phil!" he said, stepping away from the limo door and extending his hand. "What a nice coincidence! What mischief brings you down to this unholy place?"

We exchanged handshakes. Barger said he heard I'd been at Sally's. Smiling, he said he heard I'd made a great impression. Smiling back, I told him I didn't know what that meant. Meanwhile I was watching McCloy out of the corner of my eye, and Barger saw it and started to introduce us.

"You don't have to tell me who he is," McCloy said, waving the lawyer away and eyeing me coldly. "I've already met him. What's your name again?"

"It's Phil Revere," Barger said before I could answer. "He works for Charles Camelot, the famous attorney? The one who's married to Nora Saroff? But I didn't know you'd already met. Hey, maybe this isn't a coincidence after all, huh, Phil?"

If my connection to the Counselor's Wife came as a revelation to McCloy, he didn't show it. He simply stared at the two of us. Stared down, I should say, and in more ways than one, for he was inches taller than Barger and me.

"It's not a coincidence," he said in a put-down tone. "It's just that some people can't take a joke."

I've thought about that line a lot since. I've concluded he was talking about the letters and the Counselor's Wife. If so, that was as close as he ever got to an oral confession of anything.

Roy Barger was in the midst of keeping a conversation going. He didn't know the details of what had happened, he'd only gotten a call at the crack of dawn from Carter's father telling him the police were . . .

But McCloy wouldn't let him go on.

"He's not my father," he said with cold and scornful anger. He looked like there was a lot more in him to say. Instead, though, his jaws clamped shut hard, and he pivoted on his heels and headed up the sidewalk away from us. His hands were jammed into his blazer pockets and the ends of that damned scarf blew out behind him.

Barger made no effort to follow him.

"Strange young man," he said, unperturbed. "A little confused, I gather, but that doesn't make him a killer, does it? The cops must be desperate." Then, turning back to me and kicking his head up at the building: "Are you the reason they've had him down here, Phil?"

"Not really," I said.

"Well, let me give you some advice anyway, as a friend to

a friend." He smiled at me, that ingratiating and polished Southern smile. "I may not know the details yet, and if Carter's in a little trouble, it wouldn't, I gather, be the first time. But Stew Collins, that's Carter's old man . . . actually Stew's his stepfather . . . can be one mean and vindictive son of a gun, and I say that even though I'm his attorney and friend. He sounds, to put it mildly, fit to be tied. He wants to go after the police for false arrest and harassment and to sue anybody else in sight. Whether he'll actually insist on going through with it, I've my doubts, but however you're involved, my friendly advice to you is to stay out of the way."

I thought of a lot of things to answer, but I kept my mouth shut.

Barger offered me a ride uptown. I turned it down. He said he had to call the Counselor anyway to find out how his summit with the Magister boys had gone the day before, and he left room, with a wink and that same Southern smile, for me to comment. I didn't. Then he repeated his offer, that whenever I got tired of working for the Counselor, I had only to pick up the phone.

"Don't you forget it, huh, Phil?" he said, shaking my hand.

I said I wouldn't.

He drove off in the limo. I turned and looked north after Carter McCloy, but he'd disappeared by then.

I never saw him again.

CHAPTER 10

I know at least two people did see him, neither being Bobby Derr nor me. As for us, we did talk to Intaglio and Walters that same day by phone, but otherwise we were effectively out of the hunt. Intaglio always claimed the Task Force stayed on it. In view of what happened, I wonder.

Of the two people who did see him, one wasn't identified till later. The other was Linda Smith.

Linda Smith's real name was Linda Vigliotti. I'd met her on the Bowery, that night after the Rosebud, and I'd never have guessed she was Italian from the freckles on her nose. Anyway, sometime the afternoon of that day, Linda got a call from Carter McCloy. She wasn't home. Either she was still at work or en route home by subway, but he left a message on her answering machine. He wanted to see her again. He was sorry things had turned out badly that night, it was his fault, but he hadn't been able to get her out of his mind ever since. Would she meet him at Melchiorre's? Alternatively he'd come pick her up, but she'd have to give him instructions how to get there.

Linda got home, heard the message, and decided she didn't want to go out that night. She did call Melchiorre's, but McCloy wasn't there. One of the bartenders took down a message for him: tell Cloy Linda called.

McCloy called again. They talked quite a while. She really hadn't wanted to go out that night, she was too tired, but McCloy was very persuasive, very sweet, and she let him talk her into letting him come over.

It was after eleven when he finally showed. He came loaded down with stuff. He had a bunch of flowers and a kind of picnic basket of delicacies. He had to go back out to the car for an ice bucket filled with white wine.

From this point on, Linda's account went blurry. She claimed the struggle started almost immediately, that McCloy attacked her in the living room, but some of the food had been eaten and the police found half a bottle of wine in the pool of water in the ice bucket plus an empty on the floor. No signs of struggle in the living room. Plenty, however, in the bedroom. Then Linda, reversing her story, admitted that she'd agreed to have sex with him. What choice did she have, she said, he was acting so weird. How weird? Well, he told her he loved her more than any woman he'd ever met, but he also threatened her. How threatened? Well, he told her that if she didn't, he'd fix her so she'd never have sex with anybody else. Then they took their clothes off and got into bed where McCloy, according to Linda, couldn't get it up. That was what drove him really crazy, she said. That was when he really started to abuse her, in words and physically, and you could see the physical evidence of it all right, on television late the next day, when she was still in the hospital and they let her give some interviews.

She fought him as hard as she could, as long as she could—there was evidence to corroborate this too—but he was too strong for her. She started screaming, she screamed her head off, until he stuffed the pillow into her face, crammed it into her face and she couldn't get rid of it no matter how hard she kicked and scratched. She quoted him saying to her: "Time to say your prayers, l'il Linda."

She thought she was about to die.

Then she thought she actually was dead when the pressure stopped.

It wasn't that though. It was that he'd let go. He must have thought she was dead too.

She saw him stagger out of the bedroom, blood streaming out of his forehead.

She'd tried to scream. Instead she threw up.

She thought she must have passed out then. Not for long, though, because when she managed to get out to her living-room window, she saw him getting into a car in the street below. That's what she claimed. How could she be sure, three flights up, in her condition and when it was dark outside? She didn't know, but she was sure. She was also sure somebody else was driving because she saw McCloy get in on the passenger side. What kind of car was it? She didn't know. Some kind of foreign make, she thought. Sporty. She could tell that much from the taillights.

Then she called 911, and that's where the police found her when they got there, sitting on the floor under her living-room window, wearing a T-shirt and nothing else.

At about 1:45 that morning, after Linda had identified him but before the police could get the word out, Carter McCloy went off the balcony of his ninth-floor apartment on the Upper East Side. The proverbial dive of the swan. Nobody saw him go; nobody saw him land.

The police found the following statement, handwritten, taped to the mirror above the living-room mantel. Most of it looked like some kind of poetry—not much of a poem, I suppose, if that's what it was meant to be. But I give it here in the same form:

I here
Of my own free Will
Confess to the Crimes
You choose to belittle under the Name

Pillow Killer.

Why I did
Is Anybody's Guess
But I did.

I head for the long final Sleep.
Will it be welcome?
Anybody's Guess.
I apologize to
dr. nora saroff.
She did her best but it was irrelevant.

No Apology for my Parents
adrienne douglas mccloy collins and james carter mccloy.
They never did theirs.

As for mr. stewart m. collins, my stepfather, the family and friends of my last victim have him to thank for rescuing me from the Law in time to kill her.

I hope my Friends will hoist a Cup
To me
In time.
Hold them blameless.

Now I lay me down to Sleep
I pray the Law my Soul to keep
If I should die before I wake
I pray the Law my Soul to take.

Carter Douglas McCloy

As to when exactly it had been written, well, that, to quote McCloy, was anybody's guess.

PART THREE

CHAPTER 11

Mop-up and cover-up.

Most of the mopping up was done in and by the media. Linda Vigliotti and Carter McCloy both had their proverbial fifteen minutes' worth of limelight. Actually a little longer. In and out of the hospital, Linda Vigliotti was the heroine of the day. Without her pluck and guts, (1) she would be dead, and (2) the Pillow Killer might still be roaming the streets. But heroines, I guess, make dull copy, particularly heroines from Queens who aren't very photogenic, and Linda didn't last more than a week or two. I think she sold her life story to *The Enquirer*, but I don't know if it ever ran.

Carter McCloy had more staying power. For one thing, he was rich, or at least of rich and privileged background. And good-looking. And wayward: the broken home, the scandals in school, the shrinks, the suicide, etc. And, last but not least, he was a writer. Well, maybe not a writer, but a creative person. Carter's confession, or poem, or whatever it was, was widely reprinted and discussed. It wasn't that he didn't deserve to die, or that he wasn't psychotic, or crazy, or a psychopathic killer, or sociopathic if not psychopathic, but the more the media pored over his remains, the more you got the impression that somehow the blame for Carter was ours. Society's, with a capital *S*. It may have helped, in this connection, that his parents—mother and stepfather—refused all interviews, refused even to say how Carter's remains were disposed of after it came out that the Catholic Church had refused to bury him. It helped too that Carter's friends, most prominently Vincent Angus Halloran, were much more forthcoming. Vince, or Hal as his buddies called him, was the star, at least the living one, of the segment "60 Minutes" devoted to the case. When asked if Carter McCloy and his friends belonged to a new kind of Lost Generation, he answered: "Yes, I guess we do. Yes, definitely, that's who we are." It was on this show that somebody, I think it was Diane Sawyer, said: "If F. Scott Fitzgerald were alive and writing crime stories today, he would have created Carter McCloy."

The cover-up involved a certain degree of collusion, some of it unconscious. Nobody pushed the Nora Saroff connection. Partly this was the Counselor's Wife's own doing. While it was known that she'd been McCloy's last shrink, she went pretty much into seclusion after the suicide and managed to duck the media. The whole subject of McCloy's videotapes, for instance, never came out. At the same time, somebody on the Task Force understood that they could put themselves in the best public light by simplifying. They'd gotten on to Carter McCloy, they maintained, as part of the dragnet operation they'd spread over the whole city. That they'd let him go only a few hours before his last crime wasn't due to any negligence on their part. They'd been hamstrung by the law, and they'd been put under terrific pressure to release him. Similarly the whole issue of McCloy's alibis, which could in theory have led to accessory charges, was left buried. The Task Force dissolved itself with haste and efficiency.

As for me? Well, nobody asked me anything.

It seemed just as well at the time, for by then we were caught up in a limelight of a very different sort.

CHAPTER 12

"I didn't think it was possible to overestimate their intelligence," the Counselor said, standing at his desk in his shirtsleeves and glaring down at the morning's *Wall Street Journal*. "I was wrong, Phil. I was goddamn wrong."

He'd called for me first thing, and I was surprised to see him in shirtsleeves and suspenders that early. Usually he came downstairs as dapper as the Counselor's Wife's tastes could make him, all the way to a matching handkerchief tucked in the lapel pocket of his suit coat, and it took at least a few hours for disarray to set in. This morning, though, the suit coat had been flung over a nearby chair, the bow tie was already lopsided and his shirtsleeves folded a couple of times over his forearms and then abandoned.

He was, to put it simply, in a towering rage.

"Myrna!" he shouted at Ms. Shapiro through the open door. "I want McClintock! I want him right now!"

And when, moments later, Ms. Shapiro stuck her head in to say that Mr. McClintock was in a meeting: "I don't care if he's meeting with God, Myrna, tell them to get him on the phone!"

It took a few minutes, but then McClintock came on and the Counselor, jabbing at a button on his desk, put him on the speakerphone.

"What's going on, Charles?" said McClintock's even, cultivated voice.

"That's what *I* want to know," the Counselor thundered back. "Did you see the paper? What your clients have done?"

"Yes, I saw it."

"Well? Don't you think you ought to have told me about it?"

"We learned about it the same way you did, Charles. We read it in this morning's paper. The Magisters never saw fit to tell us."

"Is it true?"

"I see no reason to believe that it's not."

"Well, what are you going to do about it?"

"I've got a call in to Young Bob," McClintock said soberly. "But I don't see what you're so worked up about, Charles. I think the white knight was even your recommendation, if I re—"

If McClintock had said that face-to-face, I think the Counselor would have swallowed him whole. As is.

"You're damn right it was my idea. I think I even said: 'a white knight on a white horse.' But for God Almighty's sake, if Raffy Goldsmith's a white knight, then I'm the Angel Gabriel!"

A word of explanation:

The Wall Street Journal, in that squibs and rumors column on the front page that everybody reads first, had reported that Steelstar Investing Corporation was allegedly buying shares in Magister. Furthermore, according to an informed but unidentified source, Steelstar was about to make an SEC filing, with a formal tender offer to follow. Neither Raphael E. Goldsmith, president of Steelstar, nor any of the principals of Magister could be reached for comment by press time.

I knew a little about Raphael E. "Raffy" Goldsmith, and I was about to learn more. Some years back, a relatively obscure outfit called Starlight Investing Corporation had pulled off what some at the time called "the folly of the century" by acquiring control of Inland Constitution Steel, the first of the major steel companies to flirt with bankruptcy. "Raffy's folly," though, soon became the model for corporate raiders of all shapes and sizes, for by a combination of financial juggling and the dismembering of Inland's assets, Goldsmith had made millions for his shareholders—meaning, principally, for Raffy Goldsmith. Though he'd since gone on to numerous other takeover ventures, he'd kept the name "Steelstar" for his company, as a symbol of his first big score.

"I still think you're reacting prematurely, Charles," Doug McClintock said. "We're not even sure that this is the Magisters' doing. It could be the other side. Or even Goldsmith on his own. Why don't we wait and see?"

"We're not going to have to wait long," the Counselor predicted. "And let me tell you this, Douglas. If the brothers did go to Goldsmith, then my advice to you is to get off the sinking ship while you still can. *If* you still can."

"I don't know what you mean by that," McClintock said, but you heard a certain quiver in his voice.

"Think about it then," said the Counselor coldly, and he punched the button, canceling the call.

We spent much of that morning on the phone. The Counselor had excellent sources down on Wall Street, and I had a few of my own. We also had Charlotte McCullough, our resident guru in financial matters. Charlotte's a big and blowsy and frankly sloppy-looking redhead whose appearance belies one of the sharpest analytical minds I know. A CPA, she's officially our staff accountant, but the Counselor uses her in a variety of ways and she spent much of that morning at her computer, running through various scenarios based on Magister Companies numbers.

We confirmed the Steelstar story early. Raffy Goldsmith had open-to-buys at various brokerage houses, at supposedly any price. But very quickly he had company. As the automatic sell levels hit in computer systems all over the Street, insiders snapped up the available shares of their own accounts while their heavy-hitting customers—the institutional portfolio managers, the investment banks, the arbitragers—clamored for a piece of the action. It was, in short, one of those crazy, paper-castle mornings when the Street pros made small fortunes in a matter of minutes, and the stock, which had opened the day at 32 and 1/8, hit 49 just before lunch.

Just before, that is, the Exchange suspended trading in Magister.

Just before, that is, Margie Magister announced a press conference for three o'clock that afternoon.

Charlotte McCullough had, so to speak, run behind the ticker all morning, and a little before noon she threw in the sponge.

"Forty-five tops," she said, leaning over the Counselor's desk to point to numbers on a spreadsheet she'd prepared. "At least based on past performance and current management. Beyond at forty-five, you're betting on the twenty-first century."

The Counselor had just taken a call telling him that Magister had broken 48.

"Well, I give up," Charlotte protested, throwing up her arms. "It makes no sense."

"It doesn't have to make sense," the Counselor said. "Besides, nobody says Goldsmith is still buying. He's been known to bail out before."

We learned later that Steelstar had in fact started to sell in the hour before lunch, and the SEC filing, a legal requirement when you reach five-percent ownership of a publicly held company, never happened that day.

The call about the press conference came in to me from a reporter I know on one of the major business magazines. I'd been talking to him all morning, and he was smart enough to figure out how I connected to the Magisters without my telling him. He'd just gotten an invitation from a PR agency which, he said, often worked for Roy Barger and his clients.

"How big is Margie's apartment?" he asked me.

"I guess it's plenty big," I said. "How come?"

"Because I think they ought to have rented Grand Central Station. They told me they're limiting the invitations, but this is one hell of a story. What do you think she's going to say?"

"Beats me," I answered.

"Come on, Phil. You've got to give me some *quid pro quo*. Can you confirm that it was the brothers who brought in Raffy?"

"I wouldn't know," I dodged, although by then I could have confirmed it.

In the end I managed to get off the hook with one of those if-I-learn-anything-you'll-be-the-first-to-know promises. Then I told the Counselor.

"I knew this was coming," he said, "or something like it. The stupid bastards jumped the gun. I want you there, Phil."

"Where?"

"The press conference."

"But it's by invitation only. Besides, you know I don't have press credentials."

"You don't?" he said, glowering at me as though to say: Why the hell not? Then: "Well, get yourself invited. Be resourceful. Call Roy Barger, tell him you're interested in his job offer. But I want you there."

To each his own needle, you could say. I hadn't been able to resist telling him about Barger's offer.

I made some calls: no luck. Then I did call Roy Barger. Surprise surprise, Mr. Barger wasn't available. But—further surprise—he called me back a little before two.

"Well, Phil, how nice of you to call," he said in his usual drawl, as though this was a day like any other and he had nothing better to do than chat on the phone. "What can I do for you, my friend?"

"I understand Mrs. Magister is meeting the press this afternoon."

"You do? Boy, news travels fast in this town."

"I'd like to be there," I said.

"You and everybody else," he answered, chuckling. "There hasn't been a hot-ticket event like this since the pandas had a baby at the Bronx Zoo. I'm afraid I can't help you, though. The people who're organizing it are trying to keep the numbers down, you can understand that. But I'll tell you what: Tell Charles I'm going to have the press release delivered to him by hand the minute the conference is over. Will you tell him that for me?"

Clearly he was enjoying the situation. The Counselor, equally clearly, would not.

"But I'm not asking for Mr. Camelot," I said. "I'm calling on my own account. It's for me."

"Is that right?" He sounded surprised.

"That's right," I said.

I had no idea, right then, what he was calculating. But then he said:

"In that case, Phil, let me see what I can do. I'm not promising anything, but I'll call you back. Are you in your office?"

I told him I was and sure enough, a few minutes later, he called back. He'd gotten me on the list—"just above the *New York Times*," he said—and all I had to do was show my card downstairs.

That was how I ended up pushing my way through the jostling, irate crowd of press and curiosity-seekers that bulged out onto Fifth Avenue, stopping traffic that afternoon outside Margie Magister's apartment house. And if I wasn't so naive as to suppose Barger didn't have some ulterior motive, well, it's still nice, every once in a while, to think you're appreciated.

Margie Magister's living room wasn't quite Grand Central Station, and you'd have to give credit to the people who'd handled the arrangements, down to the microphone set up in front of the central fireplace and the straight chairs set out in arcs with the media overflowing outside the open terrace doors. But it was still Margie's show. Even, I assumed, to the positioning of the three generations of Magisters in attendance. Margie herself spoke from center stage. Sally Magister towered over her to her left, with three of her children. And Vincent Angus Halloran stood to her right, also towering, next to a representative, I learned, of one of the Wall Street proxy firms, the people who orchestrate campaigns aimed at stockholders' votes.

Their clothes looked like they'd been carefully chosen.

Sally Magister had exchanged the overalls I'd seen her in for a tailored business suit, and Halloran wore a navy blue suit, striped shirt with suspenders and maroon foulard tie. But it was Margie, again, who set the tone. How she did it I've no idea, but she managed to look chic and corporate at once. She wore a black suit that pulled in tight at the waist, with wide lapels and the collar turned up around her neck, and a figured scarf, and large round glasses, slightly tinted, for reading her speech. Later, during the questions, she perched the glasses on top of her head and then, yes, you really could *see* her in a corporate boardroom, listening intently and answering decisively. The media laughed in the right places as though her smile was their signal, and when she spoke, you could hear the proverbial pin drop.

She'd also, I gauged, been carefully coached. Barger, probably. While she talked about Magister stock having been put "in play," she was careful, then and later, not to blame the Magister brothers for it. As for the brothers themselves, she said she had repeatedly held out the olive branch to them, in public and privately, but they continued to act as if the rest of the family simply didn't exist. And that, she thought, was wrong. Wrong for the family, obviously, but also wrong for the thousands of employees who worked for Magister Companies, the thousands of investors, large and small, who owned stock, wrong even for the American people. Why was it wrong for the American people? Because Magister was a communications company. It made profits out of the airwaves, which were owned by the American people. Beyond that, she thought anything to do with communications—magazines, movies, newspapers, books, recordings—was of public concern. And when the financial vultures came in, looking for a new carcass to tear apart for their own profits, then it was time everybody took notice.

"You know," she said, looking up at her audience through the round glasses, "where I come from . . . in Europe . . . they do these things differently. They do them behind closed doors. You would never know what happened, good or bad, until it was over. But I am proud to be in America, to do things the American way, to work to find an American-style solution."

She paused, her arms spread out. Damned if her eyes weren't moist and if that wasn't the picture most widely used by the media.

"This is why we, members of the Magister family, make the following announcement," she went on. "We are asking the Board of Directors of Magister Companies to convene a special stockholders' meeting no later than forty-five days from today. We are prepared to put forth our detailed plan for the restructuring and reorganization of the Company and the election of a new Board of Directors. At this meeting, and then only, we recommend that the stockholders consider and vote upon any other serious proposals concerning the future of Magister."

Another pause. Then (tilting her glasses up on her head): "Thank you again for coming. We will be glad to answer any questions."

There were a lot of questions and they came in a hurry, monitored by one of the PR people who ran the meeting and who also organized the so-called photo ops when the questions were over. What was in their detailed plan? It would be exposed at the proper time, to the proper people. Had the request already been submitted to the Board of Directors? Yes. Had the Board responded? Not yet. How did she think they would respond? She didn't know, they should ask the Board that question. How well did she know Raffy Goldsmith? She'd never met the man. Had she ever heard of him? Yes, she thought she had, but she'd never heard of Steelstar Investing before that morning. Did she consider him a financial vulture? She thought the media would have a more informed opinion of that than she would. Had the Magister brothers invited him in? If they had, they hadn't told her.

Sally Magister, though, drew the biggest laugh.

She was asked what she thought of her brothers.

She said she'd already been widely quoted on the subject.

"But what do you think of them today?" came the next question. "Has there been any change in your attitude?"

"Yes," she answered, stony-faced. "I think there's been

some change. But if I told you what it was, you wouldn't be permitted to print it and we'd be bleeped off the 'Six O'Clock News.'"

Vincent Angus Halloran, meanwhile, seemed to suffer through it all, standing next to Margie with little change in expression or posture. He didn't look like he was paying attention. He also, I thought, didn't look like the type who beat people up in school yards. I tried for eye contact with him and failed, even though from where I was standing, right behind the last row of chairs, we had a clear view of each other.

Only then . . .

I'd been distracted, I guess, by what somebody in the audience was saying. But when I glanced back at Halloran, he was staring at me all right, eyes locked on mine, and I saw him half-smile, not so that his lips came apart but enough to break one plane of his face. But what it meant—recognition, mockery, challenge, whatever—I couldn't have told you.

Chairs scraped, people stood up between us, there were outbreaks of applause, and somebody in front of me called out, "Give 'em hell, Margie." The media had gotten their story, and by that time Roy Barger had worked his way through the crowd and joined me, hands clapping enthusiastically.

"What did you think, Phil?" he asked.

"It'll make good copy," I answered.

"Is that all?" He looked at me in surprise.

"No. She's good at it."

"Good? I'd say she's terrific! Look at her now, she has them eating out of her hand."

Even though Margie had declared the meeting over, she continued to hold court by the fireplace, talking animatedly and posing without seeming to pose, while the cameras closed in on her.

"If you've got a few minutes, Phil," Roy Barger was saying, "please stick around. There's something we'd like to discuss with you after everybody's gone."

I told him I had a few minutes. Then he left me, and, curious, I watched him glad-handing members of the media he appeared to know, escorting them through the French doors toward the entrance hall with his arms around their shoulders.

Halloran had disappeared. So had his mother. So, finally, had Margie. Even so, it took a while to clear the room, and some workers had already come in and begun to fold and stack chairs by the time Barger waved to me from the French doors.

In the entrance hall, people still clustered by the elevator doors. Barger led me past them, down a hallway and into another room where Margie Magister, in stockinged feet and minus her glasses, came toward me, hands outstretched to take mine and saying:

"Philip! I'm so glad you could come."

It was either her bedroom or her boudoir, I've never exactly understood the difference between the two. At least it contained a bed, a large one with a brocade cover and an inlaid wood canopy above it, but also an arrangement of upholstered chairs and matching loveseat in front of French windows which gave out onto the terrace and a stunning view of the city skyline heading toward sunset. That's where we sat, Barger and I in chairs, while a young and good-looking houseman offered us tea or drinks from a bar trolley.

Margie Magister ordered tea, Barger a Perrier with lime, I a beer.

"I'm exhausted," Margie Magister said. "At least it's over. Forgive me for taking my shoes off, but I'm . . . how do you say? . . . all in. Now, Philip, before I forget: How is Charles?"

"Mr. Camelot?" I started, but that's as far as I got.

Halloran had just walked into the room.

"Ah, Vincent, there you are!" Margie called out, pronouncing his name in French. "Pour yourself a drink and come join us."

She watched him approvingly while he made a drink at the bar trolley. It looked to me like straight gin on the rocks. With a twist.

"Do you two know each other?" Margie asked, crossing her legs and patting the empty space on the loveseat.

"We've met," Halloran said, sitting down next to her. He'd taken his tie off and unbuttoned the top buttons of his white shirt. He lifted his glass to no one in particular and drank.

"Well, now," Margie said, looking across at me, "where was I? What did you think, Philip? Of the press conference?"

"I thought you were wonderful," I said back. As for her being "all in," maybe so on the inside, but you'd never have known it from her quick gestures or the flush in her cheeks. If anything, being in public seemed to have turned her on.

"Let's get to the point, Margie," Roy Barger interrupted. "Our friend Phil is a busy young man, and if he's kind enough to give us these few minutes out of . . ."

"*Ach*," she said, flinging her hands up, "you Americans and your schedules, you're worse than the Germans. Well," with a pout and tossing her head, "go ahead then, Roy. Get on to your point."

Barger shifted in his chair and leaned toward me, hands on his knees.

"This may come as a surprise to you, Phil, but we have a proposition to make. It may have been pure luck that you called today, but we agreed—Margie and I, Vince too—to seize the opportunity."

I didn't immediately understand, and then, a moment later, I understood less.

"We're ready to entertain a buy-out," Barger went on. "All our combined interest in Magister. At the right price, of course, and under the right conditions."

"You're what?" I think I said. Then, after he assured me they were serious: "But what was all this about? The press conference and all the rest of it?"

"Come, come, Philip," Barger said with a smile, "you can't expect us to put all our eggs in one basket. Mind you, we're fully prepared to go through with a proxy fight if we have to, and we believe we'll win if it goes that far. But we don't want it to go that far. We don't want to force the price so high that nobody will be able to buy Magister without selling off pieces of it."

"My husband would never have stood for that," Margie put in softly. "I don't think even Young Bob would want that to happen, would he?"

"You know as well as I do," Barger went on, "that anything is for sale, at the right price. So the question is: at what price and under what conditions? I'll tell you straight out. Based on our analysis of the company's fair value, we want $72 per share. We don't insist on all cash up front. We would be prepared to take, say, today's closing price in cash . . . I believe that was $49 a share . . . and be flexible about the manner and timing of the balance. Our main condition is that Sally remain in charge of the magazine division and that, if the magazines are to be sold off, she be given first option to acquire, at fair market."

"I take it she's agreed to this?" I asked, looking across at Halloran.

"She doesn't know about it yet," he said. "But she'll do what we tell her to do."

I wondered about that, also the scornful confidence with which he said it. How loyal a member was Sally of the Margie Magister Fan Club? I did some quick calculating, though. At over 200 percent from what the stock had been worth the day before, maybe she would have no argument. Magister had never, even in its best days, ever traded anywhere near that high. But given what she thought about her brothers, would Sally sell to them at *any* price?

I could see one reason they hadn't told her. Once Margie sold out, Sally could either accept the same terms or be left at the mercy of the new owners.

And if I'd had any doubts which side Vince Halloran was on, I got the answer when, in the course of conversation, I saw Margie take his hand in hers.

I still didn't get it, though. I'd heard her say she wanted to run the company, and I'd just seen her hold forth before the media. True, the Counselor thought she was capable of losing interest, but losing it even before she'd gotten started?

I remember looking at her and she looking straight back at me, unblinking.

"I think I'm unrealistic, Philip," she said, like she'd

just read my thoughts. "If the company cannot hold together . . . ? Roy and Vincent think it cannot. What do you think? Wouldn't I rather have my money and enjoy it and be finished with lawyers and fighting and everything?"

"I'm not sure I take that as a compliment," Roy Barger said with a chuckle. "Of course, Phil, any contest over the will would have to be dropped and releases signed to that effect. But that's lawyers' work and I see no problem. More important is that, if word of this leaks out, we will simply deny this little meeting ever took place. It would be just another lie, invented by the Magister brothers, in an attempt to discredit us."

That, it went without saying, was the reason they'd picked me as their messenger rather than trying to approach the brothers directly.

"Well, what do you think, Revere?" Vince Halloran said. "Do you think it'll fly?"

He said it without any particular emphasis, like he didn't much care what my opinion was.

"I don't know," I said. "It sounds expensive."

"That it is," Halloran said.

"It could also turn out to be cheap," Roy Barger put in.

And that, I thought, would be up to the brothers to evaluate, not me.

"I also think they may want to see it in writing," I said.

Barger shook his head.

"No way," he said. "For obvious reasons. Not at least until we get a yes in principle. But you can take it as *bona fide*, Phil. We won't back off."

In that case, I said, I thought it was at least worth passing on to the brothers, though how they'd react I couldn't predict.

"That's all we ask of you," Roy Barger said. "I also happen to think it'll fly."

"I do too," echoed Margie, standing to escort me out, while Halloran got up too and headed for the bar trolley. "It will fly because Philip and Charles will make it fly."

Alone with her in the entrance hall, waiting for the

elevator to come, I remembered the effect she'd had on the Counselor that other time. Now it was my turn. Still in stockinged feet, she held both of my hands firmly and gazed upward at me from under the bangs. Then she stood on tiptoe, as though for a closer look. Her eyes were animated pools, and when you were alone with her, when that dark-eyed concentrated intensity was focused on you, well, she wasn't the kind of woman you could say no to easily.

As for me, it was impossible.

"I want to see you alone, Philip," she said. "Without the others."

Somewhere, from way out beyond Pluto somewhere, a voice was calling: Do you really want to be added to her life list?

"Well, and why not?" she said, laughing, like she could hear the voice too. "But anyway, I need to see you alone. I am troubled, Philip. Tonight, could you come for supper? I've the theater. I will come home immediately. Say, eleven o'clock? Here at eleven?"

Like I said: for me, impossible.

CHAPTER 13

The Counselor encouraged me to go ahead. In addition, no sooner had I reported Margie's offer to sell than he was on the phone to McClintock, and within the hour McClintock and Hank Rand were sitting in his office.

McClintock saw the offer as a breakthrough.

The Counselor thought it was a trap.

Why a trap?

"Because nobody's going to pay $72 a share for Magister," the Counselor said. "Nobody in his right mind, that is."

"Then maybe she'll take less," McClintock said. "At least it's opening the door to negotiation, isn't it?"

"I doubt it," the Counselor said. "Did they say anything, Phil, to indicate they'd negotiate the price?"

"No, they didn't," I answered.

"Then why . . . ?" McClintock asked, leaving the question hanging.

"Because Barger's trying to smoke out how high the Magister boys will go."

"Or Goldsmith?"

"Or anyone," the Counselor said. "As for Mr. Goldsmith, my information tells me he may have decided to cash in early."

I noticed that McClintock had started to sweat, even though the temperature in the Counselor's office was on the cool side. He'd heard the same thing, didn't know whether to believe it or not. Did the Counselor believe it? The Counselor shrugged. Raffy Goldsmith had been known to bail out on deals and take his profits in paper. Besides, he reminded McClintock, Goldsmith hadn't been his idea.

This unexpectedly set off a shouting match between them. More than anything, I think, it reflected the peculiar history of their relationship. Both had made senior partner at the Firm at roughly the same time. Then the Counselor had "gone private," as he liked to put it, taking some of his clients with him but maintaining that loose relationship with the Firm I've described elsewhere. This meant, among other things, that the Counselor could pretty much wheel and deal as he chose, whereas McClintock was responsible for an organization of over a hundred attorneys. The loss of a client like Magister Companies would be devastating to the Firm.

This was why McClintock had called the Counselor in on the Magister situation, in which the Firm wanted above all to maintain the appearance of neutrality. But if anyone had managed to stay neutral, it was the Counselor. The Firm, willingly or not, had chosen sides. Worse, and this was clearly what McClintock was afraid of, they might have chosen wrong.

Whence the shouting match.

"Well, what the hell *should* we do?" McClintock said finally, his face flushed.

I think it was the first time I ever heard him curse.

"Tell them the offer," the Counselor answered.

"And recommend what?"

"Recommend nothing. Just hope, for your sake, that they say no."

The way it worked out, I got to Margie's first. I drove the Fiero over to Fifth Avenue in a chilling rain and parked among the Mercedeses and the BMWs, then identified myself to the doorman who sent me right up. The blond young houseman who'd served us that afternoon let me in, took my London Fog (the lining now in) and ushered me into that same boudoir room, where he asked if he could make me a drink. I told him I'd help myself, which I did. Then I sat by the French windows, by the table which had been set for two with a vase of flowers in the middle, and watched the rain sleeting across the terrace and the dim towers of downtown trying to fight off the murk.

I thought about why Margie wanted to see me. Margie with a hard *g*. I thought about how "the other half"—actually the other one percent—live and how their habitats always seem lonesome to me, too big, too empty, for regular human beings. Then I thought some more about why Margie wanted to see me.

No answer.

Then Margie herself.

She was already talking as she came in, wearing a wet mink coat that came down to her ankles, something about how her driver hadn't been able to get into the block where the theater was and how she'd half-drowned finding him, apologizing meanwhile for being late, the more so since the play she'd seen had been positively abominable. Abominable pronounced the French way, with the accent on the second *ab*. She took off the mink as she talked, shaking it like a terrier, then draped it carefully over a wooden valet. She shook her hair too, which sparkled from the rain, and kicked her shoes off and came toward me, once again in stockinged feet and with hands outstretched, to kiss me first on one cheek, then the other.

"Ah," she said, smiling up at me from under the bangs, "a fellow beer drinker, would you pour me one too?" Then, picking up a telephone and buzzing, she ordered that supper be served.

The houseman, I remember, wheeled supper in, but then Margie dismissed him and served us herself.

I'm embarrassed to say I don't remember a thing we ate. I guess that was the effect of Margie, Margie with a hard *g* and a high-necked black dress of some gauzy material, with a large round diamond pin at the neck and round matching earrings, which I remember her taking off at some point.

The small talk didn't last long, maybe because it had to do mostly with me. Margie said she was naturally curious about people she liked: who they were, where they were going. So? Who was Philip Revere and where was he going?

I didn't answer well. I don't when I'm asked about myself.

Margie said that was usually a sign that people were dissatisfied with themselves.

I worked for an attorney, I said, though I wasn't one myself. The work was interesting; I was reasonably well paid. No, I'd never been married. Yes, I'd had my share of girlfriends. Why had I never gotten married? Well, I thought that was something you had to want to do pretty badly, maybe I'd never wanted to badly enough.

Did I think Charles was a great lawyer?

I thought he served his clients extremely well.

That's not what she'd asked, though. She'd asked if I thought he was a great lawyer.

I said I wasn't sure I knew what "great" meant when it came to lawyers. He was smarter than any lawyer I'd ever met, and more resourceful, but he stayed out of courtrooms, which was where most famous lawyers made their reputations. He served his clients extremely well, I repeated.

"Do you see what I mean?" Margie said. "You find it easier to talk about him than you do about yourself, Philip. I have a theory, you see. That is why I ask if you think he's great. It is that most young men who work for great men, or men they think are great, tend to underrate themselves. I think this is true of my husband's sons. Maybe they are better men than people think, but how will we ever know if they don't think so themselves? And I imagine this is true for you, how can you ever find out who you are yourself?"

She waited for me to answer, but I didn't.

"I'm sorry," she said, reaching out and touching my hand. "I don't mean to make you uncomfortable."

"You're not making me uncomfortable."

"Oh yes I am. You're . . . how do you say? . . . fidgeting. I see you fidgeting inside. You're also smoking too much. Do you want to kill yourself with tobacco?"

"No, I don't."

"Well, why don't you stop then? Maybe this will be my job—Margie's job—to make you stop. What do you think?"

She laughed at that, and I joined her, and if in fact I had been fidgeting inside, well, I stopped when she laughed.

"Maybe this is *my* real role in life," she said. "To help young men find themselves. Like Vincent. Tell me, Philip, what do you think about Vincent?"

For just a second I didn't recognize who she was talking about. It was her French pronunciation again: *Van-sahn*, sort of.

"Vincent Halloran," she said. "He says you know him."

"I hardly do," I said. Then I started to say: He helped beat up one of my friends. Then, a little to my surprise, I went ahead and said it.

"This doesn't surprise me," Margie said, shaking her head thoughtfully. "He is so violent sometimes. It isn't just *macho*. He has that too, the *macho*, all you American men have that, but this is something else. There is so much anger in him. Such scorn. You must have seen that."

"I haven't," I said, shaking my head. "But I hardly know him."

"But you knew his friend, didn't you? The one who killed himself after he killed all those girls? Carter?"

"Yes, in a way," I said.

"He is so strange about his friends, so . . . *scornful*! But they *were* friends, for a very long time. Do you know why Vincent says he committed suicide? He says it was because he couldn't even kill the last one. You know, the girl who survived? Do you know what Vincent says? He says Carter never killed all those girls, it had to have been someone else because Carter didn't have the nerve. He says it is the biggest joke of all time that Carter was the Pillow Killer."

I found myself reaching for another cigarette. It wasn't so much what Halloran had said, and in fact he wasn't the first to have said it. One of the tabloids had been running a series called *Was McCloy the Real Pillow Killer?* They'd raised the same question: If he was, why had he flubbed it with Linda Vigliotti? They'd sent out a team to investigate the earlier murders again, and while the reporters hadn't actually proven anything, they'd found a witness, the one in the Costello murder, who said, yes, she thought McCloy could have been the one she'd seen with the victim. *Could have been?* the paper had headlined that particular episode.

". . . changed since then," Margie was saying. "I can't even tell you how he is changed, but there are times when I think I don't even know him, and I *do* know him. I know him very well. He has been moody always, but I thought he has . . . potential. I *still* think he has potential."

For the first time, I was aware of her hesitating, like she was avoiding some point.

"Does he live here?" I asked.

"Sometimes," she said, with a sly smile. "When he wants to. He is a free man, free to come and go. He used to spend much time in that dreadful apartment they all shared. I went once, but I swore never again! The filth was horrible. Now I don't know where he goes. But this is all right."

Clearly, though, it wasn't all right. She reached across and grasped my forearm.

"He needs help, Philip. I mean to say, serious help. Professional. I don't think I can do anything more for him. Today, for example, it was all I could do to make him be here for the press conference. And he belonged there. But then the whole time I was afraid he was going to say something absolutely terrible. Did this show? That I was afraid?"

"No, it certainly didn't. But what were you afraid he was going to do?"

"I don't know," she said. "Something destructive. He used to work there, did you know? He hated it. I think I encouraged him to leave. Now all he says he wants is the money."

"But not that much of it is his, is it?"

"Mmm? Not so bad. For a young man in his twenties?"

"But what's going on between him and his mother?"

"Sally?" she said. "Ach, Sally adores him. But it is so typical: the more she adores him, the more scornful he is."

Vincent the Angel, I thought. Somehow, though, it didn't ring right. I remembered the display of photos in the Tribeca loft and how Vincent the Angel appeared to have dropped out around the age of five. I told Margie about it.

"This doesn't surprise me at all," she said. "It's so typical of doting mothers. Sally must still think of him as five years old, her little boy. She doesn't want him to grow up."

"Or to live here?" I asked.

"Well, yes," she said, smiling quickly, then making an expression of disapproval with her mouth. "Yes, there is that. I doubt she likes that very much."

Which, from what I'd heard in Tribeca, seemed the understatement of the month.

Little by little it'd begun to dawn on me that the real reason I'd been invited for supper was Vincent Halloran, and putting aside what that did or didn't do for my ego, I didn't see where I fit in. The more so with Margie's hand still grasping my arm and her eyes fixed on me, large and watery.

"I'm sorry," I said, "but I don't understand what you want me to do."

"Oh, I think you understand," she said with a teasing smile. "But seriously, Philip. Number one, I do want Vincent to have help. Number two, it cannot come from me anymore, I recognize that. And so? Well, I thought that, maybe, Charles's wife . . . ? You know, Nora Saroff? I've never met her, I've only seen her on television. She's very beautiful on television. I didn't even know she and Charles were married till Roy mentioned it. I thought: How lucky for Charles Camelot to have such a beautiful wife. But then, when I met Charles, I thought: How lucky for Nora Saroff to have such a handsome husband! They must be very happy, no?"

I didn't answer. The question, just then, seemed a little complicated.

"I thought maybe you could talk to her," Margie said. "Could you?"

"Well, yes, I could, but . . ."

"You see, it's because she was Carter's therapist. Even though she couldn't help Carter, or at least she couldn't stop him, Vincent says he liked her. Once he said to me: 'Carter thought she was great.' And I am thinking of myself: If it is someone who knew Carter and at least tried to help him, then maybe I could convince Vincent to go to her. But I don't want even to try if she wouldn't see him."

"I see," I said. "But that would be up to her. You know she's mostly a sex therapist, don't you?"

"Ach, you Americans, you and your Dr. Freud! Everything is sex for you, sex and the orgasm. Well, I will tell you the scandalous truth, Philip: I think I was good for Vincent. In making love he was . . . how shall I say? . . . so exuberant? Many young men are like that. I think I helped him." She pinched her lips together. Then: "I think I want him to go now. I think he is tired of me now, and if it is only that he is tired of me now, then he should leave. This is what I tell him. It would be terrible for me, yes, I would be hurt. Of course. But I would understand. If that was . . ."

I remember, though, that her voice trailed off. We were still sitting at the table near the darkened terrace, and it was raining hard outside, and the meal was over, the houseman must have cleared the dishes away, because we were drinking coffee from demitasse cups and cognac from a pair of those balloon snifters. And that was when suddenly—no warning—Margie started to cry. Big tears at first, welling like bubbles, no sound. Then her shoulders started to shake, and she moaned, and turning her head away, she tried to hide her eyes with her hand.

I watched her pull herself together. It didn't take long. She took deep breaths. Then she dabbed at her eyes with a white cloth napkin and looked at me again, her face small, saying:

"Something I just thought of made me cry. I'm sorry. It is so embarrassing. I shouldn't tell you—I shouldn't be telling you any of this—but my instinct is that I can trust you."

She glanced down at the napkin she'd been using, then up at me again, tilting her face toward the light.

"Is it okay?" she asked. "My mascara?"

It looked pretty fine to me, and I told her so.

Another deep breath.

"I will tell you what made me cry, Philip. You know, I'm frightened of AIDS, is that so terrible? It is the plague. People are dying every day all around us. I know some myself, talented young homosexuals. It is a terrible thing. So I am afraid of it, but not for me. For Vincent. And I told him this. We had a terrible row. He was going out, I know those awful places he goes to, those discos and places like that. I've been there too. They're really very banal, you know? Normally who would care if he went there? But there are people who take drugs and who knows who they sleep with? He accused me of being jealous. I said I was not jealous, that it was only because of AIDS. And do you know what he said?"

Another deep breath. She pinched her lips together, and I thought she was about to cry again. She didn't though.

"He said: 'Not to worry, Grandma'—this is what he calls me sometimes when he hates me' . . . He said: 'Not to worry, Grandma. When I get AIDS you'll be the first person I give it to.'"

She paused, her face small and tense, as though looking for my reaction.

"This was not a joke, Philip," she said. "He meant it."

My first, and only, reaction was to wonder why she didn't throw Vincent Angus Halloran out the door.

Yet clearly she hadn't. "I am very worried about him," she said, her dark eyes fixed on mine. "You must believe me, Philip, this has nothing to do with the company or the money or Charles Camelot or anything. I ask you for me. It is between us. I want you to persuade Dr. Saroff that she should see him. If she agrees, then I will work on Vincent. Okay?"

"Okay," I said. "I don't know how persuasive I can be, but I'll at least talk to her."

"Good," Margie said. Then she smiled again, the teasing smile. "But I think you can be very persuasive, no?"

We'd reached the awkward moment. The meal was done, the coffee, and so was the business she'd invited me for. The brandy, I guess, could have gone on forever.

She was aware of it too, though: the awkward moment.

"Normally I would ask you to stay, Philip," she said, still smiling. "I think it would be good for me now to be with a man my own age. I think I would be good for you, too. But not tonight. I think he will be back tonight. I don't mean that I am his prisoner. I, too, am free to do what I want, with whom I want. But right now, he's . . ."

Whatever she was thinking, she seemed to catch herself. The small, tense look again. But then she shook it off and shrugged in that philosophical way Europeans have and said:

"Never mind. I have said already more than I should have. What can I tell you, Philip? I'm trying to help him. I know this is stupid. But perhaps there will be another time for you and me?"

She led me to the front door for the second time that day, again in her stockinged feet. The hallway was dark, silent, cavernous. She watched me put my coat on. Then went on tiptoe once more. Only this time she put her arms fully around my neck and kissed me firmly on the mouth.

I kissed her back.

She pulled away. In her stockinged feet she didn't even come up to my shoulder.

"Another time," she said softly. "But you'll call me, yes? About Dr. Saroff?"

"Yes, I will."

"And quickly?"

"As soon as I can."

I remember sitting in the Fiero at the foot of Margie Magister's tower. I'd stuck the key in the ignition but didn't turn it.

It was like I was waiting for something. Or: all dressed up—again—and no place to go.

In time the rain lightened into one of those cloaky wet mists you can hardly see, the kind that coats the windshield with little droplets and soaks the pavements and the long lines of cars parked by the curbs in the night. All dark, all empty except for the Fiero.

I smoked.

I remember thinking about Vince Halloran and Carter McCloy. Then I drifted back to Margie, Margie in stockinged feet on tiptoe, and how she'd gone all the way in the

Magister chain from the grandfather to the grandson without so much as stopping off, and how she seemed capable, had been capable, of doing both. Which was weird. And such was her own power of persuasion that, whatever I'd said, I'd left her absolutely convinced that I'd convince the Counselor's Wife to take Halloran on as a patient. Why? Because it had seemed at once so logical and so crucial to Margie.

But why (in the Fiero) was it so logical? Because Vince Halloran was a friend of McCloy's, who'd been her patient and who'd killed himself after killing a bunch of women? Assuming he had in fact killed them all? Or just because Margie Magister, who was Halloran's lover and was so worried about him, had asked me to?

Maybe it was that I've always had trouble with women in tears.

In time I drifted off these subjects to a touchier one.

Meaning yours truly.

I can't say I lose a lot of sleep over the Great Burning Questions of Human Existence. Like most working stiffs, I'm too busy earning a living and just getting along, and the who-am-I-what-am-I-doing-here stuff a lot of people my age wasted a lot of their youth over just kind of passed me by.

Still.

Still on the safe side of forty but not by a lot. Still a non-lawyer, working for hire, because I never passed the bar. Still unmarried, still unloved, still and still.

Put it that Margie Magister had touched a nerve.

And yes, Laura Hugger, wherever you were that night, I thought of you, too.

Anyway I sat, sat in the dark Fiero on Fifth Avenue, in the cold misty middle of the night, with the key in the ignition. I smoked, probably I fidgeted, while the traffic lights went from red to green to red in the wet. Waiting for something to happen. No place better to go.

Then I saw Vince Halloran.

At first I didn't recognize him.

Someone was coming north along the building line, not hurrying, just walking. No coat, no hat, the collar of a jacket turned up, fists jammed in the jacket pockets. Face indistinct. Wet hair plastered to the head, head down.

Big, broad, a tight-end build more or less.

Jesus Christ, he wore the same white scarf, McCloy's, the ends trailing behind him.

Vincent Angus Halloran and then, out of nowhere, the dislike I felt for him hit me like a physical reaction. I saw that half-smile of his in my mind.

I remember my fists balling up. As quickly, though, he ducked inside the entrance to Margie's building and disappeared.

I snapped the ignition key. With a lurch, the Fiero headed onto Fifth Avenue.

I drove home.

For the record, the Counselor's Wife said no.

I ran into her the next morning, on my way to work. I'd gotten up at the crack of dawn and gone jogging, the long route, pushing myself along the sodden cinders and pavements of the park. The rain had stopped, and a strong cold wind was blowing out of the west, drying the city and shoving the bad weather into the Atlantic. I made myself run all the way home, then took a long hot shower, shaved, dressed and ate while I listened to the news. No news is good news. For good measure, I decided to walk to work.

Male makeover time, you could say.

I'd almost made it to the Fifth Avenue side when I heard somebody calling my name from behind. I turned and saw her. Muffin, the spaniel bitch, was pulling her this way and that, chasing after fallen leaves which the wind was pinwheeling along the ground. The Counselor's Wife had on a long off-white raincoat, duster-style, with a fur collar turned up and brown leather boots muddied from the ground. The cocker bitch had on none of the above, and her short legs were mud-covered all the way up to her body.

"Hi, Phil!" the Counselor's Wife said, panting as she drew abreast of me. "What a fabulous day! A fabulous day for spaniels too, right, Muffie?"

The dog, however, paid no attention.

I'd seen little of the Counselor's Wife since McCloy's suicide and had talked to her less. Probably this was more intentional than accidental, because I knew she'd been spending more time than usual at home. Somehow I was aware that what had happened to McCloy had hit her hard. Also that what had happened, or hadn't, between her and me must have embarrassed her some, because it did me.

That morning, though, you couldn't see a trace of trouble in her. Her cheeks were rosy from the wind, and her blonde hair blowing and sparkling, and a glint of gaiety, even excitement, lit up her eyes. Whether she's actually beautiful or not I'll leave to the Margie Magisters, but she has a kind of style, when she's on her game, that makes you stop and take notice.

"There's something I need to talk to you about," I said as we walked stride for stride toward the avenue.

"Well, why not right now?" she answered.

"Well," I said, glancing at my watch, "why not?"

We were both, I realized, behind our normal schedules, she more than I, but we sat on a damp bench just this side of a park wall, and she hooked the end of Muffin's leash through a wood slat, leaving the cocker spaniel bitch to root in the wet grass and dash at stray leaves that blew through the territory.

I told her about Halloran. She remembered the name from her sessions with Carter. She'd had the impression that, in addition to their having been close, Halloran had been a stabilizing influence. Didn't he at least have a regular job? He used to, I told her. Had I met him? Yes, I had. And . . . ?

"I don't like him," I said.

"Why?" she asked.

"I don't really know," I answered. Maybe a few sessions on her couch would have gotten a better answer out of me, but I wasn't in the market, Margie Magister was—on Halloran's behalf. So I asked her, for Margie, if she'd take Halloran on as a patient.

A little to my surprise, she said no.

"I don't think so," she said. She reached down and brushed some debris from near the hem of her coat. "If anything, Phil, I've been phasing down lately. I mean, I'm still seeing my old patients, but I haven't taken on anybody new. I've moved my office, did you know that?"

"No, I didn't."

"Well, I don't need so much space if I'm phasing down. It's too expensive. I've moved into a time-sharing situation."

I'd never known the Counselor's Wife to worry about expenses of any kind.

"What about the TV show?" I said.

"Oh, I wouldn't give that up," she said with a laugh. "At least not for the time being. Or as long as they still want me."

She brushed again at her coat. "Look, Phil," she said, shaking her hair, "I once said I owed you an explanation for what was going on in those crazy days. I still do. But part of it is that what happened with Carter caused me a lot of pain. I've even . . . here's a small confession for you . . . I've even gone back on the couch myself because of it."

"You?" I said.

"Oh, it's not that unusual. The self-analysis of an analyst is ongoing, it never really ends. But the profession doesn't allow you responsibility, you know? You're supposed to be totally neutral in the therapeutic situation while the patient works through it himself. Or herself. If he or she does something terrible in the outside world—commits a crime, commits suicide—well, noogies, you're not responsible. Only, as it happens, I've a lot of trouble with that."

"You mean you feel responsible for McCloy?"

"Yes, I do. I think I could have stopped him somehow. Should have. I think I was too frightened to."

"But how?" I said. "You tried."

"Not really," she countered. "This is no criticism of you, Phil, and that other guy . . . what was his name?"

"Bobby Derr?"

"Bobby Derr. But if I really believed what I said I believed, then I should have gone to the police. As it is, I went halfway—to you—which was worse than doing nothing at all. Do you know why it was worse?"

She looked at me like she wanted me to guess. But I couldn't guess.

"I think the reason Carter stopped coming to see me," she went on, "is that somehow he knew I wasn't on his side anymore."

"But that hadn't kept him from killing any of the earlier ones," I objected.

"If he *did* kill them."

"What does that mean?" I said. "He confessed to them."

"I know he did," she said. "But I'll tell you something, Phil. I've gone back over the tapes, the notes I kept of the sessions, and do you know what? I'm not convinced he killed all those women. I don't think he could have hidden it that well, that long."

"But he *confessed* to it!" I repeated. "And he certainly did the last one."

"Exactly. Only he didn't kill her, did he? Why didn't he?"

"We'll never know for sure," I said. "Maybe something scared him off. Maybe she fought back where the others didn't. But I don't get it, Nora. You were the first one to suspect McCloy, and you thought you had a strong basis for it. Then he goes off and kills another one, or tries to, and gets caught, or at least identified. Then he commits suicide, and he leaves a confession behind him. Now you're saying you were wrong in the first place? Even somehow that you might have driven him to it?"

"I know it sounds weird," she said, smiling ruefully. "My shrink's pointed out the same things."

She stood up then.

"Anyway," she said, "there's more to it than that, other things going on in my life, but I have to say no. I just don't think I'm up to taking on anybody new and complicated right now. Call it job burn-out if you like, and please tell Margie Magister I'm sorry. What's she like, by the way? But if she wants me to, I'll try to give her a referral."

We headed east from the park then, pulled by the dog and pushed by the west wind. By the time we reached the house, she'd managed to worm out of me that I'd been to Margie's the night before for supper, alone, which got me my usual dose of teasing. Normally the Counselor's Wife irritates me no end when she gets off on my alleged philandering, but that morning I gave back as good as I got, and I guess that was because I was glad to see her back in her usual form.

Even if, in a way, she wasn't.

I tried Margie Magister as soon as I got to my office. She wasn't there, or at least not available to me. I left a message that I'd called and my number.

Later that day we got the answer to Margie's proposal back from the Magister brothers. It came from Young Bob to McClintock to the Counselor to me. The answer was no, no deal.

"Pass it along," the Counselor instructed me.

"Who to?" I asked. "Barger or Margie Magister?"

"Either one. Or both."

"What should I say when they ask me why?"

"Say you're just the messenger, that you don't know. For your own edification, though, McClintock says they were outraged. Young Bob says he won't be stampeded, not by Margie or his sister or anyone else. He's calling the stockholders' meeting."

"That sounds like war," I said.

"So it does."

"And which side's going to win?" I asked.

"Neither, probably," came his reply.

I tried Margie Magister again, again had to leave a message. I got Barger, though. In his typical way, i.e., by asking me what I'd do next if I were advising his client, he tried to pump me.

Without success.

Then, sometime that afternoon, the news broke.

The local television stations had it on special bulletins. I first became aware of it myself on my way home, when I stopped on Broadway to pick up the Wall Street Extra of the *Post* which had it in three-inch headlines on the front page, and the evening television news ran on-the-spot coverage, including a pickup from, as it turned out, my own neighborhood precinct.

There'd been a murder the night before, a particularly

brutal one, in a high-rise co-op on Central Park West. Just another murder, you might say, in a city which has another murder every few minutes. But what made this one front page was that we all knew the victim.

CHAPTER 14

Somewhere in New York City, you might have found somebody who didn't know who Suzi Lee was, but you'd have been hard pressed. People said she actually owned the local channel she worked for, a reflection of the multimillion-dollar contract she'd been given when the networks tried to hire her away, and she anchored their nightly news, anchored her own weekly interview show, and did heavily promoted woman-in-the-street specials which regularly outperformed the network shows in the local ratings. She was pretty in that big-eyed Asian way, smart, sharp-tongued, as New York as the mayor and, at least in the play the media gave her, every local bachelor's dream.

She was also dead.

She was also, as I realized with an immediate shock, one of the celebrities we'd discovered on tape that night in Carter McCloy's apartment.

According to the first reports, there was no sign of a break-in at Suzi Lee's apartment. Her maid had discovered the body when she showed up for work that morning, and the police were looking for an unnamed suspect who'd allegedly been with Suzi in the apartment the night before. That suspect was subsequently found but never publicly identified, because by that time there was evidence that the killer had let himself down from the roof of the building onto Suzi's terrace and had entered through the terrace doors.

This time the media, especially Suzi's own TV channel, had a field day. Somehow they got hold of copies of police photos of Suzi's bedroom, including the one of her corpse sprawled on her bed, and they aired them despite a temporary restraining order. They were the ones who, in the face of police uncertainty, decided that the killer had mutilated her body before he strangled her, not after, and that the murder "weapon" had been her own pantyhose. They were the ones who debated the question: did the semen traces discovered on Suzi belong to the unnamed visitor or the killer? Or both?

And how had the killer gotten in? The doorman in the main lobby of the building swore categorically (for the television cameras) that he hadn't left his post once during his tour of duty, nor had he let anybody in he didn't know or hadn't announced, finally that he'd announced nobody to Ms. Lee after she'd come in, accompanied, around ten o'clock in the evening.

That left the underground garage, which you entered from a ramp on the side street. The garage also had a round-the-clock attendant, but the attendant spent at least part of his time jockeying cars in and out, and it would have been easy enough for someone to slip through unobserved, gain access to the elevators, ride to the roof and let himself down two stories to Suzi's terrace.

But how had he gotten out after?

Television (again) voted for the garage. But the garage attendant swore on the air that he hadn't seen anybody he didn't know.

The killer had also left a message, in lipstick, on the dressing-table mirror in Suzi's bedroom.

It read: "In Memoriam."

Nobody knew what that meant.

Maybe I was the only person in the city, that first night, who thought he might.

It took me a while to find him. Not that the Manhattan phone directory was rich in Intaglios, Andrew. In fact it didn't have one, nor did 718 Area Code Information. I worked my way through much of the tristate area before I located him, in a place called Woodbridge, N.J., which I knew only as an exit from the turnpike.

I got Mrs. Intaglio on the phone. No, her husband wasn't home yet, and she had dinner waiting for him. Was it that urgent? Couldn't he call back tomorrow?

Then I heard commotion at the other end, what sounded like children's voices, and a moment later Intaglio himself came on.

"I only just got in, Revere," he said. "What can I do for you?"

It turned out he knew less about the Suzi Lee murder than I did. He'd only just heard about it on the car radio, driving home.

Then I asked him the question that had been bothering me: "How tightly did you button down the McCloy investigation?"

"What do you mean, how tightly? McCloy's dead, isn't he?"

"Yes, he's dead, but there were a lot of loose ends lying around after he jumped."

"Such as?"

"Such as the business of the alibis, for one. You sweated McCloy one whole night and you couldn't break him, remember? The reason was that you couldn't bust his alibis. Well, either somebody had to be lying to the Task Force or McCloy didn't kill all those women."

"That's right, he only confessed to it," Intaglio said sarcastically.

"Exactly, he only confessed. But if he *knew* he was going to kill himself, what difference did it make? He could've confessed to anything, couldn't he?"

Intaglio went silent at the other end.

"Halloran was one of them, wasn't he?" I went on. "One of his alibis? Vince Halloran? Vincent Angus Halloran?"

"That's right."

"Well, you could've had Halloran at least for aiding and abetting, couldn't you?"

Another silence. Maybe he was doing a slow burn, but it was hard to tell over the phone.

"What can I tell you, Revere?" he said. "I only worked there. Being on the Task Force was like being in a war. You ever been in a war?"

"Actually I have, yes."

"Then you'll understand what I'm talking about. Once the war's over, it's over, and all anybody wants to do is go home."

"What you're saying is that nobody buttoned it down."

"I don't know that," he said. "Once we had McCloy's confession, the Task Force kind of disintegrated. I was back in my own office the next week. Maybe the police kept people on the case, maybe . . ."

"And maybe they didn't?" I finished for him.

I guess I could understand it. The Pillow Killer had put all law enforcement in New York under tremendous pressure. Once the case was "solved," nobody wanted to unsolve it. Not, in addition, when it would have meant going after rich kids from influential families.

Case closed, war over.

"Look, Revere," Intaglio said, "if you've got evidence to reopen the McCloy case, I'll tell you who to call. But you've got the wrong guy. Anyway, my wife's calling me for dinner."

"I don't know if I do or don't," I said, "but what about the tapes?"

"What tapes?"

"The videos. The ones Dr. Saroff and I found that night in McCloy's place."

"Yeah, I remember them. But we never found them."

"You didn't? I told you to look in the garbage."

"Maybe I'm missing something," Intaglio said, "but what do the tapes have to do with it?"

"One of them," I answered, "at least one, was of Suzi Lee."

Silence again. I could hear a voice, or voices, in the background. Then:

"Jesus Christ," I heard Intaglio say softly. Then: "You got anything else?"

I summarized it for him, editing out most of the Margie Magister part. Even as I spoke, though, it sounded pretty flimsy to my own ears. So I'd seen Vincent Halloran arriving at Margie's in the rain, in the wee hours of the night before, wearing Carter McCloy's scarf or a replica of same. So what?

When I was done, Intaglio said: "Let me get off now, Revere."

"I understand," I said. "Dinner's waiting."

"No, it's not that. I've got some calls to make. I'll get back to you. Give me a number."

I gave it to him.

"This may take a while," he said. "How late do you stay up?"

"I'll wait," I answered.

It was near midnight when my phone rang again. In between I'd done something I rarely do: I called the upstairs phone at the Counselor's and had the following essentially stupid conversation.

Althea, the cook and housekeeper, picked up.

"Cam'lot res'dence," she said.

"It's me. Phil. Are they home?"

"Phil who?" she asked suspiciously. Then, her voice brightening in recognition: "Oh, it's you, Phil. Which one of them do you want?"

"Neither," I said. "I just wanted to make sure . . ."

Then the Counselor's deep voice broke in:

"It's all right, Althea, I'll take it. Who is this?"

"It's me," I said again. "I'm sorry to call this . . ."

"That's all right, Phil. Did you get Margie Magister?"

"No," I said, switching mental gears. "But I talked to Barger. But that's not why I'm calling. Is Nora there?"

"Yes, she is, but she's already gone to bed. I think she's asleep. Did you want to talk to her?"

"No, I didn't."

"But then . . . ?"

"It's all right," I said hastily. "I just wanted to make sure she was home. I'll explain in the morning."

I stumbled my way out of it and hung up. It was a little after 10:30. God knows what the Counselor thought, but I saw no reason to alarm them as long as she was there. The whole building was wired, all the way up to and including the fifth floor, and once the systems were turned on, there was no way anyone could break in without bringing the whole security service down on their heads.

Besides . . .

That's what I was telling myself: *Besides . . . ,* when Intaglio called me back.

"I want to talk to you," he said. "When can we meet?"

"What's up?" I said.

"Look, it's late."

"I know it's late," I said, "but I've got to sleep nights too."

I heard him sigh into the phone.

"All I can tell you is that the Lee woman got one of those letters too, the same one Saroff got."

I didn't say anything.

"Tomorrow morning," he said. "Where and when?"

The one the Counselor's Wife had gotten, I remembered, had said: WHAT MAKES YOU SO SURE YOU COULDN'T BE THE NEXT ONE, and it had been signed: A FRIEND. The receptionist had found it slipped under their office door.

The one Suzi Lee had gotten had been identical.

So were the two others which had been received by prominent television personalities, both women.

There may in fact have been more. These were the ones the Task Force had known about.

All had been typed on a little portable called a Canon Typestar which the Task Force had never found, never been able to trace. All of them had apparently been delivered by hand, but in only one instance had anybody recalled anything about the messenger. One of the doormen—Suzi Lee's, in fact—had thought he remembered a black teenager on a bicycle.

"Of which," Intaglio said, "how many do you suppose there are in the city?"

We met at the Roosevelt on the Upper West Side at 8:30 the next morning. I was beginning to think I should buy stock in the joint, given the number of times I'd been there recently, but Intaglio hadn't wanted to meet at his office. He didn't come alone either. His companion was a large-format cop in plain clothes, with hooded gray eyes. His name was Martindale. I gathered from the conversation, and later confirmed, that he was pretty high up in the NYPD hierarchy, also that he'd been pretty high up in the Task Force. This explained, among other things, why we met uptown instead of down. If in fact the Suzi Lee murder could be linked to the Pillow Killer, then the Task Force had certainly blown its investigation. Whoever brought the connection to light might win gold stars up the kazoo; but whoever brought it to light would hate like hell to be wrong.

"What you're telling me," I said to Intaglio over coffee, "is that you never really focused on the letters."

"That's not true," he answered. "They just didn't take us very far. We weren't even sure they connected to the Pillow Killer."

"Until you found out Dr. Saroff had gotten one too?"

"That's right. But that was late in the day. By that time we already had McCloy."

"Except that you let him walk away," I said.

Up till then, Martindale had said little, concentrating instead on a double portion of coffee cake.

"Don't be a wise guy with us, Revere," he said, wiping crumbs from his mouth with a brush of a paper napkin. "If there's one thing we've already got enough of, it's wise guys. Have you got any idea how many threatening letters and phone calls got reported to the Task Force? It ran in the thousands. We ran all of them down. I mean every last one of them. Did you know we had eleven people who tried to confess to the crimes? I said *eleven*. Eleven goddamn wise guys."

At least I wasn't that kind of wise guy, I thought.

"Let me tell you something," Martindale said, washing the last of the cake down with light coffee, generously sugared. "The Pillow case is officially closed. Zipped up tight. Now we've got another homicide on our hands, Suzi Lee. I watched Suzi Lee, I liked Suzi Lee. We're going to find out who killed Suzi Lee. But now, along comes a wise guy who says the killer's one and the same . . ."

"I didn't say that," I interrupted.

". . . and that we must've blown it on the Pillow case," he went right on. "And what've you got to prove it? A bunch of threatening letters?"

"Plus the videotapes," I said.

"The videotapes we never found," Martindale said.

"The videotapes I saw," I said. "And I wasn't the only one who saw them. Dr. Saroff did too. Somebody in that apartment, either McCloy or Halloran, taped Nora Saroff, Suzi Lee, and the others. Everyone who got one of the letters was on tape there."

"Why don't you tell us what you know about Halloran?" Intaglio put in.

I took a deep breath and launched in. Most of what I had, in fact, I'd already given Intaglio the night before. That Halloran and McCloy were close friends from way back and part of a gang of well-heeled party boys who went in for the "bridge-and-tunnel bunny" type of playmate, which corresponded to the Pillow Killer's first victims and his last. That some of them, Halloran included, seemed to like to beat up on people. That Halloran was clearly estranged from his mother who, I thought, might know things about him she wasn't telling. Then there was Margie Magister, who was at the least worried about him and maybe, I thought, afraid of him. There was, finally, the question of where Halloran had been the night before while Suzi Lee was having her nipples worked over and when I'd seen him on Fifth Avenue in the rain.

I tried to tiptoe around the Margie part, but that didn't work out too well.

"I bet he's balling Margie Magister, isn't he?" Martindale said with a weather-beaten grin.

"You said it," I answered sharply, "I didn't."

"Aren't we touchy?" he said back, still grinning. "What's the matter, you jealous?" Then the grin went away. "So? What else you got?"

The truth was I didn't have much else, except for one thing: my own, please pardon the expression, intuition. Intuition and the proverbial dollar will get you on the subway, I know that, and I've long since learned to distrust people's intuitions, my own included. Which means that I don't have many. Only with Vince Halloran, I did.

"My own conviction," was how I put it. "I believe he may have committed at least some of the Pillow murders. Him and McCloy probably. And I think he may have killed Suzi Lee."

"The M.O. is totally different," Martindale said.

"Maybe so, but the Pillow Killer's wasn't that consistent either."

"Yeah, and that's what makes you think there wasn't just one killer, right? But what else you got? What's there that makes you so convinced?"

I could, in hindsight, have answered this several ways. "In Memoriam," for one thing. "In Memoriam" is Latin for "in memory of." In memory of who if not Carter McCloy? And there was McCloy's white scarf. And Bobby Derr getting the shit kicked out of him in a school playground. And other items, more and less farfetched. But what I saw—all I saw—was Halloran's half-smile.

"I can see it in his face," I answered.

This made Martindale laugh. Rumbly sounds. But his head didn't move, nor did his gray eyes.

"Gee," he said, "that's great. We sure could use somebody like you on the force, somebody who can tell a killer just by looking at his face. But since we don't have one and you not being a cop, what do you suggest we do?"

"Pull Halloran in," I said. "Shake him."

Martindale shook his head.

"No way," he said.

I glanced at Intaglio. When I first met him, it had been with a cop too, Walters from the DA squad, and Intaglio had clearly been the one in charge. Now he clammed up. Clearly, even though they came from separate areas of law enforcement, Martindale outranked him in somebody's pecking order.

Maybe that was what got me sore.

"Come on," I said to Martindale. "If he was black or Hispanic, you'd pick him up and throw away the key. I know that and you know that. I thought you guys had quit working the old double standard."

Which, I guess, is what got Martindale sore in turn.

"I told you I can't stand wise guys," he said disgustedly. "Do you really think that if you weren't who you were, didn't work for who you work for, that we'd be wasting our time listening to your cockamamie?"

"What I'm hearing," I retorted, "is that you're going to do nothing about it."

"I didn't say that."

"The least you could do is put the women on the hit list under protection."

"We've already done that."

"You have? What about Nora Saroff?"

"Her too."

Oh boy, I thought to myself, remembering the reason for my call to the Counselor the night before.

"Have you told them that you're doing it?"

"No way. There's no need for them to know. They won't feel a thing."

Sure, I thought, and pigs really do have wings.

"What about Halloran?" I asked.

"What about him?"

"What are you going to do about him?"

"Whatever we're doing about him," Martindale said, lowering the shutters with a clank, "is our own business."

I looked at Intaglio, then back at the cop. End of conversation. Or almost.

"Let me tell you something else, Revere," Martindale said. "We live in a free country, that's the truth. Anybody who wants to go around chasing murderers can go around chasing murderers, and nobody's going to stop him. But if you've got any ideas about this Halloran and you get yourself into trouble, don't go looking to us for help. You'll be on your own. This meeting never took place."

No, Virginia, pigs don't have wings. By this I mean that the unmarked car parked next to the fire hydrant across the street from our office stuck out like a sore thumb, and so did the plainclothesman sitting behind the wheel reading a newspaper.

"Is she in there?" I said to him as I walked past his half-open window.

"Yeah, she . . ." Then, looking up at me in surprise: "Hey, who the hell are you?"

"Never mind," I told him. "I only work here."

I went straight up to the Counselor's office and reported in. He hadn't noticed the car across the street yet, but he started a slow burn when he learned that the NYPD had put his wife under surveillance without telling him. He didn't know Martindale, but he took notes while I talked. Knowing the Counselor, he'd go in at the top, and I'd have given a week's pay to be there when friend Martindale got called in on the carpet.

I gave the Counselor everything, suppositions as well as facts, and I could feel anger building in him as I went. With him it takes the form of stoniness. His face turns gray, like stone, and the jaws work, and by the time I was done, he looked like he was biting granite.

"We live in a slaughterhouse, Phil," he said when I'd finished, the eyes lifting in his immobile head to meet mine. "People get murdered every day, and we pay no attention. We either can't, or we don't know them, or it's not our job. That's what we pay the police for. But when it gets this close to home, Jesus Christ Almighty, that's different. I'll tell you what I want from you. I don't know if you're right or wrong about Halloran, but I want you to drop everything else till you find out. You're to pull in whatever resources you need."

"I'll get Bobby Derr for one," I said.

"Up to you."

"He already knows the scene, including Halloran. Also he's got some personal motivation, remember?"

"Up to you," he repeated. "But I also want protection for Nora for as long as it takes. I don't even want her walking the dog without somebody else out there. Whether that's Fincher's people or another organization is your responsibility."

"But what about the police?" I said. "It's going to get awfully crowded out there."

"Do you want to leave this to the police?"

"No," I said.

"Neither do I. Don't worry about the police, I'll get them off your back."

"And what do we tell Nora?"

"Nothing," the Counselor said. "We tell her nothing. She's not to know what's going on."

"But that's going to make a close surveillance job pretty tricky, isn't it?"

"You heard me," he said, his jaws working. "We tell her nothing. She's been upset enough lately, I don't want her upset any more."

I still didn't like it. He didn't care whether I liked it or not. He told me to spend whatever I had to spend.

He was on the verge, I thought, of telling me something else, but maybe that's with the benefit of hindsight. In any case, he didn't. All he said was:

"Get it rolling, Phil. And just one word of advice: If it turns out you're right about Halloran, then you're dealing not only with a crazy but a smart crazy. Whatever you do, be careful."

Such words of solicitude from the Counselor, needless to say, are rare enough to be underlined.

By the end of that day, I had it rolling all right. Maybe the Counselor's Wife could accidentally slip through the system Bud Fincher and I set up, but it was as good as we could make it, down to the two people we had planted in the studio audience when she did her show that night.

Along the way I tried to get through to Sally Magister and

failed. Ditto Margie, who'd called me that morning but was gone when I called back.

She found me, at my desk, late in the afternoon.

"You must be very busy, Philip," she said. "I've been trying to reach you."

"Me too."

"I need to talk to you," she said.

"Funny," I said, "but that calls for another 'me too.'"

She didn't laugh though.

"As soon as possible," she said. "Right now if you can."

She didn't want me to come to her place. She didn't want to come to the office either. We settled on a Madison Avenue saloon I knew, which was about equidistant from the two of us.

Oh yes. When I walked out into the chill dusk, I noticed that the unmarked car was gone from across the street, and I spotted no replacement.

CHAPTER 15

Mostly, when you live in New York, you wear blinkers. You go to work; you go home. You go to the same neighborhood stores, the same eateries and saloons. The garage. The jogging routes in the park. You're hot in the summer, cold in the winter, and sure you know in some vague way that there's an in between from one to the other, but that's the same way you know there are eight million other entries, give or take, in the daily New York rat race. They're there all right; but you don't see them.

That's what happened to October that year. Carter McCloy jumped off his ninth-floor balcony, and Suzi Lee got strangled, and somewhere along the way the leaves on the trees must have turned gold and red and dropped and been blown into piles and carted off on trucks to wherever the trucks take them, and we got an extra hour's sleep on Sunday when the clocks went back to standard time. The World Series happened, but don't ask me who won. The Giants got whipped a couple of times on TV, and the Rangers opened another dreary season at the Garden.

Blinkers.

Only then, in November, looking for Vincent Angus Halloran, the blinkers came off. The rains came long and steady and, certain days, just a few degrees from snow on the thermometer. The holiday season was just around the corner, and everywhere you turned there were people, college kids and tourists adding to the jam. The bars, the restaurants, the nightclubs, the stores. Getting around—morning, noon, and night—was like climbing through mud. The whole town took on the smell of wet wool and the angry sound of car horns, and it was a great season for umbrella peddlers and muggers. The whole world, in sum, seemed to have poured into the city. The whole world, that is, minus Vincent Angus Halloran and his friends.

Bobby Derr and I followed their footprints everywhere we could think of and came up empty-handed. Melchiorre's, the Rosebud, Willy's, plus a number of other joints Bobby knew about. It didn't seem to matter how much green we dropped along the way. A $50 bill to the super of the building in the East Eighties bought us the news that the apartment was empty and, so he'd heard, was going to be put up for sale. The girlfriends we could find hadn't seen Halloran either, though a couple of them seemed to like the idea, and Bobby, who insisted on taking on the friends of Vincent Halloran himself, drew a similar blank. As far as we knew, the only ones who had regular jobs were Sprague Fording and Shrimp Stark, both down on Wall Street. But Messrs. Fording and Stark, Bobby was told, were both on vacation.

So where did the sons of the New York rich go for vacations in November? Wasn't it too early for skiing? Or the Caribbean?

Early, we crossed tracks with the police, but then their traces grew faint and disappeared altogether. I tried calling Martindale a couple of times, but he never called back.

I did, though, get through to Sally Magister once.

The ruse I used, I admit, was pretty lame, but it worked. Briefly. I gave Sally's secretary the name of a writer of some prominence around New York, one I figured they wouldn't mind adding to their roster, and sure enough, Sally came on all milk and honey.

I let her soften me up a little. Then I said:

"I wonder if you could help me on another subject. I'm trying to locate Vincent Halloran."

"Well, I'd be the last one to know that."

"But he works for you, too, doesn't he?"

"He used to, not anymore. But what on earth would you want Vincent for?"

"I don't myself," I said, "but a mutual friend does. Somebody who thinks your son might be in serious . . ."

"Wait a minute," she interrupted, her voice shrilling, "who *is* this? Some kind of impersonator? You're not . . ." Then, before I could say anything else: "Oh. I get it. I know who you are. I told you once before, mister, I don't like cute. Well, you can tell that double-dealing . . ." Then, catching herself: "Never mind. Just tell her I don't care if he beat her up. If he beat her up, she probably deserved it."

"She might not be the only one he beat up, Ms. Magister," I said as calmly as I could.

"That's nice," she said icily. "Are there any other accusations you'd like to make?"

Before I could answer, though, the phone went bang in my ear.

Each day, I got a full rundown on the Counselor's Wife from Bud Fincher. I felt like I knew more about where she'd been in a given week than she did herself: the patients she'd seen, the stores she'd been in, two doctor's visits (one her ob-gyn; the other a psychiatrist—her own shrink?), one lunch with Dr. Biegler (the shrink who shared her office, or her old office), another with the producer of the show, but home every evening excepting the night of her show, and then, home right after the show. And no entertaining. A low profile, in sum, which was hardly her style. I wondered if she suspected anything.

Each day too I reported to the Counselor. As time went by, I kept expecting him to pull the plug. I even predicted what he'd say: *For all we're getting out of it, Phil, you might as well be handing out dollar bills on the street*. But he didn't. On the contrary, he pushed me to keep going.

And each day, sometimes several times a day, I talked to Margie Magister.

You could say that if anybody had concrete reason to be afraid of Halloran, she was the one. Back on that October afternoon, when she'd called me and we'd met in the Madison Avenue saloon, not even her dark glasses had hid what he'd done to her. An ugly swelling almost closed her left eye, and Halloran had given it to her—a kind of going-away present—that same night of the Suzi Lee murder, when I'd sat waiting for him in the rain on Fifth Avenue.

I learned she'd waited up for him too that night. When he came in, she'd wanted to know where he'd been. He refused to tell her. It wasn't that he wasn't free to come and go as he chose, she'd told him, but she worried about him. It was, he'd answered, none of her goddamn business.

Then he'd wanted to go to bed with her.

She'd turned him down. She'd told him she wasn't his whore.

He'd laughed at her for that. If she wasn't his whore, then what was she?

Then he'd tried to force her.

She'd slapped him, as hard as she could.

In return, he'd beaten her. Apparently the swollen eye wasn't the only evidence of it, simply the most visible. And what good had it done her to struggle with him? In the end, though that wasn't the word she used, he'd raped her anyway, and then he'd gone off.

"I don't know what to do," she'd said to me that afternoon, at a table in the back of the darkened bar. "I haven't seen him, he hasn't called. I have no idea where he is. What should I do?"

"Who else have you told about it?"

"Nobody. I just tell people I had an accident."

"The first thing I'd do," I told her, "is change the locks on your doors and hire a security service."

"Oh that," she said, waving the idea away. "I don't care what he does to me. He can kill me if he wants to. But I still want to help him. He needs help so badly."

She'd taken my hand, squeezing it so hard her nails bit

into the skin. I didn't know what to tell her, other than to stay away from him. That the Counselor's Wife, in turning Halloran down as a patient, had offered to give Margie a referral was no longer relevant, though I told her anyway.

"Do you really think he's dangerous?" she asked me in the bar, her face upturned toward me.

"I think he may be very dangerous," I answered. I thought, but didn't say, that she'd might have been lucky to get away with bruises.

She looked away.

"I do too," she said in a low voice. "I will tell you what he said. If it means I betray him, then I betray him. He was very angry. I have had men say terrible things to me before, but not like this. It was while we were . . ." She stopped, bit at her lip, then plunged on. "He said: 'Keep it going, Grandma. You want to end up like all the others? Keep it going, keep it going.' I didn't dare ask him what he meant by this. I was too afraid. And now he's gone."

I guess there's no telling about women, though. Margie may, like I said, have had more reason than anybody else to be scared of him, but that didn't keep her from calling several times a day to see if I'd learned anything. I wasn't the only person she called either. And no, she still didn't change the locks on her doors.

Into November then, and still nowhere. We felt like fools, Derr, Fincher, myself, the Counselor, outsmarted, reduced to listening to the news, scanning the crime headlines. The city had its normal run of same, sure enough. An off-duty cop got gunned down in Washington Heights, and the next day the police had to cordon off a couple of blocks in the Twenties when somebody set off a bomb in one of the welfare hotels. Drug-related crimes, it was said. Not our line.

Waiting, I guess, for the proverbial shit to hit the fan.

And then it did, unexpectedly, the Monday before Thanksgiving, when Intaglio called.

Here's how it went:

Intaglio: "I'm not supposed to be telling you this, but some friends of mine down here have had a visit from somebody you know."

Revere: "Oh?"

Intaglio: "That's right. He didn't come by himself either. He brought an attorney. Seems like they want to swear out complaints against my friends and your friends, including some people who work for you and who you work for."

Revere: "On what basis?"

Intaglio: "Oh, harassment, slander, false accusation, a few other goodies. They claim my friends and your friends are going around town saying this person's been implicated in a certain criminal act. They claim my friends are doing it because we've got an unsolved case on our books. They claim you're doing it because of another matter you're involved in."

Revere: "What do you mean? What other matter?"

Intaglio: "Say, the takeover of a certain company."

Revere: "But that's a lie!"

Intaglio: "I wouldn't know. That's what they're saying."

Revere: "Let me ask you something. This attorney, do his initials happen to be R. B.?"

Intaglio: "I'm unable to answer that."

Revere: "But is it somebody I know? And who knows me?"

Intaglio: "I think that's a fair guess. He also says he's planning to go public with it."

Revere: "I think that's baloney."

Intaglio: "I wouldn't know. But they produced alibis for the criminal act in question, complete with written statements."

Revere: "I'd like to see those."

Intaglio: "Sorry, can't help you there."

Revere: "Why not?"

Intaglio: "Because my friends don't know you. They don't know a thing about what you're up to."

Revere: "Jesus Christ."

Intaglio: "It's serious, I think. I think you're going to be served. That's about all I can tell you."

Revere: "Thanks a bunch."

Intaglio: "No problem. Gotta go now."

End of conversation.

I sat at my desk, momentarily stunned. Not by the fact that the police would disavow any connection to me. Martindale had already warned me, in the cafeteria, and no matter what else he'd said, it's pretty obvious the the NYPD is intimidated by rich and influential people with high-powered lawyers. It wasn't either the no-names-mentioned, paranoid tinge to the conversation. Intaglio, I guessed, had been calling from downtown. Maybe their own phones were tapped. Hell, maybe ours were.

No. What floored me was Halloran himself. Would any of us in a million years, if we'd committed a murder or murders, actually go to the police and make a grandstand play like that?

Maybe the answer is that, since only a few of us have committed a murder or murders, we don't know.

Except that I did, or thought I did. Because I saw in my mind's eye Vince Halloran's smile. That arrogant, rich kid's smile.

I reached for the phone. I had something else I wanted to ask Intaglio. But then I thought better of it. The timing was wrong: he'd made it clear in the conversation that there was no way he was going to do anything else for me right then.

Instead I went upstairs to see the Counselor.

I half expected him to land on me. After all, if Barger did carry through on his threat to take the story public, the Magister brothers would scream like stuck pigs. The Counselor heard me out, and I watched the smoke curling and eddying upward from the bowl of his pipe while I talked. His eyes seemed fixed on an envelope on his desk and meanwhile he was playing with one of those oversized paper clips, turning it on one flat edge, then over on the ones with the points, then back again.

"How did he know?" he asked when I was done.

"How did who know what?"

"Halloran. Unless you've been going around telling people he murdered Suzi Lee? You haven't, have you?"

"Of course not. At least not in so many words."

"What does that mean?" he said. "Did you or didn't you?"

I thought about it. We'd greased a lot of people, asked a lot of questions. Maybe Halloran had outgreased us? But I didn't think I'd ever mentioned Suzi Lee by name, and Bobby Derr, I figured, was too slippery a talker to have done it either.

"The closest I could have come," I said, "was with one of the bartenders at Melchiorre's. He knows me from when I was in there with McCloy. I gave him fifty bucks to call me if Halloran showed up. He has my card. I also asked him some questions about the night of the Lee murder. Had Halloran been in there, or any of his pals? But that's as close as I got. I'm pretty sure I never even mentioned the murder."

"That was the same night he beat Margie up, wasn't it?"

"That's right."

"So you could have been asking for that reason too, couldn't you? Or any number of other reasons?"

"That's right."

I watched the paper clip fall over, and he leaned his pipe against the telephone console.

"One of two things, Phil. Either you or Derr—or just conceivably the police, though I doubt that—went too far. Or you've got Halloran feeling the heat. I'll go for number two. He's got to know you're looking for him by now. You've scared him, and he's trying to scare you back. With Barger's help. If he so much as sees you again, he'll be able to shout 'Harassment.'"

"Do you want me to lay off?" I asked.

"No. We'll keep the heat on him. I even want you to take it up a notch if you can."

"But what if Barger carries through on his threats?"

"I hope it happens," he said. "I think it's time we went to the mat with Roy Barger. But I doubt it'll happen."

I looked at him questioningly.

"I think Barger's got a problem," he went on. "He put together the coalition, the three generations, but now it's breaking up and he's stuck with a proxy fight. I think he's trying like hell to hold it together. But you can't represent the whole world, and it looks to me like he's got the makings of a nice conflict of interest."

"You mean between Margie and Halloran?"

"Exactly. That's why he won't go public with Halloran's story, at least not directly. Innuendo's more his style anyway. He may have gone this far, going to the police with Halloran, but if he has to choose, and we're going to make him choose, he'll drop Halloran like a hot potato."

"Because Halloran's a murderer?"

"Hardly," the Counselor answered. "Because the bucks are in Margie."

If I'd expected criticism, I hadn't gotten it. On the contrary. But there was another reason for that.

"There's one other thing you'd better know," the Counselor said, handing me the envelope that had been sitting on his desk. "Without telling you, I've just tightened the security around Nora. I've already told Bud to close it up."

"But won't she find out?" I asked.

"I don't want her to," he said, "but if she does, I'm not sure how much that matters anymore."

I looked at the envelope. It was a plain white #10 job, with the top slit open. Roger LeClerc, the Counselor told me, had found it slipped under our front door less than an hour before and had brought it upstairs.

No name on the address side of the envelope. Inside, a single sheet of typewriter paper, folded in three, with only the words "In Memoriam" on it.

We argued over giving the new letter to the police. Even though it hadn't been typed on the same Canon machine, I wanted to take it to Martindale, confront him with it and try to explode the case. But the Counselor said no. He'd already been in over Martindale's head. The Pillow Killer file, he'd been told, was closed, and nobody downtown was going to reopen it on a theory, no matter how interesting the theory. The more so now that Halloran had claimed harassment. The best he'd gotten was an offer of police surveillance for Nora, but that was only because he was who he was, and as far as that went, he'd still rather use Fincher.

It remained, therefore, for us to prove my "interesting theory."

I waited till that evening to put in my call to Intaglio. I figured he'd be more forthcoming at home than at the office, but I was only half-right.

No amount of persuasion could budge him on the subject of the alibis Halloran had given the police that morning for the Suzi Lee murder. I told him about the "In Memoriam" letter, and he promised to check on whether any of the other celebrities had gotten one, but beyond that I couldn't budge him. All I did, in the end, was piss him off.

"Give me a break, Revere," he said finally.

"What do you mean, give you a break?"

"Just what I said. Do you know what they do to people in my office who get caught leaking information? I'd spend the rest of my career in Traffic Court, prosecuting scofflaws. I've already crossed the line once today by calling you. That's enough."

"But you told me Halloran and Barger are going public with the story themselves, so what difference does it make?"

"When they do that," he said, "then give me a call."

Back at square one. But when I tried him on another aspect of my "interesting theory," to my surprise, he unbuttoned. Maybe it was because he'd done some of the interrogating of Carter McCloy himself and felt he'd blown it. Maybe it was because he didn't have to open a file that was closed but could pull it out of his memory. Or maybe—just maybe—his memory wasn't that good and he'd been doing a little investigating on his own.

What I was after wasn't that complicated in fact. And when I was done transcribing onto a grid the notes I'd taken from talking to Intaglio, plus some data of my own on the Pillow Killer, the pattern became crystal clear.

The Task Force, lest it be forgotten, had had Carter McCloy in its hands for almost twenty-four hours and had let him go.

Why? Pressure from a high-powered attorney, yes, but more because they hadn't been able to break his story. Or stories.

And why was that?

Vincent Angus Halloran.

He wasn't the only one, of course. That might have been too obvious. The Task Force had had statements from other people too, among them Messrs. Stark, Fording, Villiers, and Powell. For every single murder in the Pillow Killer cycle, Carter McCloy had had a multiple alibi. From his friends.

With one exception, I discovered. The next-to-last murder, the one before Linda Vigliotti. The one that had taken place just a few blocks from McCloy's apartment. The victim herself had been different: an elderly woman who lived alone, and in this one case her body had been brutalized either before or after her death. According to Intaglio, some people on the Task Force had thought at first that it was an unrelated crime. Furthermore, McCloy had left Melchiorre's alone that night, and angry, and there was only one witness who'd identified him as having been drinking in another Third Avenue saloon at the time of the murder.

Guess who?

Vincent Angus Halloran.

If the Task Force has somehow gotten on Halloran's trail, would it have been Carter McCloy who'd have come forward to cover up for his buddy?

McCloy or Halloran, Halloran or McCloy?

Old friends, from way back. They'd even gone to the same schools according to Bobby Derr's reports, a Catholic school up in Rhode Island called Portsmouth Priory, then Choate Academy in Connecticut. Halloran had actually graduated from college, a small school in Maine; McCloy had dropped out. Halloran with his back to the camera, McCloy facing with the towel draped around his neck.

Linda Vigliotti had stated she thought somebody else was driving the car that night, that McCloy had gotten in on the passenger side.

A foreign car, she'd thought. Halloran owned an Alfa.

Then McCloy had gone off the parapet, nine stories up, and they'd buried it all. Case closed.

If I should die before I wake.

If I should die before I *die*.

Jesus Christ, he'd said he'd been talking about a friend on Nora's tapes. She and I had assumed he was talking about himself. Maybe we were both wrong.

How well did Halloran sleep nights?

Did McCloy go off the parapet to protect his friend? The ultimate alibi?

Or had they taken turns: I'll kill this one, you kill that one?

Did they flip coins for Linda Vigliotti? And McCloy won?

In Memoriam.

I woke up like a shot for at least the third time that night. I was sitting in the easy chair, papers strewn across the couch and the coffee table, and one forearm ached from where my head had been pressed against it. I'd been dreaming one mess of a dream, which had the Counselor's Wife in it, and Halloran, and Carter McCloy. The ancient radiators in the building I call home were bonging and gurgling with the first morning heat.

It was 6:10 A.M. I felt rancid, sober. Worn out and keyed up at the same time. Almost forty, with a stubble beard and the first signs of thinning at the temples and a job without prospects, blaw blaw blaw. Why is it, when you wake up like that and the first shock wears off, that you end up feeling sorry for yourself?

Too many cigarettes.

I changed into hooded sweats and running shoes, wrapped a towel around my neck and hit the streets.

It was still dark outside and cold as a bitch. I jogged east, shivering inside, across the deserted avenues where the WALK and DON'T WALK signs blinked at nobody in particular, and, entering the park, did my reservoir route. The cinder paths, which had been sodden for days because of the rains, had gone hard, resistant, and I had trouble finding my rhythm. I wasn't alone out there either. I guess the reservoir oval is never altogether deserted. There's always somebody trying to run off, or run away from, something: fat, booze, years, anxiety, loneliness. Males only, in the dark; women runners tend to wait for the sun to come up.

But something wasn't right. I could tell it from the way my body struggled against me, the muscle aches in my thighs and shoulders, the heaving of my lungs when I hit my street again, homeward bound, and slowed to a walk ahead of time, letting the cold dry my sweat. Had McCloy actually killed them all, with Halloran's help? Or had he and Halloran taken turns? Only two witnesses had identified McCloy: Linda Vigliotti at the end, and the woman in the Brooklyn Heights supermarket some six months before. What would have happened if the Task Force had taken Halloran's picture around, a selection from his family album?

Only there was no family album to select from, not at least on Sally Magister's wall. Just the one picture: "Vincenzo" with his back to the camera, and Carter McCloy face front.

Something wasn't right either with the Suzi Lee murder, if my "interesting theory" had any basis. The one suspect—a celebrity, to judge from the silence surrounding his identity—had already been cleared. The doorman had seen him leave, and his departure had preceded the estimated time of the crime. The question remained: how had the killer gotten in, and out? For a time, attention had focused on the garage attendant. I'd seen him on TV. He'd sworn that he'd seen nobody enter, or leave, whom he didn't know.

Still, the timing fit Halloran. The same Halloran I'd watched in the rain, hunched under his jacket collar with the white scarf around his neck. *In Memoriam.* The same Halloran who'd gone upstairs and beaten his mistress black and blue, then raped her, then disappeared, then resurfaced in Roy Barger's tender custody.

But Halloran had claimed alibis the length of his shirt sleeve. And how could he have gotten in, and out?

I checked my chart again, from the Pillow Killer murders. No answers. But then, in the shower, trying to heat some life into the body, I got the glimmering of an idea. Not even that, more like the glimmering of a glimmering. Even so, it made me sick to my stomach.

I was in the midst of drying off when the phone rang. It

was the Counselor. I glanced at my watch: an unprecedented hour for him to call. Maybe he'd been up half the night too.

"I tried before," he said.

"I was out jogging."

"Oh," he said. I knew he was of the opinion that any form of exercise was life-threatening. "Where are you with it now?"

"I don't know," I said. "Nowhere really." I told him about my second conversation with Intaglio and the chart I'd worked up. Halloran, Powell, Fording, Stark, Villiers. Except for that once, never had just one of them been with McCloy and never all. Overkill and underkill. You could go several ways with the fact of it, at least one of which was pretty unthinkable.

"Get Derr on it," he said. "If you can't find Halloran, find the others."

"We've been trying that," I said.

"Try again," he said. "And get on to Margie Magister. Halloran's got to be somewhere. Get her to squeeze Barger. If you can't, then I'll come behind you."

I'd never known him to be anxious like that. I'd never known him to be leaning over my shoulder that closely.

I hung up and called Bobby Derr. I had to go three times through his answering machine: *Wake up, Bobby, it's time to get up; Wake up, Bobby, it's your mother calling; Bobby, get off your goddamn ass, Bobby, I need you,* and shouting, before he picked up, his voice blurry from sleep.

"Jesus Christ, Phil," he said, "what time is it?"

"Never mind. Remember: they kicked your ass in. I'm giving you the chance to get even."

"They didn't do it at eight o'clock in the . . ."

"Never mind."

I told him what I wanted.

Then, judging it was still too early to call Margie, I had breakfast and scanned the morning papers and found—what do you know?—a gossip-column item as follows:

> The battle for control of Magister Companies is heating up again, the dirtiest part yet to come. It

> may even involve the wildest of accusations against a hapless member of Margie Magister's slate. (Raffy Goldsmith, where are you when we need you the most?) With the special stockholders' meeting scheduled for next month—you asked for it, Margie!—stay tuned in for further mudslinging.

Like most such items, it managed to fill up space by saying nothing, and it could have come from any number of sources. Sure. I wondered if the Counselor had seen it.

I gave up waiting then, called Margie and got one of her blond youths on the phone.

Mrs. Magister wasn't available, he said, could he take a message? No, I said. This was Philip Revere; I wanted to talk to her; it was urgent. He was very sorry; Mrs. Magister had left orders not to be disturbed.

"I think you'd better disturb her," I told him. "I think she would want that. In fact, I think if you don't disturb her, you're going to end up very disturbed yourself."

"Okay, sir," he answered. "I'll see what I can do."

I had time to clean up, pour a second cup of coffee and light a (first) cigarette before the phone rang again.

"What's happened, Philip," Margie said anxiously, without preamble. "You and Charles both called. Has Vincent done something? Have you seen him?"

"We wanted to ask you the same question, Margie."

"What do you mean?"

"Halloran was in the city yesterday."

"He was? How do you know that? Did you see him?"

"No. But we both know somebody who did."

"Who is that? Philip, please don't tease me, tell me what you know."

There is—at the risk of repeating myself—no accounting for women. The last time I'd seen her, she'd been wearing his bruises and convinced that he was dangerous. Now, at least in tone, she sounded like a . . . like a . . .

Well, like a lover. A jilted lover, maybe, but still an anxious one.

"Philip? Are you there, Philip?"

"Yes, I'm here." In fact I was debating with myself what to tell her and how much. "Apparently he went to the police yesterday."

"The police? Why the police?"

"He claims he is being harassed. By me, among others. It's even in the papers this morning."

I read her the item from the gossip column.

"But what does that mean, Philip? What 'wild accusations'?"

"He claims he's being accused of murder."

"Of murder? What murder?"

"The Suzi Lee murder," I said.

Whatever I expected, I didn't get it. No screams, no protest, no tears. Nothing.

"We thought you might have known about it, Margie," I said.

"Why should I?"

"Because your own attorney, Mr. Barger, went with him to the police."

"Roy?"

"Come on, Margie," I said. "Do you expect me to believe you didn't ask Roy Barger to help him?"

"Ask Roy? No, I didn't. Well, yes, but only in the same way I asked you. I did tell him I was worried about Vincent, that I thought Vincent needed help. Was that the wrong thing? But not for Roy to go to the police with him. That's crazy."

I wondered why she thought it was so crazy if she thought Halloran hadn't done anything. But I already knew the answer to that one.

"I want to see him, Philip," she said.

"I do too."

"Yes, but I think you and Charles only want to hurt him."

"*Hurt* him?" I think I started to shout. "For God's sake, Margie, we think he killed someone! And not just one!"

"What does that mean: 'not just one'?"

"The McCloy murders," I said. "His great friend, Carter. I think he was involved in them up to his eyeballs!"

I'd gone further than I'd intended to. I didn't think it mattered. I thought she knew it too, enough of it, whether she'd admitted it to herself or not.

Silence. Then, softly:

"Why are you telling me this, Philip?"

"Because I want your help this time. I want to know where he is."

"I don't know that."

"Then I want you to find out."

"How?"

"It should be easy. All you have to do is call Roy Barger. You're still his client, aren't you? In fact, his principal client in the Magister situation? If you insist on it, I'm sure he'll tell you."

"You're right. Yes, you're right. I'll call him now."

"And then you'll call me back?" I said.

"Yes, Philip. I promise I will."

I didn't believe her then. I didn't entirely believe her later, at the office, when she called to tell me Barger didn't know where Halloran was. According to Barger, she said, Vincent had always called Roy, not vice versa, and only once had he left a number. Roy hadn't kept it. He thought it might have been a 516 number. 516 was Long Island, wasn't it? Yes, Margie, 516 was Long Island.

In addition, the previous day it had been Vincent who picked Roy up at Roy's office, then left after they'd had the meeting downtown. It had been Roy's impression that Vincent had driven in from outside the city, but that's all it was: an impression.

And that, per Margie, was all Barger had been able to tell her. He'd had no idea how she could reach Vincent.

Maybe so, maybe not.

My focus was on Barger. It didn't even occur to me that he wasn't the only person she'd have called. In any case, the Counselor had walked into my office while I was still talking to Margie and stood in the doorway, listening. When I hung up, I told him what she'd said.

"Try it," he said.

"Try what?"

"The 516 number. Call 516 Information. Doesn't his mother have a house somewhere on Long Island?"

I remembered it then, from the pictures in Sally Magister's loft: a large and rambling Victorian-style affair on a bluff, kids sitting on the broad front steps, and water in the background.

I called the 516 Information while the Counselor stood there. Sure enough, they had a listing under S. Magister.

I punched out the number.

Five, maybe six rings. Then it picked up, and a male, probably black, voice said:

"Magister residence."

"Who's this speaking, please?" I said.

"This is John, the caretaker. Who's this?"

I told him I was working on a research project for the Census Bureau. I said we were trying to determine how many people were actually living in the homes in his community.

"Actually living?" he said. "Well, there's only me in this one."

"You mean you're the only one who lives in the house?"

"Well, not all the time. It fills up in summer. Sometimes holidays."

"But right now you're the only one?"

"That's right."

"So I should put down a one?"

"If that's what's best."

"And your name's John Magister?"

This drew a chuckle from him.

"Heck no," he said. "I'm John Jackson."

"But I don't get it. If you're Jackson, who's Magister?"

"They *own* the place, mister. They're the summer people."

"And how many are there?"

"Well . . ." He hesitated. Maybe he was getting suspicious.

"Isn't there a Vincent?" I asked him.

"Yeah, there's a Vincent. He doesn't come around anymore. But he's not a Magister either. His . . . hey, who did you say you was?"

"I think I'll just put down a one," I told him. "Thank you very much, Mr. Jackson."

And I hung up.

"He says Halloran doesn't come around anymore," I told the Counselor.

"Then keep trying," he said.

"Trying what?"

"Maybe he's not the only one with a house on Long Island." He turned to leave. "I'll be upstairs," he said. "Let me know when you've talked to Derr."

I got to spend a lot of time with Information while I waited for Bobby to call in. After 516 I went through 203, which is southern Connecticut, and 914 (Westchester) and 609 (the south Jersey coast) for good measure. And drew blanks. Yes, there were Powells, Starks, Villiers, even one Fording. But none we were looking for.

Where do the rich go in November, the week before Thanksgiving? When it's too soon for skiing or the Caribbean?

On a hunch, I called Intaglio at his office.

"This is an old friend of yours," I said to him when he answered. "You don't have to say anything incriminating. I'm going to read you a list of names, with regard to certain written statements I know your friends have. If I'm right, just say: 'I can't talk to you now.' If I'm wrong, say: 'I'll call you back later.' Got it?"

"What is this sh—?" Intaglio started to say.

"Here goes," I interrupted. "Wilson 'Booger' Powell. C. Sprague Fording. Arthur A. 'Shrimp' Stark. Michael A. Villiers. That's it. Over to you."

He didn't say anything for long enough that I thought he might have hung up. Or was thinking. Or waiting for somebody to get out of earshot.

"Hello?" I said.

"I can't talk to you now," he answered. "I'll call you back later."

And though I said: "Wait a minute!" the phone went dead in my ear.

I took him to mean that I was part right and part wrong. Maybe my list was too long? It didn't matter, I thought.

It mattered even less, though, when Bobby Derr called in.

"I can't find a single one of them, Philly," he said. "I even went over to Powell's old man's office. Zero."

What I'd set Bobby to doing was to find one of the others on the alibi lists: Powell, Fording, Stark, Villiers. All the party boys. I'd figured we'd find at least one and start there, shaking a tree as we went.

In a funny way, that fit too—that he'd come up empty-handed—but I didn't see it right then.

"What do you mean, zero? You mean they're *all* out of town? That can't be, can it?"

"Beats me," he said. "Remember: Fording and Stark are the only ones who have jobs. The rest could be anywhere. I checked the addresses we've got. Like I said, I even went to Powell's old man's office. Nothing. Nobody's seen them around."

"Well, what did Powell's father say?"

"I didn't get as far as him. I only got his secretary."

"And?"

"She laughed at me. She said she didn't think Mr. Powell had seen his son in a decade. I told you, Philly, it may be your nickel, or Camelot's, but we're wasting our time."

"What's Powell's mother's name?" I said.

"Mrs. Powell," he answered, laughing.

"Are you sure?"

"Sure I'm . . ."

But then he hesitated. With good reason. Vince Halloran's mother wasn't Mrs. Halloran, and Carter McCloy's wasn't Mrs. McCloy either.

"Weren't Powell's parents divorced?" I asked him.

"I think so."

"Well? What name does she go under now?"

"I don't know. If anybody has that, you do, Philly. We did a rundown on McCloy's buddies, remember? Maybe it was in there, but you've got the file."

"Hold on a second," I said. "Let me look."

"It's your nickel, babe," he answered.

I rummaged through the file drawer of my desk and came up with the report he was talking about. And found the name. It wasn't Powell.

"Bryce," I said into the phone. "Mrs. Harmon P. Bryce. No address or phone number, just the name. Have you checked her out?"

He hadn't. He started to protest, but I cut him off.

I found the listing right in the Manhattan phone book. I jotted down the number on a pad and was about to pass it on to Bobby when I noticed the address. *Noticed* it? Jesus Christ, it was like it was printed in bold type.

Central Park West.

"Jesus Christ Almighty!" I shouted into the phone. Bobby tried to say something, but I went right on. "It's the same address! That's how they did it! Powell drives right in, his mother lives in the same building!"

"Who did what?" Bobby was saying. "What are you talking about?"

"The Lee murder. Suzi Lee. She lived in the same building as Powell's mother! That's how they got in. They drove in. What did the garage man say? He said he didn't see anybody he didn't know, right? Or course not! But he knew Powell. And he saw Powell. Powell drove in and Powell drove out, I'll bet the house on it!"

"Hold . . ."

"Never mind, Bobby. Find him. Find that garage attendant."

"How the hell am I supposed to do that? It's eleven in the morning. He's the night man."

"I don't give a damn. Find him where he lives. Try Powell on him. I'll bet he saw him. Then call me here."

Bobby started to say something about my nickel again, but I hung up on him.

And sat, with the adrenaline running.

And decided I couldn't wait for Bobby.

I tried the number in the phone book, Mrs. Harmon P. Bryce, and got the maid. No, Mrs. Bryce wasn't in, the maid said. Mr. Powell? No, of course he wasn't there. Yes, she knew Mr. Powell, but Mr. Powell didn't live there. Now who was this calling, please?

I said I was an old friend of the family's, but then I blew it without even knowing it.

I asked for Mr. Bryce.

Mr. Bryce, I learned, had been dead for four years.

And that was all I got out of the maid.

I had nothing to do till Bobby called in again, but I couldn't stand the waiting. I went back to the area code game I'd been playing before, and what do you know, the Information operator for 516 asked me to spell the name. I did. A moment later, the melodic computerized voice came on with: "The number you are looking for is . . ."

I wrote it down. I stared at it for a minute. Then I took the stairs, three at a time, to the Counselor's office, the slip of paper clutched in my hand.

Ms. Shapiro was with him when I burst in. I knew the scene well. Whenever the Counselor was trying to get away—as he was that Tuesday, for I knew he and his wife were due to leave, midday, for the house in the Hamptons—he drove Ms. Shapiro half nuts. Normally he'd be throwing papers at her, instructions too, and in the end, somehow, the mess on his desk would have been transferred to hers. But this time she was just standing there, steno pad and pen in hand, while the Counselor looked like he was having trouble concentrating.

I told him what I had.

"I think we've got it," I said excitedly. "I can feel it in my bones."

"Well, go ahead," he said, motioning. "Use the other phone." Then, to Ms. Shapiro: "Myrna, it'll have to wait."

"But you'll be late leaving," she protested.

"Then I'll be late," he retorted, and she went out, shutting the door behind her.

The so-called other phone was one of the Counselor's Wife's touches. When she'd redecorated his office, she'd put an easy chair, table and swing-over reading lamp in the far corner, next to the windows which gave out over the back of the house. The Counselor, as far as I knew, had never used it, but every once in a while the second phone came in handy, particularly when we didn't want people to know they were on the speakerphone.

I sat down in the chair and punched in the Bryce number.

Halfway through the fifth ring, it picked up and a sleepy girl's voice said: "Hullo?"

I went through my Census Bureau routine again. It didn't work so well this time. She bought it all right, but since she didn't live there, she couldn't answer the questions.

A young voice, I thought. A little blurry-sounding.

"Is Mrs. Bryce there?" I asked.

"Who? Oh, I guess that must be Booger's mom." A soft giggle. "No, she's not."

"Well, what about a Mr. Wilson Powell? Is he there?"

"You mean Booger? Yeah, he's around somewhere. You want to talk to him?"

"Yes, that would be very helpful. If you don't mind."

"Well, hold on. I'll have to go look for him."

She went off. I covered the mouthpiece with my hand and explained to the Counselor:

"It's some girl. Maybe Powell has a kid sister. She's gone to look for him."

Come to think of it, she was gone a long time. She never did come back on. But we didn't have to wait anywhere near that long.

I guess Vincent the Angel's ego just couldn't stand it. He must have picked up on another phone and heard my spiel, but now his young ego simply couldn't stand having me there and not revealing himself.

I heard the start of a laugh. Then, suddenly, his voice broke in:

"It's you, isn't it? Revere? I thought I recognized your voice. What a coincidence, that's beautiful! I've been waiting for you, amigo. What took you so long?"

I covered the mouthpiece again. "Halloran," I mouthed at the Counselor. He covered his lips with a finger and gently picked up at his desk.

"Hello, Vince," I said.

"My friends call me Hal."

"Hello, Hal," I said.

"Better," he said. "But you're sure some lame kind of investigator. What took you so long?"

"I guess I had other things to do," I said calmly.

"Other things? What other things?" He actually sounded indignant. Then he laughed again. "Oh yeah, I almost forgot. I heard somewhere you've been chasing after Margie. How're you making out?"

"You know she's worried about you," I said.

"Worried about me? Why is everybody so worried about me? *I'm* not worried about me. Let me tell you something, amigo. The whore's not worried about me, she's worried about the company. Do you know what I told her? I told her to sell it and let's party."

He seemed to find that funny.

"I saw what you did to her the last time you had a party, Hal," I said.

"Did you now? Well, let me give you a tip, amigo." His voice dropped. "Between us, she likes that stuff. The rough stuff. It turns her on. You ought to try it."

I didn't say anything.

"Most of them do," he said. "I bet it turns Nora on too, doesn't it?"

Oh Jesus, I thought. I glanced at the Counselor. Head down, listening, the brows hanging heavy over his eyes.

"Is Dr. Saroff next on your list, Hal?" I said.

"What list?"

"Your 'In Memoriam' list?"

"My what?"

"I think you heard what I said."

"Is that some kind of accusation, amigo? Hey, are you taping this conversation? I heard the click at the beginning, I know you're taping it. Well, why don't you bring your tape and we'll go downtown together with it, what do you think?"

I paused. The Counselor had his hand over his own mouthpiece and was motioning me to cover mine.

"Smart crazy," he said in a low voice. "Tell him you have to talk to him. Get him to come here."

I took my hand away.

Halloran was laughing again.

"Did you know Margie was trying to fix me up with her?" he said.

I didn't answer right away. Then:

"I think we ought to talk, Hal."

"Talk? Well, like that's what we're doing, isn't it? Aren't we talking?"

"I mean face to face."

"You mean *mano a mano*? That's great! Like who gets to choose the weapons?"

"No weapons," I said, trying to keep my voice level. "Just talk."

"Just talk," he repeated. "When do you want to make it?"

"Today," I said. "Why don't you come in to the office this afternoon? There'll be nobody else around. Just the two of us."

"No, man. That's not happening. You come out here, we'll have a party."

I hesitated. The Couselor was shaking his head in disapproval.

"What's the matter?" Halloran said. "Don't you like parties?"

"Okay," I said. "How long'll it take me?"

"That depends on whether you're flying or crawling, amigo."

"Driving," I said, feeling the urge—not a new one—to twist his neck and gritting it back.

The Counselor was gesturing at me. I tried to ignore it.

"Well, two and a half," Halloran said. "I do it in less; it'll take you more. Say, three o'clock if you get started soon. Who're you bringing? Let me guess. It won't be the cops, I guess. How about some broads? Nora? No, I guess not Nora. Too bad, I can't wait to meet Nora. Hey, what about Bobby? You know Bobby Derr, don't you? We haven't seen him in a long time. If you brought Bobby, we'd make it a real old-fashioned reunion."

"I'll try to bring Bobby," I told him. "Now give me the address."

This set him to laughing again.

"The *ad*-dress?" he shouted into the phone. "Like what kind of lame investigator are you, amigo? *You* find out the *ad*-dress!"

I did, as it happened, find out the *ad*-dress. That is, I got Ms. Shapiro to, by calling back the maid at Powell's mother's. In between, though, after I hung up on Halloran, I had a knockdown drag-out with the Counselor.

He didn't want me to go, plain and simple. He thought Halloran was too dangerous, even if I took Derr along.

"What's the alternative?" I said. "Anyway, I want this one for myself. For a lot of reasons."

"That's exactly what I'm worried about," he said.

"But what's the alternative? That we sit on our hands?"

"No," he said. "That we go back to the police with what you've got now."

"With what?" I said. "Maybe I've got enough for them to pull Powell in, but that's all. And meanwhile Halloran's out there, laughing at us. For Christ's sake, you heard what he said about Nora! He's taunting us with Nora!"

Needless to say, I don't often talk to the Counselor that way. He took it. Then he thought about it for a long minute, head down.

"All right, Phil," he said, looking up at me, running his hand through his hair. "This is what's going to happen. Nora's due back right after lunch. We should be at the house at five, five-thirty. No later. I'll give you till six. If I haven't heard from you by then, you'll have company."

I didn't ask him who. I was already on my way.

But he called me back.

"Do you still keep the gun in your car?" he asked. He knew perfectly well I did, with permit, in a locked glove compartment. Also, that I'd never used the damn thing beyond target practice.

I told him I had it.

Then he called me back again.

"What about Derr?" he said. "I don't want you going alone."

In fact I'd forgotten about Bobby.

"I'll take care of it," I said from his doorway. "I won't go without him."

"All right. But for God's sake, Phil, watch what you're doing and don't take chances."

On my way to grab my coat downstairs, I told Roger LeClerc to tell Bobby to meet me at my garage, but that if he wasn't there by twelve forty-five to forget it.

At 12:40 I had the Fiero out and idling on the street next to the garage. Then I spotted Bobby getting out of a taxi at the corner.

I honked at him, and he ran down the block and got in.

"You were right, babe," he said, breathless. "We just struck gold."

CHAPTER 16

He was right about one thing: it took us longer. Blame it on the Long Island Expressway, that graveyard of first gears and nerves. Blame it on whoever it was that had declared Thanksgiving a five-day weekend that year. Or so it seemed. Everybody out of the city and onto the highways. After a while we zigged over to the Northern State, then zagged back to the expressway. Stop and go; hurry up and wait. Finally, with the sun behind us and the shadows already stretching out, we got to the end of a long line of cars waiting for the Shelter Island ferry.

I piloted the Fiero around the line and pushed it in close to the front. Horns honked in outrage, and one guy in a business suit got out of his car, shouting. We brandished fists at each other, and he thought better of it. Still, we waited. The ferry ride takes all of a few minutes, once you get there. You can practically jump across. But all there is between the mainland and the island is this dinky ferry, and you wait.

We drove at last into the town of Shelter Island, a quaint-looking hamlet with lots of Victorian gingerbread and tall bare trees. Nobody had heard of the road we were looking for until we stopped in front of an old geezer who was sitting on some porch steps in a ragged sheepskin, watching the passing parade.

"Keep going," the geezer said, pointing, "till you can't go no further. Then you're there."

We kept going. Glimpses of water on one side. The trees taller, the houses bigger, the piles of dead leaves immense. Then we ran out of road.

A dead-end street to the left. At the end of the dead end, a sweep of lawn, a couple of acres' worth anyway, down to a half-timbered, Tudor-style mansion that looked more like a school than somebody's home. Beyond the mansion, the water. I thought it was the sound. Later I found out it's called Gardiner's Bay. Big house, big bay. To the right of the house, a smaller but still imposing Tudor structure with a dock running out behind it.

Not bad to be rich.

"This has got to be it," Bobby Derr said.

"If it isn't," I answered, "we're in trouble."

We drove in and parked in front of the arched doorway. No other cars, and no answer when we rang the front bell. I couldn't hear the bell inside. I rang again and banged the knocker, a big curved wrought-iron job, for good measure. Nothing.

"Shit," I said, wondering if Halloran was playing games with us.

As if in answer, a voice called out from a distance. We looked in its direction. Off to our right, maybe fifty yards away, a girl was waving to us from the doorway to the boathouse.

"Yo, you guys," she called. "Over here. There's nobody there."

We walked that way, down a graveled extension of the driveway. I noticed an old VW van parked just beyond the boathouse. No Alfa. The girl, when we got closer, looked not much more than sixteen, and she was all sweater. Straight blonde hair that came halfway down her back, denim shorts, bare feet, but mostly the oversized white sweater. Pretty. She looked like somebody's kid sister. She ought to be cold, I thought, even in the sweater.

"Hi! I'm Lucinda, what did you bring us?" Then, turning back inside and shouting: "Hey, Boog? They're here!"

We went inside. Some boathouse. The downstairs had been converted into one enormous glossy pine living area, complete with kitchen and bar and a whole wall of window giving out over the water. The upstairs was loggia or loft style, narrow staircase leading up with, from the glimpses I got of it, a lot of mattress on the bare floors. The decor? Well, you could call it party-time, or Carter McCloy Modern, take your choice. The mess reminded me of the apartment in the Eighties, so did the posters pushpinned to the pine.

Or Booger Powell Modern.

Powell was standing at the far end near the window, a beer can in his fist. He too was barefooted and in shorts, and with a gray sweatshirt that looked like he'd been wearing it a whole lot. He'd been nicknamed, I assumed, after the ballplayer, and in fact he resembled the one-time Orioles star, though in a slightly smaller version. The same tow hair, broad shoulders, tapering waist. Big hands. He had a ruddy, beefy face, our Powell did, and a blond stubble and small blue eyes, and I remembered him from that night in the Rosebud men's room, when McCloy had thrown up and Powell had taken a shot at me. Our Powell had a chirpy sort of voice, higher pitched than you'd expect. He also didn't look so hot: red in the eyes and a little wobbly on the pins.

"Help yourselves to a brew," he said by way of welcome, gesturing in the general direction of an oversized freezer-refrigerator combo.

"Aren't you going to introduce us?" the girl called Lucinda said, draping herself on him.

"This is Bobby," he said. "This is Revere. Now get lost."

Lucinda didn't seem to like the idea of getting lost. She turned to me, asked if I was sure I hadn't brought any coke. I said I was sure. Then Powell picked her up with one arm, deposited her halfway up one of the staircases to the loft and, patting her on the ass, told her to get lost again.

"Sit down," he said to us, waving to a large round table

near the window. "You're early. The party won't start for a while, but have a brew anyway." With that, he finished off the can he held, belched, squeezed and tossed the can, took another from the refrigerator and popped it. He made as if to toss cans to us, but we turned him down. He shrugged, then sprawled in a chair with his back to the window and drank, and we sat across from him.

"Well, how you doing, Bobby?" Powell said. "Long time no see."

"Not bad," Bobby said.

"Wish I could say the same. My mouth feels like the bottom of a birdcage. Life's a bitch, no kidding."

"And then you die," Bobby finished for him. "Party last night too?"

"You got it," Powell said with a groan.

I wondered how many others there were above our heads, where Lucinda had disappeared. I wondered too how long I'd be able to listen to their small talk.

"Where's Halloran?" I asked Powell.

"I don't know. He'll be back."

"When?"

He shrugged, a heavy gesture.

"Beats me," he said. "I only got up a little while ago. He said you'd show up, asked me to make you feel at home. He'll be back for the party. So make yourselves at home, will you? Pour yourselves a brew."

"I don't want a brew," I said.

I measured him. I think he saw it, because his eyes went small, wary, and then he looked at Bobby Derr, then at neither of us, and took a long pull on his beer. Something about him pissed me off. Maybe everything about him pissed me off. His style, or lack of. The way he looked, talked. Maybe it was that I was tired of the way they jerked the world around, and not only Halloran and McCloy but their kind, the golden boy set who can afford to get up in the middle of a Tuesday afternoon with hangovers and sit there complaining to you about it. With, in their case, a little murder now and then, when life became too much of a bitch.

Maybe I'd driven too far.

Maybe it was time to play the one hunch I had.

It didn't hurt any, I admit, knowing that Bobby had nailed Powell to the wall that morning.

Party time.

"How many did you kill yourself, Booger?" I said matter-of-factly.

"What? What did you say?" he chirped at me.

"Just what it sounded like. How many did you yourself kill?"

"Hey, wait a minute. That's not very funny."

"It's not supposed to be," I said. "Let's start with the 'In Memoriam' case. Suzi Lee. That one was you, wasn't it?"

Out of the corner of my eye, I saw Bobby Derr staring at me in surprise. This wasn't how we'd agreed to play it. But we'd expected Halloran, not Powell.

"You've gotta be out of your skull!" Powell said. "I think Suzi Lee was great!"

"I know you did," I said calmly. "You even taped her shows."

"That wasn't me. That was Mc—"

"I know, I know," I went on. "McCloy taped her, right? And McCloy's dead. So what difference does it make?"

"Well . . . ?" he said.

I measured him again. I thought he was scared a little, but not enough. Taken aback more than scared. And wide-awake. And beginning to wish, probably, that he wasn't there alone with us.

"We've got you dead to rights on Suzi Lee, Booger," I went on.

"What're you talking about?"

"Dead to rights," I repeated. Then, turning to Derr: "Tell him, Bobby."

"It's the garage attendant, Booger," Bobby said. "He puts you there the night Suzi was murdered."

He didn't tell him how much the garage attendant had cost us. At $100, he thought he might have seen Powell that night. At $200 he was sure of it. Going in and coming out.

"So what? My mother lives in the same building."

"We know that, Booger," I said, taking it back from Bobby.

"A very convenient coincidence. How else could a killer get in and out of the building without anybody paying attention? But let me ask you something, Booger. What do you think your mother has to say about whether you were there or not that night?"

I stared at him, not blinking, not budging.

"Go ahead, feller," I said. "Take a guess."

He stared back at me. I'd taken a shot in the dark, all right, but Powell and his buddies didn't exactly strike me as the type who went home for Friday night dinner.

"You bastard," he said in that chirping voice. "You talked to my mother?"

I didn't answer. I just looked at him.

"You dirty bastard," he said.

I let it lay there like that for a moment, then said:

"How else do you think we found you way out here in the boonies?"

No answer. He looked away from me, looked up, down, aside. I'd like to say some of the color drained from his ruddy complexion. Maybe it did at that.

"I think I better talk to a lawyer," he said finally.

"A lawyer?" I said. "What do you need a lawyer for? We're not cops. We're just here making ourselves at home, like you said."

He looked at his beer can, started to take a slug, then put it down. He stood up and, joining his hands, cracked his knuckles. Then sat down again.

"Maybe I'll take you up on the beer at that," I said, standing. "You want one, Bobby?"

"Why not?" Bobby said.

I went to the refrigerator. The bottom shelves were solid Bud.

"How about you, Booger?"

"No thanks," he answered from the window.

"Come on," I said, bringing him one anyway. I popped mine, and Bobby his, but Powell just let his sit, the condensation dripping slowly down the sides.

"You know, Booger," I said, sitting down again, "I hate to say it, but I think you're being a real jerk. Do you know what we really think, Bobby and me? We were talking about it on the way out here. We don't think you actually killed anybody, at least not Suzi Lee. We don't think you're the type. But we know you were there, and we can prove it. So what's the big deal? You helped somebody, that's all."

For a second I thought I'd gone a little too far. He seemed to pull himself inside, and his blue eyes went small, ugly.

"Who wrote it on her mirror, Booger? 'In Memoriam.' In memory of who, Booger? Carter McCloy?"

He shook his head, not so much denying anything but like he was trying to clear the cobwebs.

"You bastard," he said. "Hal said you'd do exactly what you're doing."

"What's that, Booger?"

"He said you'd try to split us up, pit one against the other. That's exactly what you're doing."

"Not really," I said, shaking my head. "If you ask me, that's Hal trying to save his neck. Maybe it's time you started doing that too."

I took a sip from the can. It tasted dry and empty, flat in spite of the bubbles. Budweiser standard.

"If you ask me, Booger," I went on, "you're being pig-headed. Do you realize the difference between murdering somebody and just being there? It's life and death, literally. You may think you're covering for Halloran, but you're the one who's got the problem."

"You can't prove anything," he answered.

"*We* don't have to prove anything," I said. "It proves itself. *You* were the one who was in the building."

"Hal wasn't with me," he said doggedly.

I gave Budweiser a second chance. Better, but not much.

"That's funny," I said, putting the can down again. "I'd've sworn I heard somewhere that you two were together that night, you and Hal. Didn't you hear that, Bobby?"

"Seems to me I did," Bobby said, starting to grin.

Powell got it then: the alibi game. To his credit, he didn't break. He just grunted.

"The statement, you mean?" he asked.

"Yeah," I said. "The statement. The one Halloran took to the police."

"Doesn't mean anything," he said. "So I made a mistake."

"Why'd you make a mistake?"

"Well, maybe Hal asked me to. He wanted people off his back, you included."

"But the police have it now."

"Big deal," he said. "So I made a mistake."

"You don't seem to get the point, Boog ole buddy," I said. "If you weren't with Halloran, you were still in the building. Either you were there alone or with somebody else. And if you were there alone, that makes you a suspect in a murder."

"You bastard," Powell said for the umpteenth time.

"I've been called worse," I answered. "And if you think I'm bad, I'm a pussycat compared to the cops when they'll think they've got the Suzi Lee killer in their hands. You tell him about it, Bobby. And tell him about plea bargains while you're at it. I've got to take a leak. Where's the john, Booger?"

He pointed up above. I went up the little staircase to the loft. I did in fact need the bathroom, but I also wanted to see what else was up there. And to give Powell time to think about what I'd said before I hit him with the rest of it.

Something wasn't right, though. Maybe Powell had been too easy. Obviously we were getting to him, and I thought there was a better-than-even chance we'd crack him right there and then. But where was Halloran? He was too smart to have left Powell alone with us unless he'd wanted to. Was this another Halloran joke, that we'd break Booger and still not be able to prove anything?

Party time.

Unlike the downstairs, the loft had been broken up into smaller rooms, some of which were separated by partitions which slid back and forth along floor and ceiling tracks. Curious, I pushed a couple open. Empty.

And then a third. Almost empty.

A girl was lying on a floor mattress, not Lucinda but of about the same size and age. Her back to me. Light brown hair. For clothes, a tie-dyed T-shirt. Bare ass. A portable radio was playing softly, something classical.

At first I thought she was asleep. Probably she was just a little stoned.

She rolled over in my direction, giggling a little. Pretty, except for the dark red contusion which ran off one cheekbone into the temple. A slurring voice.

"Hi," she said. "I bet you're the one from the Census Bureau."

"That's me," I said. "Were you the one I talked to?"

"I thought that was pretty neat, that trick you pulled."

"Thank you," I said. "Who told you it was a trick?"

"Hal did."

"Speaking of which, where is Hal?"

"Who cares?" she said, making a face.

"Did he do that to you?" I pointed at the bruise mark on her cheek.

"Who cares?" she repeated. "You're cuter than Hal. Why don't you come play with me?"

"Not now," I said. "It's not party time yet. Where's the john?"

By way of answer, she flung an arm in the direction behind me, then rolled back over away from me.

"Where's Hal?" I repeated, but she seemed to have gone back beyond hearing.

I found the bathroom and relieved myself. No, it wasn't right. Halloran had gone off, leaving us a couple of underage bimbos to play with and Powell to work over. Up to you, take your choice. As if he didn't care.

I remember glancing at my watch. It was a little after five. Already dark out. I had to call the Counselor before six, but to judge from the traffic we'd run into earlier, they wouldn't be at their house in the Hamptons till even later.

I went back downstairs. By then, Powell was working on the beer I'd brought him, and Bobby Derr looked glad to see me.

"You know," Powell said to me, "this is all so much baloney. So I was in the building that night? Big deal. My mother lives in the building."

I shrugged.

"It's all the same to me, Booger. The police have already interviewed everybody who lives in the building. Your mother didn't mention anything about seeing you that night."

"So what?"

"So, for one thing, what were you doing there?"

"That's my business."

"Yours and Halloran's, you mean."

"Hal wasn't there."

"So you say now. But that's not what you attested to."

"Like I say, maybe I made a mistake. Maybe I saw him later."

"You didn't see him later," I said.

"How do you know?"

"Because I was there," I said. "I know what time he got to Margie Magister's."

He stared at me, his lower lip curling out over his upper, like he didn't know whether to believe me or not. Then he shook his beer can and, finding it empty, crushed it in his ham fist. A show of macho, I thought, for his own benefit.

It was his turn to get the beers. He did. Then I said:

"Okay, Booger, have it your own way. But let's talk about something else. Let's talk about Cloy."

"What about Cloy?"

"Well, I've got an interesting theory about him. Actually more than a theory. I don't think he killed all those women."

Surprise, surprise, Booger Powell didn't say anything. He just continued to stare at me rigidly, like if he turned his head, he might be giving something away.

"I'll take it a step further, Booger: I don't think he killed *any* of them. Except for Linda Vigliotti, but he blew it. That was no surprise either, was it? That he blew it? Carter McCloy may have been a lot of other things, but he wasn't too accomplished at murder. Or even willing, was he? He kept putting it off and putting it off until the rest of you pushed him into it, and then he blew it. Linda Vigliotti was supposed to be his turn up at bat. Only he missed his turn the first time around, and Hal let him because he was Hal's old friend, and it blew your minds."

I paused to give him room to react. He didn't at first. He simply held my stare, or tried to. His version, I guess, of *mano a mano*.

"You're full of it," he said finally.

"Am I, Booger?" I went on. "Ask Bobby. Remember I was there the night Cloy was supposed to put the pillow to Linda. At Rosebud's, remember? In the john? When McCloy got so drunk he threw up? I was the one you knocked on his ass, remember? What you don't know is that I followed you out of Rosebud's that night. I know what happened and what didn't happen. Who do you think it was who put McCloy to bed that night, when he was too blind drunk to stand up and the rest of you, Bobby included, were off balling the Staten Island girls?"

I was so convincing at it, I even had myself convinced, but I couldn't quite break him. So I took him through the alibi game. For each of the Pillow Killer murders except the last ones, McCloy, when the Task Force interrogated him, had come up with multiple alibis. But never the identical cast of characters. I knew Powell was off McCloy's list on two of the crimes: the Park Slope one and the Riverside Drive one. Damned if you do, I said to myself, damned if you don't, and I went for broke.

"I don't know, Booger," I said, "but I've got you down for the Park Slope murder. What was her name again? That was yours, Booger. What do you say?"

"I'd say you're out of your mind," he answered.

"Am I? What do you think, Bobby?"

"I don't think you're out of your mind at all," Bobby Derr said.

"I've got people who'll testify I was nowhere near . . ." Powell tried to say, but I cut him off.

"Sure you do, Booger. It's all part of the alibi game. Funny thing, though: for a crime that took place over six months ago—and nobody's ever charged you with anything—you're still ready with your alibis. But what're you going to do about the evidence?"

"What evidence?"

"The police came up with something in Park Slope, Booger. Physical evidence. Seems like you were a little sloppy. Of course they couldn't match it up to McCloy because McCloy wasn't there, was he? But what'll happen when they try to match it to you?"

He thought about it. He looked at Bobby Derr—no help there—then back to me.

"You're lying," he said. "There was no evidence."

"I'm a lousy liar, Booger," I answered. "I'll let Bobby tell you what a lousy liar I am. Meanwhile, is there a phone I can use?"

It was 5:45. I went down to the other end of the ground floor and tried the Counselor's Hamptons number. No answer. I tried again at six, again at six fifteen, same result.

Like I'd figured, they'd gotten stuck in traffic.

There was one other interruption. At some point, Lucinda and the girl with the bruised cheek hung their heads over the balustrade above us and asked when the party was going to start.

Powell told them to get lost. They'd be called down when anybody wanted them. When they started to complain, he told them to beat it. He said he'd pound them if they didn't get out of sight.

Nice.

The girls, though, took him at his word and disappeared. By this time Powell was on his fifth or sixth beer. Halloran still hadn't showed, but I figured we had the old Booger about ready for the count. His face was red, and he wiped at sweat with his forearm even though the room was on the cool side.

"You know, Booger, I think you're right at that," I said, sitting down backwards on a chair, my arms propped over the top brace. "You ought to get a lawyer. You shouldn't take our word for anything. But the way I look at it is this: All you guys have got your asses covered six ways to Sunday . . . except you. You're in the building the night of the Suzi Lee murder—alone, you now say—and when the police find that out, they're going to sweat you real hard. Then, when we tell them to look at Park Slope in the Pillow Killer murders, you're going to be stuck. You and you alone. They'll throw away the key. The way it stands right now, I think I could get you a deal if you'll come clean. I even know where to go. His name is Andy Intaglio, he's in the Manhattan District Attorney's office, and he was on the Pillow Killer Task Force. You can take your time deciding if you want to, but my guess is that the longer you wait, the less likely anybody'll want to give you anything, much less immunity, and good ole Hal will be doing an 'In Memoriam' for you."

"You dirty bastard," Powell said in that chirping voice.

"Maybe so," I answered. "But I don't kill women for kicks."

He came halfway out of his chair at that, his face beet red.

Bobby Derr stood up at the same time.

"Come on, Booger," he said, his fists ready.

I got up with him, lifting my chair off the ground.

At this point, though, Wilson "Booger" Powell simply caved in. He slumped back, all two hundred-plus pounds of blond Ivy League masculinity. Like the air had gone out of the balloon.

"Speaking of good ole Hal," I pressed on, "where is he?"

"Wouldn't you like to know?" he answered tightly.

"What does that mean?"

"It means he's where you bastards can't get him, not unless you've got wings."

"But you said he'd be back!"

"Yeah, but I didn't say when."

At that he started to laugh, and I saw his square sweating face laughing up at me, his shoulders shaking with it, and the sight of it, plus what he said next, drove me past the edge.

I don't remember the order of events. At some point, there was a crashing of furniture. At some point I had Powell by the throat, the top of his sweatshirt bunched in my fist, and slammed against the window. His eyes bulged above me and his tongue came out, and we slipped in the mess and went down on the deck in a crash of glass and wood. At some point Bobby Derr was trying to pull me off him—"Jesus

Christ, Phil!" I remember him shouting—and the two girls were clawing at me and the phone was ringing. Then I remember being off him, standing over him, heaving and panting, and him cowering on the floor, arms above his head, against the shattered glass of the picture window.

And lest you think I went stark and raving for no reason, let me tell you what he said:

He said Halloran had gone to the city. Halloran and Stark.

And he said it was Nora Saroff's turn for In Memoriam.

The brown-haired girl was shouting at me. It was Mr. Camelot on the phone. He said it was urgent.

"Watch him, Bobby!" I called out to Derr. "If he so much as moves, kick his head in!"

I got on with the Counselor.

"I thought I'd better call, Phil," he started, "because . . ."

"I've been trying to reach you," I interrupted. "Where's Nora?"

"She's in the city," he said. "That's . . ."

"She's *where*?"

"In the city. What's wrong, Phil? That's . . ."

"God Almighty!"

"Phil! Phil!" His voice boomed, drowning mine. "For Christ's sake, calm down. Listen! I'm in the city too. We're both still here. That's why I'm calling you out there. We never left."

"Then where's Nora? Is she with you?"

"No, she isn't. The truth is: We don't know where she is. That's why we're still here. She had late appointments. We decided to wait to go out to the house till tonight. Now for God's sake, calm down and tell me what's wrong."

"Nothing's wrong," I must have babbled at him. "Nothing's wrong. Nothing's wrong at all. Only that Halloran's on the loose and he's going after her, that's all."

"All right, Phil. All right. Calm down. Start at the beginning. Take a deep breath, then tell me what's going on."

I took a deep breath. Then I told him, as quickly and succinctly as I could, what Powell had said. And that Vincent Angus Halloran was a killer, one, I thought, of a gang of party-boy killers, and on the loose in New York. And that Nora was his next target.

"All right, Phil," he said when I was done, in a surprisingly steady voice. "Now listen carefully. I won't repeat myself. Here's what I want you to do. As soon as I get off, I'm going to call Fincher, I'm going to call in the police, I'm going to find Nora. I want you here. Get here as fast as you can. Come right to the office. It'll take you how long?"

"Two and a half hours," I said.

"You're to come right to the office. I'll have instructions for you here."

"What about Powell?" I said.

"That's up to you. Leave Derr with him. Good-bye now, I'm hanging up. Get here as fast as you can."

I hung up and went back to where Bobby was standing over Powell and the two girls. It looked like the two girls were trying to administer to their fallen hero, and Powell, propped against a wall now, was rubbing his throat. His complexion had paled out, and he looked like he was going to throw up any second.

I pulled Bobby Derr aside and told him what I wanted. Moments later he came out to the Fiero with me, and I gave him my gun. But first I had one more go-around with Powell.

"Booger," I said, crouching next to him so I could see his eyes. "I want it all, everything you know, and fast."

"What about my deal?" he said, the chirping sound gone hoarse and whispery.

"What deal?"

"My immunity. The DA with the Wop name. You said you'd . . ."

I had to fight back the impulse.

"I'll tell Bobby what to do the minute I'm gone," I said. "He'll make the call. But if you don't talk right now, no deal."

He looked at me, I guess to see if I meant it. Then his head drooped. I think he started to cry.

"*Now*, Booger," I repeated.

"You got it right," he said in the same hoarse whisper. "We

took turns. I did the Park Slope one, but that was the only one. It wasn't me who did Suzi Lee. . . . Hal . . ."

He broke into a blubber then, and I slapped him once, hard, to make him stop.

"What's the plan with Nora?" I asked him.

"I don't know. All I know is he made an appointment to go see her."

"He *what*?"

"That's right. He said he was going to see his shrink, that's what he said. He said he even had an appointment. Then he took off, with Shrimp. It was before you got here."

"When was the appointment, Booger? What time? Where?"

He said he didn't know, and I grabbed his throat again, lifting him, shook him till the tears rolled out of his eyes. But he still swore he didn't know.

I let go of him. I told Bobby to call the Counselor the minute I'd gone, to pass on what Powell had just said. Then I told him to find Andy Intaglio, in Woodbridge, New Jersey, tell him what we had, let him decide what he wanted to do about Powell.

Then I drove off, alone, headed for New York.

CHAPTER 17

Parts of it I didn't learn about till later. There are still details I don't have the answers to. But that November night, driving faster than I dared against the steady flow of Thanksgiving traffic, I was in the dark every which way. I couldn't believe Nora had agreed to see Halloran professionally, not after what she'd said that morning in the park. Hadn't she told me she wasn't taking on anybody new? Hadn't she understood that Halloran might be more dangerous than Carter McCloy?

What I had no way of knowing was that not only had Margie Magister called Nora direct, but that Vincent Angus Halloran had called her himself, that same Tuesday.

He'd introduced himself as Carter McCloy's closest friend. Carter's suicide, he'd claimed, had pretty much wrecked his life. He hadn't been able to get over it. He'd diagnosed his own problems as one of deep, deep depression, to the point that he felt paralyzed in everything he did, or tried to do. Sex included. He knew Carter had thought the world of Dr. Saroff. He'd talked about her all the time. He, Vincent, understood that she wasn't taking on any new patients, but in a funny way, because of Carter, he didn't feel like a new patient. Wouldn't she see him just once? For one hour? Couldn't she at least orient him toward what he should do next?

Don't ask me to analyze Halloran for you. They say killers have got to escalate the risk each time, that they get their kicks out of danger. They also say they want to get caught. Who knows? Maybe Halloran, feeling the noose closing on him, had some such wish. Just possibly, though, he wanted to test his own invincibility.

In the end, he'd persuaded her. She'd even agreed to see him that same day, at five. Then, when he called back, she'd agreed to wait for him till he got there.

In between, he'd talked to yours truly. We must have passed each other on the road.

Needless to say, if Nora hadn't had something else to take care of, I've my doubts that she'd have agreed to either the first or the later appointment. The Counselor, for one thing, wasn't one to be kept waiting. But neither he nor anybody, myself included, knew about this something else.

Unless Halloran himself did, and exploited it?

I wouldn't have put it past him to mix a little blackmail into his insane party plans.

The other thing I had no way of knowing was that, sometime early that afternoon, she'd given Bud Fincher's people the slip. She'd done it in the cleverest of ways and knowing, obviously, exactly what she was doing. She'd taken a taxi downtown to one of the department stores and, by changing clothes in a dressing room, had succeeded in walking out right past Fincher's unsuspecting agent. By the time Fincher's man checked with a sales clerk and found out that Nora had bought the whole new outfit *before* trying it on, she'd disappeared.

Clearly she'd realized she was being followed, if not why.

The Counselor had only heard from her once, and then indirectly. Around four o'clock, she'd called Roger LeClerc. First she'd asked for me. Roger said he didn't know where I was, or when I'd be back. Then she'd told him to tell the Counselor that she'd be later than she thought, that he wasn't to wait, that she'd drive out to the Hamptons herself when she was done. She'd hung up before Roger could pass the call along.

By the time I got there, at about 9 P.M., the house was lit up like Christmas, top to bottom, and there were two cop cars double-parked in the street outside, their lights revolving, and the Counselor was storming the premises like a caged animal. I pulled in behind the cop cars, and even as I got out of the Fiero, he was shouting at me from the sidewalk. In his shirtsleeves despite the late-November cold, the great mane of his white hair glistening and wild in the light. I glimpsed Roger LeClerc peeping out of the open doorway behind him, like some kind of scared rabbit.

"For Christ's sake, Phil," the Counselor raged at me. "Where the hell have you been?"

I couldn't get a word out. He seemed to tower over me on the sidewalk, even though we're not all that different in size.

"I've got the whole damn city out looking for her, the police aren't worth a goddamn nickel, you goddamn well better find her!" and words more or less to that effect. I'd never seen him like that, wild and bloody-eyed, never heard him curse like that at his worst moments.

I talked to him, or at him, or tried to, while he strode back into the house.

"Did Fincher . . . ?"

"Damn Fincher! I've already fired Fincher. He's hiding in your office, but don't bother talking to him, it's a waste of time."

"Margie . . . ?"

"I talked to her. I even called Barger. Sally Magister. I told them they were defending a goddamn murderer. Nothing."

"What about her office?"

"Not there. It's surrounded, but goddamn it, she hasn't been there all day!"

"But I . . ."

"Goddamn it, Phil, stop chattering at me. Find her! What about Powell?"

"He said Halloran had an appointment with her, that's all."

"What do you mean, that's all?"

"That's all he knows."

"How the hell do you know?"

"I squeezed him. I squeezed him hard. I think that's all that's there."

By this time we were standing in the middle of the reception area downstairs. All the lights were on, and there were several men, in uniform and out, moving in and out of my office, and Roger LeClerc in their midst looked like a whirling dervish.

"Where's the dog?" I asked the Counselor. "She never goes anywhere for long without the dog."

"Muffin's here," he answered. "Upstairs." Then, lowering his voice: "Find her, Phil, for God's sake. If anything's happened to her, we'll never forgive ourselves. She's pregnant, you know, in addition to . . ."

I didn't hear the rest. I don't know what I said, or didn't. The news dumbfounded me. It made a lot of things fit, but at the same time it jumped a lot of others out of sync.

"Jesus," the Counselor said, staring at me. "Didn't you know that?"

I shook my head.

"I thought she'd have told you, of all people. But she's been so funny about it. Anyway, Phil, yes, it's true, at my advanced age I'm going to be a father. Well, what the hell? Worse things have happened to people." His voice, right there, had gone gentle—a phenomenon about as common as snowflakes in July. But then it hardened, and he gripped my shoulder, saying: "For Christ's sake, Phil, find her."

I went into my office. It had been turned into a kind of makeshift command post. My old friend Martindale, none other, the bigshot cop, was sitting at my desk, listening to somebody on the phone, while Bud Fincher sat on my couch, even more cadaverous-looking than usual and holding his bowed bullet head in his hands.

"Hello, Revere," Martindale said, hanging up the phone. "Welcome to one holy mess. That was Dr. Santamaria on the phone. No dice."

"Who's Santamaria?" I said.

"Dr. Anna Santamaria," Martindale said, looking down at a notepad. "Saroff's office mate. They split the use of the place. We've been hunting high and low for her, finally found her."

"What did she say?" Bud Fincher asked from the couch.

"Nothing is what she said. Tuesday afternoons, the place is Saroff's. She hasn't seen her, talked to her, in several days. She has no idea where she is."

I'd almost forgotten that Nora had changed offices, though I remembered her mentioning it. A time-sharing deal, she'd said. The new one was in the Nineties off Fifth, and the police had already broken into it and found no one.

I asked for a rundown on what they'd done. Martindale gave it to me succinctly and a lot more politely than the Martindale who'd tried to bite my head off in the Roosevelt. They had a list as long as the telephone book, he said, for people Nora knew, and a shorter one for Halloran. They'd been calling and, in some cases, sending people out to make contact. He showed me the lists in case I had any additions. I ran them down, noticing the checkmarks where they'd found the individuals in question. Margie was checked off; so was Sally Magister. In addition, they were checking the bars for Halloran and Stark and looking for the car. They'd gotten a description of the Alfa from Powell, who was still out in Shelter Island along with Bobby Derr and, within the last hour, the Suffolk County police.

Bud Fincher was clearly rattled. I guess the Counselor had hung him out to dry. In a way, I couldn't blame him. We'd known and used Bud for a long time, and once he himself had been a top-notch investigator. But he was less good at running an organization, which is what he now mostly did.

All Bud wanted to do was apologize. I didn't have time for that. I went over his rosters with him, all the places Nora had been in the days he'd had her under surveillance, all the people she'd seen or been seen with. Between Bud's operatives and the police, they'd located a good number of them but not all. But if the answer was in the ones they hadn't yet reached, then I failed to spot it.

The last person to have talked to her, as far as we knew,

was Roger LeClerc. The last one before Roger was the Counselor himself. She'd called him around one to tell him she'd be unable to leave till late in the afternoon. They'd discussed it. She'd wanted him to go on to the Hamptons himself; he'd decided to wait for her. Then nothing, for around three hours. Then the call to Roger LeClerc.

I called Roger in.

I think I've described him before. He's a spare and, I guess, good-looking black man from the Ivory Coast in Africa, by way of Paris, France. An impeccable, if rather exotic, dresser. He speaks English with an indescribable accent and has a manner which can be either ingratiating or high-handed, depending on who he's dealing with. Except, that is, when he blows his cool.

"Roger," I said, "I want you to calm down now. I want to hear exactly what Mrs. Camelot said when she called."

The fact that he'd been the last one to talk to her had clearly affected him. He seemed to take it as his personal responsibility that the Counselor's Wife was missing and in danger.

"Madame she says: Let me talk to Philippe. I tell her you are away. Madame she says: When will he be back? I say: I don't know, I don't think he'll be back. I say: Is there any message? Madame she says: 'Never mind, Ro-jay, I will find him elsewhere.' Then Madame she says I am to tell Monsieu' Camelo' she . . ."

"Wait a minute," I said. Roger jumped as if I'd set off a firecracker under him.

I told him again to calm down, simply to repeat the last part.

"'Never mind, Ro-jay,'" he quoted, "'I will find him elsewhere.' Is there anything wrong with that, Philippe?"

"Nothing wrong. But what did you think that meant?"

"I don't know," he said.

"It sounds like she knew where I was, doesn't it?"

"I don't know. She says: 'I will find him elsewhere.'"

"Okay," I said. "Now go on. Run through the rest of it."

He did, the part about the message she'd left for the

Counselor. Then she'd hung up on him, and he'd gone upstairs to deliver the message personally.

"Did she seem nervous?" I asked Roger.

He didn't think nervous. She'd sounded in a hurry, he thought, but Madame Camelo' usually sounded in a hurry.

I let him go then. Martindale by this time had vacated my desk and gone outside. I was alone with Bud Fincher.

I thought about it, then turned, punched out my home number on the phone and worked my beeper against the mouthpiece. It was a longshot all right, but that's what we were reduced to, and every once in a thousand days and nights longshots come home.

Like this one did.

There was only one message on my answering machine.

"Phil, where are you?" Her voice on the tape was hurried but calm enough. "I think I may have done something stupid. Please call me. Please don't tell Charles—I think I'd die—but I'm at my old office. I'll explain."

Then she'd given me a number.

Then nothing.

Then the three beeps signifying that the machine had run out of messages.

I hung up. The number she'd given me didn't sound familiar, but I punched it out. Seven, eight rings, no answer. Still. I think I started to sweat, inside and out. I made some excuse to Fincher, like going to the bathroom, and got up from my desk and went out into the reception area where I remember seeing the Counselor in discussion with Martindale and somebody else. I ducked around them, and Roger LeClerc, and out the front door.

But once I was outside in the street, I ran like hell.

I ran the blocks to the building on Park like I was Jesse Owens and the Nazis were coming after me to take their gold medals back.

No, delete that. There's no point trying to make a joke out of it.

I was scared witless.

No, not that either.

I kept thinking: She must have left that message hours before, probably right after she'd talked to Roger. By now she could be anywhere. But if she was anywhere, why hadn't she turned up? Why had nobody heard from her?

And what the hell was she doing in her *old* office, the one she'd shared with . . .

Jesus Christ in spades.

I burst into the lobby past the startled doorman and down past the elevators to the corridor that crooked around to her office door. I rang the bell, and banged, and was about to rear back and give it a battering-ram charge when I gave the doorknob a try.

Surprise, surprise. It turned in my hand.

I walked into the reception room. The lights were on. A chair had been knocked over right near the front door.

Nora's old office to my right.

I could hear sounds, but I couldn't place them. Soft crooning sounds, not menacing.

I went in.

My first impulse was to back out, tiptoe away. I thought I'd interrupted a love scene. Then, when Nora looked up at me, I saw thin streaks of blood coming out of her scalp, down one side of her face to her neck.

She was sitting on the floor, legs crossed under her, cradling someone in her lap. She'd been bent over him, rocking back and forth a little, talking or making sounds while she cradled his head.

The office was an unholy mess.

The guy with his head in her lap was Bill Biegler, a short shrink with a reddish blond mustache and a ruddy bald top. Except the top wasn't so ruddy right then.

Her one-time office partner. And more than that, I now guessed.

"Did Halloran do this?" I said.

She nodded, not saying anything. She'd lowered her head again. She just went on rocking slightly and crooning that low soft sound.

"When?" I asked.

She shrugged by way of an answer, then said quietly: "I don't know."

"Where did he go?"

Another shrug, and she went on rocking.

I examined her first. I'm no doctor, but the wound in her scalp seemed to have stopped bleeding, and the stains on her cheeks were as much from tears as blood. Her clothes were torn, but I saw no other signs of physical damage.

I eased Biegler off her lap, and she let me help her up. I led her to the patient's couch, and the only argument she gave me was when I tried to make her lie down.

"I'm all right, Phil," she said in a close-to-normal voice. She arched her neck down, then up. "A little in shock, but I'm all right. I'm worried about Bill. He had him tied up, in the chair. I got him free, but then I think he passed out."

I turned to Biegler. He was out all right. The color had drained from his normally ruddy cheeks, but when I took his wrist, I readily found his pulse beat.

"I think he needs mouth-to-mouth," Nora said behind me. "Do you know how to do that?"

I did know. I kneeled over Biegler, working his arms backward and forward while I breathed air into his lungs. He came to pretty quickly. I helped him to a half-sitting position, then supported him while, turning away, he threw up on the carpet.

He wanted water.

"In the bathroom," Nora said.

I went into the bathroom, filled a cup and brought it back to him. By that time he was sitting up, rubbing at his wrists.

"Just sip it," Nora told him.

I helped him hold the cup. He sipped some water, then handed it back to me. I put in on Nora's desk. Then I reached for her telephone.

"What are you doing, Phil?" she said.

"I'm calling for help. You two need to see a doctor."

"Not yet," she said.

"Nora, for God's sake, we've got the whole city out looking for you. There's a killer on the loose. The Counselor's half-crazy with . . ."

"Not yet," she repeated.

I stared at her from the desk. She sat on the patient's couch, supporting herself on her palms. One shoulder wing of her blouse flapped loose where it had been ripped from her body, and her hair looked frizzed and wild, but her gaze held mine.

"Here's what happened, Phil," she said, her voice slow but steady. "I'd made an appointment with Vincent Halloran. He was late. When he got here, he tried to attack me. Bill was working in his office. He heard me call for help. He came in, tried to stop it. Halloran slammed him against the wall, knocked him out.

"That's when I got this," Nora said, touching her head near the wound. "He knocked me down, my head hit against the edge of the desk. I think I was out for a minute myself, or dazed. By the time I came to, he had Bill trussed to that chair there."

I followed her pointing hand to a straight chair which lay on its side.

"He used my own tie, my own fucking belt," Biegler said. "He gagged me with that thing over there," pointing to a place on the carpet where I saw the white silk scarf. Then Biegler went back to massaging his ankles. "He tied me so fucking tight I still can't feel a thing."

"Then it was my turn," Nora said, her eyes still on mine.

"I'm amazed you're still alive," Biegler said.

"I am too. He told me he was going to kill me. He was doing it for Carter, he said. In Memoriam."

She stopped talking then. I watched the planes of her face break up, and she started to laugh. A weird laugh, like she'd been holding herself together barely and now it was time to let go.

"What happened?" I said.

"I think I scared him, Phil," she said, catching her breath. "It's unbelievable but I actually think I scared him. Actually I . . ."

Whatever she was going to say, though, she couldn't. She shook her head, more shudder than shake, and then I saw the shudder run down into her shoulders.

She hugged her torso with her arms, rocking a little on the couch. I watched her slowly regain control. Then she said, flat out:

"I told him he was going to have to rape me first, Phil. That's what I said. I said: 'Okay, go ahead and kill me, Vincent, but you're going to have to fuck me first.' Those were the words. I said: 'If you're going to kill me, fine, Vincent, but I want your come in me when you . . .'

"God," she said, interrupting herself. Her eyes went big. "I don't even know where I got it, where it came from. It's not instinctual, and I'm sure it's not what they recommend in rape prevention. But that's what I said, that's what was *in* me to say. I even . . . I even . . ."

I started toward her and Biegler, still on the floor, did too. The shuddering was back, and I thought she was about to break down.

"You don't have to talk about it, Nora," Biegler said.

But she waved us both off, hands gesturing.

"It's okay," she said. "I'm all right. Just a little shook, that's all."

She looked away from me, though, the one time in telling it.

"I don't think he believed me," she said. "Maybe he didn't know what to believe. But it stopped him, at least for a minute. Then I walked over to him—he was where you are, Phil—and I . . . I put my arms around his neck. I just put my arms around his neck and . . . I swayed. I said: 'Lucky Vincent. You're going to get to make love to me first, and then you can murder me.'"

She looked up at me somberly.

"It freaked him out, Phil," she said. "My touching him, I think, more than anything. Totally. I didn't know what was happening. One minute I literally expected he was going to kill me, the next he'd flung me down. I ended up on the floor. He ran out. He fled."

She paused, still staring at me like that wasn't all of it.

"When did this happen?" I asked them.

"It was sometime after eight," Biegler said. "I remember looking at my watch before."

"I honestly don't know," Nora said. "I lost all sense of time. Maybe it was after eight. I remember untying Bill, but I have no idea how long we were sitting here after that."

Nobody said anything for a minute. Nora was eyeing me oddly.

"There's something else I'd like you to know, Phil," she said finally, her voice small. "It's that I'm pregnant. I should have told you before now."

"It's okay," I answered. "I just heard that. Congratulations."

Maybe it wasn't so okay, I thought, maybe not at all okay. But that, I guessed, wasn't my lookout.

"I only hope to God I'm not going to have a miscarriage."

I didn't know how to answer that one. It was Biegler who ventured that she wouldn't. How he knew I've no idea.

"Go ahead, Phil," Nora said then from the couch. "Make your call now."

I'd had my hand on the phone without realizing it. I didn't lift it for a moment. Instead I looked at Biegler, then back at her.

"One thing, Nora," I said. "How much of what you've told me is the truth and how much did you just make up?"

"It's close enough," she said steadily. "Go ahead and call."

"Then what were you doing here, in this office? I thought you'd moved."

She thought about that briefly. Then:

"I was afraid of being alone. I'd agreed to see Halloran. However mistakenly, I thought I had an obligation to. At the same time, I knew he was dangerous. You yourself had told me you thought he was dangerous. I wanted someone nearby, in case there was trouble."

"That's not exactly . . ." Biegler began, but she cut him off.

"Yes, it is, Bill," she said firmly. "That's what I was trying to get through to you all afternoon."

Biegler didn't look any too happy about it, but he bought it.

And so, looking at it the way the rest of the world would, did I. She hadn't known about the "In Memoriam" letter we'd gotten because the Counselor hadn't told her. She hadn't even known about Halloran's possible connection to the Suzi Lee murder. Yes, she might have realized she was under surveillance, but maybe that had been the Counselor's doing for entirely other reasons.

"Go ahead, Phil," she said, staring at me again. "It's okay."

I made the call. And I stayed with them in silence till the Counselor showed up a few minutes later, followed by the police, followed by, unnecessary though it turned out to be, an Emergency Medical Squad complete with ambulance. The media, I figured, wouldn't be far behind. And I sat there, silent witness, during their first interview in her former office, while the Counselor sat next to her on the patient's couch, holding her hand.

Then at the first break, when the police started taking photographs of the scene, I slipped out and went into the night, past the revolving lights of the vehicles on Park Avenue, to look for a killer.

I'd have liked to have done it in style too, what Halloran had called the old *mano a mano*. To have gone back to the family castle, buckled on my mail and sword and ridden off into the night to bring the villain to justice. At lance point.

What did they call my adopted namesake's horse, old one-if-by-land Revere?

Maybe I'd have taken Fincher along, for redemption. He'd have looked better that way, his pointy head clanked over by a vizored helmet.

All for the fair Nora's honor.

Mixed metaphors anyway. For one thing, Paul Revere didn't wear armor. For another, I wasn't born Revere.

Besides, I was already too late.

I did get as far as the castle, its lights still ablaze in the night. The "family retainers," you could call them, were all gathered in the reception area, along with a couple of leftover uniformed cops. Roger was there, and Myrna Shapiro, and Charlotte McCullough, who I hadn't even realized was still in the building when I'd been there before, and

Althea from the residence upstairs, Bud Fincher, even Muffin. It was like our annual Christmas party, minus the king and queen.

"How is she, Phil?" Charlotte McCullough asked, worry lines creasing her broad florid face.

"She's okay," I said. "She's safe. Unhurt."

"Where did you find her?" somebody else asked.

"It's okay," I repeated. "I think they'll be back soon."

"Thank the Lord," Althea said, and then there was a rush of questions which I ducked, and I took Bud Fincher into my office.

I briefed him on what had happened. I guess he was relieved. He told me a couple of calls had come in in my absence.

"Derr's on his way into the city," he said. "He said to tell you the local police have Powell, also somebody called Fording?" I nodded. "But no sign of Halloran or the others. He said the Powell house is under surveillance, just in case."

"Who was the other call?" I asked.

"Somebody called Intaglio?"

"That's right."

"He's on his way in too. He was just leaving. He said to tell you he thought everything was under control in Shelter Island. He said: 'Tell Revere I owe him one.' He wanted to know where he could find you later, and I told him I didn't know but to try here."

I wanted Halloran. Bud said he had half a dozen of his people on hold, that he could put them into the field at a moment's notice. He suggested they start working the saloons and nightspots.

"For Christ's sake," I said, "we won't find him there. By this time he's got to know the whole NYPD is out looking for him. He's got the car. He could have just taken off, could be anywhere by now. Do the police have the car's description?"

"Yes, they do," Fincher answered. "Derr phoned it in before you even got here."

If Halloran had done anything rational, I figured, and there was no saying he had, then there were only two possibilities I knew to pursue, and neither required Fincher's help.

I told him so.

He went thin in the mouth, but nodded and left me alone.

Heads or tails. It came up heads in my mind. I punched out Margie's number.

She herself picked up, but only after a number of rings. Her voice was fuzzy.

"It's Phil," I said. "Are you all right?"

"Who? Me? Yes, I'm fine. I must have dozed off."

"Have you heard from Vincent?"

"From Vincent? No. Is he . . . ?" Then suddenly, catching herself, as though she'd only just remembered: "My God, Nora Saroff! Is she . . . ?"

"She's fine, Margie," I said. "I just saw her. He was there, but she's all right."

"Mon Dieu," she said. Then a long pause. Then, in a faint voice: "And Vincent? Where is he now?"

"I don't know. I thought he might have come to you, but if he hasn't by now, I don't think . . ."

Just then, though, Bud Fincher rushed back through my doorway, his eyes bright and motioning with his hand when he saw me talking.

I covered the mouthpiece.

"They got him!" he shouted at me. "It's on the police radio! He's been shot and . . ."

I shut up, took my hand away, and said into the phone:

"I'll call you back, Margie. Something's come up. I'll call you back."

I think she was trying to say something, but I hung up.

I went outside with Bud. The one remaining cop in the reception area confirmed it, and we headed out into the street where I heard it again, leaning in through the open window of the cop car.

The call had come into the downtown precinct that includes Tribeca. I'd had the right idea but, not that it mattered anymore, I'd flipped wrong.

Vincent Halloran had gone home all right, but all the way

home. To the converted loft building, with the posh duplex on top. Where his mother, Sally Magister, had greeted him with a bullet in the face.

Then she'd put the gun down and called the police.

PART FOUR

CHAPTER 18

It'd have been better if she'd killed him.

That's what Intaglio said. He invited me to lunch the next week, and we went to one of those Italian restaurants down off Grand Street where the fare can vary all the way from high-priced mediocre to reasonable sensational, depending on which menu they give you and whether your last name ends in a vowel. Like Colombo or Gambino.

Or, to judge from our meal, Intaglio.

In between, I had a quiet Thanksgiving, and that's putting the best face on it. The Counselor and his wife finally got off to their Hamptons house late on Wednesday. They even invited me to come along. Though I had no plans, I declined. I figured, rightly or wrongly, that they had plenty to sort out, and I didn't want to be a part of it.

I called Laura Hugger that Wednesday afternoon. I knew, from a couple of previous calls, that she'd been seeing someone, but I didn't know how serious it was. Plenty, apparently. Her secretary told me she'd already gone away for the weekend. I left a message that I'd called. I thought better of it the minute I hung up but decided against calling back, lest the secretary leave a second message, like Phil Revere called again to say he hadn't called the first time.

In the end I took Bobby Derr to Thanksgiving dinner. No, we didn't eat at the Roosevelt. We timed it so as not to interfere with the football games on TV, and I got a couple of bets down with my friendly neighborhood book. Then we went to one of New York's more famous traditional American joints, which had advertised all you could eat for a fixed price. No way of knowing, but I've a suspicion the Roosevelt would have been better.

I broke even on the games, so I lost on the vigorish.

The rest of the weekend I just sort of hung around. I thought about calling some of the other numbers in my book, but the thought passed. I jogged every day and swam in the health club I belong to but never get to. I went to the movies. At some point I realized I'd never called Margie Magister back that Tuesday night, but I didn't call her either. Nor she me.

"It'd have been better if she'd killed him," Andy Intaglio said.

"How so?"

"Well, if she'd killed him, he'd be dead and your friend Powell would be in the headlines. He'd never have gotten immunity."

"He what? You're giving him *immunity*?"

"That's what the man said."

"But why?"

"If I knew the answer to that one, pal, I'd be a partner in some big firm and I wouldn't be living in the boonies."

By this time we were into a platter of *vitello tonnato,* as good a version as I've ever encountered, having already worked our way through fresh oysters and a minestrone so thick you could eat it with a fork. I wasn't about to let the workings of Justice, New York City style, stunt my appetite. Still . . .

The argument, the way Intaglio explained it, worked like this:

Without Powell, they had nothing on Halloran other than aggravated assault plus breaking and entering, this in the Saroff/Biegler episode. Not even attempted murder; he hadn't actually tried to kill anybody. Without Powell, Suzi Lee went unsolved and Halloran's role as mastermind, or co-mastermind, in the Pillow Killer case got lost in a murk of alibis true and false. With Powell, though, they not only had Halloran but all the other members of what somebody in the media dubbed The Silver Spoon Gang, and the powers-that-be in New York City law enforcement could tie a ribbon around their files and get on to their next fiasco.

I had two glaring problems with it:

One was that, of all the members of the gang, the case against Powell was the most ironclad. Not so, according to Intaglio. The forensic evidence from the Park Slope murder had turned out inconclusive. It didn't rule Powell out, but it wouldn't convict him either. And if the testimony in the Suzi Lee case would put him irrefutably in the building at the time of the murder, nobody could prove he'd been on the roof, much less in Lee's apartment.

"But Jesus," I protested, "he *confessed* to me and Derr!"

"That was you, Phil, and according to Powell, you got it out of him under duress. By the time we got him, he had representation, and all he'd talk about was a deal."

"Don't tell me," I said. "Was it Barger again?"

Intaglio laughed and said no. As far as he knew, Roy Barger had dropped out of sight.

I happened to know better, but in a field other than murder.

What stuck in both our craws, though, was the near-certainty that Vincent Angus Holloran himself would never stand trial.

The way Intaglio put it, the bullet Sally Magister had fired might have failed to kill her son but it had pretty thoroughly rearranged his head. By the day we had lunch, his condition was called "stable," but even if the doctors pulled him through, their most optimistic medical prognosis for him was an institutionalized future. In no event would he ever be "competent" to stand trial.

"I don't know if I buy that," I said. "Hell, in a couple of years they'll probably even be able to transplant brains."

"Sure," Intaglio said, quoting me without knowing it, "and if pigs had wings they could fly."

He predicted better results on the other members of the gang. Wrongly, as it turned out. The granting of immunity to Powell brought on a veritable stampede of plea-bargaining attempts by the attorneys representing Sprague Fording, Shrimp Stark, and Michael Villiers. The DA's office resisted for a time, but public interest in these cases inevitably waned, and at the end of the day all three were allowed to plead guilty to crimes short of murders one and two. All three would do time. All three could expect to live long enough to try to hide it from their grandchildren.

The most interesting open item, at the time of that Grand Street lunch, was the legal fate of Sally Magister.

"Provided they can make her keep her mouth shut," Intaglio ventured over a stemmed glass of *zabaglione,* "self-defense ought to do it. Strictly between you and me, though, that's so much bullshit. I looked at the police report. No sign of a struggle, and Halloran was unarmed. If you ask me, she took one look at him when he came in the door that night, and then she shot his face off."

"I've got it a little different," I said. I was thinking of Halloran's half-smile and Vincenzo the angel. "I think he bragged about it first. I think she confronted him with it, and he said 'Mom, you don't know the half of it,' and then she shot him."

"Either way," Intaglio said, "premeditated or not, it's still attempted murder. But what jury will convict her? They'll say she was doing society a favor. They'll say her son's getting the best medical care money can buy, and it'll be her money. I'll bet they never even have to put her on the stand. Hell, I'll go a step further and bet it never even goes to a jury."

In this, Intaglio was right on the money.

In Memoriam.

I remember us standing on the sidewalk with our coat collars up, and feeling the cold air on my skin but warm in the belly. We'd been talking about what made people like McCloy and Halloran, who'd been born with everything, kill strangers for kicks. But we'd run out of answers, and I had a meeting to get to that afternoon—the full-scale one at the Firm, a follow-up to our tête-à-tête with Roy Barger.

"Thanks for the meal," I said. "Hell, thanks for the feast."

"Don't thank me," Intaglio said. "It was the least I could do. Remember, you gave us the case, pal."

What case? I thought. I didn't say it, but I didn't have to.

"What's the matter?" Intaglio said.

"Nothing. It's sort of depressing, that's all. All of it."

"Depressing? Come on, Phil, you weren't born yesterday. We'll come out a lot better on this one than we usually do. It's the same old story: most of the time people with money don't pay for their sins. What more can I tell you?"

Nothing more, I guessed.

"Besides," he added, grinning, "there are the fringe benefits."

"Like what?"

"Like you and I got to know each other. Like maybe you found out we're not all of us plastic and polyester down here."

I started to protest but then grinned back at him instead. We shook hands.

"Keep in touch," Intaglio said.

CHAPTER 19

Roy Barger, as I've mentioned, had already been in to see us. He'd asked the Counselor for a one-on-one meeting and the Counselor had agreed, except that his "one" had to include me.

"Congratulations, Counselor!" Barger had said with a broad smile, hand outstretched, as soon as Ms. Shapiro ushered him in.

"Congratulations for what?" the Counselor replied, standing to shake hands.

"Why, I read in the papers that you're going to be a father. I think that's marvelous! It's not your first, is it?"

"Thank you," the Counselor said while Barger turned to shake hands with me, "but it is my first. I suppose I'm a late starter."

"Nonsense," Barger said. "It'll keep you young."

"That's just what my wife says," said the Counselor, smiling back benignly.

I should put in that, whatever had gone down between them or hadn't, the Counselor had returned from Thanksgiving in high spirits. Nora had stayed in the Hamptons. She was fine, he'd said. More important, she'd been to her gynecologist and all was well on that score. As for the media, well, the headline PREG SHRINK THWARTS KILLER pretty well summed it up, and from everything I'd seen, they'd swallowed Nora's version whole.

"I've come with hat in hand, Charles," Roy Barger said, sitting down and gesturing with his manicured hands. "My client wants out."

He wasn't, for the record, holding his hat or anything else, but I guess his hands were up in the air to show that everything was going to be aboveboard this time.

"Who're you representing these days?" the Counselor asked.

"Why, Margie Magister. Who else?"

"Well, Phil tells me you've had a very active client list lately."

"What . . . ?" Barger didn't seem to get the point at first. But then he shifted in his chair and, reaching across, touched my arm. "Oh that," he said. "You mean Halloran?"

"Yes, Halloran," I answered.

"Well, look, I only got involved with Halloran for the family's sake."

"Is that so?" I said. "Margie told me she didn't know anything about it."

"Well, but it's what they would have wanted. Look, Phil, Charles," glancing from one to the other of us, "if what you want is an act of contrition, then you've got it. I apologize to both of you. I made the mistake of believing Vincent, strange as that may sound now. It's a tragedy, a terrible tragedy for the family. Well, we all make mistakes, don't we?"

For Roy Barger to admit that he'd ever made a mistake in his career chalked up one for our side. At least that's what the Counselor said later.

"To business," Barger said. "Gentlemen, my client is prepared to sell her entire interest in Magister Companies to the brothers at a reasonable price to be negotiated, and to settle all outstanding differences between them."

The Counselor worked at a pipe and, rare event, got it lit on the first try.

"The word 'reasonable' is yours, Roy," he observed.

"What do you mean?"

"You said 'a reasonable price.' When Margie called me this morning, she gave me to understand that what's happened has been such a shock to her that she wants out . . . at any price."

Barger struggled with it. He said nobody could expect Margie to sell at "any" price. The price ought to be reasonable; it ought to bear some relationship to value. The Counselor asked him if he had a figure in mind, knowing full well, as did Barger, that Margie had said she'd accept any figure the Counselor himself thought was fair.

Barger suggested market plus a premium. When pressed, he mentioned $60 a share. This, he pointed out, represented quite a significant sacrifice from the figure his client had originally put on the table.

The Counselor said he could just as logically defend market *minus* a premium. The stock, which had peaked at just below 50 the day of Raffy Goldsmith's semi-raid, had since trended downward to the low 40s.

Roy Barger suffered in silence—another first. Then, clearing his throat:

"So, Counselor. Name your price."

"It's not for me to set a price," the Counselor answered.

"Well? What's your recommendation going to be?"

"All I'm going to recommend is that a meeting of the principals be convened as soon as possible. Let's get on with it. Also that Bob Magister come to the table with an offer, his best and only one, and that it be submitted on a take-it-or-leave-it basis."

Barger waited for more, but there was no more. He didn't shake hands when he got up to go, which may also have been because his palms were sweating.

"One other thing," he said at the door. "You should know, Charles, that I no longer speak for Sally."

"I know that, Roy," said the Counselor.

The main conference room at the Firm, I've always thought, would make a fine argument for socializing the legal profession. The art which hangs on its walls is, I understand, worth a hell of a lot more than most of us working stiffs can expect to earn in a lifetime. The room contains a full-scale film projection unit, a bar which would rival the Plaza's, and heavy mahogany furniture with leather and brass trim which can be arranged in various configurations, depending upon the event.

They'd decided on a horseshoe arrangement for the Magister meeting, so Hank Rand had told me that morning, with Doug McClintock and the Counselor presiding, as informal co-chairmen, from the closed end. Margie, Hank Rand expected, would be there. They weren't sure about Sally, who'd been in seclusion since the shooting.

It turned out differently.

By the time I got there, the room was already more than half-filled. Lawyers mostly, and their staffs. A lot of commotion and paperwork and handshakes and huddled conversations. Then the Magister brothers came in, escorted by Doug McClintock and a retinue of advisers I mostly recognized, and the Counselor motioned to me to come sit next to him at the head of the horseshoe.

But still no Margie, no Sally.

Then Roy Barger stood up.

His client, he said, had chosen not to attend the meeting, but she had empowered him to act in her behalf with respect to all matters.

"I have here," Barger went on, "a power of attorney which grants me said rights. I apologize for the fact that I only have two copies but—small confession—my copier broke down this morning."

This brought laughter from the room, and the Counselor, leaning toward me, said: "He's decided to play the poor relative in the midst of luxury. I doubt it'll work."

A staff member disappeared with one copy while another worked the center of the horseshoe, showing the document to whoever wanted to inspect it.

I saw Doug McClintock bend over the Counselor, wearing a worried expression.

"What do we do about Sally?" he asked in low tones.

"Find out if her attorneys are similarly empowered."

"I don't think they are."

"It never hurts to ask," the Counselor said.

McClintock straightened, but he never got to put the question. Just then a door opened and Sally Magister herself was ushered in.

A far cry, I should say, from the frizzy-haired redhead in coveralls who'd once showed me the door of her Tribeca duplex, even from the press conference at Margie's. She had on a tweed suit, predominantly wine-colored and severely tailored, the skirt short and the jacket long, high heels, and a little hat, with veil, of the same material as the suit. She carried a black leather portfolio under one arm. The heels made her seem even taller, and the face beneath the veil looked chiseled, intense.

The Magister brothers rose, three as one, and encircled her. Somebody said it was her first public appearance since the tragedy. Somebody else said it was the first time the family members had seen her since then. I watched her lift the veil over the front lip of her hat and allow each of her brothers to kiss her, but her lips never touched their cheeks. Then there was some confusion about where she was to sit. Her attorneys were on the far side of the horseshoe, near Barger, but Young Bob wanted her with him. He insisted on it. Finally, several of the brothers' lawyers changed places with Sally's, making room, and then McClintock called the meeting to order.

"I think it appropriate," he said in a somber voice, "given the circumstances, that we take a moment to thank Ms. Magister for joining us and that we express our deepest sympathies to her."

I heard a couple of hear-hears, but Sally Magister herself cut them off.

"Thank you, Douglas," she said, staring hard at him, "but that's not necessary. I learned a long time ago, in this family, that when an animal goes bad and betrays its breeding, you have no choice but to put it down. That I didn't succeed in this regard is what's truly reprehensible. Now let's get to our business, please."

A conversation-stopper, needless to say. A hush fell over the room. I studied the Magister faces, all in a row, and thought about something Intaglio had said, to the effect that self-defense would play as long as Sally Magister stayed off the witness stand.

Amen.

"Very well," McClintock said, recovering. "The purpose of this meeting is for Robert Worth Magister, Jr., president of Magister Companies, Inc., and with the approval of his board of directors, to put forth an offer to buy the outstanding shares in the corporation held by certain members of his family or which would accrue to said members under the terms of the will of Robert Worth Magister, deceased. Bob?" McClintock looked up from his notes and found Young Bob. "It's your show."

Bob Magister's lawyers then worked the horseshoe, distributing copies of the so-called deal memo, while Young Bob summarized its contents.

"Putting aside all the fine print," he said, "our offer is for market value, whatever that may be, at the end of trading today on the New York Stock Exchange."

I glimpsed the look of relief on Roy Barger's face as he listened and skimmed the memorandum. Market value was a far cry from 72, even from the 60 he'd ventured in our office, but it could have been worse. In fact I'd expected it would be.

"Was that your number?" I wrote on a scratch pad, which I then handed to the Counselor.

He shook his head, leaned over and whispered at me, cupping his hand by his mouth:

"No. I recommended market less five. But they said they didn't want to hurt Sally."

I looked at him in surprise.

"Does she already know the number?" I asked him softly.

He shrugged.

"What do I know?" he whispered, cupping his hand again. "But it's their money."

McClintock was asking Roy Barger if he was ready to respond, but Barger wanted Sally to go first. Ms. Magister, he said, was a member of the family after all, whereas he was just a simple attorney. But, Sally's attorneys argued back, Barger represented the larger stockholder. They went at it across the horseshoe until somebody suggested the Counselor arbitrate.

"You've made your point, Roy," the Counselor said. "Now let's have your answer."

"Do I understand," Barger shot back, "that if I choose not to respond, the offer is withdrawn at the end of this meeting?"

"Come on, Roy," the Counselor answered. "You agreed to this meeting. You knew it was going to be take it or leave it."

"Right," Barger said. He paused, his eyes scanning the room, like he couldn't resist a small moment of suspense. Then: "I want it known that I personally have strong reservations. But on behalf of my client . . . I accept."

Even two seats away, I could hear Doug McClintock's sigh. Of relief, presumably.

Then it was Sally's turn.

One of her attorneys tried to say something, but she shut him up.

"Well, I don't accept," she said peremptorily, fixing the Counselor with that determined, chiseled gaze. "It's not the money. I leave it to you men to argue dollars. But I've made my position clear from the beginning. The only way I'll sell is if you'll sell me the magazine division."

A moment—a long one—of stunned silence. Apparently nobody, much less her own lawyers, had known this was coming.

Then Young Bob was standing, his brothers with him, looking down at his sister.

"You realize, Sally," he said, "that this means the break-up of the family?"

She didn't stand, didn't so much as shift her gaze.

"The family, Bob," she answered, "has been a sick joke for as long as you or I can remember."

She too, it turned out, had a proposal in writing. She took it out of the black portfolio and put it on the table in front of her brothers. I learned later that it was based on whatever her brothers' offer turned out to be, prorated to match the magazine division's share of the company's revenues. Fair enough, it seemed to me. But then, like Sally said, it wasn't about money.

Young Bob asked for a recess, and the three brothers left the room, followed by their personal attorneys, followed by Doug McClintock and, at a signal from McClintock, Hank Rand. The Firm, it seemed, had decided not to be left out.

At some point in the wait that followed, the Counselor wrote the figure $7,000 on his pad and pushed it in front of me. That, he said, was a conservative guess at what Young Bob's recess had cost the family so far in legal fees. A little later, he crossed out the 7 and changed it to a 10. Then I saw Sally look at her watch, and she sent one of her attorneys out with the message that she would stay no more than another fifteen minutes. The attorney came back immediately, accompanied by Stafford Magister, who asked Sally if she would join them outside, and Doug McClintock, looking worried, who did likewise with the Counselor.

Sally Magister left with them, the Counselor too. And Roy Barger started to sweat. Maybe he thought the Magisters would pull the offer if Sally refused. Maybe he thought that might mean a lawsuit, possibly a lucrative one, but who knew what his client would decide? By this time, the stock market had closed for the day. The last quote on Magister, we learned, had been 42 and 1/8, and Roy Barger could do the arithmetic. He—or his client—stood to make millions. But the decision was being made outside his control, and this drove him crazy.

The Magisters never did come back to the conference room. I guess they felt they didn't have to. All the power people, after all, were outside, and only the spear carriers (namely the attorneys) were left behind.

They left it to Doug McClintock to make the announcement.

"Gentlemen," he said from the doorway, the Counselor towering next to him, "Bob Magister has asked me to thank you all for coming and to tell you that he and his sister have reached agreement. The Magister magazine division will be sold to Sally Magister. They've left it to us," with a McClintock sigh, "to draw up the paperwork."

And so it ended.

CHAPTER 20

For the record, the Magister brothers did have backing. It came, sign of the times, from overseas, and by the end of the following year, the German-based communications conglomerate which had financed the family buyout had swallowed up all the remaining outstanding shares in the company.

The Firm, nevertheless, has managed to hang in there. They still represent the so-called Magister Division and are angling—"positioning themselves" is the phrase they use—for more of the new owners' legal business. On the rare occasions when I talk to him, I like to ask Hank Rand how his German's coming, but he takes teasing less well since he's made senior partner.

Another prediction come true: Sally Magister never did stand trial. Her oldest son, as far as I know, remains what people call a "vegetable," although I've never understood the term. Vegetables, it seems to me, lead healthy and useful lives, if short ones; Vincent Angus Halloran will never be of use to anyone, and he died long before he died.

I've left the personal parts for last.

Roy Barger mentioned, that last afternoon at the Firm, that Margie wanted to see me. She took to phoning me too. I ducked her for about a week—I guess I'd had enough of the Magister clan—but one dark afternoon, in the trough between Thanksgiving and Christmas, her call found me at my desk.

"Philippe!" she said, with the French pronunciation. "Haven't you gotten my messages?"

I said something about having been awfully busy.

"Busy with what? Busy with women, I would bet. But I must see you before I go away. Why don't you come to dinner tonight?"

The difference between dinner and supper, she explained provocatively, was that dinner left you with the rest of the evening free.

I told her I was sorry but that I had a date, which was true. She asked who it was. I said nobody she knew. Finally we agreed to meet for a drink that same afternoon. I suggested the Madison Avenue bar we'd been to before. No, she thought that was bad luck. The Pierre, she thought. The little bar at the Pierre. That was much more romantic. If I'd give her forty-five minutes, she'd meet me at the Pierre. Her treat, she insisted.

I walked down Madison, then Fifth, in the enveloping gloom of those shortened afternoons and waited for her in the Pierre bar. She came rushing in some fifteen minutes later, in a chic black cloth coat with a fur collar high around her neck and her cheeks rouged either by the cold or makeup. She flung her arms around my neck and kissed me on the mouth. She'd done something to her hair. The bangs were gone, the black hair swept back off her forehead. The full-face look, I thought, made her older but somehow more beautiful.

We sat at a little table near the window, and she held my hand while she told me about her plans. I'd thought, over the phone, that she was just going away for the holidays, but she meant more than that. In fact, she'd already put her apartment on the market.

"I'm leaving New York, Philippe," she said. "There's nothing here for me anymore. It's not that I made a mistake—I love New York—but it's over, all that. I'm going back to the south of France. I have that house there, you know, Bob's house, but," making a face, "I'm going to sell that one too. But the Côte d'Azur is marvelous in winter."

"It sounds like you're cashing out," I said.

"Yes, cash. One can do everything with cash. Tell me, Philippe, what would you do if you suddenly had all the cash in the world, all you could ever imagine needing? What would you do?"

"I don't know," I said with a laugh. "That's one thing I've never had to lose sleep over."

"Of course you haven't. Do you think it was any different for me? But imagine yourself with all Margie's cash. What would you do?"

"I don't know. Probably I'd travel, go to all the places I've never seen. I'd want some time to figure out how to spend the rest of it."

"Exactly," she said. "This is exactly what I am going to do now." Then, squeezing my hand and eyeing me excitedly: "But here is the thing, Philippe. Why don't you come spend it with me?"

I took it as a joke, spur of the moment, but she looked serious about it. One hundred percent serious, in fact. I was sufficiently taken aback to blurt out the first thing that came into my head:

"Why me, Margie? I'd have thought I was too old for you."

I saw her wince a little, but her eyes held mine.

"Touché," she said. "But you know, ever since what happened, I've thought and thought about that. About Vincent. The others too but mostly Vincent. I have asked myself: Margie, Margie, what did you think you were doing? And do you know what I think? Well, I was trying to help him, yes. Somehow I knew he was in big trouble. But more than this, I think I was trying to stay young too.

"Now, though," she went on, "that's over. It was a terrible time for me, believe me. Terrible like a bad dream. But what

Sally did woke me up from the bad dream. I'm a different person now. I think I'm ready for what you Americans call a 'mature relationship.' With," smiling at me now, "someone my own age. Someone such as you, my dear Philippe Revere."

She rushed on before I could say anything. Why was it such a crazy idea? What was wrong with people acting on an impulse? We would have all the money we could ever imagine wanting. For two people who had worked most of their lives, we would never have to work again if we didn't want to. We could go anywhere, live anywhere, buy anything, do anything. Do nothing. She thought she would love doing nothing with me.

She tried, as she described how it would be, to gauge my reaction. Apparently she misread it.

"What will happen if it *doesn't* work, is that what you're worried about? Why, that's so simple, darling. We'll have Charles or Roy work up an agreement, they'll know what to say. If it doesn't work and we split up, then you will still have far more money than you'll ever have slaving for your stupid Charles. But it *will* work, darling. I know it will. I can be wonderful for a man, the right man, believe me, Philippe."

I did believe that, and I told her so. I also believed there had been times before, and maybe there would be again, when an offer like Margie's would have had me running to the nearest drugstore to buy a toothbrush and then onto the plane, no looking back, and I told her that too. But the timing was wrong, at least for that season.

I remember standing outside the Pierre with her, after I'd succeeded in paying the bar bill. It was dark, cold, and the avenue was jammed with taxis plying the rush-hour trade. She'd asked me to walk her home anyway, and we headed up the sidewalk, her arm tucked inside mine.

"So there is someone else, is there?" she asked, matching her stride to mine.

"Yes, in a way," I answered.

"What do you mean, 'in a way'? Is there or isn't there?"

"Yes, there is."

"Well, tell me about her, this lucky other woman."

"Her name is Laura," I said.

"Yes? And is she pretty?"

"I think so."

"And how old?"

"A little younger than I am."

"And is she rich too?"

"No," I said, laughing. "She works for a living."

"And where does she work?"

"For an advertising agency."

"Well, what's so wonderful about all that?" she asked irritably. "What is it then that makes you love her?"

I didn't know that I did, at least up till that minute.

By this time, we'd reached the canopy over the entrance to her building. She turned to face me under it, taking both my hands. The rouge was in her cheeks and the smell of her perfume rising from the fur collar of her coat.

"Why don't you come upstairs anyway, just for a little while?"

In spite of myself, she must have read my expression. I'd realized, or thought I'd realized, that not all the money in the world could keep Margie Magister from the fear of being alone. Realized it, I should add, because I knew the feeling well. And so, just for that minute, I felt sorry for her.

She read that all right. The dancing light went out of her eyes.

"Good-bye, Philippe," she said tersely. And turned and was gone, and I haven't heard from her since.

The Laura Hugger part.

Like I said, I'd called her just before Thanksgiving to learn that she'd already gone off for the weekend. I spent the nothing weekend as described and also, which I haven't mentioned, got through my own short stint as a celebrity: the guy who'd helped the police crack the Pillow Killer and In Memoriam cases, etc., etc.

Laura called back the following Monday and missed me,

and I called her back and missed her, and back and forth we went, answering machine style, till one night I found her at home.

"So how's the famous Phil Revere?" she said for openers.

"Not so famous," I answered.

"What's wrong? From what I've seen, you've practically become an urban hero overnight."

"Maybe that's what's wrong," I said. "Other than that I'd like to see you."

She didn't respond to that one.

"How was your Thanksgiving?" she said.

"Nowhere. Yours?"

"Equally nowhere."

"Really? I heard you'd gotten away."

"True."

"Well? Not alone, I assume. Who was the guy?"

"Never mind," she said.

"That bad, huh?"

She started to laugh. Then I did too. Then I said:

"Can I come over?"

"When?"

"Right now."

"But it's the middle of the night, practically."

"So what? We've got six hours left. Seven if I hurry."

"You're crazy."

"No, I'm not crazy. I think I was for a while, but I'm not now."

So we started up again, as we had other times, and I took to sleeping most nights at Laura's again, carrying my jogging gear in a plastic bag so as to make the dawn run and be able to start the new day from home. Only this time it was different from before, somehow, and I think we both knew it. Call it caution; call it tenderness even. Or maybe age, the sense of two people growing older and finding themselves together again in spite of everything. Or maybe at that it was nothing more than the look in Margie Magister's eyes that evening I've described; the fear of being left alone again, and Christmas was coming, and for God's sake please let's not spoil it this time.

Was that enough?

I guess not, at that.

The night I came home to Laura's after meeting Margie at the Pierre bar, I found myself, to my surprise, suggesting we set up housekeeping together.

Second surprise: she turned me down.

Which leaves the Counselor's Wife.

It's no accident, she'd say, that I've left her for last. She'd say there are no accidents in interpersonal relationships, only unresolved conflicts.

She'd even say it was because I was in love with her, a little.

How do I know what she'd say?

Easy.

I think I've mentioned the feeling that we were avoiding each other. Well, once she came back from the Hamptons, that became, I'll admit, pretty much a one-way street. A couple of times she even invited me to have lunch with her, but I begged off. Once I had another appointment, the other time a backlog of work I was determined to get behind me. Both true enough. For some reason, it seemed to be my season for people inviting me to meals.

Etc., etc.

Then one morning she stopped by my office again. It was, I remember, one of those incredible December days: cold, brisk and, for New York, a totally unreal blue sky, and the Counselor's Wife, who'd been out with the dog, looked positively blooming. Though you couldn't yet see that she was pregnant, you'd have to say it agreed with her 100 percent.

"Phil," she said, "this time I won't take no for an answer. I don't care what else you have on, you're having lunch with me today. We'll eat upstairs, in the solarium. Okay?"

I started to invent some excuse, at least in my mind, but she shook her head firmly. Then I grinned at her, saying: "What time?"

"Any time you're ready," she said. "Just call up fifteen minutes ahead."

I did, and at one, after the Counselor had gone off to La Gonzesse, his favorite bistro over on Lexington, I rode the little elevator up to the top floor.

That top floor is the Counselor's Wife's pride and joy. If you said it's a little too perfect for living, I wouldn't argue, but that day, with the louvered shutters and the awnings at just the right angles, the sunlight diffused the room with warmth and gave a picture-postcard shine and sparkle to the facades and rooftops of the neighborhood. Unreal, like I said. The fare might not have been quite as elaborate as Margie Magister's, but it wasn't far off, and the Counselor's Wife served it herself. Furthermore, I ran into the first dog of my acquaintance who has an appetite for smoked salmon.

"As I've told you before, Phil," the Counselor's Wife said, holding a platter of smoked fish while I helped myself, then the side dishes of capers, diced onions, lemon wedges, and a mountain of rye and pumpernickel bread, thinly sliced, in a wicker basket with a napkin bottom, "I owe you an explanation. I don't like the way things are between us now. We're too good friends to have unresolved conflicts between us."

I said, more or less obligatorily, that I didn't think she owed me anything.

"Oh yes, I do," she answered. "I used you. I used you in the most flagrant way."

"Well," I said, "at least I didn't feel like I was being used."

"You didn't? Well, then, let me ask you this: What do you think that was all about, that night we went to Carter's apartment and I asked you to make love to me?"

She has, needless to say, that way of cornering you with direct, even blunt questions.

"I guess I haven't thought about it all that much," I answered.

"The truth is that I was scared. Scared stiff."

"You had every reason to be."

"Why?"

"Why? Well, we thought McCloy was the Pillow Killer, remember? And we'd just seen the tapes of your shows in his living room. I remember the look on your face when you found them. You were like stunned, blown away."

"Wrong," she said.

"What do you mean, wrong?"

"I don't mean I wasn't thrown by the tapes," she said. "You're right, they made me go numb. But there was something else going on. That's what I want to explain. Or try to explain, because I'm not sure anyone who's not a woman can really understand."

She caught herself then, saying that, and started to laugh.

"I'm sorry," she went on. "Most men can't stand to hear that, but it happens to be true. Anyway, let me tell you something about myself. I'm the kind of person who likes to run things, to manage things, to be in control. I think I've always been that way. I *manage* this house, I *manage* our parties, I chose a profession which requires you to *manage* therapeutic sessions, and I even think that's why I'm good on TV and why I still do it: because I get to *manage* my own program. The only thing I haven't entirely been able to manage is my own marriage. Your boss and my husband is probably the most difficult and least manageable human being I've ever met. In fact I think that's one reason our marriage is so successful: the challenge, for me, of Mr. Charles Camelot. And by the way, I *do* think it's a successful marriage."

Up to here, I thought she'd described herself to a T. She could even have added me to her list.

"But I found out this past year that there was something else I couldn't manage. Do you know what that is? Or was?"

I shook my head.

"My own body," she answered.

She went on about the "biological clock" inside every woman, about how she'd only really heard hers ticking that past year, and how it had brought on the realization that if she was ever going to have a baby, it was now or never. And how if she didn't, she'd come to realize she was going to miss out on one of the great events in a woman's life. Irrevocably. And that, she said, was a little like dying ahead of time.

"It drove me crazy, Phil," she said. "It was like an obsession. Suddenly nothing else mattered. I'm afraid I more or less sprung it on Charles. If there was ever something I *mis*managed, that was it. He reacted badly, for which I don't blame him in the slightest. He said he was too old to have children, which isn't true, but he also said our marriage bargain, unwritten though it is, didn't include children. And that *was* true. We had some terrible arguments—I don't know if you knew about that or not—and in the end, I walked out. I left him, Phil. You know about that part. I actually thought I was leaving him for good."

Here was where I came in. Here too came the unanswered question I probably didn't want answered, much less asked.

She seemed to spot it. She paused, expecting me to say something.

I didn't.

"Where do you think I went that night?" she asked then. "That night you turned me down? And thank God, by the way, that you did."

"To Biegler?" I guessed.

"That's right. When did you know?"

"Know what?"

"That we were having an affair?"

"I didn't," I said. "Not till the night in his . . . in your old office. The Halloran night. It was pretty obvious that something had been going on between the two of you."

She laughed then, a downbeat kind of laugh.

"Actually, it was over by then. It had been for quite a while. One problem—not the only one—was that Bill was trying to manage me. Did you know he was the one who'd called the police? Remember? When you thought it was Charles?"

I shook my head.

"Anyway," she said, "our sordid little affair dragged on longer than it should have. I tried to stop it—that was the main reason I changed offices—but he kept after me, and finally I agreed to see him. I thought I owed him that. To top it off, I did something very stupid. That was when I tried to reach you, remember? The message I left on your machine?

I honestly think I agreed to the appointment with Vincent Halloran to rescue me from Bill, and I wanted Bill there, I think, in case I couldn't handle Vincent Halloran. I'm not proud of it, Phil. I almost got the two of us killed. But that's what happened."

"And at the same time you'd realized somebody was following you?"

"Of course," she answered. "But for the wrong reasons. I actually thought . . ." This was the one time she looked away from me. "I actually thought Charles was trying to find out if I was seeing someone else."

I remember gazing out at the sparkling rooftops of the neighboring houses and, beyond them, the towers that abut onto Madison. I'd polished off as much as I could eat and was working on an expresso which she'd poured from a long-handled silver pot.

"I told you I'm not proud of it," she repeated, reading my reaction. "But that's what happened."

Okay.

"Come on, Phil," she said. "Something's still bothering you. Tell me, please. I want everything out in the open between us."

"Okay," I heard myself say, still not looking at her, "but whose baby is it really?"

She didn't answer at first. She waited for me to look at her. When I finally did, she was smiling at me.

"You're so sweet, Phil," she said. "It's all right, I promise you. I could even get you proof if you insisted. Bill had a vasectomy a long time ago. He already has four children, two by each marriage—he's single again now—and he decided four was enough."

Which is why, I suddenly realized, she'd said Thank God it wasn't me.

"Then why him?" I asked.

"I don't know," she said, shrugging. "Because he was there. Because I needed someone who wanted me. Because I was crazy."

Clearly she'd finished. It bothered me still, though. I didn't know altogether why. I was thinking about the

Counselor, about her. About me too, I guess. It was like she'd just put more slugs into the pool table, emptying the pockets, and you could hear the balls riding down the chutes, and it was my turn to rack again.

"How much of this does he know?" I asked.

"Who, Charles?"

I nodded.

"Some," she said. "Enough. Not as much as you do now, though."

"Then why are you telling me?" I asked.

She hesitated. Then she looked at me forthrightly, her blue eyes taking me in that confident way of hers.

"Do you really want to know?" she asked. "Even though you may not like it?"

"Yes, I would," I said.

"Because I think you were in love with me. A little."

She was right about one thing: I didn't like it.

"And because," she went on, "I want us to stay friends. That's very valuable to me."

She lifted her glass of Perrier, smiling at me.

"To our friendship," she said.

I didn't say anything. But I lifted my glass too then, and clinked it against hers, and drank what was left.

Laura Hugger's refusal turned out to be like nothing more than a passing hiccup in our relationship. We went through the holidays together and on into the new year of our dwindling century. I have asked her, in passing, if she ever thinks about children. She says she's too busy living right to think about it. She still has time left, she says.

Nothing else has changed much.

Except for the Counselor.

As an expectant, then an actual, father, he has mellowed out to an extraordinary degree. To put it another way, he's become insufferable where his daughter is concerned.

She was born on schedule in the early summer. They named her Diana. Three weeks later, the Counselor's Wife threw a rooftop bash in her daughter's honor—the first party she'd given in over a year.

"Diana the Huntress," the Counselor has taken to saying when, holding the baby gingerly in his arms, he introduces her around the office, and you can make his day by telling him how much she looks like him.